AN INTIMATE OBSESSION

AN INTIMATE OBSESSION

Elizabeth McGregor

HEADLINE

Copyright © 1994 Elizabeth McGregor

The right of Elizabeth McGregor to be identified as the Author of the Work has been asserted by her in accordance with the Copyright, Designs and Patents Act 1988.

First published in 1994
by HEADLINE BOOK PUBLISHING

10 9 8 7 6 5 4 3 2 1

All rights reserved. No part of this publication may be reproduced, stored in a retrieval system, or transmitted, in any form or by any means without the prior written permission of the publisher, nor be otherwise circulated in any form of binding or cover other than that in which it is published and without a similar condition being imposed on the subsequent purchaser.

All characters in this publication are fictitious and any resemblance to real persons, living or dead, is purely coincidental.

British Library Cataloguing in Publication Data

McGregor, Liz
   Intimate Obsession, An
   I. Title
   823 [F]

ISBN 0-7472-0961-8

Typeset by
CBS, Felixstowe, Suffolk

Printed and bound in Great Britain by
Mackays of Chatham PLC, Chatham, Kent

HEADLINE BOOK PUBLISHING
A division of Hodder Headline PLC
Headline House
79 Great Titchfield Street
London W1P 7FN

AN INTIMATE OBSESSION

Imagined worlds.

More real than life.

His fingers paused on the diary page. This coming year would alter everything. He smoothed the thin pages with care, avoiding cracking the spine of the little book.

Under his nails there showed a faint rim of dark oil and earth; frowning, he bent his fingers until the joints rested on the paper and the nails were hidden. His two large, reddish fists showed their white knuckles, shining hard against the skin. Here on the table lay all the days to come; they were within his grasp. Silence pressed in on him, as intimate as a shroud.

He thought, fondly, of his hands on her neck. Bending and cracking. For a second, the thought – her under his thumb – was too violent, too extreme. He rubbed at the image with that thumb and mended it. She softened and melted. He could feel the outline of her throat, the pulse of the artery. He stroked her willing face.

In these last weeks, it had come to him what he had done wrong. Why she always just turned away. It was not that she thought herself too good for him. Not at all. It was just that . . . too many years had passed while he stood at the sideline, waiting. Too stupid to know that there were no prizes for patience. No prizes for the also-rans. But he knew *now*. He knew.

They also serve who also stand and . . . no. No serving. *Winning.* That was all that mattered. That was the only way. You never got what you wanted by standing in the crowds, watching.

Too much waiting, too much time.

He would think of it soon . . . His hands turned the blank pages of the New Year. He would think of a date.

One

She went to the door and listened to the end of the year.

The sea was still up, rushing in the distance. It had a voice, the blunted voice of the water throwing itself in the darkness at Chesil Bank. Hidden behind the last rise of hills before the coast, the farmland that belonged to Hugh Scott was a dark body lying on its side; the fringe of bare trees, spokes of branches in the gloom, lining the long garden.

Eve stood on the doorstep, waiting.

The darkness, below the first hill, was whistling and hammering. Two miles away, in the village, the dog at the post office was barking hysterically at the volley of unaccustomed sound. Ghost voices wailed up through the blackness. Standing at the crown on the hill, looking down into the dark, Eve realised that they were chasing out the old year. She had forgotten the custom . . .

She, too, started whistling breathily between her teeth; the air picked it up and froze it into moth-like clouds. The wind came rolling up the long hill and up through the trees at the edge of the lawn, picking up the tin trays and hammers of the village in its fist, and carried her own melody away.

Her patience gave out. 'Come on,' she called. 'I'm freezing. I'm waiting.'

Until ten to twelve, she and her father had been playing cards. The kitchen table was littered with them: he had thrown them down when he realised that he could not win. The kitchen was a warm pool of cream light, a circle in the darkness. The oil boiler ticked away the time, the gearing of its enamel clock worn down. It sent its minutes methodically whirring and falling along the pipes of the wall. She walked back, sighing, turning her head and listening for her father. But he was nowhere near the door.

Each day a game. More horrible than the last.

It had begun about a year ago. Her father, retired six years from his teaching post in the secondary school, had begun to get up at night in the house they shared.

She would come down in the morning and find some peculiar

anagram of shapes facing her: glasses of all different sizes lined up, for instance, on the kitchen sink, each with varying degrees of milk or fruit juice in them. Or pairs of socks lying in a row on the floor. Or the newspapers cut into pieces and stacked neatly on the table. The absurdity of the tableaux could make her laugh. In fact, she remembered one morning when she and her father had both stood at the kitchen door, staring at a perfect display of flour, scrolled and patterned on the worktop. They had both been baffled; they had looked at each other. He had had only a vague memory of having done it, and she had patted him on the arm as he'd rubbed his forehead in exasperation. *Your dreams are getting out of hand*, she had said, and – worse still – as they had stepped forward to clean it up, *You're going a bit potty in your old age, you know, Dad* . . .

The memory of those remarks now were uncomfortable. They were not in the least funny. They had looked into the future as neatly as any clairvoyant.

By the spring of this dying year, he had begun arguing with her about which day it was. He would pick a fight over a television programme, or something she was wearing, or the fact that he couldn't find his own clothes. And it had been – she tried to recall exactly – probably June before she had mentioned it to her doctor. The diagnosis had been quick.

'But it's been so sudden,' she remembered saying, sitting in the consulting room at the hospital, while outside, through the panelled glass, she could see her father sitting upright, only his wringing hands a sign of inner confusion. 'Last year he was fine, absolutely fine . . .'

The consultant had been all sympathy. No practical bloody use, of course. No use at night, or in the mess of the mornings, or in the evening when her father sometimes became so aggressive she could feel his breath plastering her face. But sympathetic, yes.

Actually, the consultant had been rather attractive. Blond, about forty-five, conservatively dressed, with a good, unpolished smile. As he had leaned forward – Aramis, cigarettes, ink – she had blushed a little. He had neatly manicured nails on pale fingers, she noticed. Sensitive hands that she had deliberately drawn her eyes away from. 'This can sometimes go on for many years,' he had said. Modulated voice. Public school and Oxbridge. 'In your father's case, it's come rapidly. That might be the pattern for him. A rapid escalation, a rapid demise. But no one can say for certain.'

She'd met his eyes, smiled, and fought down a sudden and completely irrational desire to kiss him between the moist, bedside-manner eyes. Either that, or slap him – just there, on the smooth, babylike cheek. Something to make him take notice. *I'm not a professional carer, you see? I don't know how to do that. I just happen to live in the same house as my father.* Beside him she saw the neat pile of case notes: other people waiting for his decision, his life sentences.

She'd walked out of the hospital, arm-in-arm with her father. This tall, imposing man who had always guarded and dominated her. They'd walked past roses, very pretty – yellow and full of scent – to the car. The sun had been shining. It had been a glorious spring day. And somewhere between the roses and the car, she'd let go of the arm of her father and taken hold of the hand of a child.

Her father was now, seven months later, markedly worse, and a stranger. In the past – even in her father's past – the doctors would have called his illness by a different name. Crueller, more succinct. Those great Victorian redbrick mausoleums would have put a clean tag on it straight away. No cloudy talk of displacement or stress or neurological failure then. They would have had a name that the relatives could catch hold of. *Lunacy. Madness.* Something nice and gritty to set your mind to. Something unshakeable. Something both harder and easier to take.

The label tacked on to her father's file at the hospital made it sound clean and tidy: all the things, in fact, that it was not.

Alzheimer's had ambushed him; the bandit in the rocks, the highwayman flourishing his pistol in the path of age. A beast had opened its mouth and swallowed him, effortlessly: he lived in its stomach, a Jonah calling for help.

At sixty-six, her father was far from old. He loomed larger than life, as he had always done. He was six foot three and powerfully built: his hands were freckled and very large, easily capable of crushing her own. His face was flattish, broad and rather crude, a Mr Punch-like face, with thick eyebrows over large green eyes. His yellowish-pink hair had once been wiry red. His voice matched his build: a voice that filled you with guilty dread; a great sergeant-major's voice. He still carried himself very straight; no shuffling. But inside the big body lived a furious, violent and bewildered baby.

That night, shortly before midnight, he had got up unexpectedly from the card table. He had taken the chrysanthemum plant, an armful of little bronze suns swaying in his grasp. And a piece of coal from the bucket. And a slice of bread. And rattled money in his trouser pocket. For a minute, he had banged about in the hall.

'Here, you, let me out! I want to go first-footing! It's lucky . . . Where're the keys? Here, you . . .'

She had known better than to cross him in this high temper, and had taken the key from the top ledge – the new place – and opened the door.

Now, Eve turned on the radio.

The local station was crammed with static, but they were broadcasting the chimes of Big Ben from London. For some unfathomable reason, she turned off the light and listened hard. Clearer. It was up to the fourth or fifth chime, that dark rumbling note of the clock.

Almost midnight.

Eve put her hand to her throat, and, in that second, panic charged down at her, trampling her, until she had to lean on the frame of the door just to breathe normally. All the year draining out of the clock, all the time going away: March, August, December. The dry spring, the garden flowerbeds going grey with the chalk rising to the top of the soil; the rings of Bronze Age barrows in the field beginning to break through. And then that drenched Easter. Frost in May. Heat in May. Their trip to Brownsea Island. Foam-grey sea. Wildly electric blue sea on a sunny day in November.

All those days.

Her father had never been her friend. Her father had never been *Daddy* – there had never been anything remotely approaching that between them. They had lived, inclined upon each other in their lives and proximity for more than thirty years in that same house; but that did not mean there was any kindliness in their relationship. It had been more like a thirty-year truce in a war. More like thirty years of fencing and scoring points; two intelligent combatants too tired actually to fight. There was, of course, a sort of comfort in that. They knew each other; they could make each other laugh. But there was no sharing of secrets or intimacies, no breaking down before each other. Eve had grown up adult and serious before her time, aping her father's sardonic smiles, his breathtakingly hard criticisms of other people.

When she had gone away to college, the yoke of him had gradually fallen off her. She had flourished, enjoying herself, and some part of her personality that she always considered similar to her mother's had risen up from under his influence.

This last year, watching him, seeing the layers peel from him, seeing his tears for the first time, trying to find a place to put this new unpleasant, embarrassing, helpless person who was her father: the sensation had been dizzying, bending mirrors and reeling paths. She had tried to walk straight through the unwinding months: by some freak, she found that she had succeeded more often than not.

All the days of the year.

All those colours and shades running wildly out of the clock. All those days lost: the night when she had opened the window and the warm harvest had rolled in, blond crop rippling in the curious half-light that was not darkness at all, that July . . . All those moments bleeding out of the clock, vanishing for ever.

All year she had gone into school, into the classroom where she taught thirty-two six-year-olds; had seen their faces turned up to her from their cross-legged position on the floor as she held the register; seen their absolute faith in her as the keeper of law and order. No matter what farce she had just stepped from at home, here she was the woman who knew more than their mothers and the prime minister and the vicar put together. 'Miss Ridges' to them. Miss infallible Ridges who knew just fractionally less than God and who was infinitely more powerful than Him. And sometimes she thought, *Hey, let me sit down there. You come up here. I'm dizzy up here . . .*

She had kept going all year. Made jokes about Dad in the staff room. Accepted help where she could. Got him into a day centre once a week. Made do and mended, always hoping for a change. Always hoping to step outside the spiral of the illness; to wake up, perhaps, and find it was nothing more than a dream. Complained over coffee and stolen gin-and-tonic half-hours in the pub to Sarah. Laughed and stormed a little. Talked to the doctor, the consultant. Had her hand on the phone to call a support group several times – had never rung them, hoping for the miracle.

She'd always hoped for the knight on the white charger who would gallop through the gloom, loop Dad over his arm and carry him away. Not carry *her* away . . . oh, no! Her fantasies were far more practical. Just let him carry *Father* away. Sarah had roared laughing at that.

Now, in the darkness of the year's end, Eve put both hands to her face. The room seemed to tilt a little, and in that single second she felt the scent of something coming. Something huge, some immeasurable change, something terrible, casting its shadow before itself in time.

In the village, they began to ring the church bell.

She straightened up, shaking her head. 'Mustn't drink Scotch,' she said, wryly, to herself. 'Somebody's got to stay upright in this house.'

She smoothed back her hair, sighed. Midnight was past, as was the terrible sensation of vertigo. The next year was waiting on the step.

She went to the door again.

'Dad!' she called. 'Dad!'

There was no reply.

'Oh, you bloody fool,' she whispered, under her breath.

The dip of the land was dark.

Somewhere down in that dip, over that rise, Hugh Scott sat in his farmhouse. She wondered if he was by himself. Perhaps, as his nearest neighbour, she should have invited him up to play cards; it wouldn't have been much fun, but it might have been better than being alone on New Year's Eve. And then, smiling to herself, she dismissed the idea. It was bad enough sharing today, alone, with Dad. Not Hugh as well.

She stepped down on to the path.

'Dad! Come on now, Dad . . .'

It took a moment for her eyes to accustom to the utter blackness of the garden. At the far end she could make out the large, white-painted gate that was propped permanently open. Humped, dug-over furrows where the vegetables would be. Strips of green path. She squinted about.

'Dad!'

Beyond the hedge was their lawn, sheltered from the wind on the east side of the house. She went to the gap in the privet and peered through.

Something was on the lawn; something crouched there. Her heart leapt for a second – Christ, what *is* that! – but then died down. Only her father had that shock of hair. His shoulders were perfectly rounded, hunched, so that he looked, funnily, like an immense tortoise stranded there in the dark.

'What're you doing?' she called.

He did not reply, so, wrapping her arms protectively around herself, shivering, she went to him.

His forehead was almost touching the ground, and he was passing his hands across the grass religiously, slowly, with almost loving care. She thought he was combing the grass. Combing with one hand, smoothing down with the other.

She touched his arm.

And then the truth hit her.

Around him, on the lawn, were fragments of . . . stones? Shells. The curled spiral shells of garden snails. The big ones that plagued their flowerbeds. The place was rife with them. Her father was cracking . . . cracking the shells and . . .

'*Qu'est-ce que tu voudrais?*' he asked himself. He was back in class, taking his French lesson before a sulky group of fourteen-year-olds; talking in that classroom-stilt he used, the tone that completely vanished when he went to France itself. '*J'ai faim . . .*' he whispered. *I'm hungry.* '*Je voudrais des . . .*'

She suddenly understood what he was doing.

'Oh – Jesus!'

Her father looked up at her vaguely. The hand on the lawn made a scraping motion, like the move you would make scraping food together on a plate.

He was not *combing* the grass. He was . . .

Oh Jesus, Jesus.

She swallowed down a sudden, urgent sickness.

'*Oui, je veux bien . . .*' said the bland, white-framed face beneath her. Without a trace of recognition. *I would like to . . .*

'God,' she whispered. She neither laughed nor cried. Some sick jokes went beyond being funny, even blackly funny. 'What next?' she breathed. 'What next?'

She tried to get her father to his feet, trying not to look in his face, holding her breath. Gritting her teeth unconsciously. But he tore her hands away, punching at her.

She cradled her bruised forearm, cursing. In the end, there was no alternative but to wait for him to finish.

'Happy New Year,' she whispered, closing her eyes.

It was cold in the solitary house, but Hugh Scott had not noticed it. The stove burned perilously low in the kitchen, a door banged loosely overhead in the dark. The window revealed a yard and a farm field and a narrow road without lights. It was New Year's Eve, but there were no callers at this house. He was utterly alone. But he had his little book. His important little book. And that was all that mattered.

He considered carefully. This was the most important date he would ever fix. He had to get it exactly right. Women liked you to get things right. To know. To be in charge. And it was to be a surprise, just before the time. To sweep her off her feet.

Because they liked that too.

Not winter or autumn: too cold. And summer was too busy, with the harvest. What did every woman want for a wedding? May, or June.

A June wedding.

His wedding. *Her* wedding.

He wanted to do this for her. He was right and, up till now, she had been wrong. Keeping them apart the way she did. Keeping him at arm's length.

She would see how wrong she had been.

He knew what he had to do. He would book the church, the hotel, the honeymoon. The flowers. He would think of everything. Even the dress. She would not have to lift a finger. He would give her this gift, whole, entire and perfect. The greatest gift of her life.

And once she saw how right he was, she would be grateful.

In the darkness, he looked at the clock.

It was almost midnight, and the old year was dying. He glimpsed his forty-seven-year-old face – dullish complexion, grey-sprinkled hair cropped fiercely short – in the shadowy mirror. He stood up and went over to it while the year fell soundlessly to its death. He drew himself up tall, peered with his head poked forward, and smiled. The empty grin sheared the dark in half.

On the table behind him, the diary lay open at the first page. January the first was half full of his writing already: a blunt pencil, letters rushing into one another.

Help me, it read.

Over and over and over.

Help me. Help me. Help me. Help me . . .

Two

Four months later. An April morning in a bright dry spring. The phone was ringing as Eve came downstairs.

'Hello, Eve.'

'Matthew! Hello.'

It was Eve's headteacher, Matthew Streatham.

'I just thought I'd ring to remind you that Ashley's parents are coming in today. Half-past.'

'I'm leaving any moment – I'm waiting for Hugh Scott to collect Dad.'

Out of the corner of her eye, Eve saw her father come into the kitchen. He stood just on her side of the door, looking rather like her six-year-old class on the first day of term: pressed smart trousers, clean shirt, very stretched smile. One hand fumbled at his belt. He looked washed out, yellowish. He was in – not remission, that sounded too optimistic – but a kind of lull. A bleak patch of calm water in the middle of a storm. In such patches he would, for days at a time, wander helplessly about, never cursing, never raising his voice or hand. Sometimes weeping. Always confused.

'How is he?' asked Matthew.

'Oh – fine. You know. Up and down. But we're fine.' She made a face at the phone. She never gave away the real picture, just a poor-quality print of domestic harmony. She had never told Matthew about her father's rages or insults or wanderings in the last four months, because she was afraid it might affect his opinion of her. Afraid he might suggest that she leave or go part-time. Afraid that he might watch her too closely. And she needed that school – those faces turned to her, those small hands in hers. They kept her afloat in this slipping, slithering sea.

She glanced at the clock. It was ten past eight. As she did so, she caught sight of Sarah's scrawled message about the PTA meeting that afternoon. She grabbed it with her free hand.

'I shall be with you in fifteen minutes . . .'

She put the phone down, and at once saw a faint plume of dust along the track outside the house: the mile-long panorama of field and hill, through which a rutted path threaded. Hugh's Land Rover was negotiating the bend, coming towards the house.

'Good old Hugh,' she murmured to herself. 'Always on time.'

She gave her father a drink, and, seeing that he could not recognise what to do with it, she urged it gently towards his mouth.

She looked from his face to the vehicle bouncing along the track. The Land Rover was coming up the slight gradient to the front gate, and she could see Hugh's face with his smile – it always reminded her of a ventriloquist's doll's – in place.

Since January, a minor miracle had happened. Hugh had started to come here often: three, four, five times a week. He had taken it upon himself to look after her father, giving him odd jobs to do while she was working.

Hugh was eight or nine years older than she was. He had always come to the house, even as a boy – a thick-set fifteen-year-old hanging over the fence, carrying in his hand a punnet of raspberries, a quart bottle of cider; or helping her father in the garden, digging up the potatoes, cutting the grass, mending the fence. She had barely spoken to him then. Really, she had only noticed him at all when she had come back here to work. That would have been when she was twenty-two, and he was thirty or so. Hugh and Father had got along – a kind of odd couple. Sometimes they even went to the pub together. Hugh would laugh at her father's jokes; never a great deal to say, prone to blushing, he rarely exchanged a word with her.

He would look at her, though: behind her father's back as they stood together in the garden; as he stood at the fence or the gate; as he turned the tractor at the bottom of the field.

Just looking.

That's what people said in shops, when they couldn't afford to buy. *It's all right. I'm just looking.*

Waiting at her father's side now, watching the Land Rover, Eve remembered the glances, and a chill ran down her back for no apparent reason at all. After all, there was no harm in Hugh, she told herself. He was an ordinary man, a hard worker, a man without passions or many interests. He lived alone, which was sad; alone in the house beyond the hill, since his parents had died. But one day, no doubt, he would marry. She imagined it would be some straightforward girl; a large, dull, heavily built girl devoted to morning television as she washed Hugh's clothes and cooked Hugh's dinner.

What nonsense, she thought wryly. *He'll probably marry a*

professor of philosophy in a size eight frock.

Still, the thought didn't completely erase her unease. Hugh was waving through the driver's window. Her hands hung by her side. She did not wave back.

It was the same, this eerie feeling, whenever Hugh came here. First, gratitude that he had come at all; that someone was helping her. But then, rapidly, this unspoken unease. It was nothing she could put her finger on. It was just . . . The expression in his eyes, perhaps. The hangdog expression, like a dog that has been chained up for hours on end. The unerring, unblinking, rather accusing look of those eyes. The way he listened when she spoke, with his mouth slightly parted, his neck blotchy, his hands hanging loose.

Eve shook herself. There was no time for reflections today. She looked into her briefcase, checking its contents, stuffed the note from Sarah inside with the PTA minutes, drank the last gritty inch of her coffee. Her father was sitting before a slice of toast, unscrewing the top of the marmalade in incredible slow motion.

The Land Rover stopped outside. The door slammed: she heard Hugh's heavy step on the path.

She had a thousand reasons to be grateful to Hugh, she reminded herself, as she waited with something like a knot in her throat for him to knock on the door. He had told her in January that he could see her father was getting worse, and that he would help her whenever he could. There had been no need for him to offer like that, had there? It was kindness; it was generosity. 'Just being a good neighbour,' he had explained. 'Don't like to see you struggling.'

'Oh, you're very thoughtful,' she had exclaimed, that January day. 'But it's a burden, you know. You mustn't tie yourself to helping, it's a tremendous effort . . .'

Hugh hadn't smiled. He had simply sat there, hands on knees, and his voice had had a closed intonation, as if the subject were at an end. 'I'll come and check on you most days,' he'd said.

She had been surprised and a little unnerved. Boundlessly grateful though, especially when Hugh got into the habit of taking Father for days at a time. So very, *very* grateful.

'I don't know how I shall ever thank you,' she had told him.

He'd managed a smile then.

The most curious, childlike smile . . .

And so, from a casual and awkward neighbour-to-neighbour acquaintanceship, she seemed to be increasingly dependent on him. There was nothing, it appeared, that she could do about it. Hugh was often passing, so he said. And it was so lonely up here. Nothing but the stretch of fast road into town fringing the edge of Hugh's land. And the fields themselves: immense rectangles of single colours.

At her back, her father spluttered and spilt the tea. She rubbed her forehead, frowning.

Hugh's knock came at the door. Always the same: three loud, steady blows. She kissed her father on his forehead – getting no response – and went through to the hall.

Three

The staff room, after school, was in a companionable fog: fourteen adults squeezed into a twelve-by-ten box that smelled alluringly of feet. Eve was late, flushed from loading Class Three into the school bus. A crayon was stuck behind her ear, which she removed with an apologetic smile.

Sarah was already in full flow: gossip at Warp Factor Six. The topic was Davina Beech.

'Why'd they throw her off the parish council anyway?' Matthew was asking. His hooded eyes drooped over the PTA minutes. He was only half listening.

'They didn't,' Sarah retorted. 'She resigned. She tore up the AGM accounts and called them a bunch of wankers!'

There was a sharp intake of breath, followed by a ripple of laughter. No one could stay shocked at Sarah for long: she had a round, schoolgirl's face that beamed reddishly, begging a response. Eve supposed Sarah was about forty-two, forty-three, though she had never asked. Sarah was also a size eighteen, blanketed today in a navy blue skirt, navy blue striped blouse and navy blue Pringle sweater. She looked like a head girl, but you forgave her the moment she began to speak: marbly vowel sounds rolling over each other in a constant stream of conversation, her voice pitching up and down. She itched with frustration in PTA meetings, hyper because smoking was banned.

Eve only knew Davina Beech vaguely: she had noticed her sometimes walking through school to playgroup, dragging her children by both hands behind her. Davina had once been a systems analyst in Holborn, but was now a mere mother pinned to the microwave by three-year-old twins, and was known to possess a temper of tigerish proportions.

Sarah was snorting happily at the image of Davina erupting. Eve settled back with a coffee, grinning at her friend's show: Sarah had a laugh that sounded for all the world like a donkey being hit with an accordion.

Matthew, meanwhile, was trying to begin the meeting, moving through the tangled web of the school's summer barbeque, which was coming up in eight weeks' time. Sarah raised her eyebrows at Eve. 'Don't rush off,' she mouthed across the room.

As they waded on through the hiring of bouncy castles, the buying of beefburgers and the emotional blackmailing of local businesses, Eve's mind drifted. She looked around the faces: nine mothers, three teachers and one unemployed father who sat, chewing his nails in boredom, his Minutes scrunched in his lap. As he glanced across at Eve, she gave him a sympathetic wink. 'I hope them Bright lads don't come down,' he said. 'I'm on back fence duty. I'm no bouncer.'

'You see life here,' Eve replied. 'But then, you lob so well.'

He grinned. 'Likely,' he replied.

The meeting passed on, and Eve's thoughts drifted back to Sarah. They had known each other three years, since Sarah's youngest – horribly named Sydney, for which he paid in the school playground and had to be protected by a scrum of dinner ladies – had started in Eve's class.

Sarah had been the sort of smiling and overbearing mother that Eve dreaded. Her child had been mercilessly hothoused, and Eve was given an avalanche account of how Sydney could count to twenty and add up and play the violin and could say 'My name is Sydney, where am I?' in five languages. Eve's heart had sunk; such children were the odd ones out and often had high opinions of themselves. And yet, as Sarah spoke, and poor little Sydney gazed up at her with his gingery hair and his mother's glowing round face, something in her softened. She felt Sydney's little damp paw on her wrist, and Sarah's hot dry hand on her other arm.

'Will you come up for drinks this Saturday?' Sarah had asked that first day. 'Should be fun. Assorted pillars of society. Don't let me be bored on my own.'

Eve had agreed, laughing. And seen the household for the first time.

Three or four times a year, Sarah and Duncan Marsham held these dreary bashes that Sarah thought essential to advancing Duncan's career. Yet nothing could crank the local dignitaries up to be even mildly amusing at these – or any other – events, not even Sarah's accordion braying. Eve stood to one side, enjoying it all with a kind of fascinated horror. She found herself admiring Sarah's bowling-ball charm. She liked eccentrics; and Sarah's oblivious enjoyment was so breathtaking, so careless, so howling, that it was a joy to watch.

Sarah and Duncan lived in a peeling Georgian monolith that they could not afford. The unheated house always stank of Benson and Hedges. That night, opening the kitchen cupboards, trying to find a bottle opener at Sarah's request, Eve had found a bottle of expensive claret, an empty bottle of gin, water biscuits, a packet of tea, and an ancient sealed Easter egg: Sarah's children were not allowed sweets. The cavernous living room had a painting of a misshapen horse that Sarah said was worth a fortune – but the room had no carpet; the downstairs loo, similarly, had a collection of National Geographics three feet high, but no towel and only one clattering cold tap.

Duncan was in insurance, and worked away from home most of the time. Sarah was left to bring up the children. They thought it best for Sydney to come to a village school – a village state school was acceptable, a town state school was not. Sydney was the youngest of three. Sarah had, at some point in the past, studied the art of swearing as anyone else would take up Italian or macrame. One of the results of this was that Sydney had taught the Infants Reception to say 'Sod off, you bitch' in his first week. Sarah was called in. She apologised, and said that he had probably heard her say it when she was driving. And Eve, who knew the feeling, always being herself five minutes late, her car littered with illicit chocolate wrappers, paper bags and books, felt an immediate pang of companionship.

Eve glanced at her watch. Abruptly her train of thought jolted away to her father. Hugh would be bringing Dad home soon. She ought to go. But the drone of the voices around her was pleasant: busy and rolling and soft, like a smothered hive. She would have loved to fall quietly asleep, her cup in her lap.

The meeting ended at five.

Sarah walked with her to their cars: Eve's yellow Volkswagen, Sarah's battered blue Volvo. In the car park, they sat on the Beetle's warm, sloping bonnet.

'I volunteered to wrap one hundred and twenty Lucky Dip parcels,' Eve said, thinking aloud. 'Why did I do that?'

'It's that staff room,' said Sarah. 'The Japanese used it in the war. You agree to anything after half an hour of Matthew's socks.'

'Is it him?'

'I was next to him. I should know.'

'No wonder his wife's got that expression. You know . . .' And Eve wrinkled her nose, rabbit-like.

'Listen, Duncan's not back till Friday. Why don't you bring those what's-its round tomorrow, after school? I'll help you wrap them.'

The next day was Eve's father's day at the centre: she didn't need to collect him until five. The thought of gossiping with Sarah until then was pleasant, an analgesic. An aspirin against the evening.

'Fine,' she agreed. 'Thanks.'

They watched some mothers go past: pear shapes in leggings, thin legs in jeans, two voluptuous ones in short skirts.

'I had a bum like that once,' Sarah said.

Eve opened her car door. 'No you didn't.'

'Bitch.'

'I was going to say you were like a Reubens painting, but I won't now.'

'No, I wouldn't. It would be crawling.'

'It's a knack, though, isn't it? Lying and crawling at the same time.'

She grinned at Sarah, who turned away, smiling and shaking her head.

Eve shoved the car into first, and drove away, waving goodbye out of the driver's window.

It was a warm spring day – grey rather than sunny, and humid. As she got close to the house, nestling in its fold of fields, she felt the fizz pass from her, like a drink going flat. Duty loomed up through the wheat and the hedges. Her father was ahead: her father, and Hugh. Unknown to her, her face wore a frown, her mouth tightened to a line even before she slowed to turn in at the gate. The look of the house was so familiar, she could probably have walked around it, through it, blindfold, never bumping into a single wall or piece of furniture.

After all, she had lived here – with him – for thirty-two years.

She had not meant to come back here to work: *that* had been one of life's accidents. Just after her Finals, her father had been ill with flu, and she came home out of pity after hearing his voice over the phone sounding throaty and frail. To her surprise, he had been very grateful, almost loving: he'd actually told people, with some pride in his voice at last, that she had passed her exams. Then, the following week, at a fête, she had met the then head of the primary school, who had offered her a job. She had hesitated, thinking, *I might have to live with Dad for a while.* And that had been all those years ago, and she had stayed put, always promising herself she would move out, move on . . . And here she was still. As isolated as she had been at the age of ten.

As she turned off the car's engine, she smiled half-heartedly at the thought. It was longer than most marriages. Certainly longer than her parents' marriage.

Eve remembered flashes, distinct and preserved, as if on archive film, of single days in early childhood. Single hours. Single words. Her mother was reduced to one photograph, and a disconnected scent.

One such flash belonged to the year when her mother had died. Some time after the funeral. Not long after.

She had been eight years old, chasing Rice Krispies around the rabbits on the china rim of the plate. Her father had worked outside that day – *all* day, he had told her, with a dark and irritated inflection. She sensed, incomprehensibly, that it must be her fault if her father had to do some job that he hated. A job, he'd repeated darkly. Like a magistrate giving out a prison sentence.

In this case, it was the garden. The remains of her mother's beloved garden around the house. As he worked, he whistled.

He whistled 'Nick-nack-Paddywhack, Give a Dog a Bone'. He whistled 'My Old Man Said Foller the Van'. It was like hitting himself over the head. The enforced jollity, the exact opposite of his mood. Better to hide when her Dad whistled or sang.

Infuriated beyond belief at the green kingdom that had been her mother's, he would sometimes feel pressed to tell her his favourite story. Today, as she finished the cereal and gazed at him, a stringy nervous sensation fluttering in her throat, was no exception. He glared at his small daughter, saying, 'Do you know, when Alexander The Great invaded India, he went to a kingdom near Lahore, and do you know what they did with children there?'

The first time that she had heard that story – one of his favourites – she had shaken her head, thinking it was some kind of fun, some kind of game. Listened wide-eyed, smiling with expectation. He lowered his head – those beetling eyebrows, green eyes that speared her, that very fleshy mouth; the hair, red then, that shone like a wiry halo around him.

'They loved beautiful things,' he went on to explain. 'And if a child was not beautiful, was not . . .' He stroked her shoulder. 'If a child was not perfectly perfect at eight weeks old, they would hold a meeting of the elders to decide. The mother would have to bring the little baby. She would give the baby to the elders, and they would pass it from hand to hand, inspecting it, and if it was not beautiful, do you know what they did?'

He brought his face, grinning, to hers.

'They chopped it up.' And he chopped his fork, expressively, on the tablecloth. 'Chop-chop-chop. Poor baby!'

He was a trespasser in that garden, forever tweaking at the shapes Eve's mother had made, the beds and the trees, forever hauling them back more or less to the original pattern. But the garden no longer seemed to have any life in it. In the summer, the plants fell about in various postures of failure; he never watered them, never fertilised them. The vegetables – the beans, the thin yellow strands of the broccoli – dying before his eyes, pleaded for water. He ignored them, sending her out at night instead.

It was one of the most arresting memories of her childhood – watering the garden at night with the four-litre green bucket. The evening coming in from the coast and her, alone, miles from another child, miles from another house, watering in the twilight, the whispering hush of the water disappearing into the soil, the veiny leaves turning their undersides, the fragile stalks fluttering in the temporary downpour.

'You practise the piano while I'm doing my job,' he would say. 'I'll be listening. Open the window.' His back lumped over the mower – a clattering clockwork mower, stop-starting, stop-starting. 'I'm listening.'

She had gone into the room and opened the window.

'I'm listening!'

The mower clacked along the border, teeth chewing the grass. She had turned away from the window and the rattling blades and her father's hands gripping each side of the mower bars, and looked at the piano.

It was mahogany, a lovely thing. A piece of wood with a life of its own. Livid bright wood, brass pedals and lock. They still had it in the living room, even now. She had lifted the lid and sat down on the stool, and put her hands on the keys.

Clack-clackerclack-clack.

He had come to the end of the row.

She began to play, softly. That was on purpose, to make him strain to hear. Only when playing the piano did she have any feeling of authority over him – the power to make him really listen. And so she would deliberately string out the practice.

Out of the smooth flat pellets of ivory came an adult's voice: a German, singing a polka. German feet raced, stumbling from time to time, up and down the soft felt hammers and strings. At the end of a headlong rush down the ballroom, at last, the German stopped, breathless, and tripped over his own feet.

'No!' shouted her father from the lawn.

She started again.

This time, in the rose light – her mother's ash-grey roses leaning over the sill like languid girls – the German moved more solidly, more correctly, about the dance. He crushed the soul out of the steps and planted himself in front of his audience, sweating inside his collar. His face the high colour of pressed meat . . .

'No . . . NO!' shouted her father.

She started again.

The sun moved a little higher, and its light touched the room. Slowly, very slowly, it crept past the picture of the two Venetian women who waited, one holding a handkerchief, one bending forward and leaning towards a dog, in shades of brown and gold, for something unseen past the left-hand side of the picture . . . Slowly, illuminating them, it fastened on the frame, and passed in a margin of bright light to the wall alongside. The roses on the sill freshened. Out of the corner of her eye, she thought she saw a leaf, like time-lapse photography, unfold in two palms of green. Her father was standing motionless at the top of the slope. Quite suddenly, his body seemed to shudder.

'Stop . . . stop . . .'

She wondered if she had heard properly. The fingers went fumbling about the scale on their own.

'Bloody well stop, then!'

She stopped.

He stumbled to the window like an invalid taking tentative steps after a long illness. His face wore an injured expression. He leaned on the sill, and looked in on her.

Her hands on the piano felt huge: giant's hands. Great awkward fleshy things that had settled on the little ivory keys by accident. She shrivelled inside as he watched those hands, felt the familiar strangulating apprehension. The house rang with that pressured silence, with his silent displeasure.

'Eve,' he had said quietly, leaning on the sill from the garden. 'Must you murder it like that?'

'I'm sorry,' she had said.

'I mean . . . must you?' he ranted on. In his sarcastic stride now. 'We did this all last week. Don't you remember? Think what Mrs Morrison said. What did Mrs Morrison say?'

Eve stared down at her lap, her hands still stuck on the keys. She had an urge to rest her head on her extended arms. It was as if she would never again be able to take her hands off the piano. Stuck there for life.

'She said to let it run,' she murmured.

He nodded. 'Let it run like . . .'

'Water,' she had said.

He had walked away.

Her father was moving some lever at the side of the mower to lower the blades. He was still listening to her, though. Waiting. He looked like one of those irate professors in a cartoon strip; his hair, needing cutting itself, fanned on either side of his head in waves that threatened to turn to curls.

She had run out into the corridor while her father was still attending to the mower in the garden. Had run into the hall.

By the door – a pool here of stained-glass blue blue blue on the beige linoleum – was a washroom. Once, this had been a Victorian house of some prestige, enough anyway to merit a butler's pantry (wooden racks for drying the plates, wooden draining board, stone sink), and this cloakroom. It was a real cloakroom – plenty of brass pegs, their winter macs and boots smelling of rot. She had run in here, swift as anything, like a breath, like a fairy, she thought to herself, a water sprite – the smile pulled at the corner of her mouth – water sprite, eight years old, water sprite . . .

She filled the jug to the top and carried it, splashing the floor, into the room, and got to the piano and she poured she poured she poured . . .

She locked the lid.

'Daddy,' she asked, hanging from the frame of the window, holding her plait twirled around one wrist, 'Daddy, can't I come and help?'

He sighed.

A blackbird flew across them, dropping song.

'You can rake up the grass, dear,' he said.

Dear.

Oh, God!

Where had that word come from? Now, now of all times, while the water dripped out of the piano at her back, and the blackbird gushed on the top of the hedge like a faucet, and the carpet soaked up the oozing lake from the jug, he called her . . . that thing. That word of affection.

She crawled under the window, into the folds of the long brocade curtain, put her hands over her ears, and began, uncontrollably to laugh . . .

'Getting it cut,' said a voice.

Eve – the adult Eve, cleaning the mower, weeding the garden, lost in reverie – nearly leapt out of her skin.

It was late that same afternoon after school, about six o'clock. She leaned back on her heels, rushing back to the present out of the past. Hugh Scott was standing behind her.

She pushed back her hair. 'Where did you come from?' she asked, laughing. 'You frightened me to death.'

He watched her, still as a soldier on guard duty. He would suit a bearskin hat.

'Talking to yourself, you were . . .'

'No. Was I?'

They smiled at each other.

'I was remembering something,' she admitted. 'Something awful I did to my father when I was a little girl.' And she smiled up at him disarmingly as he raised one eyebrow. 'And I know what you're thinking,' she said, waving the gardening glove at him in reproof.

'About talking being the first sign. But don't worry. It's not catching.'

She got up. Hugh looked steadily at her. 'Did you forget something?' she asked.

'No . . . I just walked down to the dewpond. Thought I'd come back this way.'

She looked at him, trying to work it out. It was barely an hour since Hugh had left her, after depositing her father. It seemed odd that he shouldn't have gone home yet, but had spent that hour walking the farm. In aimless directions, if what he had just said was right. She got to her feet. 'Father's gone out,' she said. 'Town.'

'Town.' Hugh repeated it solemnly.

'It wasn't five minutes after you left. After I got in.' She sighed, shrugging her shoulders. 'I can't stop him when he gets a bee in his bonnet. Short of lashing him to a chair.'

'He was all right all day.'

'Was he?' She considered. 'He was going on about the car. My car. Something I needed.'

A light dawned, slowly, on Hugh's face. It was rather comical, it was so slow. 'We was talking about the Motor Show in Birmingham,' he said.

'That must be it. It was something he wanted to buy . . . Would you like a drink . . . coffee?' The stillness with which Hugh remained there, not a muscle moving, as though he had been momentarily turned to stone, unnerved her.

'I'd like a drink of water.'

She laughed; then, seeing he meant no joke, she said, 'Water, water,' to herself as she gathered up the gloves and trowel. 'Yes, all right, OK,' she said, and led him into the kitchen.

Four months had passed since the incident on New Year's Eve. It would come to her at the oddest time, just as now, filling the kettle and watching the field sloping away from the house, and the thread of road where the cars passed, too fast, shards of colour appearing and rapidly disappearing between the hedges. But then, Hugh. Something about Hugh – maybe the blandness of his face, the fixed look in his eyes – had reminded her of New Year's Eve. The pair of them – Hugh, and her father – had this big, block-like obduracy. Two great obstacles standing in her way.

She turned back after plugging the kettle in, glanced at Hugh, and immediately felt guilty at the thought. Poor Hugh. He wasn't stone. He had been as helpful as he possibly could over her father. It was unfair to think badly of him. After all, he couldn't help the way he looked. He probably didn't even realise the expression his face could assume – that blank mask.

He stood deferentially now to one side, following her movements with a slight rolling of his head. The grey strands in his hair framed his face like highlights teased out by a hairdresser. It made him look older than his forty-odd years. His skin looked very soft – unnaturally soft, really, for the work he did outdoors. His eyes were grey, too.

Today, in the spring heat, he wore the farmer's uniform of cord trousers, wellington boots, checked shirt and a frayed brown sweater. He must have washed his hands, because they were not as dirty as usual. Nevertheless, his nails were outlined in grease and earth. He stood permanently hunched over, apologising for his size – six foot two, six foot three – and a small smile on his face. Last week, he had caught her as she was running out to the library van that had stopped in the gravel lay-by. He had told her that, when he was younger, he would go to the library in Wraughton and get those thin little romantic novels for his mother: six at a time. They would last her a week. Blushing and looking very pleased, he had said that he used to read them himself when she had finished. And the image of Hugh, with his hunched-over posture and his small smile and boy-like, uncreased face reading the little books in the chair of his living room at the farm . . . Well, it had made her smile.

No. Not smile. It missed the smile and went sinking down, sinking down, into the dark. She felt sorry for him; the idea of him reading them, absorbing them, was rather sad.

I wonder if you're lonely, she thought. Then mentally corrected herself. *I wonder how* much *you're lonely.*

He seemed to fill the kitchen. She edged past him and got down the biscuits from the shelf.

'How is work going?'

She asked him this every time she saw him. Their formality.

'"Tsfine.' All one word, thrown away.
'I saw you doing the track yesterday.'
To her surprise, he grinned broadly; his face lit up. 'You were watching?' he asked. 'Watching me?'
'Just glancing out of the window. I thought it was you . . .'
'That's right,' he told her animatedly. 'I cleared the dewpond. We got ducks there this year. One pair. You ought to walk down and see 'em one day.'
'Yes, I might.'
'I'll show you.'
'Yes . . . I'll see.' She spooned coffee into the cup for herself, gave him the glass of water, offered the biscuit. The dewpond, in the hollow of the track, was a good mile's walk. There could be flamingoes in the wretched place for all she knew.
It was then that she noticed the time. 'Is that right?' she asked Hugh. 'Is it really half-six?'
He sipped. 'Yes.'
She tapped her watch face. 'This is going slow. It stopped yesterday. I put a new battery in it.'
'You shouldn't. Jeweller should do it.'
She grimaced. 'I know.' She leaned on the worktop and stared out of the window.
Then, to her absolute surprise, Hugh reached out and took hold of her hand. He made a little fluttering motion towards the watch. 'You need a new one,' he said.
She gazed down, uncomprehendingly, at her fingers clasped between his. His hand was rather warm and sticky. Looking up at him, she saw a pulse flicking in his throat, a silent Morse code of excitement. Or maybe anxiety, or even embarrassment: which, she had no idea. His hand on hers seemed ludicrous and funny all at once; she wondered how on earth she could extricate herself without seeming rude.
'Oh, no. No, that'd be a waste.' She tried to joke. 'I'm always forgetting to put it on, get it mended. I take it off at school and people find it and bring it back – it's quite a joke . . .'
She tried laughing. Hugh was watching her so intently, it was almost as if he were lip-reading. Her thumb was at an awkward angle: she managed to prise herself loose. There was a second of excruciating silence: Hugh was standing, looking rather agog and stupid and flushed. The moment had amazed her.
'Have to remember a new watch when it's your birthday,' he announced, abruptly. 'A real good one.'

'But Hugh, thank you, but . . .'

Maybe he hadn't heard what she said. She started to deny again that she needed a new watch, then thought better of it. She gave herself a mental shake.

'Yes, he – he went on the bus,' she said, loudly. *For goodness' sake, change the subject.* 'He insisted.' She made a whirling gesture in the air with one hand. 'In-*sis*-ted. I suppose I ought to go and look for him.'

Hugh looked down into his glass. The pursing of his lips was the nearest he came to an outright criticism. 'He was wearing a tie yesterday, and no shirt,' he said.

It was said with the utmost gravity: so much so that she burst out laughing. If only that were all.

Hugh frowned at her. She waved his remark away. 'Oh, that's nothing,' she said. 'It's just the latest. Do you know that they have a word for it, it's so common? It's called "dyspraxia". Dad's got this thing about buttoning anything up. He's hated buttoning for the last ten days. I'm waiting for it to pass.'

As if it would!

They used to pass, these phobias, and Father would come back, his old awkward self. But now the obsessions returned, roaring into his face, within days.

She snatched up her handbag from the side. 'I'd better check,' she said.

'Shall I come with you?'

'Oh no. Thanks, Hugh, but I'm fine. You've devoted enough time to him today. Also . . . well, he might think it's a search party. He'd get outraged. You know him. But thank you anyway . . .'

Hugh followed her out. Solid, doglike padding, rubber boots squeaking a fraction on the floor at her back.

She was *always* thanking him. She wondered if the recurrent sound of her thanks irritated Hugh as much as it irritated her. Lord, the equations! She hated this trap she had been pushed into, this small secret prison. And constantly seeing Hugh; the visiting at every hour of the day that she dare not say anything against for fear she would be left without help . . . God! She couldn't stand this feeling that her life was out of her control, unravelled, unpredictable. As soon as she got her hands round one problem, it all altered and she had to think again. It was like wearing clothes that had not been sewn together properly: nothing *sat* right.

She tried not to think of the future. After all, the situation could change from day to day. Her father might suddenly become so bad that he had to be admitted to care, if she could find anywhere. Alternatively, he could go on for years, steadily getting worse: if he did so, she would eventually have to give up work.

And that was the option she dreaded.

Leaving school meant leaving the real world. Leaving her class, and their triumphs over matching sets and understanding words, and climbing four feet up a rope, and making hand shadows, and catching bugs in a bottle.

All life was like that. Catching things in a bottle, trying to preserve things. If only it were possible to bottle some pleasant experience; to capture it in every detail, its sounds and tastes. To capture wind or sun on your face, and the colour of a scene laid out before you in every dimension. A kind of hologram of the past. If only she could have bottled some of her holidays when she was twenty and twenty-one, at college: bottle the summer in Italy which remained in her mind as a perfect memory. The walk to the hilltop village, the coldness of the gin-and-water in its lime-scented glass, the warmth of the evening rain that fell, a soft, yellow-tinted curtain around the terrace of the café, weighing down the flowers. If only she could feel again the texture of stone and grass under her feet, and see that odd, ochre light as the evening began, rolling over the red roofs below, the winding stairs, the olive trees. If only it were possible to bottle all that, and have it stored somewhere in this house. So that she might go to the cupboard and uncork a day, perfect in its sense of optimism and a sweet, drunken drifting feeling, and release the same light. Release and live again the spaniel lying in the shadow at the side of the café, and the kerbstone rubbed smooth to a gleam like glass. The smell of blossom and sand. A day out of the past: a talisman. Warding off the present.

She thought of this, unlocking the car, brushing her long hair back from her face. Forgetting Hugh, who stood at the house door, smiling to himself.

As she backed her car out of the gate, turned it around, she could not see Hugh. The inside of the car smelled of the hot fabric seats. It was like an oven. She wound down the window. The view of the house and its back door was cut off by the field hedge.

She revved the accelerator, put the car grindingly into gear, and passed into the long straight lane. She looked into the driving mirror, and her thoughts flew out, forward along the road, wailing for escape. But she knew that she was not going to escape. She was going along this three-mile stretch of road looking for trouble.

She did not look back at the house.

* * *

Hugh went back down the track.

It was a quarter of a mile to the top of the track hill. Then the land sloped sharply away. At his back, Eve's house perched on the side of the road, surrounded by his crops. Nothing behind it. Nothing in front of it. Just the red-brown roof and the church-like arched window that looked south, and the patch of lawn trimmed with red and white and yellow, her sewn trimming at the hem of the garden, the flowers.

She was shut inside his land. He had her here, in the palm of his hand.

Soon now. Soon.

An immense swathe of hairy-headed winter barley fanned out behind the house all the way to the Sherving road. She and her father looked lost, forgotten, hidden from the road by their hedges. He had planted those hedges himself twelve years ago.

He looked away from them, and all around himself, with quiet possessiveness.

Straight ahead, a mile further down, was the road between Petherell and Winterbourne Beck, just at the edge of his own house and outbuildings. Just as Eve's house was sheltered from the road by her hedges, so his was hidden by the contour of the land. You came upon his farm and its decaying outbuildings all at once, a surprise, after negotiating a right-angled bend in the B-road. A horseshoe of thatch and a new white house behind trees. Then it was gone. The next turning of the road swept it away.

Up on this ridge, it was different. Exposed, highest of the rolling low hills, you could see the sea. There was its grey line, a line painted over the top of the next rise. This too was his land: his field of spring wheat yawned upwards in a great arc; two hundred acres. Flash, it was called. A hundred-year throwback to the time that the stream had run along the side of the lane. Flash was an eerily bright green now, a superb colour, and perfect. He sometimes stood for minutes at a time, anywhere on the farm, but particularly here, admiring the unerring sweep of the lines he himself had ploughed. Beautiful strong deep sections: parabolas, arcs, angles; a geometric exercise in soil.

The breeze blowing over the land today was fresh and strong. Salt was in it, and green, green, green . . . A lark was bubbling frantically, a liquid clean clamour. He felt a sudden, suffocating rush of feeling. A kind of impatience, so drawn out, so overused . . . He was accustomed to shutting it down. Treading on it to stop it. The feeling for Eve. It would come without warning, like a seizure, a pain in the chest. At times like that, pinpricks of light blotted the fields. He would even have to switch off the engine of the car or the tractor and wait for it to pass, like a woman in labour waiting for a contraction to pass, squeezing the life out of her. It stuck in his chest, at the bottom of his throat, just above the rib-cage. It stuck there like a weight, and took his breath away.

It rolled off him at last: he put one foot down, then another. All he had to do was walk, the feeling would go away. Impatience and longing . . .

He must not rush her. *He must not rush.* Now that the decision was made, now that the course was set, he must go steadily and firmly and calmly. Like schooling a horse, accustoming it to the saddle. Steady and firm. That was the way he had schooled his own three horses, so that they would not shy away at the crucial moment; the moment when he put his hand across their eyes with the bridle that tied them to him for ever, and to his desires. Gently, gently, gently, never letting the rein go slack.

His face suffused with colour, his mouth clamped shut, Hugh began to walk fast. Reaching the crest, he looked down at the thousand acres running down to his house.

Just on this top, he had planted a narrow rectangle of linseed rape. He squinted against the low sun and looked at it. A car was parked, humped on to the verge of the track. In the centre of the field, about forty yards away, two figures were moving.

He walked towards them and, after a minute or two, the smaller one stood up and waved to him.

'Hello, Hugh,' the man called.

He lifted his hand by way of reply, and threaded his way carefully down the line of crop. As he got up to them, the second man straightened up, too. He was a lad of about nineteen or so, of average height, and dark. He looked almost Indian: the American-Indian of cowboy films. A wide forehead and flat cheekbones and dark liquid eyes: the kind of face that women would find handsome. The curve of the lips had a satisfied, sexual line. The two of them watched him.

'All right?' Hugh asked.

'Yes. Not much more now.'

'That's good. Everything all right?'

'Yes. See you got the whole lot down.'

'Yes.'

Hugh's eyes wandered off Latham, on to the bags beside them. They were taking a trials test, looking at the quality of the crop. His eyes strayed from the ground to the boy again. He gave the lad a nod. 'Now then.'

The boy said nothing, but the sensual smile never went away.

'This is Jonathan Davies,' Latham said. 'Helping me out for a week or two . . . Good fine weather, isn't it?' he added.

'Yes, good and fine.'

The desultory conversation came to a stop. Jon twirled a tape at his side, a tape like a white plastic whip. Hugh watched it tapping against the boy's leg.

'Coming down for a sandwich after?' he asked Latham.

'Thank you. Maybe we can go over the few bits of paperwork.'

Hugh nodded. He was already moving away. 'Look down along the stream if I'm not in,' he said over his shoulder.

They watched him plod away, across the green and gold rape, to the track; watched the solid squarish body disappear past the rise.

'So that's him,' said Jon.

Latham grinned.

They bent down again, the lad handing the tape and the plastic bags. In the silence, the wind stopped. Jonathan looked up at the sky, along the ridge, and out in the direction that Hugh Scott had taken.

The dark came along the hill softly, in all the muted colours of the day.

Eve stood at the back door watching it, the red and grey washing across the empty sky. There was going to be a thick mist tonight: they always caught it up here. Spring mist late for the time of year. Petherell's spire could just be seen, the tip of it, above trees. She watched as it was drowned in shadow.

Above her and to the left, she could hear her father running water for his bath.

She had found him that afternoon sitting on a bench right at the bottom of the town, on the corner where there was a garage and the start of an industrial estate. He had been sitting watching the traffic pass, perfectly content, swinging his crossed leg. A woman was talking to him.

Eve had parked the car in a sidestreet, taken her bag from the seat, and slipped into the garage shop, all the while keeping her eye on the bench and the talking couple. She'd bought milk and two packets of tissues, neither of them needed, paid the girl, and stood uncertainly on the doorstep. A lorry had come in, parked by the nearest pump, and obscured the view.

When Eve had at last reached the bench, she could hear her father saying, 'And when they excavated Brewer's Walk they found a bit of Roman wall . . .'

So he'd been all right.

There was a Roman town house – the remains of it – just a hundred yards up the road. Perhaps the woman had stopped and asked about it: the tourist sign was just on that corner pointing the way. And he would know: after all, he was still a member of the Archaeological Preservation Society, though no longer secretary, of course. Still, he remembered some things with uncanny clarity. The excavation that he was now talking about, for instance, had been last summer. Pre- worst of illness. Pre- this. For a week, he had helped: scraping, digging, sorting. He had been thrilled to bits. Proud of himself.

The woman was listening, very politely, her hands folded in her lap.

'Hello, Dad,' Eve had said.

He'd glanced up. She'd sat down beside him on the seat.

'And they say that a Roman road must run somewhere between here and the coast,' he had continued. He'd shifted his body so that he was looking directly at the woman, turning away from his daughter. Eve stared across at the sign for tyres and exhausts and diesel. She saw the edge of the woman's face, under its border of felt hat.

'Of course . . .' her father's voice had rattled soothingly on.

The lorry had pulled out of the bay, and stopped on the junction. The driver had looked down at Eve, chewing something slowly as he'd gazed. The vibration of the lorry shook his body, gently, gently, in the cab. He'd grinned at her and winked.

'Pouring tonnes and tonnes of concrete . . . They never allowed long enough, to my mind, before they built on it. They never do . . .'

Quite suddenly, the woman had stood up. She'd looped her shopping bag over one arm, and given Eve a helpless, bewildered look.

'I think I've got my breath back now,' she'd announced, and shuffled off, crablike, retreating, to the side. 'So nice to talk to you,' she had said.

'Tonnes and tonnes,' said Eve's father.

The woman had picked up speed and made an adroit swerve, crossing the road to the accompaniment of car horns.

'Going east to the harbour in line with the aqueduct,' Eve's father had continued, barely breaking rhythm.

He had put his hands on his knees and sighed deeply.

They had watched as the cars had changed gear, shuffled up together in the road like a pack of cards. Air brakes hissed. The nearest driver, behind his windscreen, had mimed a furious curse. Then the whole stream of them had accelerated and unravelled again, whipping away along the by-pass. The woman who had been cornered on the bench had merely put up her hand to steady her hat, squared her shoulders without looking back at the traffic, and walked away.

Eve had smiled at her father. She'd touched his arm. 'Coming?' she'd asked. 'I've brought the car. Give you a lift home.'

He had stood up, giving her a surprised look, straightened his jacket, and gazed around himself.

'I'm sorry, but I've got to get the bus,' he'd told her. It was in a tone of the utmost deference and kindliness. 'You see,' he'd added, 'I've got to get to my own house. I'm expected there for tea.'

She went upstairs quickly, shutting every door behind her, locking the outside ones in particular, and putting the keys into the pocket of her jeans.

At the curve at the top of the stairs, she could hear that the water was running into a full bath. She knocked, pressed the door open. Her father was standing at the sink.

'Shall I turn off the water?' she asked.

'Oh . . . yes, do.'

She swilled her hand around in it. 'You'd better hurry,' she told him. 'It's run a bit cold now.'

'Has it . . .?' He was looking in the bathroom mirror.

'What's the matter?' she asked.

He gripped the side of the sink. 'Nothing.'

'What is it you want to do?'

'I—'

'Is it something you need? The soap's on the bath. Your comb—'

'I don't want my comb. I don't want nothing.'

He heard the ungrammatical sentence at once: it jarred on him, jarred on her. 'Anything,' he corrected himself.

'All right,' she said. 'OK.' She went out.

On the stairs, she paused, and picked up her father's socks and shoes, which were standing neatly on the landing, as if tucked under a bed, or as if he had – as in a hotel – put them out for cleaning. As she did so, she caught sight of her mother's photograph.

This image dominated the upper part of the house and stairs. It was only a small picture, about five by seven, in a silver frame. It perched on the windowsill, and one could see it from right along the landing and from the bedrooms. It had been there as long as Eve could remember. As Eve went up to bed at night, her mother's face laughed down at her as she climbed the stairs. She had a tight high collar, so tight that it seemed to threaten to choke that long neck. Or perhaps it was just the straining of her mother's head as she had pitched her head back to laugh.

Eve had often wondered about that photograph. Her father said it had been taken on holiday when Eve was still a baby and, although it was only head and shoulders, Eve's mother had actually been leaning over the push-frame of the pram, after straightening the cover. Wind had brushed back her hair. Sun shone directly in her face. She had a high forehead, light hair, a large mouth, a cleft, very deep, in her chin.

Of all those characteristics, Eve had only inherited the blonde of the hair, translated in her to a shade that was almost white. She had memories, tantalisingly fleet, sharp, clear – like the sharp tart taste of lemon which she always associated with her mother. Perhaps her mother had drunk that lemon juice that was so popular in the early sixties; perhaps she had worn a lemony perfume; but the strong prick-taste of lemon always accompanied the image: her mother in a crepey dress, gondolas in Venice wrapped around her body, ribbons, water, written in blue and red on a white background, her mother leaping forward and snatching her up in the watery folds of that dress, the material so soft, the smell of lemon, acid and clear, her mother's brown arms with the tendons in the wrists corded with effort.

Her mother in a field, religiously picking dandelions to make wine. Her mother, laughing, stretched on a lilo and her feet in a paddling pool, all the long border behind her hot with nasturtiums. Her mother digging fiercely in the vegetable plot, on some indefinable day before she became ill. Brilliantly alive in her daughter's head.

She wished so much that her mother was with her now. Not just to halve the awful burden of her father's illness, but to talk to. To share with. Looking in the photograph was like looking into a puzzle – if only she could see round the edges of the image. It was almost impossible to deduce anything from one faded photo. But she felt they were alike.

She paused, staring past the frame now and out through the arched window into the last twilight of the evening. Maybe that was why she irritated her father so much, why he could never bear her touching him. Perhaps she was like her mother; so much so that the sight of her hurt him.

She looked back at her mother's frozen smile. Simple psychology. Too simple, too easy. And it gave her father the benefit of the doubt. No; the answer was far more prosaic. She knew what other people thought of him; knew the reputation he had had at the school where he'd been head for years. Knew he was considered an impossible personality: difficult; unpredictable. And that, more than anything else, was likely to be the explanation of why he had kept her at arm's length all her life. Because he was simply an angry, unpleasant, unapproachable man.

It had been about a month ago, she recalled, when Hugh, talking of the time when he'd altered the route of the track and put up the barn, had suddenly said, 'Course, your Mum was furious at us. She come down to the farm and tore us off a strip. Mind, she had a lot on her plate.'

Eve had stopped what she was doing and looked at him in surprise. 'Did she?' she had asked. 'Why?'

Hugh had blushed. 'Nothing. Nothing particular,' he'd said.

She'd smiled. 'But there must have been a reason to say that,' she'd insisted. 'What was the matter?'

'Well, your Dad . . . You remember . . .?' he'd begun, then stopped.

'Remember what?'

He'd looked at his feet. 'Well . . . well, you know him – what he's like. That's what I mean. He weren't ever any different.'

She'd thought no more about it at the time. After all, Hugh was right. Her father had few friends and used roundly to declare that he didn't want any. Well, he'd got his wish. Nobody wanted *him*, now.

Tonight, however, just for a second, staring out at the growing gloom, she wondered what it was about her parents – about her mother – that she was supposed to remember.

Mother . . .

She looked so friendly in the picture. An extrovert person. You could imagine her talking breathlessly; fidgeting as the focus was altered on the camera; laughing and making fun of herself. The hair was all loose and unstyled, unfashionable for the time. She looked happy. Capable, outgoing.

I wish you were here, thought Eve passionately. *I wish you were . . .*

'Oh, fucking hell!'

Eve whipped around, jolted from her thoughts. She ran back to the bathroom, shoes and socks still in her hand.

'What is it?'

There was no reply, so she pushed the door.

'Fucking, fucking hell!'

He had pushed a chair against it. She pounded on the wood, 'Dad!'

No reply.

'Dad!'

At last came his muffled response. 'What?'

'What's the matter?' she asked. 'What's up?'

He came to the door very slowly: she heard him shuffling on the other side and dragging away the chair. Gradually, he opened it, and she saw that he was undressed. Naked grey-haired legs. She deliberately tried not to look at his small wrinkled genitals, the matted grey pubic hair. His body was long, slightly flaccid, bony-shouldered; his neck thin, his face flushed. Face put on top of body. Mismatched.

'What's the matter?' What's happened?'

He pointed to the sink.

There was nothing in it: no razor or blood, which was what she had feared.

'What? What is it?'

His face collapsed quite suddenly. Crumpled up. He looked at her baffled, furious, defeated.

'I want – I want to do that thing with my face,' he said.

'What? What thing?'

His mouth turned down in a small boy's cry. 'You *know* that thing, whaddya call it, whaddya call that thing with the face you do . . . you know . . . you *know*, you know . . .' He slapped his hand on the sink in impatience, then sat down finally on the edge of the bath, his hands hanging between his knees. His voice, when it came, was far, far away. 'I want to cut the hairs on my face,' he whispered.

She said nothing, but went to the bathroom cabinet and took out the razor.

Four

Eve walked to Sarah's house the following afternoon. It was about a quarter of a mile from the school: set back from the road, it looked out over the river valley. The very last of the forsythia was blowing in the garden, the cherry blossom rotting on the ground, the daffodil leaves lying about abandoned and yellowing. Sarah was no gardener. Eve came in the gate, struggling with two full carrier bags; at the same moment, a lad of about nineteen came round the side of the house. He went to a ladder lying in the grass, and started to pick it up; the sound of her footstep on the path distracted him.

'Is Mrs Marsham in?' she asked.

'Yes. Round the back,' he said.

He watched as she came towards him, and as she went past, and then followed her.

Sarah was sitting on a rug on the lawn, a tray of tea at her side. Sydney was head-first in the rhododendrons, and Eve could hear Sarah saying, 'Darling, you mustn't do that. Frogs like to be left alone. Darling, you mustn't do that – bloody Nora! – frogs don't like—' as she walked down the slope of the grass.

'I'm here.'

'Oh, Eve. Look at him. He *won't* come out. In a minute I shall tell him you're here: that'll terrorise the little beast.' She gave an exasperated shrug, and then waved her hands over the tea things. 'What d'you think of this? I've got proper saucers and everything.'

'I'm impressed. I'll swap you. I've got fifty cap guns and things with elastic on that go whee-boing.' Eve dumped the bags, smiling, on the rug, and looked behind her.

The dark-haired lad was setting the ladder against the back wall. There was some problem with the catch: it kept slipping, and they could hear him cursing softly to himself. She knew then that she had seen him before; but where, exactly, momentarily escaped her.

Sarah was already pouring.

'Who's that?' Eve asked. She sat down and was handed a cup.

'Jon – I think *Jonathan* – Davies. Don't you recognise him? He was helping Latham last week up at Hugh's. And he's been doing odd jobs for the Witchells. He's trying to fix that bloody pane in the bathroom. It's driving me potty.'

Together, they tipped the lucky-dip toys on the rug and portioned them out; it came to fifty-four each. They made a face at each other, sighed, and began wrapping and taping. The afternoon was cool and the paper kept threatening to blow away. Jon was, by now, at the top of the ladder, scraping paint from the window.

'Who does he belong to?' Eve asked.

'Eh?'

'Jonathan. Whose son is he?'

'Nobody's. I mean, nobody's here. He's taking a year off from college – somewhere in Kent, I think – and he came down here because of his course. Geography. Geology? I can't remember. Witchell said he's a first year and something went wrong and he's having to go back in October. He's doing odd jobs. Got a room in town. Don't think he gets on with his mother.'

Eve began to laugh. 'And that's all?'

'What do you mean?'

'No star sign, no inside-leg measurement? You're slipping.'

Sarah smiled, a piece of Sellotape between her teeth. 'Well, one likes to know.'

Eve glanced across. She realised, now, that she *had* seen him – the previous week, in Latham's car. They had stopped at the road entrance and were writing something. She had watched them for a minute as she'd stood at the sink, peeling potatoes. That day, she had noticed the absolute darkness of him: the hair, the sallowish skin, his whole Latin colouring. Now, as she looked, she saw that he was about six foot tall and solid. Not muscular, but broad, slim-waisted, slim-hipped. He wore a pair of denims and a white T-shirt: toddler clothes, with dirty white trainers. He was all squares in the way he looked: blunt-shouldered, square hands, that squarish face. Very young. *Very* young.

'Talking of Hugh,' said Sarah.

'Were we?'

'Not really. But anyway, I just remembered, I meant to ask you . . . Did you go in to town on Saturday?'

'Town? Why?'

'Did you park in the library spaces?'

Eve tried to think. Early on Saturday, she'd gone in for half an hour to get a few pieces of shopping.

'I was there about nine o'clock, first thing,' she said. 'Why?'

'And by the library?'

'Yes.'

'Well, bugger me.' Sarah sat back, picked the packet of cigarettes from the tea-tray and lit one, drawing in the smoke with an air of relief and luxury. 'He's a bit gone in the head, I reckon,' she said.

'Who is?'

'That Hugh Scott.'

'Hugh? What makes you say that?'

Sarah was gazing at Eve, her eyes narrowed, as if she, too, were trying to work it out.

'Well, I was crossing at the top of the High Street, I had a dentist's appointment at nine. I glanced across at the library and, just by that wall, where they put the telephone cables in last month, the bit they dug up?'

'That's right,' Eve said. 'I was parked behind there. It was a corner gap. It's not a real space. Not marked out.'

'And there was Hugh.'

'Doing what?'

Sarah stared to laugh, then stopped, her brows furrowed. 'Well, that's the strange thing,' she said. 'He wasn't doing anything at first, particularly – he was just standing, looking at your car.'

'My car . . .?'

'And I got to the pavement, and looked again. There was something just – I don't know – *peculiar* in the way he was staring at it. I thought, surely he's not going to break into it, and then, damn me if he didn't just . . . put his hand on the windscreen. Just the damnedest funny thing. Put his hand on the windscreen, and *stroked* it. Like a cat. Stroked it five or six times.'

The two women sat staring at each other.

'But why?' asked Eve. 'It wasn't dirty or something, was it? He wasn't wiping away a fly, or a leaf . . .?'

Sarah shook her head, definite. 'Nope. Just stroking. Very very gently.'

A ridiculous shiver ran straight up Eve's back.

'Is he a brick short of a bloody load, d'you think?' Sarah asked.

'Hugh?' Eve sighed, still puzzled. 'He's just . . . solitary. He keeps coming round, you know, helping with Dad, asking if I want anything. I think he's lonely.'

Sarah stubbed out the cigarette. 'I should keep an eye on that one,' she observed, drily. 'I wouldn't mind betting he's sickening after something. Mind out it isn't you.' She looked up at Jon, perched on the ladder outside the house. 'Hey, Jon,' she called out. 'Do you want a cup of tea?'

Jon climbed down and walked towards them. He had none of the round-shouldered, apologetic way of an adolescent; he walked upright, smiling, slightly hurried, as if he were anxious to get to whatever lay ahead. He looked at Eve and nodded as he took his tea, holding the saucer carefully between fingertips.

'It's Miss Ridges, is it?' he asked.

'Yes.'

'At the school.'

'That's right.'

'You live up near Mr Scott's.'

'Yes.' She had to smile back at him: he was gazing at her with an innocent expression, like a child from her class, the eyes widened. It was as if she had just revealed some fascinating piece of information, or told a joke that delighted him. He looked ridiculously fresh, untouched and green, rather like a fruit, picked too soon, peeled to show its soft green flesh and laid in her hand.

Something in her moved into life, and she immediately banked it down, thinking inwardly, *Don't be stupid, don't make a fool of yourself, he is nineteen* . . .

'Sit down,' Sarah said.

He hesitated. 'No – I won't thanks,' he told them. 'See you're busy.'

'You could wrap a few,' Sarah said.

He laughed. 'No thanks.'

'Are you coming to the fête?'

'I don't know.'

'Come and help. We always need able-bodied men.' She was into her stride now: Sarah's best bantering, hectoring tone. 'Go on . . . Give you a free cream tea.'

'I might,' he said. 'When you say cream, is it anything that comes out of a can and melts?'

'Heaven forfend.'

'How many scones?'

'Oh, two.'

'Sold.'

Sarah laughed. Jon handed back the cup, smiling. All the time he was talking, however, he had barely taken his eyes off Eve. He hesitated for a second, looking down at her as she held the hair back from blowing in her eyes.

'Is it your dad – Bill?' he asked, his voice much lower now. 'Who was with Mr Scott?'

She was momentarily taken aback. 'I expect so,' she replied. 'Tall, in his sixties . . .'

'Yes.' And he gave her a smile, so very adult, so direct and understanding, full of kindness, that she stared for a second at him.

'My Nan was a bit forgetful,' he said, quietly. 'It must be a worry for you.'

She didn't quite know what to say. It was obvious he had seen her father, obvious that he had known exactly what was wrong – and probably Hugh and Latham had given him more than enough detail – and yet here he was, barely nineteen, sparing her the indignity of making a joke of it; saying, in a quiet voice, *forgetful*.

Bless you for that, she thought.

'Thank you,' she said. 'It is.'

Jon looked at his feet. She thought he was going to say something else; but he obviously thought better of it.

'I'll get on,' he said. 'Thanks for the tea.'

When he walked back, Sarah said nothing. She had looked from Jon to Eve while they talked with an expression of amusement and intrigue. Eve, similarly, said nothing. The pile of the gifts grew higher, the wind blew steadily, infuriatingly, across them. Somewhere in the undergrowth they could hear Sydney smashing stones together and digging. Jon moved the ladder to the next window.

'He keeps looking,' Sarah said.

'Who?' Eve thought Sarah meant Sydney. Sydney was fond of getting into inextricable corners and then keening plaintively for help.

'Jon-boy. Him up t'ladder.'

'Is he?' Eve replied.

'No – no! Don't *you* look. Blast.'

Eve smiled. Jon had been diligently scraping the sill.

'He was,' Sarah insisted. She poured them another cup, the last in the pot, and sat back on her heels, staring with frank interest at Jon's turned back.

'He's quite appealing,' she said, suddenly. 'Don't you think so? Wouldn't you like something like that?'

'Sarah!'

'No – no. I mean, purely hypothetically. Not *him*. He can't even be twenty. I don't mean him. You'd have to get his inoculations done and tie his shoelaces. But – hypothetically now – someone like that, someone uncomplicated.'

'Everyone's complicated.'

'No they're not.'

'They are. They are. It would just be a lot of trouble.'

'Why?'

Eve shook her head, smiling. 'Oh, you know. You meet this person, and you go through all the meals and phoning and whatever, and then you find he's got a fetish about string or a phobia about trains, or he likes birdwatching, or Gilbert and Sullivan, or he has to win arguments, or is funny over money, no no . . .' Sarah was beginning to snort, the dangerous forerunner to the flattened accordion.

'No, but, that's right, isn't it?' Eve persisted. 'You get your legs waxed, or you drive a hundred miles to watch him play cricket . . .' Now Eve started to laugh, too. 'Oh, I just couldn't stand it,' she said. 'It takes up all this *time*. I haven't got the energy. I'm just happy if I can get a night's sleep without Dad roaming the countryside – that's all I want.'

Sarah sat back and considered her. 'It's a shame,' she said.

'No – no. I've got enough on with Dad.'

'Forget your wretched father for a second. What about you?'

'Well, what about me?'

'When do you get to have fun?'

'Well, I – just . . .' Eve cast around her for a way to put it. 'I just enjoy what I do at school. And it's *enough*. It really is.'

'You liar.'

'It's not a lie. I'm just too worn out to care.'

'What if it wasn't trouble?'

'There's no such relationship.'

'Oh!' Sarah made a sign of crossed fingers in front of her. 'Take that back, you cynic! I mean, is Duncan trouble?' She put her hand to her head as if suddenly ill. 'What am I saying? Of course he's bloody trouble.'

She sighed, glancing round in time to see Sydney pulling faces at Eve, who – mercifully – hadn't seen him. 'Look,' she said. 'You know what's the matter with you? You've forgotten. You've forgotten! That's the pity of it: a young – well, ish – woman like you, and all your own teeth and a regular income, too. It's criminal. If you're not very careful, you'll get all bitter and twisted and end up looking like that woman on the patisserie in Fowlds.'

Eve shrugged, picking up the very last parcel with a sigh. 'When *I* get in bed, the only thing that I lie awake thinking about is whether Dad is trying the downstairs doors, lighting the gas, running taps.' She taped the last parcel with satisfaction, then gazed about her.

Sarah put a hand on her shoulder, and gave it a sympathetic squeeze. Eve didn't look for much practical sympathy from Sarah – nothing more than the hand on the shoulder, and listening when it became too much. Sarah had told Eve roundly the year before that she ought to have her father admitted to some kind of care: 'Before he drags you down with him,' she had said. Eve, still refusing this option in her own mind, was acutely aware that Sarah's advice hung permanently in the air between them whenever Bill was mentioned.

But apparently Eve's father was not at the forefront of Sarah's mind today. She leaned forward, her hand dropping from Eve's shoulder. Her voice fell a shade, becoming serious.

'It isn't that you don't want anybody, or that they'd be any trouble. It isn't that you don't need anyone.' And, as Eve opened her mouth to object, Sarah laid a hand on her arm. 'You're all . . . walled in, shut up. Closed down. You're showing it, here,' she said, pointing a small, plump finger at Eve's face. 'As if you've given up . . .'

Eve stared at her, resisting an urge to put her own hand to her face to feel the constriction that Sarah said was drawn over it. 'Well, thanks,' she responded, finally. 'That's really made my day. That's given me confidence.'

Sarah leaned forward, across the rug, the tray, the paper and parcels. A flood of Diorissima engulfed Eve, and a smile that was more characteristic of her than the depressing verdict on Eve's expression lit her face. 'Listen,' her friend murmured. 'I've got the perfect remedy. Won't take five minutes. Pop up that ladder a minute. Just for research purposes. See if everything you've got still works. Do you a world of good. And I won't tell a soul – except the Education Authority. Brownie's honour. Honest.'

Just at that moment, Jon finished, coming down the ladder in one rushed chain of steps. He glanced over at them as they exploded into laughter.

'Damn,' said Sarah.

'For God's sake, shut up,' Eve told her.

And they both looked carefully in the opposite direction as Jon stood, hand on one hip, smiling across at them.

It was evening, in the last of the light.

Hugh Scott stood in his kitchen, by the window, listening intently, as if cataloguing the sounds.

For a long while there was no noise on the lower road, then, reeling out of the dark and silence, a car rushed through. He heard its swishing as it turned the corner. In its wake, a soft, ballooning silence. Then, down on the fields, he heard the horses moving about. He could actually hear the sound of their hooves thudding through the grass: they must be running. He went to the door and looked out.

Sure enough, there on the lower field, the mare was cantering aimlessly about. She got as far as the fence and kicked up her heels, then danced down the division, almost indistinguishable in her dark coat from the darker border of the trees. She was bringing her head up and charging it down again. Probably just escaping the flies, he thought. They massed like nobody's business down there in the flat. Great clouds of them: moving blocks of insects hovering in the air. No wonder the horses charged around like that in the evening. Maddening. He ought to go and bring them in.

Hugh went back inside. He reached up and closed the curtains. He went through into the kitchen and made himself a cup of cocoa. He put the cup on a tray, and spent a good five minutes wiping the surface of the cupboards and the sink, wiping the taps in particular until they shone. Satisfied, he took the tray and went upstairs.

At his bedroom window, he laid the tray on the table next to it. His room looked forward to the fields, only giving a glimpse of the rise of the hill. He sat on the chair and sipped his drink.

He thought it had all gone very well, really. Despite the date. He had got over that now.

Of course, it had been late when he had got to the vicarage. Later than he had agreed. But that was Bill's fault: all his aimless wandering and fussing about. It had been the devil's job getting him into the Land Rover and up to the house. Hugh had wanted to go in and be with Eve, if only for a few minutes, but by then he was already behind time. Eve had asked him if he wanted to come in – she'd seemed rather distant, as if thinking of something else – and he had had to refuse her. He didn't like to do that. Refuse her *anything*. Still, in the future, they would have all the time in the world together.

The vicar was young: thirty-five, maybe. He was new to the parish. He had a younger wife, and four children. Hugh envied him that. The two eldest boys were playing in the hall as Hugh came in, and the vicar gave them a friendly telling-off, ushering Hugh into his study. Somewhere back in the rear of the house, Hugh could smell the evening dinner being cooked. He wanted to say, 'That's how it's going to be for me, soon – a wife cooking dinner, children in the house.' But he had not. He had kept the details of his secret. They were precious.

The life they would make together, their children: it belonged just to him and Eve.

'What can I do for you?' the vicar had asked.

Hugh had sat down in the squeaky plastic chair that was offered. 'I want to get married,' he'd said.

'Married! Well, that's a nice bit of news, I must say. Congratulations.'

Hugh had blushed with pleasure. 'Yes. In June.'

The vicar had paused a second, eyeing him. Then he'd reached to the desk for his diary. 'Right, let's see,' he'd murmured. 'What date?'

'The last Saturday.'

'Right . . .' He'd flicked the pages. 'That'll be the twenty-fifth. Saturday . . .' He had begun to write. 'Saturday twenty-fifth June, next year.'

Hugh had sat forward. 'Not next year. This year.'

The vicar had looked up and smiled. 'This? I'm afraid that's not possible. It's barely eight weeks away. We're fully booked.'

'Eh?'

'Booked. All booked up. It's a rather pretty church, ours. People from all the four parishes apply to be married in St Swithin's.'

'But I want June. Got to be June. I live here. I've a right.'

The vicar had put his book down slowly. 'Yes, I know that you live here, Mr Scott. But you have to plan way ahead for a wedding, you know. A long way ahead. We're full every Saturday from now to September.'

Hugh's face had fallen. This was something he had not expected. Not for a moment reckoned on. It had never dawned on him that he couldn't be married, on the date he chose, in the same church where his own parents had been married and were now buried. 'I want this June,' he had repeated.

The vicar had frowned. 'I'm awfully sorry.'

There had been a silence. Hugh had looked out of the window, flushed an angry red, his hands working on his knees in silent frustration.

'Who is the lady?' the vicar had asked.

Hugh had not looked back. He was sulking. 'Eve Ridges. My neighbour.'

'Eve . . .' The vicar's voice had trailed away momentarily. Hearing the inflection of surprise, Hugh had looked back accusingly at the younger man.

'The teacher at Petherell?'

'Yes.'

'Oh. I see . . . Of course, I don't know her. Just to say hello, perhaps. Not got my bearings quite yet.'

Another silence. The boys had run out from the hall into the garden, squealing. Their small sister, four or five years old, had followed them. They'd all rushed past the window, and Hugh had heard their mother shushing them from the kitchen door.

'It is, er, it would be usual for the bride and groom to see me together.' The vicar had smiled his best and most concerned smile. 'Will . . . will Eve be coming along to see me?'

'It's a surprise,' Hugh had said.

'Sorry?'

Hugh made an impatient movement with his hand. 'A surprise. The wedding's a surprise.'

The vicar had stared at him, then offered a brief laugh. 'Not *too* much of a surprise, I hope,' he'd said. 'Not a shock?'

Hugh had shot him a furious glance. 'I want June,' he had said.

The vicar had scratched his head. 'If we had a cancellation, I would fit you in,' he'd said. 'Of course, those are rather rare. They do happen. But rare. Now, September . . .'

'September's no good.'

'Well – all I can suggest is that you try another parish.'

Hugh had got to his feet.

The vicar had risen too. He'd kept a chair between himself and Hugh, as if afraid that Hugh was about to hit him. 'I'm so sorry. Really. If you'd let me know earlier . . .'

Hugh had gone to the door. He'd got down into the hall, almost to the front door, with the vicar, giving him a strange glance behind his back, in his wake, before he turned round.

'Well, what day in September?'

'The – er – fourth, I believe. In the afternoon.'

Hugh looked at his feet, wrestling with some inner demon. 'The fourth.'

'Yes.'

'All right.'

'There are banns to call, of course. And I run a "Getting Married" course, three evenings in the month before the day . . .'

'All right.'

Hugh had opened the door himself, and gone out into the porch.

'And you'll bring Miss Ridges to see me?'

'All right.'

'If you give me a call, I'll be only too happy to—'

But Hugh had turned and gone. He'd ignored the vicar's wave from the doorstep.

All the way home, he had fought down his fury. Little bloody pipsqueak of a man like that telling him what he could and could not do. Booking out *his* church, *his* day, *Eve's* day, to strangers . . .

Getting out of the Land Rover in the yard, he had slammed the door, muttering, 'Jesus H. Christ,' to himself. In the kitchen, he had spent a long time gazing out at the road.

His temper had taken an age to go away.

Remembering it now, he gazed in the twilight at the little dark horse cantering about. He sighed to himself. Things were never easy. Not for him.

He saw the mare coming down the centre of the field as if she were doing dressage, performing some odd kind of polka in a neat line. Then, quite suddenly, she stopped and looked – he thought – up at the window where he was.

He stopped drinking and held the cup, chest-high, mid-movement, watching her. She looked like some book animal in the dark. Some fairytale animal. She might have a horn and wings there in the dark. She looked up at the window of the farmhouse with a steady, unflickering inclination of the head. He wondered if she knew that he was in there: he had not put on a light at all at the front of the house. He leaned forward.

No, she was not moving. She was looking at him.

He had on a dark blue shirt. She would not even be able to see his shape. Except, perhaps, for the shape of his face in the glass. He wondered if she was looking at the shape of his face. If she had caught the movement of him drinking. The dark came in full now, cloudy, soaking up the grass and the line of the fence in the field. Still the horse stood motionless in the centre. Then she lowered her head and began to crop at the grass. He could make out the great muscles along the line of her neck. He put his hand on the glass of the window, and felt the increasing cold out there, and very faint rims of heat surrounded his fingers on the pane. He took his hand away and stared at the impression of his hand on the fading picture of the horse in the darkness.

He stood up and, without moving away from the window, he undressed.

It took him a long time, as usual.

He was scrupulously careful.

Everything he took off, he laid in a neat line on the bed. He folded them just so. Then he went out of the room and along the corridor.

The last part of the corridor upstairs was uncarpeted. The sensation of the wood under his naked feet, and the coldness just here, past the last radiator, coming to the unheated closed room, was just unpleasant enough to be delicious.

It meant her.

That discomfort and cold.

He liked it even better when it was winter: then he almost froze approaching this door. And she would appear in the front of his mind with an extra clarity and the sharpness and the hard cold of it would be . . . oh, very nice.

There was a picture rail running around the wall. He took a small key from the top of it, and unlocked the door.

It was a very good room. Nobody had a room like this room.

It had very little furniture, and no floor covering. The floor was board. That was not how he really wanted it, but it would have to do. There were lots of things in this new house that were not as good as the old ones, the thatched ones in the little semi-circle that he now used for storage. Floorboards was one of them. For instance, in the nearest cottage, the floorboards upstairs had at one time been pasted with some thick black tarry stuff – it lay in patches, where carpet had been stuck to it. It was disgusting to look at, but it was dry and it gave a wonderful gritty, textured feel under his feet.

Still – Eve would never live, as he and his parents had once done, in a run-down place like that. That was the reason he had built the new farmhouse six years ago. Now the cottage thatches had gradually decayed, and he did not quite know what to do with them.

When Eve married him and came to live here, he would let her do whatever she liked with the house and the cottages. He would let her have her head.

The image of the horse intruded for a second, shaking her head, dancing in the dark along the fence of his field. Standing and staring up towards his window. The wriggling of the neck.

He was master of that horse.

He would be master here . . .

The pink plaster walls had never been decorated in this room: they bore a fine tracery of settlement cracks. He would allow her to choose her own colours.

In the middle of the room, on the chipboard floor, stood two packing cases, several cardboard boxes, a trunk – very old, peeling – and a small table. On the table was a telephone.

No directory. He didn't need a directory.

He went over and stood next to the trunk. He stood there in the dark, accustoming himself to the blackness that was not quite black when you got used to it: a rectangle of light spread on the floor from the window. He thought of opening that window so that it would be colder still, but could not quite bring himself to move. It would spoil his moment.

The first few minutes could be very good indeed providing he was perfectly still. Like stepping into a theatre or a museum or a shop, where there was something you liked and wanted to see, and savouring having found the right place, and seeing that it was exactly what you had anticipated and needed: that could be very good. He stood, cold but not shivering yet, feeling the pleasant secrecy of the room coat him from head to foot. He was the master . . .

Finally, he had to reach down to the trunk. He had waited ten or fifteen minutes, listening to the cold and the silence and thinking about opening the window. As he shifted, his foot ached. That told him that he had been standing there quite a long time – otherwise he would not have known. He had no sense of it while he was here. He had finished his obsequies now.

The trunk was a leather one, once maroon, now black streaked with faded red. He opened the lid. Inside was a photograph album – a good one, not the plastic kind. A good one with leaves of tissue between. Then there was a whole folded pile of clothes. Then there was grass in a Tupperware box. Stones in a Tupperware box. Remains of a picnic she had once had – not with him, of course, but on the farm land. There was a coat. There were children's books. There was an oil can and an oil filter: she had asked him if he would service her car once. There was a woman's underslip, with a cotton border with a ribbon in it. There was a sheaf of music for the piano. There was a pair of nylon popsocks still in their packet, now over ten years old, dropped as she had got out of the car coming back from town once. There were worn pairs of shoes from the dustbin. And a bus ticket. And there were his postcards.

Eight postcards, dating from about twelve years previously and stopping eighteen months ago. That was the last time she had been on holiday and sent him a picture and a polite message.

He had probably read those postcards at least a thousand times. Now he read them again.

As he finished with each one, he leaned down and stacked it on top of the packing case, facing him. When there was no more room against the case, he laid the rest carefully in a fan shape on the floor. The very best ones – the ones where she mentioned him – he placed with the writing facing him and the picture turned away. The other scenes were reduced to black and white lines in the shadow. Malta and Majorca. One of Venice. How she'd gone on about Venice. She said that her father had spoiled it for her with all his complaining and ranting. She'd loved that place... He had this dream, this dream of taking her by boat out to one of the islands, and surprising her by knowing all the names of the streets and why it was famous...

You should see the colours.

Terracotta and green.

Faded red. That blue!

Coccina Tiepolo Papadopoli Palace. He could say it like a native. The look on her face he conjured up when he thought about the future...

Hugh! You never told me you knew all about it! All the time! You dark horse...

Built by Guglielmo dei Grigi. Then the Dona Palaces and the Businello and the Barzizza... He knew more about Venice than she did, now. One day – very soon now – he'd surprise her. He surely would. He'd surprise her. The idea of her surprise and the exact – *exact* – line and contour of that expression on her face, fuelled his fantasies for weeks.

You never told me you knew all about it. Why, Hugh! Why, Hugh!

He replayed it again and again in his mind to get that inflection in her voice just right.

He knew what she liked, all right.

The Tiepolo Papadopoli Palace slowly drowned in the darkness as he watched. Only the three central arched windows showing like black eyes against the side of the trunk. Only the words Puerto Soller showing in any other picture. The rest were her words, turned to face him.

He refused to touch himself, though it half killed him.

Look at Hugh, Eve.

See me.

Don't edge past me with that half-smile. Don't say thank you on the doorstep. He wished – oh God oh God – he *wished* she would not be forever thanking him. Don't always thank me. It's not what a lover would do. Don't take that road into school in the morning without even glancing down the track. I stood in the field and you never even saw me. I stood in the turn of the track and I willed you to come to me and you never came even though your bedroom light was on for hours and hours.

Frowning, he corrected himself.

That was not the way to go on. You never got a woman interested by complaining. If she hadn't noticed him, it was his own fault. He must do something else.

He must think of something else.

Something to please her.

Something to free her.

He looked at the telephone and then squatted down, facing it. It was a red phone. See that, Eve? Red. Show me another place round here that's got a red phone. See that!

He had been popular at school. Same school she taught at now, in fact. When she told him that she had found some lad down by the blackberry hedge, he knew exactly where she meant. Where it had all gone away, those easy friendships of school, the nights with girlfriends and mates, he didn't know. They had all got married, had children, moved away. There wasn't many he knew now.

Taken a lot of girls down that track alongside the Capricorn field, specially in summer.

Last one was . . . Last one was . . .

But he couldn't remember who the last one was. Eve's face intruded when he tried to bring back the girl in the back of that old Ford truck.

Hugh took a breath.

In the cold and the dark, he held it, enclosed inside him. While the world stood perfectly still.

Five

Eve woke with a start, and stared into the black.

For a moment, disorientated, she could not think where she was – the sound had interrupted a dream. Then, turning her head, she saw the bedside clock. It read 3.30 am.

The noise was coming from along the corridor, from her father's room. She sat up, listening, and again the sharp crack leapt through the night like the noise of a gun. Quickly she pulled on a wrap, and went out, and ran to his door.

His light was on, but she could not get in. He had put something heavy against the door. She managed, by shoving hard, to push it open just a little. In the segment revealed, she saw the floor littered with paper.

'Dad, what are you doing?'

Nothing. She pushed harder.

Her father was sitting in a sea of chaos. Clothes were pulled out of the wardrobe. The bed was stripped, the sheets tangled at one end. Everything in the bedside cabinet, the drawers, the bookshelves, had been thrown about. In the centre of this disorder, her father squatted on his haunches, the old wood trunk open. He was holding a book that Eve had never seen before: a big desk diary.

'Dad . . .?'

He shot to his feet, staring at her, the book clasped to his chest.

'What's all this?' she asked.

His face contorted. 'You get out!'

'I can't – look at this mess. What the hell are you up to?'

He took a step forward. 'Get out . . . get out!'

She started picking up clothes. 'Look at this. My God—'

The blow took her completely by surprise. He had reached out and caught her on the side of the head with the book, taking her breath away, making her head ring. She stumbled backwards, putting up an arm to defend herself, but he made no other move. He stood in the middle of the room.

'I can't find it,' he said.

She rubbed her cheek and ear. The ringing became a dull buzzing.
'Where is it? I can't find it.'
She closed her eyes. *You old bastard*, she thought. *One day, I'll kill you.*

'I can't find her. Where did she go?' His voice droned on, became twisted with the sound inside her skull. Downstairs, in the locked cupboard, she had the prescription that the doctor had last given her. Sometimes the drug worked, sometimes not. Instead of making him sleep, he could pitch forward into overdrive for perhaps an hour or more, before dropping where he stood. She weighed up in her mind whether she could bear him in overdrive tonight. She had to work tomorrow.

He was wagging his head from side to side, looking around him.
'Can't find her . . . can't find her . . . looked everywhere . . . can't find her . . .'

She couldn't put up with this all night.
'Who?'

He opened the book, flicked the pages. 'She never said anything,' he muttered. 'She never said she was going. It wasn't my fault.'
'Who?'

'I wasn't to know,' he continued, his voice wavering. 'How could I know? One day she's all right, the next day . . . I provided for her. It proves that here.' And he hugged the desk diary closer. 'Proves it. What she asked for. Within reason. It wasn't my fault . . .'

Suddenly, the old man collapsed inwards, like a house of cards folding in on itself. He slumped to the bed, and then, slowly, to the floor. He threw the book to one side and pressed his knuckles into his eyes. 'Can't find her, can't find her,' he whispered, agonised.

Eve pushed the table backwards, away from the door. 'I'm getting you a drink,' she announced, in a voice not entirely her own. 'If I get a drink, will you have it and go to bed?'
'Not till I know,' he said.
'If I help you find her, will you go to bed?'
He wiped his mouth, snuffling. 'Yes.'

She went out. She had no idea what – or who – he was looking for. The probability was that he didn't know either.

At the top of the stairs, when she stopped to listen, she heard him weeping.

Six

It was the second time that Hugh had been back to the shop.

The town was busy, flooded with shoppers; but the place that he had chosen was in a small side street. A street that, in the last century, had been almshouses for the poor of the parish, and had now been converted into an exclusive row of small boutiques. In the centre was a small stone yard, set with tables. He had been sitting here for over half an hour, sipping at a cup of cold tea, watching the shop out of the corner of his eye.

It seemed to be the right kind. At first glance it had looked deserted; a few women with pushchairs and a few older mothers had paused by the window, but passed on. No one seemed to go in. Probably because the prices were so fantastically high. Then he had noticed activity at an upstairs window. There was a spiral staircase in the downstairs room, and a girl with her arms full of cloth ran up and down it. Finally it dawned on him that the upstairs was a fitting room: they not only sold the dresses, but they made them too.

At this revelation he ordered a second cup of tea.

That was good. It was not just churning out dresses off the rail. They produced originals: ones that were never repeated. That was what he wanted for Eve. A dress that would never be repeated.

He glanced up again at the window.

Two girls, now, stood at the glass. The one who worked there was showing a piece of fabric to another, a redhead with bare shoulders, who peered down at the design. He saw a flash of breasts barely covered with lace. The curve of the neck. The way the hair fell forward. As the material moved in the other girl's hands, it gave a momentary, fleeting sheen in the sunlight.

His heartbeat doubled. ·

He wished he could be there, invisible, between those girls. Hear what they talked about. Watch as one worked and the other peeled off her clothes. He would like to sit in the corner and just watch. Women – that foreign, mystifying, seductive species – fascinated him. Perhaps just a little touch – if he could freeze them for a moment and touch them without their knowing; a little touch on the shoulder, the thigh. A fingertip. Imagine being able to do that. Step into a room and watch, and then slip a hand, a finger . . .

A man sat down opposite him and opened a newspaper, but Hugh did not notice. He was breathing in the cloud: fabric from the roll, a mixed scent of starch, cotton, and satin. The cold clean kiss of cotton as thick as a shroud.

Eve . . . Eve, in a silk dress.

Eve standing still while he did whatever he wanted.

He put the money for his tea down on the table, and walked to the door of the shop.

As he pushed the door open, the smell that he knew would be there assailed him, powerful as sorcery.

A woman walked forward. 'Can I help you?' she asked.

Seven

On Friday, there was a meeting at the school. It was the Annual General Meeting to which the parents were invited. Eve stood in the doorway to the school hall – a hall festooned, high above them all, with the ropes and ladders of the gym equipment – and ushered them in.

As she handed out the minutes to them, she thought of the children that the faces belonged to. Here and there a couple stood out who were so dreadful that your heart sank horribly. There was Joe Marshall, a cigarette turned inwards towards the palm of his hand, the receding hair combed over the bald crown of his head, a black polo shirt three sizes too small stretched over his stomach. His wife, next to him, painfully thin and nervous, also had a smoker's dark circles around her eyes. And yet little Andrew, aged six and in Eve's class, was a fragile little boy with the face of an angel. In twenty years, he would no doubt emerge as a carbon copy of his father.

The mum grasped Eve's elbow. 'Is it all right if I come in Monday?' she asked. 'I got a problem. He says some boy steals 'is shoes.'

Eve smiled. 'Of course . . . I need to see you anyway. Any time before assembly.' She made a wry smile to herself as the Marshalls passed. Obviously angelic Andrew hadn't told his parents he'd discovered an effective response to the shoe-stealer already. He tried to strangle him at lunchtime.

Eve glanced down the corridor. Here came another challenge: the low-cholesterol liberals. You heard them before you saw them, speaking twice as loudly as anyone else. He in a Viyella shirt, blazer and flannels; she in a floaty sixties frock with her hair down to her waist. They had no TV in their home, allowed no rock music, no sweets, no comics, and had drilled the children into playing the bassoon and the cello. As a result, the two eldest boys ran riot at school, stealing sweets from lunchboxes and begging to be allowed to watch videos. They also had another dreadful vice: the overwhelming urge to call parts of the body by their correct names, and to announce them at every opportunity. Youngest LCL had, on his very first day, declared that his 'penis had wet his trousers'. The middle LCL, aged eight, wrote in his news that,

'Mother had a pain in a vagina and took it to the doctor's'. The staff room waited with bated breath each week to see what the LCL genitals had achieved over the weekend. They were rarely disappointed.

Here, at last, came someone sane. The Blythes, all smiles, were coming down the corridor in full sail: they both weighed at least sixteen stone, and moved with the unassailable grace of two galleons.

'Hello, hello,' said Catherine Blythe, grasping Eve's hands between her own. 'I was just telling Harry, *aren't* Eve's paintings *marvellous*, you're so talented, why don't you show some of your work? I know La Gallerie in Foxwell Tarrant, you *must* . . .' She turned to her husband, a bearded and cheerful-faced twin. 'And Eve has done marvels with Caroline's piano playing, hasn't she?'

Without waiting for an answer, she swivelled back to Eve. 'Honestly, I wish I were creative, like you, it's a blessing, *marvellous* . . .'

And they passed on, bequeathing equal amounts of praise on other lucky recipients down the long rows of wooden chairs. Their two little daughters, one in Eve's class, one in Year Two, were adorable. As they sat, they waved at Eve, and she, smiling, waved back.

A contrast if ever there was one, Eve thought. Some parents had a special voice they reserved for her, a voice meant to impress. That, or they hardly ever looked her in the face. She had long ago decided that it must be a residual reaction to their own childhood teachers, gorgons they had once feared. They looked as if they half expected to be rapped over the knuckles with a ruler as they held out their hands when they met her. She sympathised, though; she herself had had a terrible Infants teacher when she was five. She remembered Miss Darling to this day – a witch in a chestnut wig, who relished the cane.

The meeting itself was a mind-paralysing amalgam of budget, ethics and governor-speak. Most sat with their brows furrowed. A new parents' committee was elected: the same brave few as last year, facing another twelve months of desperate money-raising via jumbles and fêtes and car boots.

Eve was glad to get to the glass of wine at the end. She circulated, purposefully avoiding Sarah, who was arguing with a governor about violin lessons. Surreptitiously, Eve ate most of a bowl of crisps. It was the best thing about the whole two hours. Finally she went round the tables, tipping one bowl of rag-end Ritz crackers and peanuts into the same bowl. As she did so, she inadvertently overheard two women discussing a third.

'And he's gone up to Two Trees to move in with *her*, and then Gayle came down here and moved in with *Tony* . . .'

Eve paused in her tipping and straightening. Did Matthew know anything about this? Be sure to get it right. The husband had moved out to set up house with one woman, and then that woman's husband had moved in with the other wife. A swap.

Eve realised that her mouth had dropped open like a trap-door. She suddenly clamped it shut. Good God! And the husband looked like five foot nothing of spit and fresh air . . .

'I say! Somebody got something against red?'

The man at her side was leering happily at her, holding up his glass. 'Somebody got something against red?'

'Oh, well, I don't know. Perhaps there was a special offer on the white.'

He wrinkled his nose. 'Not that special. Are you the Reception teacher?'

'Yes. Eve Ridges.' She held out her hand.

His returning grasp was flaccid, weak. 'Tony Sanders. Mine's in St Bertram's next year, little bastard.'

'Is he?'

'What, a bastard?'

'No. St Bertram's.'

The father was still laughing at his own joke. 'Little blighter.'

She placed him. 'Oh, you came last term, didn't you? From abroad.'

He drained the last of his glass. 'Yer . . . Germany. Ever been there?'

'Not lately.'

'Don't. Bastard place. Flat as a board, north Germany, *mein Herr*, flat as a board.'

'Yes.'

'Yer . . .'

She considered him. He was blond and thirtyish, and flushed with the drink.

'And now you're back here. For long?'

He shrugged uninterestedly. 'Year or two.'

'Are you a pilot?'

She saw him straighten up suddenly. 'Yer.'

'Oh – that's interesting.'

He began to laugh. He made a hawk-hawk-hawk noise. 'Yer . . . crack the bloody rooftops. That's us, that's me. One of those buggers. Ooooops! No, mustn't say that, eh? That's what we *don't* do. No, not us!' And he began to laugh again, hawk-hawk-hawk.

'You didn't have to go to this terrible thing in the Gulf?'

'I bloody well did,' he said proudly. 'I went out for four weeks, but I missed the show. Can you believe it? Bloody Bush chickening out. Hot rain. Ever felt hot rain?'

She had. But it had been long ago, in Italy.

'Yes . . .'

He wasn't listening. 'Tore up the engines.'

'I heard that on the news. It must have been – well . . .' She was going to say 'awful', but she could tell that it hadn't been awful, quite the reverse. It had been the high point of his life to date. She adjusted what she had been going to say. '. . . an experience.'

'Yer.' His eyes had glazed over. He was cracking the rooftops over Kuwait, and dragged himself back to the school only with the greatest effort of will. Abruptly, he grinned. A small boy playing at war beamed at her from beneath the flushed face. 'Quiet round here, I should say? Village life. Crikey!'

'Oh, it's not so bad,' she said. 'Have you managed to get around much?'

He put the glass down on the table. 'Seen a lot of insides of houses,' he said. 'Dinnering.'

'Dinnering.'

He snorted. 'Yer. Dinnering. You know . . . *They* give a dinner, *you* give a dinner. Suppering. Got to, you know. All on the jolly old report, socialising. Wife gets marked on the vol-au-vents and my brandy gets inspected.'

'Ah.'

'Yer . . . ah. Fucking boring.'

She smiled.

'Sorry, sorry,' he snapped. 'Out of order. Sorry.'

'That's OK.'

'No, not the thing. Sorry. Hate white. Doesn't agree with me . . .' He gave himself a mental shake, looked around himself. 'Well, nice to meet you, Mrs Rhodes.'

'Miss Ridges.'

'Yer . . .' He gave her an exaggerated wink and walked away.

Smothering a smile, she turned back to the table. She shoved all the bowls up together, took a cloth off one end. Hinting. *Go home.*

It was only as she walked out of the school forty minutes later that Sarah grabbed her.

'Hi, where are you going?'

'God, you gave me a shock.'

'Sorry. Think I was Hugh Scott?'

They smiled, rather wanly, at each other. 'I must get home,' Eve said. 'Hugh's with Dad.'

'What, right away?'

'I have to, really. Dad's been bloody awful today. I had to go home at lunchtime. He's had this thing this week . . . looking for something. Some woman. I can't make it out.'

Sarah pulled a face. 'You're a martyr to that man, aren't you?'

'Who – Hugh?'

'No, you arse. Why'd you say that?'

'I don't know, why did I? Freudian slip.'

'I'm not surprised. It dawned on me what Hugh looks like, you know.' And she made an attempt at a gargoyle expression. 'Death's Head,' she announced. 'Like this.'

Eve laughed. 'You're terrible to him.'

'He makes my flesh creep. How can you stand him in the house?'

'I've got no choice. Dad . . .'

'You poor cow.' Sarah had a way of consoling you that was rather akin to a slap in the face. She squeezed Eve's arm. 'I say, can't you bunk off for half an hour? We're going to the pub. I've got Duncan's underwriter staying with us. Meeting tomorrow or some such thing. Did you see him in school? He's absolutely loaded, house in Liliput, boat, the whole lot.'

Eve smiled and waved her hand, *no thanks*. 'Oh – I don't think so. Look at me. I'm not dressed up. And Hugh . . .'

Sarah laughed. 'Bollocks. Hugh will hold Daddy back. Or in, or whatever you have to do. Come on. Twenty minutes is all! We're only in the Half Moon across the road. Oh, Eve. Come *on* . . .'

Hugh looked at the clock.

Ten to ten.

He looked across the card-table at Eve's father and, as he did so, the old man surprised him by looking up, directly at him.

'Do you know what day it is?' Bill asked.

'Friday.'

Bill made an angry face. 'Not the bloody day of the week. The date, man. The date.'

'It's the sixth.'

Bill grinned. Tonight there was very little hesitation or confusion about him at all. Hugh could see the younger man, the man without illness, staring through the older face. Aggressive, randy, foul-mouthed.

Eve had told Hugh about the night before. As a warning, in case he did the same tonight. She made it sound as if it were a joke. But it was no joke to Hugh. More and more, Bill Ridges appalled and disgusted him. He'd been frightened of him as a lad – the big, loud-voiced man who made Eve silent – now it had distilled to a quiet loathing. Eve said that last night there had been a terrible mess in his room, and that he had been rambling on about a woman he could not find. It had been the same this lunchtime. She described the frustration, the tears. She said that her father would not let her see the red book; that when she tried to take it from him he had abruptly locked it up in his trunk. Hugh now stared at the man across the table. It was close on thirty years since he had seen this man destroy the woman who was his wife.

It had been covered up well enough.

The village rarely talked about Bill Ridges any more. He had weathered a slight storm at the school where he taught, and there had been whispers, but to all intents and purposes, that terrible year when Eve was eight had been obliterated without trace. Eve never talked about it – he suspected she had no memory of it. Adult tongues had fallen silent to save Eve pain; now, few remembered or cared. And thirty years ago secrets stayed secret. No dirty linen washed in public. Hugh's parents even tried to cover it up from *him*. When she was ten, Eve was moved to a school in another town, keen on music. By then, her mother's death had been swallowed up by time.

The things this man had done. The suffering he had caused.

Hugh would never hurt Eve by telling her of that time. Daddy had come home to live with and look after his little daughter. Devoted tragic Daddy. Never a mention of why he had gone away in the first place . . .

Eve had once said – in passing, with no great concern – that she knew her father had been away a lot, that she and her mother had spent a lot of time together when she was very small, that Bill in the house was no great part of her memory. She said it casually, implying that fathers often worked away from home.

Hugh's mouth tightened into a bitter line. The bastard.

He looked at him now, shuffling the cards.

About half an hour ago, Bill had been showing Hugh a picture of a topless model in a newspaper. 'Look at that prozzie,' he'd said. 'Just look at that bike.' It was a matter-of-fact statement, without lust, but with deep aggression.

'It's my wife's birthday.'

The sudden announcement jolted Hugh from his thoughts.

'Oh. Is it?'

'She'd have been sixty. Sixty on the sixth.'

Hugh considered. Hard to imagine that woman who used to stand waiting for the school bus – hair blowing back, who always looked so stubborn and erect and strong – as a woman of sixty.

'Can you imagine it?' Bill said, as if he'd been reading Hugh's mind.

'No,' said Hugh.

'Neither can I,' came the response.

There was a prolonged pause, during which Bill picked at a loose piece of skin on his face with his fingernail. 'Peas in a pod,' he said, at last. 'Mother and daughter. Ungovernable.'

This so shocked Hugh that he said nothing at all. Bill began scratching, scratching, at the cheek. Words came running out of his mouth, as if a tap had been turned; they came bubbling softly one over the other.

'What did she go out for?' Bill started. 'What did she go out tonight for? I don't know where she goes. She's forgotten it's her own mother's birthday. Should have seen that child at ten and twelve. Used to go down to the church three or four times a week. Flowers for Mummy, flowers for Mummy. Never see her go now. Never said a word to me about her mother's birthday . . .'

It was not delivered with any malice or regret or annoyance. Rather, the old man's voice had a tone of amusement in it, as if Eve had made some ghastly error that was sure to find her out and make her suffer agonies, and he could not wait to see it.

Hugh unconsciously clenched his fists. 'She went to the church yesterday,' he said.

The old man met his eye, and the grin burst into a deep, throaty laugh. 'Ungovernable women,' he repeated.

His hands suddenly grasped the deck of cards, splayed fanlike before them where it had been left after the last game. Bill was still laughing, slow and deep down. Bubbling water.

'Beggar My Neighbour now,' he said.

It was so long since she had been out anywhere at night socially that Eve hesitated a moment on the darkened doorstep of the pub. There were obviously a lot of people inside; a blanket of raised voices. She glanced down at her naked legs beneath the cotton skirt, the wide leather belt, the patterned shirt, her brown arms. She ran her fingers through her hair. 'God, I feel like a square peg,' she told herself. And, realising suddenly that she was acting as if she were sixteen, afraid of a crowd, self-conscious, she lifted her head, took a deep breath, and went through the door.

'Here!' called Sarah through the smoke.

Eve negotiated the crowd. 'What're you having?' Sarah's face, pushed towards her in the red gloom, looked puffy and out of proportion.

'No, it's all right. Here . . .' Eve searched for her purse in her bag.

'Don't be daft, darling. Vivian is buying you a drink. What're you having?'

Eve hadn't noticed the man standing to Sarah's right. He was tall, mid-forties, thin and wiry-looking, with piercing yellowish eyes in a freckled face. He had red hair, like a red cottage loaf stuck to the top of his head. The yellowish cat's eyes were fringed by almost white lashes. He stuck out his hand to shake hers, and the grip was light and delicate. She felt she had squeezed him dry when she took her hand away.

'And you are Miss Ridges.'

His voice was a contrast to Sarah's: it was low and soft.

'Yes. I'm afraid I must look a wreck. It's been quite a long day.'

'I don't see your medals.'

'Medals?'

'Your medals and war wounds. Dealing with all those children, you must have some.'

She laughed. 'Wounds, yes. But no one gives teachers medals any more.'

'Oh, my goodness. That sounds bitter.'

'Does it? Oh dear. My mask must have slipped.'

He laughed, then smiled at her thoughtfully. The drinks arrived, Sarah wobbling them purposely on a tray, singing tra-la, tra-la for a joke.

'Here, orange juice for Eve. I'm ashamed to ask for it. Viv's gin.'

'Vivian isn't driving,' he said as he took his.

Sarah pushed him heartily on the shoulder. 'You insurers. She won't have a bloody accident on one drink, will she?'

'It has been known.'

'She's only half a mile up the road.'

Vivian said nothing. He was watching Eve, rather expressionlessly, as one watches a TV programme one has switched on by accident and is too tired to change.

Quickly, Eve looked round the pub.

It was certainly packed tonight: the small timbered bar was a sea of faces. All slightly out of focus for Eve, who was short-sighted. In the corner, the enamel arc lamp lit up the darts board. There was a game in progress between a crowd of young lads and girls, whose voices had risen to shouting pitch.

Eve looked at Vivian. 'So, you're in the same business as Duncan?' she asked.

'Vaguely.'

'Insurance.'

'Rather boring.'

'Well . . . it *sounds* important. That's something.'

Vivian laughed. He had a laugh that was almost a whisper, which was blown away by the waves of sound lapping around them. 'Oh yes, I'm most terribly important,' he said.

She refused to be crushed. 'And you live along the coast.'

'Yes . . .'

'All those lovely houses. Huge places with gardens and moorings and everything.'

'That's us. Huge everythings.'

With any other man, this might have sounded like an attempt at a joke, but Vivian said it listlessly, twirling the glass by its stem. Occasionally he would look over her shoulder. She thought it must be someone that he liked the look of. The glance had that trailing recurring interest.

'Do you sail?' she asked.

His eyes flicked back to her, as if he had been caught out. 'Not really. I mean, I don't haul things about, keelhaul the mizzen mast, or whatever it is they do. I know someone who sails the thing properly and I sit on deck and drink and wave to people.'

She laughed, putting her drink on the nearest table. 'Would you excuse me just a second?' she asked. 'I must . . .' And she gestured towards the loos.

'Oh, please,' he said. 'Do, do.'

She turned, biting her lip to stop herself smiling. Sarah knew the most weird and wonderful people, some so outlandish that they were almost caricatures of themselves.

In the gloom, walking with her head down, trying to avoid the edges of the tables, she suddenly bumped into someone standing, his back to her, across her path.

'Sorry,' she began.

He turned round. It was Jon Davies.

'Oh, hello,' she said.

'Hello,' he replied softly. And she was amazed to see a violent blush suddenly colour his entire face, spreading, like spilled paint, down his neck. The colour faded almost as rapidly as it had come. She found herself pressed close to him in the crush, looking slightly up at him.

'Are you playing?' she asked.

'What?'

'Darts.'

'Oh, yes. I'm a stand-in. Got roped in, sort of thing. Not much good.'

She smiled.

'Who's that you're with?' he asked.

She glanced over her shoulder. 'Oh, that's Mrs Marsham's friend. A Vivian something.'

'Viv? That's a boy's name?'

'Well, it must be. Like Vivian Richards. The cricketer.'

Jon's mouth pursed expressively. 'Funny sort, is he?'

She laughed. 'Actually, he's a bit of a one-off, yes. Why?'

'He's been staring at me.'

'Has he?'

'Yes.'

'Oh Lord. Well, take it as a compliment.'

'I will.' He squared his shoulders, jokingly. 'I'm a new man. I can handle it.'

'Oh, yes?'

'People should be free to express their preferences.'

'Go on.' Eve was grinning back at him.

'Even if it means you get a squint like Quasimodo's. He needs glasses. He looks like the White Rabbit. Is he blind, too?'

'What, to ogle you?'

'No, to ignore *you*.'

She blushed. 'That's why I like Mrs Marsham – Sarah,' she said. 'Her friends are all eccentric. Oh, excluding *me*, naturally.'

He laughed. 'I like eccentrics,' he replied. 'I mean, they're a bit like Christians. You know, you wouldn't exactly like to *live* with one, but the world needs them.'

'Ouch! I see you were never an altar boy.'

'Don't tell Vivian.'

They smiled at each other. Eve felt abruptly hot, and rather embarrassed, the sense of his physical presence crowding her. He was wearing a blue chambray shirt, jeans, both very clean. He smelled of soap and fresh air, even in that claustrophobic room.

'Look, I wanted to say something,' he began.

'Sorry?'

'To say—' He turned round, frowning at the noise behind him, where a girl in a short tight dress had just scored double top and was prancing about in triumph. 'I can't hear myself bloody think,' he said. 'I just wanted—'

There was another crescendo of sound. Smiling, Eve nodded towards the other far door, and they made their way to it. Here the door was propped open, into the back yard of the pub. They stood on the threshold, in a porchway, and a fresh breeze blew in on them.

'I just wanted to say that, if you ever needed any help, with your dad . . . Because I know when Nan lived with us – it was only for a few months, but it was bloody terrible. Specially keeping track of her, the way she used to wander. I thought, if you wanted a break for an hour, say at a weekend . . .'

'Well, that's very kind. Very kind. But he's a handful, you know.'

'It's why I thought I'd offer. Nan had one or two bouts where she tried moving furniture, and tearing clothes, pulling books to pieces. She didn't mean it, it was a kind of frustration. And I thought, if ever your dad got like that, you'd be hard pressed. You're not much of a match for him, physically.'

'You're right.' And she remembered the recent blow, the bruises. 'But he's like a storm that blows itself out. I'm afraid if I called you, it might be a wild-goose chase by the time you got to us.'

'I don't mind.' He smiled at her.

Strangely, Hugh's face sprang to her mind. She imagined the expression on it if she said that Jon had come to help, that she had called Jon instead of Hugh. And it was not fear that she felt; not *exactly*. Those flat calm grey eyes, fixed on her, were not terrifying – not *exactly*. They were distracting, and deeply unsettling, rather like the fixed look on a painting, a still photograph, a burial mask: the eyes that stare out to eternity on the faces of Egyptian sarcophagi, or the eyes on puppets and dolls. You could pick the paint from the eye of a doll, and the other eye would never blink, and the mouth would never scream.

Sometimes she saw Hugh's eyes in the moments after waking, the moments just before sleep, looking steadfastly ahead, never moving, never altering. That in itself was bad enough; but she was wary, for a reason she couldn't exactly understand, of saying or doing something to make Hugh angry. She thought of her hand on the phone, starting to call Jon; and she envisaged Hugh's painted eye, scratched with a fingernail to reveal a blacker paint beneath . . .

'. . . help him with the harvest.'

She looked up at Jon, picking up only the last couple of words of the sentence.

'Sorry. Sorry, I—'

'What's the matter?'

'Nothing. Just felt . . . I'm sorry.' And she laughed, not very successfully. The room had pitched and rolled; the step on which they stood ballooned like a wave and slipped back again.

Jon reached out and held her arms beneath the elbows, and then passed one arm behind her back in an effort to hold her. She recovered – it was just momentary, fleeting – and found her palms pressed to his chest. He felt dense and soft, like some sort of giant toy, warm to the touch and gently sweet-smelling, a child straight from the bath, wrapped in a towel, the kiss of soft sand, the heat from an oven. All the most pleasurable sensations coursed through her. It was not sexual, but intensely good. For a moment she felt she could close her eyes and be carried gently away.

It passed; she stepped back, confused, smoothing down her skirt, fussing with her hands. Jon remained exactly as he had stood, with his arms a little extended, and a look of indescribable surprise on his face, as though he had discovered some new sound, new colour, new scent.

'Well, I don't think I've had a dizzy spell since I was ten,' she said, making a joke of it. 'Good heavens! I'm so sorry.'

'It's all right.'

She glanced back into the pub. 'I really must go,' she said. 'Hugh is at home – Mr Scott – looking after Dad. I think he's done his penance by now, poor chap.'

A slight frown passed over Jon's face at the mention of Hugh. 'Remember – about help. If I can help.' And he reached in his pocket, taking out a folded envelope. He tore off a corner, wrote his telephone number on it, and gave it to her. 'Ring me,' he said.

She put it in her own pocket. 'Thanks. It's ever so kind.'

They stood another second in silence. Then she turned and made her way back to the bar.

Sarah was standing in deep conversation with Vivian. 'Here she is,' she exclaimed. She immediately grabbed Eve's wrist with a grin. 'You disgraceful old cradle-snatcher,' she said. 'We saw you!'

Eve smiled. 'He was just telling me about his gran – she had Dad's illness. He offered to help; it was nice of him.' She downed the last of her drink.

'Oh yes?' Sarah responded. 'No need to throw oneself into his arms in gratitude, though. Bit over the top, darling.'

Eve didn't bother with an explanation. 'Oh, Sarah, you're impossible. Look, I've got to go,' she said.

'Go!'

'Yes, I must. I really must.' Eve smiled at Vivian. 'Nice to meet you.' He bowed his head.

'But it's only half-ten.'

'I must go. Poor Hugh.'

Sarah came with her to the door. 'It's like you were married to him. I introduce you to a perfectly nice man and you waltz off.'

Eve had to laugh outright at that. 'I'm sure Viv *is* lovely: loaded with cash, great house and all moving parts,' she said.

Sarah leaned on the door as she left, taking no notice at all of the couple who were late and trying to get in before time was called.

'But?'

'Nothing! Just *but*,' said Eve.

She looked back at Sarah, who was drinking solidly, happily, glass propped in hand, cigarette waving uncertainly at shoulder height.

'Have a lovely time,' Eve called as she reached her car.

'Give my regards to the dead sheep,' Sarah called back.

Eve did not go straight home.

She was within two minutes of the house, within sight of it on its dip in the hillside, when she took a left turn abruptly and put her foot on the accelerator. Quite suddenly, although she'd been saying for the last hour that she must get back, she could *not* go back. Not just at that moment. Hugh's eyes, her father's face, seemed imprinted in the strip of grey road in the headlights. She had to leave it.

The lane came blurring past; away from the house, the school, the sea of sound in the pub, she felt better. Just a little distance between herself and them all: just for a moment. Darkness washed over the car.

Just before Hugh's own houses, she turned left again, and took another turn where the lane petered out, down a track. A gate barred her way, and she stopped the car and got out. This was still Hugh's land. There was a yellow way-marker on the post, showing that it was a public footpath. Hugh kept the paths and the stiles in scrupulously good order. She went to the gate and climbed over the stile, and walked past the deep green gloom of the copse of trees.

In only twenty yards, the coast leapt out from the shadow of the hill: a smooth rolling sketch, in the dark, of the field and the sea. Hugh had wheat planted here. It was half green and half gold, a rich ochre seamed with acid green. The water came round in an arc, muddy at its mouth. Past the curve of the land, Chesil Bank formed a straight stone and sand line. She could hear the sucking of its stones as the waves turned, that voice endlessly speaking, speaking under the soft hand of the hill.

Today was her mother's birthday. She would have been sixty. In this particular half-mile before the sea, Eve felt extraordinarily close to her: she knew that her mother had liked this place. As she walked, she felt much better – lighter, freer.

Her mother had had a terrier called Punch. The dog had disappeared after Mother had died. Her father had said it had just run off. She had always doubted that was actually true, for Punch was devoted to the garden as well as themselves: he used to patrol it fiercely, his tail ramrod straight, his little feet trotting. After her mother's death, Eve had gone out looking for him, listening for him, calling for him. She used to come down this very path. But Punch had never come back . . .

There, at the darkening arc of the water, her mother used to swim. It had been a solitary occupation. The only time that Eve remembered watching her, she had been seized with panic when she had seen her mother's shoulders disappear beneath the waves. She'd begun to call, 'Mummy, Mummy!' and her mother had turned, and waded, laughingly, out of the sea, her arms outstretched. She had picked up the towel and wrapped them both in it, and Eve could still smell the salt on her mother's skin and the warmth rising up between them.

As Eve stood now and watched this same spot in the spring-summer night, another thought raced on the heels of the towel: the dog's barking, the salt, the warm breathy dampness in her mother's arms.

Her father had never mentioned the birthday. He had probably forgotten.

She tried to imagine her mother, at sixty, striding up the path from the water now, some other small dog at her heels. She imagined her dressed in jeans and a sweater, laughing, and holding her arms outstretched as she used to. For the briefest of seconds, the image was so clear that Eve actually thought she saw someone coming up the path, a dog turning round and round at her heels, trying to catch his tail just as Punch used to do.

Then it was gone.

There was no one there. The few conjured lines of a face, figure, shoulder, hands, vanished. Anything she might have had with her mother had vanished, too. Taken away by accident: one of those illnesses that claim the unfortunate few. The statistic. The one in ten.

There was nothing she could have done about it. There had been no one to blame.

She put her hands to her face and pressed the tears back, wiping her eyes with one sleeve.

Mum, I miss you. Miss you . . .

The rushing sweet silence of the land swarmed towards her and over her. She closed her eyes and let herself feel it carrying her away.

The residue of the evening faded. The faces of Vivian and Sarah retreated; the man with the drink in his hand in the school hall; the Punch and Judy cartoons of people. Red light on glass. Only Jon's face remained with her, and the unfathomable sweetness of his touch, his arm under her arm.

Over the wheat, the dark water whispered and shrank and turned. And she stood, her hands to her face, wanting something without a name, in the warm blowing darkness.

When she got home, it was eleven o'clock.

She squinted at the face of her watch while she opened the car door, and looked up at the house guiltily. There was a light on in the kitchen. None upstairs.

Just as she was about to put her key in the lock, Hugh opened the door.

For a second in the darkness she hardly recognised him. He looked odd – taller, perhaps. Broader. Darker.

'Hugh, sorry I'm late.' Perhaps he was angry. Perhaps that was what the look on his face meant. 'I went for a drink,' she said. 'And I . . .' Her voice trailed away. Hugh was shaking his head.

She tried to get over the doorstep – put her foot on the frame sill, but couldn't step up. He had not moved. He was blocking the way.

'Hugh . . .'

Still the head shaking. Like . . . what did that remind her of? Autism. The shaking.

'I can't find him,' he said.

'What? Can't find what?'

She had misheard him. She thought he meant that he could not find some domestic thing – a can opener, a key.

'*Him*. I can't find *him*. He's gone.'

All at once, she understood. 'Dad?'

'I went to the lav, I come back . . .'

'Not in the house?'

'No. I looked all over. Twice over. And called him.'

A great sigh escaped her. 'How long?'

'Quarter of an hour. I thought I'd best wait till you came back. See what to do.'

And Eve thought – she thought – there was some inflection in the way he said it, asking her a question, asking her to do some formless thing, something she could not grasp.

Momentarily, Eve closed her eyes, leaned on the door.

'Yes,' she said softly. Then, a little more than a breath, she added, 'Yes. I see. Yes . . .'

Eight

The police came in the morning, about ten o'clock. Sergeant Knight and a young constable who Eve had never seen before. She stood with Hugh as they swung into the bumpy gravel drive.

They looked at the house and the land, and drank a cup of coffee standing in the garden looking out over the fields. Hugh had already been out in the Land Rover: he had been searching, he had told Eve, since first light. All the land between the house and the farm, he said. Even walked the fields and ditches over the top, he said. Even as far as the sea.

'They go back to places they knew. Places they used to work. And live,' Eve volunteered. She had read this in a book, and it seemed a possible solution, even though Bill had never done that before. The four or five times that he had gone missing previously, they had found him almost at once, somewhere on the road between the house and town. Only once had she found him somewhere else: reading the newspapers in the County Library.

This time, however, she herself had driven to town – tracked the route half a dozen times already this morning. But nothing. Not a sign of him.

'We'll go to the school,' Sergeant Knight said, naming the secondary school where Bill used to teach. He laid a hand softly on Eve's arm. 'Might find him trying to take a lesson, like the old days.' She smiled at the joke that was no joke. 'Don't you worry,' the sergeant added. 'We'll soon get him.'

'Like he just vanished,' Hugh said.

The men nodded together. Three nodding dogs.

'Just vanished. I went to the lav. I was three or four minutes. When I come down . . .'

'They do,' said the constable. 'Alzheimer's. It's like senility, you see. Then they turn right up again.' And with his free hand he snapped his fingers theatrically like a magician.

The half-truths, the arrogance behind this remark took Eve's breath away. Yes, I know! she felt like screaming. Don't you think I bloody know!

They all stared dumbly at the grass.

When they had gone, Eve went to her car. 'I'm going to the market,' she told Hugh.

Saturday was market day – a chaos of cars in the small town. Bill had liked to go to market when he first retired. Not lately. But he *used* to like to pick over the bric-à-brac stalls; for a while he had been fascinated by clocks, and by old tools rusting in boxes. For a while he had brought them home. It had been a routine and, outdated though it might be, she plucked hopefully at the idea. Market, routine, market, routine, danced about stupidly inside her head.

Hugh came and stuck his face in at the driver's window. He looked like a basset-hound. Small folds of skin hung down around his jawline. He had not shaved. He looked . . . strange. It was as if he were excited. As if he were holding down, keeping in check, some high-pitched emotion, like one of her five-year-olds.

'Shall I come with you?'

'No, Hugh. No thanks. I'll just whizz round – you know. I'll be back soon.' God, she was giving excuses to *him* now. Hugh and her father had exchanged places. I won't be long. I won't be long . . .

'I won't be long.' She revved the accelerator.

Hugh stepped away.

She parked at the top of the town and walked down.

It was a bright and windy day. Warm. Spring unrolling into summer, her favourite month. That smell of freshly opened leaves. The sun laid a hot hand across her back. Passing the Borough Gardens, she saw the blue Victorian clock-tower revealed suddenly between the trees, a cream-coloured face, edged with cobalt, emerging between the branches. Great sheaves of lilac were in bud over the pavement. Someone had recently cut the hedge: flat-topped, it afforded a new view of a swept lawn, bench seats, empty paths, the children's paddling pool. There was something unerringly right and comfortable about this sight. She felt like someone who had been let out of prison into paradise.

She knew that was absurd: home was not – not yet, anyway – a prison. And this town was not a paradise. Still, despite the desperate anxiety over Bill, she wanted this freedom for just a little longer. *After all, I am alive, and my father . . . is dead.* She stopped at the pedestrian crossing at the end of the road, staring across at the crowds of the market, realising how terrible and true that last thought was. *I'm looking for a dead man. He has been dead, now, for months. I'm looking for a dead man in a crowd of the living.* I'm going to take him home ... *and I'm alive* ...

But she did not even feel guilty at this insane monologue. She was alive. Alive for just the time the sun breathed on her back before she turned into another street.

For twenty minutes, she looked for him. It meant a trek twice round the square, treading over boxes, squeezing between stands and pushchairs. Colour jumped up out of the stone, smell pressed down from above. The smell of doughnuts and tea and fish.

For a minute on the third tour, she stopped at the man who sold meat from the side of a lorry. He was yelling at the top of his voice, and the crowd lined up and stared back at him in the hot morning sun and the slowly rising clouds of dust. There was a drawing of a smiling pig, wearing a butcher's straw hat, on the side of the lorry.

The butcher held up a joint of pork sealed in clingwrap cellophane. It looked like a square of pinky-beige jelly.

'Three pound, three pound, three pound,' yelled the man.

The crowd stared silently back.

'Two-eighty, two-eighty, two-seventy . . .'

An auction going down instead of up, thought Eve. Different. A woman in front of her put up her hand, and the pink joint was handed down over the tailgate, over the heads of the people in front. The money passed it going the other way, up to the butcher and his scales and his slab.

Another sealed jelly joint was held up. 'This 'un's a six-pounder. Give us eight quid. Eight quid, eight quid, seven-fifty, seven-fifty . . .'

Eve put up her hand.

The meat came down, bobbing over the heads. She sent back a ten-pound note fished out of her jeans' pocket. The change came back with a white carrier bag. She looked down at her hands and saw that they were smeared with blood.

'Hungry?' said a voice in her ear.

Jon was standing at her shoulder. She found herself looking straight into his eyes. His hair was brushed back, an impossible shade of black. 'Got yourself in a bit of a mess,' he said.

She held up the carrier bag and her tacky hands in a gesture of helplessness. 'Why did I buy it?' she asked him. 'I hate bloody pork.'

'Right word.'

'But I hate pork. Why did I buy it? I don't know why I bought it.' And she laughed. 'I'm going crazy,' she told him. 'That's what it is, I'm going quite crazy . . .'

He did not laugh at all. But he took the bag from her and gave her a handkerchief from out of his pocket.

'I can't. It'll spoil your hankie . . .'

'You can't walk round looking like an axe murderer.'

Obediently, she cleaned her hands. She stuffed the handkerchief into the carrier bag. 'I'll wash it and get it back to you. Thank you.'

'Nine, take eight, eight, eight-fifty,' boomed the salesman.

'I'll carry it,' Jon offered. 'Are you doing your shopping?'

She glanced up at him. 'I'm not supposed to be,' she replied. 'I'm looking for Dad.'

Jon looked around the crowd. 'Where did you leave him?' he asked.

'You don't understand,' she said. 'He's not here. He's gone missing. When I got home last night . . .'

Her eyes filled with tears.

He took her by the elbow and steered her out of the crowd.

They sat at a white plastic table next to a kiosk. He bought her a mug of tea.

In this backwater, next to a wall, hemmed in by the side of the tea-stall, the sun roasted them. She looked at her watch and saw that it was exactly eleven o'clock.

'I think,' she said, 'I think I'm very tired.' And she pressed one hand to her forehead and smiled.

'Shock.' He sipped his tea carefully.

Her first reaction was to ask what the hell he knew about shock, all eighteen or nineteen of him, another little-boy white T-shirt, tight faded jeans. His nails were clean and looked as if they had been manicured, they were so neat. Far neater than her own.

He's careful, she thought. *He cuts his nails and carries a handkerchief . . .*

The skin on the back of his hands was clean and tight and soft-looking. He had long fingers, she saw. Perfect pianist's hands. His eyes were ringed with dense fair lashes, utterly different to the colour of his hair. And it was this that gave him that second-glance look to his face, she decided.

He looked Indian, the Indian of American Westerns. And he had that stillness in his expression, the lack of movement that was either lack of feeling or too much feeling. She wondered – briefly – which.

The irises of his eyes were deep, dark brown.

'It is,' he said. 'That feeling you're not really here.'

She sighed down at the table with its saucer of crushed cigarette ends greying in the sun.

'He likes coming here,' she told him. 'Or did.'

'How long's he been gone before?'

'Oh – half a day. Sort of . . . ten till five, that was the longest.'

'And how long now?'

She calculated, more slowly than usual. 'Nearly twelve hours. And, you see, the worst thing—' She looked up at him. 'Overnight, you see. Where did he sleep? Overnight.'

'Not in the night before?'

'No. Never.'

Crowds pushed at the edge of their small kingdom of white chairs, white table ringed with orange juice from cups, the cigarette ash. Inside the circle they sat silently.

His arm lay along the tabletop, the first signs of a tan darkening the skin. Dark hair on the arm. He smoothed hair back from his face. She saw blue stranded in the black. He had that lucky kind of hair, the kind she had always wanted, the kind that looked like liquid when it moved. Dense dense black water moving behind his fingers.

'I don't know where to look,' she said. 'We've tried everywhere near the house. There's just no trace.'

'Maybe he got a lift. He could have walked down the road – even over the other side, to Mr Scott's. Just thumbed a lift.'

The full horror began to dawn on her; she stared at Jon as he looked sympathetically back at her.

And her father was perhaps a hundred miles away by now . . .

Hugh was alone in the dip of land by the dewpond. He lay on his back in the grass, grass decayed with weeds grown into yellowing bundles. Now that there was no one near, he could allow the grin on to his face.

He lay staring up into the bright sky, almost laughing. On either side of him, the pleats of crop shelved away. There was no sound other than a distant thread of traffic on the road.

He had looked into Eve's face and told a lie. Even told the same lie to the police. Nobody had suspected him, no one had looked twice at him. They had listened to him and accepted his word. It had been as easy as that.

Of course, it was not a *big* lie . . .

He *had* gone upstairs last night and then come down to find the door open and Bill missing. He *had* searched the house and the garden, and the couple of outbuildings. All in the dark there without a torch. Standing on the doorstep when Eve came home, he had told her the absolute truth.

But, going home along the track, the headlights snatching at the edge of the fields, magnifying every pothole, he had suddenly realised that Bill's disappearance did not worry him at all. More than that, it was a relief. Bill had always left that disgusted taste in his mouth; now, the thought that he might be gone, had really gone, leapt on him. And that relief . . . Surely as he had faced Eve last night, he had seen that same emotion cross her face too? A second of relief slipped through her before the searching. He knew. He could tell.

They had gone through the pantomime of the police, and another search out there in the blackness, and, oh God. She was so close as they went down the path together. Once she had stumbled a little, and he had reached out to take her arm, but had not been quick enough before she straightened herself up. He nearly, nearly . . .

Going home last night, at one in the morning, he had stopped the Land Rover.

The wind had been rushing at him as he had stood on the track and looked back at Eve's house. At half-past two, her bedroom light had gone out. All that remained was the small circle of light at the back door: the light that illuminated a corner of the garden and the path to the road. He'd looked at that light until his eyes ached, and the circle itself had danced and wavered and moved; until other pinpricks of light had littered the huge expanse of darkness, and he'd had to close his eyes at last and wait until the stinging in them stopped.

When he'd looked again, he'd known that he could not leave Eve alone much longer. It hurt him to see that small, lonely candle shining in the vast body of the hill: *his* land, enclosing her on all sides, but not holding her. He ought to be with her, not leaving her there without any protection. She would need him now; she would turn to him.

And he would be ready.

His fingers had closed on the precious bottle in his pocket. It was only about four inches long: plastic, with a black screw-top. He had taken it out then, in the dark, and held it up to his face to get a better look at it. The green label on it looked black in the darkness: he could only just make out the letters on it.

When he had gone upstairs to use the bathroom in Eve's house, leaving Bill alone, he had made his usual circumspect tour of the rooms: walking on his toes, like a ballet dancer, careful not to let his heels sound on the carpet. He had smoothed the cover on Eve's bed, run his hand along her windowsill, opened the wardrobe and looked at her clothes. He had even noted the title of the book on her bedside table, and stood for a full minute, breathing in the uniqueness of *her* in the room. He prided himself that he had not taken underwear. He was not as low as *that*. Not as ordinary as that. Instead, he had returned to the bathroom and taken a little bottle of foundation from the cabinet: Summer Beige, said the label. Later on, he thought . . . He had stared about him, at the night, at the tiny pool of light on Eve's doorstep for inspiration. Yes, later on, at home, he would go to his special place and open the bottle, and put a little bit of the liquid on his finger, thinking that she had done the same, smeared a little bit of the liquid stuff on her finger and then on to her face, covering each curve of cheekbone, arch of eyebrow, line of her mouth. He would put the stuff softly on his own face, on his own skin, thinking solidly, solidly of her – no other image to invade his mind, only her, and the contour of her skin, and its smell and touch and taste, as he put the stuff wherever he wanted, wherever he needed . . .

He had gone home, the bottle in his pocket, still warm when he took it out an hour later.

It had been four when he'd finally gone to bed, feeling almost drunk with exhaustion; the exhaustion of excitement and anticipation more than anything, more than any act.

In his bedroom, the wind had pushed at the window and, despite his terrible tiredness, he'd hardly slept. Five o'clock, and the dawn coming up, the thought had occurred to him. Beautiful in its simplicity.

He would not look for Bill at all. He would *say* that he had looked, but what was the point anyway? The old man had likely taken the road, and would by now be either in Sherving or heading for the coast.

Hugh did not need Bill. Hugh did not *want* Bill: the old man was no longer worth a thought.

What was more important, *Eve* did not need Bill. He was no father. He was a walking corpse, a shell, an ugly mistake that was not human.

Eve only needed *him*, Hugh . . .

He knew in his heart that Eve's relief at Bill's disappearance matched his. One day, sooner or later, Bill would die. He would probably walk out in front of a bus. Or he would drink himself to death. The illness had only one outcome, sooner or later. Bill was dying – the slow, stretched-out dying of that disease. He might hang on for years, weakening Eve and bringing her down, squeezing the life out of her.

Or he might die – the better way, the infinitely better way – by accident, much sooner.

Let him vanish, he thought, as he lay now in the grass, staring into the sky, clutching the promise of Eve's loneliness to him.

Let him vanish. Let him die. Now, sooner rather than later.

Now!

Without a trace.

At Lyme Stoke, Eve rang the police.

There was no news, they said. All other local forces had been informed. Bill had not been found at his old school.

'I've come down to the coast,' Eve shouted into the receiver, above the noise of the passing seaside crowds. 'Lyme and Charby. He used to fish here, years ago. We used to come every weekend . . .'

The line crackled. She stood looking out at the sea. The tide was up and a fringe of families lined the sand, children running squealing from the waves, digging in the sand. On the promenade above the beach, deckchairs faced the sea. It was a scene of high colour, the sea a bright blue backdrop.

Visits here with her father had stopped about twenty-five years ago, when his interest in fishing had abruptly ceased – another one of his passions that had sudden beginnings, sudden endings. She used to like them coming here. She liked the town, liked the high Victorian wall of the harbour.

I used to hold the catchnet and the bait tins. I used to pour his coffee. He was utterly sweet and kind to me on those trips. We both enjoyed them. He would forget all about the music and the piano; he would never mention it. I looked forward to those days: allowed to stay up late, fishing from the Brake, the sea turning lilac and then the darkest blue, the lights showing in the water; and then happily falling asleep in the car on the way home. He used to buy me ice-cream. Sometimes, in the evening, we would get scampi and eat it sitting looking at the sea. That was my Daddy . . .

These thoughts choked her. She stood at the door of the telephone kiosk, gulping air, looking at the horizon. The occasional sweetnesses of Bill could sting her. As if she had been eating the same bland diet for years, and suddenly these isolated tendernesses of her father would swarm into that taste, overcoming her with their flavour and keenness.

This is what it's like to be loved. This is how a father ought to be. How lovely and sweet to be held in your own father's arms, secure from pain, protected from the world. How lovely to feel that he was listening to you, that what you said had importance; to see his smile of understanding and patience. Love and patience. How wonderful that might have been; and to have only rarely experienced it was like going through life with some buried disability. She expected men to be cool, and were always surprised when they were not. Especially, she knew, she was attracted to men that laughed and made light of life. Men who were sympathetic, who were touchers. Yet their very kindness tended to confuse her: she knew that she waited, listening to any man, for the note of disapproval and distaste – her father's note – to come into their voice.

She gazed out now at the distant Brake: the wall of the harbour. The first time her father had bought her cooked fish, wrapped from the shop and smelling so good, he had peeled the batter from it to reassure her that there were no bones. He could be like that: he *could* do it. It was just that he didn't do it often enough. Not by a long, long way. And that simple careful action, his infrequent capacity for gentleness, was a taste of sharp sweetness, surprising her.

She looked away from the sea, blinking. It had been a long time since the suppers on the curved brick arm of the Brake.

She turned away. Lifting the receiver again, she tried to ring Hugh. The note of the ringing sounded over and over: no reply. He must be working. She put the phone back on the hook.

Jon came and stood outside the kiosk, carrying the newspaper he had just bought. 'He's not there,' she said. 'Hugh.'

Jon looked down at his feet.

'Where did you try?' she asked.

'Up the Gardens. Along the Brake. Asked on some of the boats. I gave them your telephone number.'

Eve screwed up her face. 'I ought to get leaflets printed. His photograph. My number.'

'Let's hope you don't get some crank ringing you in the middle of the night.'

She felt a flash of annoyance. 'Well, I have to do bloody *something*, don't I?'

They began to walk, up the steps to the main street, now in deep, late-afternoon shadow. Jon walked apart, his hands in his pockets, whistling between his teeth.

'Why are you doing this?' she asked.

He looked surprised. 'I've got nothing else to do.'

'Oh.'

'No . . . I mean, two's better than one, right? What else would I be doing, anyway? On a Saturday.'

She shrugged. 'Well, everything. You're nineteen, aren't you? Windsurfing, or something. Chasing women. Getting drunk. What do you do at nineteen? Everything. Nothing.'

He frowned at her. 'Funny ideas you've got.'

'No – that's what you *ought* to do. That's what nineteen is *for*. Nineteen!' And she said it breathily, almost longingly. She immediately heard that in her own voice, and turned her face, blushing.

They had stopped by the shop displaying fossils. Through the plate-glass window, in which she and Jon were vaguely reflected, as dim as ghosts, Eve stared down at an ichthyosaur, two hundred million years old, fish lizard, six metres. She read the title under the stone over and over to herself, trying to make sense of it. Lizard . . . two metres . . . two hundred million . . . hundred million . . .

'I know a man who digs them out round here,' Jon volunteered.

'Do you?'

'Mmm. De Franchard. He's famous. You know, de Franchard.'

She shook her head, no.

'Don't you bring your kids down here to see the fossil cliffs?'

She had not taken her eyes off the skeleton, glossily preserved in its shining brown stone. 'We've not been here in a long time.'

Jon pressed his hand to the glass. It covered the reflection of her face. 'Fascinating things, rocks. They are like stone calendars; ever thought that? A morning trapped in sandstone; two lines of footprints crossing each other, a million, a hundred million years ago . . . fascinating.'

She turned and looked hard at him. 'Is that what you're doing at university?'

'Mmmm.'

She wiped the grime from her face, tracing the eyebrow, cheekbone, jaw. 'Why did you leave there?' she asked.

'I haven't left. I'm on a year's grace. I was stupid with the first grant, and got into debt. I go back in October.'

'Oh, I see.'

'Debts.'

'Debts.' She repeated after him, not a question.

He leaned back on the glass and looked at the street, at two girls passing in Lycra shorts, bandau tops. He watched them go up the hill, and one of them glanced back at him, laughing.

'I lost money on horses.'

'What? Horse racing, you mean?'

'Yes. Horse racing.' He inflected the 'racing' sarcastically.

She said nothing, but turned back to look at the fish skeleton. What did it matter? Look at this, set in stone in this window. What did their small lives matter? Two . . . hundred . . . million . . .

'Want to swim?' he asked.

'No. No.'

'Well, don't snap my head off. It'd cool you down.'

'I don't want to cool down. I want to go home. I'm going home.'

'Mind if I do? Only five minutes. Straight in and out.'

'What – in the sea?'

This time he laughed outright. 'No, in the drains.'

She went to wait in the car for him.

She had a sudden, violent urge to shut out this place, all the paraphernalia of leisure, pleasure. She wanted to go home and close the doors, get into bed, and pull the covers over her and sleep for ever.

It had become a jumble: her father, Hugh, Jon. Duty – duty at school, to children, to parents; duty to Bill, the embarrassed heavy duty of pandering to Hugh; duty now to look, to search, to go round in what was obviously ever decreasing circles: all these expectations weighed unbearably on her. Somewhere at home she had a set of Tarot cards – some birthday present, years ago – and on one of them a man was depicted, an Atlas holding up the world. She felt like that now. Life was like a rock under which she was staggering, keeping her feet on the path and yet desperate to let go. Each step drove her feet deeper into sand. She sat thinking of the fossil in the stone, a parody of life and the living. She imagined herself dry, stripped, motionless, pressed into a block of slate two hundred million years old, becoming nothing but bone in rock. That was how they would all be sooner or later. For a minute or two she thought of herself translated to stone now: no one would *ever* expect *anything* of her again. She would not be responsible any more. She would just be slate, rock, bone. It all seemed wonderfully, blissfully appealing.

Then Jon came walking down the steps.

He was naked to the waist, whistling, and drying his hair on his T-shirt.

I don't want to be taunted by the living.

I don't want to be shown.

He stuck his head in at the open window of the passenger side.

'Got anything to put over the seat? I'm a bit wet.'

'It doesn't matter.'

'Might feel bit damp.'

She pushed open the door. 'Nobody sits on that side much,' she muttered.

And he got in.

They said nothing while the car climbed out of the Lyme valley. On the tops, they joined the main road. Eve pushed hard on the accelerator. Evening was closing in, soft and greyish and saltily warm. She was terribly aware of him at her side: his easy slouch in the next seat, his fingers drumming occasionally on the window-frame. Now and then he would sigh, the sigh of someone perfectly relaxed and calm. She stole a glance at him as he stared sideways at the view at the valley top: he had the slightness of teenage years, starting to be overlaid with muscle. His jeans were dragged low on his hips: she saw a line of black hair on his stomach and, jolted by a desire that shocked her, she rapidly took her eyes away. He turned back, as if he'd sensed her inspection of him.

'What now?' he asked.

'Sorry?'

'What'll you do now?'

She shrugged. 'Go home. Wait.'

'Looking again tomorrow?'

'I don't know where to. Maybe I should just stay near the farm. He might walk through the gate, mightn't he? And there's work on Monday. I've got these damned tests to prepare . . .' She considered, manoeuvring the car as she overtook another. The speed shot up to seventy: Jon gave her a sideways look. All the while she was thinking, *Perhaps Dad remembered it was Mother's birthday. Perhaps he was upset and wanted to go away. France was his favourite place, IS his favourite place . . .*

Suddenly, Jon's hand gently touched her own on the steering wheel. She jumped.

'It's OK,' he said. 'But did you know you're doing eighty? It's not a very wide road after here.'

'Oh God, I'm sorry.' The car rapidly slowed as she took her foot off the accelerator.

'It's all right, don't worry,' he said. Soothing and soft. She felt monumentally embarrassed, a child reprimanded.

'What did Hugh say he was like?' he asked.

'Like?'

'What mood was your Dad in last night?'

'Oh, rather rough. He became aggressive playing cards or games; anything competitive. Like a small boy wanting to win. Do you know –' here she managed a smile – 'once when we were playing Risk – this was ages ago, before he got ill – we had all these wretched cones laid out all over the board, and because he realised he was going to lose, he simply tipped up the board.' She shook her head. 'That was Dad even *before* . . .'

Jon pulled his legs up so that they rested partly on the surround of the gearstick, the casing of the stereo. 'Do you think he could have planned it?'

'No. He couldn't follow it through, even if it occurred to him.'

'You mean, he'd set out, but forget where he was going after a while?'

'Yes . . .' She looked at him, biting the edge of her lip, thinking. Yes, it was possible that Dad got an idea in his head to go to France again, and had even got as far as taking his passport. And was now wandering . . .

And he was capable too, before the illness, of deliberately not telling her where he was going. It was typical of his cruel jokes. Once, when she was in the sixth form, he had gone off for a night without a word. A conference to do with the Archaeological Society. She had been frantic, until one of his colleagues had rung to find out if she was managing OK. She had been furious, but when he came home had said nothing at all, not wanting to give him the satisfaction of knowing how worried she had been. *That* was the kind of game Bill enjoyed. Perhaps he wanted to play it again.

God damn him.

They sat in perfect silence, the road unwinding before them, the light draining away. Sun was replaced by a soft monochrome, leaching colour from the hedges and trees.

The deep clefted valley of Rag Lot passed them, with its indented circles on the turf of the summit. Bronze Age burial mounds. In the oblique light of evening, the rings showed clearly, patterns from the past, their symbolism long forgotten. Again, as Eve turned the car down the lane to Cerne Saint James, she had that feeling of being drowned by time.

Only bones in slate, all of us. All lost. All bloody lost. She felt herself slipping, slipping, slipping.

She got right to the bottom of the road before the farm before she had to stop.

She pulled into a flat place by the roadside, alongside the river. There was nothing here but rushes at waist height, a thick border of cow parsley, overgrown flat fields, and the hills on either side. She put on the handbrake, and the car shuddered to a stop, and she put her head on the steering wheel, covering it with her hands. Holding the leather rim of the wheel felt like gripping the sheer edge of a precipice, into which she was helplessly slithering, her fingers digging into the thin earth and gravel before the drop.

Jon had immediately got out, seeing the greyness of her face, and come round to her side. He opened the door and took her arm, releasing her seat belt. He helped her out as if she were some sort of invalid, easing her away from the car. She leaned on him, taking shuffling little steps.

At the fence, she grabbed the post and leaned on that. Still there was that awful sensation, like vertigo, of teetering at the edge of a void. She felt empty, bleached, filled not with blackness but with air, as fragile as a bubble being blown over that yawning chasm: weightless, empty, and as thin as breath.

The river ran beyond. It looked curiously white, like a wide strip of satin thrown down in the rushes and grass. All around it the spring evening, carrying a thousand scents, ran in, bringing smoke from a fire somewhere further down the road, the burning of leaves and cuttings, the green, sap-smelling smoke. Yet the river was white, reflecting the evening sky, from which all colour had vanished.

And it ran with scarcely any noise at all, until you were almost upon it like this. You could see the white satin of the water before you heard the noise of it, turning and whispering between the reeds. And above them the sky too was impossibly white, above the faint trails of smoke that hung close to the water . . . light, with the first dry specks of stars.

She turned to him, and put her hand on his arm. He was still naked to the waist, and amazingly warm to the touch, as if giving off heat from some inner furnace.

'And I'm so cold,' she said, surprised.

He put his arms around her. Like being enveloped in heat, the door from the oven, the door from the furnace, opening. He made a little noise, a strangled sigh of pleasure. She could feel his heart beating impossibly quickly in his chest. As he held her against him, he whispered to her, 'I've been waiting for you to cry all day. When are you going to cry?'

She traced the curve of his mouth with a fingertip, and then closed her eyes.

'Never,' she whispered.

Nine

Hugh had gone up to the house three times that day, and lost count of the number of times that he had phoned. The dull burring of the ringing infuriated him, even more than turning up in the Land Rover only to see the same dead and closed look to the face of the house. She should have been back hours ago: she had promised that she would not be long. And a promise between them ought not to be broken.

At about three o'clock, he gave up. All day yesterday he had been fencing one of the bottom pastures, and he went back to it now with a vengeance, cursing as he banged in the posts with a sledgehammer.

At the far side of the field, the horses grazed without even raising their heads to him. He could hear them snatching at the grass, tearing it out of the ground. With a mindless rage, Hugh carried on with the work until it was long past his usual time to eat. A faint fog began to drift across the course of the stream.

He finished the row, thinking of Eve, resisting the temptation to ring the house again. Jamming the tools into the back of the Land Rover, he roared it into reverse and bumped across the field. He got out at the gate and paused for a second, staring out across the yard ahead of him, at his own house and at the decaying pair of thatched cottages forty yards in front of it, their doors nailed and the 'Beware Chemical' sign fixed to them. Lichen had turned the thatches green; what was once straw hung down from the gutters. The windows were dark with filth.

It was then that he heard the noise. Like someone talking.

He listened, holding his breath. It was like a distant radio, fading in and out. Had he left his radio on in the kitchen? The TV? No, he never left anything on. He checked everything four or five times before leaving the house. Plugs, lights, cooker, taps, and radio.

The sound stopped. Hugh stood for another minute, straining to hear. He didn't like mysteries: they were untidy. A lorry came trundling along the small road, grinding gears around the bend. Exasperated, Hugh opened his gate, drove through, got out again to fasten the catch. The Land Rover sputtered bluish exhaust; smoke and mist trailed into the yard.

And it was only as he was taking his boots off at his own back door that he heard it again.

This time, hardly more than whispering.

Whispering, whispering.

Shuffling the wellington back on over his heel, he walked the forty yards to the nearest cottage.

'Hello?' he called.

He looked around. The back doors were bolted and padlocked – all those were still in place. The windows were closed, as usual. They had not been opened for more than forty years in this nearest cottage. A shred of net curtain clung to the top pane like web. Hugh cast about himself, listening. Waist-high weeds were all around him: thistles, cow parsley, bindweed choking them all. An aura, wet and heavy and warm, clung to the spot: the smell of damp undergrowth. Once there had been rats in the outside sheds... He looked, now, inside a door. Barbed wire, chicken wire, rolls of felt were picked out in the gloom.

'Hello?' he repeated. 'Anybody here?'

There was nothing in the first cottage or its outhouses. He went to the second. The roof was so low that it would not have been hard to reach up and touch it: as the place decayed, it seemed to shrink in on itself. He really ought to do something about these places. They were an eyesore, a sore in the back of his mind, too.

The trouble was that some daft sod up at the County Council had put a preservation order on them. One day, he supposed, the roof would collapse. One day...

Then came the scratching.

There was no doubt about it now: it was as clear as day. A repeated scratching and shuffling from under Hugh's feet. He looked down at the grid that covered the cellar and saw, with a shock, that a narrow path had been trodden through the weed. The iron ladder to the cellar, just murkily visible, was broken. One of the hatches hung open.

The scratching came up from the darkness.

Hugh edged through the green, got on his knees, and peered in.

'Hello?' he called warily. It was probably rats again. The size of some of those things, like cats they were—

'Hello,' said a voice.

Hugh nearly shot out of his skin.

It had come up out of the blackness of the cellar, fifteen feet below. 'Holy Jesus Christ,' he gasped. It had been a man's voice, very calm. 'Hey, that's not you, is it, Bill?'

'Hugh, I can't get out, you know.'

Squirming, Hugh managed to push his head and shoulders through the gap. His heart began to thud heavily. Below him there was a drop. As his eyes became accustomed to the blackness, he could just make out the shape of the ladder that had been attached to the sill of the hatch doors. It lay in two neat pieces directly beneath the opening.

'Bill?' he called softly. 'Bill . . .?'

There was no reply.

Hugh considered how to get down. He hadn't looked in these cellars for a long time, ever since the cottage hallways had been blocked up. There was a set of wooden stairs, as he recalled, from the cellar floor to the hallway oak door, back there in the blackness; but they would be rotten by now. And anyway, the hall door was locked and barrels stacked against it. No way out from that angle. He would have to get some sort of rope affair or a ladder and get Bill to climb out this way.

'Here, Bill,' he repeated. 'You'm a daft old bugger. What're you doing down there? What d'you go in there for?'

And, out of the gloom, Bill suddenly appeared and looked up.

Hugh had to force himself not to cry out when he saw him. Bill looked as if he had fallen into water or mud. His clothes hung damply on him, streaked with muck.

'You've not been in the silage, or what?' Hugh asked, smiling. 'Where'd you get like that?'

Bill stared up at him silently. His face was comparatively clean, with a day's growth of beard making his skin half dark and half white. His eyes were round, like a child gaping at a Christmas tree.

'Called those lot in?' he asked.

'What lot?'

Bill's fist clenched. 'You blasted well know, you little sod! Call the whole Fourth in, you cheeky bastard!'

Hugh looked at him, an expression of weary disgust coming to his face. 'All right, Bill,' he said.

'And don't Bill me! You call me Mr Ridges!'

Hugh began to wriggle back through the gap. 'All right,' he muttered. 'All right. Old bastard.'

Once up, he looked about for something to throw down. A piece of rope or a long plank of wood. Then, thinking better of it, he decided to go up to the barn to fetch the ladder. 'Hey, Bill,' he called out. 'I'm going for the extension ladder. Be a minute. You hear me?'

He heard Bill walk back, away from the light of the hatch. He was muttering something to himself. Hugh shuddered, thinking of the cellar beyond. Must be a nest of bloody spiders and I don't know what, he told himself. Get the old bastard out. Right little pit it is in there. Right little bloody dungeon. Black as hell. Like a stinkhole. Old fool. Bloody simple-minded old fool . . .

As he got to his own house, the phone began to ring. He dashed in without bothering about his boots, and grabbed the receiver off the wall.

'Hugh,' said Eve's voice.

Warmth rushed over him. She was back.

'Hugh, any news?'

He steadied himself against the wall. 'Where've you been? I called and called,' he said.

'I've been over to Lyme. You know he used to go fishing there? It was just an idea. But . . . Were you ringing to tell me anything?'

'No, but . . .' He was going to add, *There was nothing to tell you before, but guess what I've done, I've found him for you* . . . An image of her face swam before him. The supremely tantalising vision of her gratitude made him feel sick – dizzy and sick for a second – and breathless.

'Hugh?'

'What?'

'No news?'

His eyes narrowed as he stared ahead of him. Suddenly, the way she had said, 'No news', the way she had said, 'Are you ringing to tell me something?' . . . There was a real edge of disappointment in it. A dull sound. More than anything, he could not, he would not, disappoint her. He would do whatever she wanted. Always. Whatever.

Desperately, he tried to shake the pieces together in his mind. The pieces of this puzzle.

She was ringing thinking that Hugh might have a word, a clue, or *even have found him*. And there was that dead, dull sound in her voice. The sound of coming down. So – he had been right, last night. It must have been relief he had heard in her voice when he told her that Bill had gone.

He flattened his palm against the wall and looked at it, looked at its lines and dark freckles of age. Already there were liver spots on the back of his hand, like his father used to have. He would be fifty before he could turn round. Fifty and alone. If he was not careful. Not very careful.

'You've been out looking all day, then,' he said.

She sighed. The reply was terse. 'Yes. All day.'

'Terrible job.'

'Yes.'

'I'll come with you tomorrow and help.'

'No – I mean, thank you, but no, Hugh. You've got the farm. You can't neglect the farm.'

'Won't neglect for a day, will it?'

'I—'

'You ought to get some posters done.'

'Yes, I've been thinking that. His photograph. I'll look one out tonight.'

Palm flat on the wall. The tips of his fingers showed white.

Ladder . . . ladder.

'You'll be glad to see him again,' he said.

She said nothing, perhaps not for ten or fifteen seconds. In that brief silence, his heart leapt into his throat.

It was true, then! She was hoping he wouldn't come back.

'I will,' she replied, as if from a great distance. He thought, she sighed. His heart went out to her. If Bill came back, it would be as if a gate, now open to freedom, had been slammed shut in her face. She might care for him, and the slamming might be soft, but she'd still be caught, caught again in that terrible cell, nagged and slapped and driven mad by the person she had been chained to. Over the sigh, the telephone line crackled faintly with static. It was no life. No life for an animal. Let alone Hugh Scott's wife.

'We'll be all right, when this is over,' he said.

'Yes,' she responded.

There was the final sealing of a pact, of a deadly secret, in that single word.

'Well look,' she began. 'Ring me again in the morning. Will you do that? I mean, before you go looking or anything? I might stay home, I don't know. Ring me before you come out.'

'Before I come out. All right.'

'Don't, you know, don't come up here on a wild-goose chase. Or I'll ring *you*.'

He gripped the receiver with both hands. 'Shall I come up and sit with you tonight?' he asked.

Another silence. Ah, she was thinking about it. Thinking about him being with her. Wondering if that would be right.

'Well, perhaps not,' she answered. 'I'm going to bed. I'm shattered.'

'All right.' Again the unspoken contract. He felt ready to choke, to die himself, he felt so happy. This was something they were in together: she had asked, he had obeyed. He *would* obey, he would carry it out whatever the cost. The room rushed around him. He would do what she wanted.

At her own end of the line, Eve listened to the stilted, low voice of her neighbour with unease. He had been ringing all day for no reason. He hadn't found Father, and it didn't appear to be out of any concern for her especially. He'd just wanted to find her.

Frowning, she rubbed distractedly at a spot between her eyebrows where a headache was threatening to start.

'I'll ring you, then,' she said.

All she heard was his irregular breathing. His listening. His peering at her, as though through a keyhole of a connection.

Oh, for Christ's sake, Hugh. Hang up!

'All right,' he repeated.

She put down the phone.

She did not turn around for a long time.

At last, Jon put his hand on the back of her neck, stroking the line between her shoulder and chin.

'You must go home,' she said.

He flattened his hand and pressed her shoulder, working his thumb on her neck.

'You must . . .'

He took her hand, and she followed him into the hall. For a moment she thought he was leaving, and a feeling of mixed relief and terrible disappointment swamped her. Then he began to climb the stairs.

She went after him and, as she saw what he wanted, her heart quickened. Excitement rushed over her, fast and sweet. Dozens of sane reasons why she should not follow him up the pale shadow-wreathed stairs rushed in; just as quickly they shrank, fell away, and died. She needed to be touched, to be sheltered, to be wanted; she needed that now more than at any other time in her life.

She knew it was not fair: Jon was nearly twenty years younger than she was. She ought to make a joke of it and turn him out of the house. But she was incapable, at that moment, with her hand in his, of doing the *right* thing, the *sane* thing. She was no longer the adult and he the boy; she was the helpless one, being led to the eradication of pain by a man much older than herself. She couldn't have found a word to dissuade him, even if she had wanted to. He lifted her palm to his lips and kissed it. There had been no one for a very long time. God. She turned her face and put her free hand to it, trying to mask her expression. Her legs trembled.

At the landing, half-way up, with its view across the long slope of land, Jon suddenly turned and took her in his arms. The desperation in him rushed into her. His hands and body trembled too. He said her name, over and over.

Light fell down on them, the soft slanting light of evening, dark grey and gold. Dreamlike, dreamlike.

They reached for each other, clumsy with need. On the landing, in the hour between evening and night, they lay on the floor, holding each other like two drowning people. And, as at last Jon moved inside her, and everything shrank to this small piercing blade of reality – this skin, this touch, this mouth – Eve felt some distant lock ticking over, trying to find a combination long forgotten. The key in the lock of the door, the key in the lock of the door . . .

It swung open, and she saw the world bright with light, full of pleasure, free of weight. She saw the ochre path leading up the Italian hillside, the dog lying in the shadow of the restaurant, the warm rain falling, the lime-scented glass. Felt again that distant, forgotten sense of freedom and sheer joy. She held Jon to her, moving as he moved, carried along by him, lost in him.

Singing to himself, Hugh closed the door.

He went to the kitchen and switched on the radio; turned up the volume, a happy smile on his face. Sound boomed around the house.

The ladder lay on the floor of the barn, untouched.

'Hugh,' Bill called, frightened, out in the encroaching darkness. 'Hugh . . .!'

In the pasture, the mare raised her head and looked towards the cottages.

No one answered.

Ten

She slept in Jon's arms.

But she did not dream of Jon. The moment she closed her eyes, she dreamed vividly of her father. He roared, larger than life, into the dark room, pressing her back into childhood.

When he came home from work, Bill would often say nothing all evening.

She would have been about eleven, or twelve. At first she had made a joke of it. She would say something like, 'We played St Joseph's at hockey – Dad – and I was right wing – Dad – and a hydrogen bomb exploded in goal.' Bill would carry on eating.

She never had a problem coming home from school to an empty house. There was a lot of talk in the news around them about latchkey kids, but she had never felt that they were talking about her. She happily let herself in, picking the key up from under the dustbin. She rather enjoyed the freedom.

She would make wedges of jam sandwiches, a mug of tea, and then watch the television. There would be a soap opera on at half-past four; she was addicted to it. But the delicious half-hour soon wore off. She would go into the kitchen and make her father's supper, watching the road all the time for the domed blue top of his Citroën coming down the hill. The moment when it appeared between the hedges, a kind of sick worry started in the pit of her stomach, like a machine cranked up, a clock wound beyond the mechanism. The whirring and winding feeling would stop as his car swept over the gravel of the drive and she watched him get out. She would stand, waiting for the second that she ought to go to the door.

'I've been to the doctor's and I've got beriberi.' That was another one.

One evening, he finally rose to the bait and looked up from his paper. 'Is that it?' he asked.

'Is that what?' She smiled at him.

'Is that the end of these stupid remarks? Have you finished?'

There was such venom in his voice that she didn't answer. Her smile faded. He would often use that tone: an absolute venom, as if he were disgusted by her.

He put his knife and fork down at the side of his plate, and pressed both hands on the cloth. 'Because it's enough,' he said, in a low voice. 'I've been working all day. I've been listening to the abysmally stupid remarks of idiot children all day. It's called work. Work, you understand? When I come home, I don't want to work any more. I don't want to come in and have to listen to my own daughter full of the same cretinous remarks. Am I getting through to you?'

'I just was trying to get you to say something to me,' she said. The adolescent climbed out of her throat, letting her down, embarrassing her. She hated him to hear her tearful.

He gave a deep sigh. 'And what is it that you want me to say, exactly?'

'Well . . . school. Anything. You never ask.'

'What d'you want me to ask? I see Charlotte Benson regularly. She tells me about you. I don't need to ask about your schoolwork. I already know.'

'But you don't ask about . . . the day – or anything . . .'

'What do you want me to ask? Tell me in words of one syllable.'

'I want . . .'

But she didn't really know what she wanted. It had no name. She had never been given it. The previous week, at a friend's house for tea, her friend's father had come in, put an arm round her shoulder, kissed his daughter lightly, and said, 'Hello, sugar. How're things with my favourite girls?' And sat down and *listened*, joking with them, and telling them about his own day . . . It had been lovely. She had felt ill with longing. But it had no name.

'I don't know,' she said.

And she didn't. It would be another ten years before she understood the concept of love at all. She would suddenly come to understand, in one of those flashes of recognition, how you could selflessly give yourself or something, just to revel in the delighted expression on the other person's face. She would suddenly understand that to love is to defend against life, to deflect the hurts. Not to demand. Not to inflict them. Not to expect any standard, only the other person's complete happiness . . . At that moment, ten years in the future, she would feel outrageously cheated and fooled by her father. Because all the time, inflicting his hurts, he had said that he loved her. Had called the coldness and guilt, love. *Fraud!* Because love was wildly simple and pleasing, if one loved well. It was a gesture of trust without flinching. No turning the light back on yourself. No *look at me, look at me.*

And for the whole of her four years at college, after discovering his lie, she visited him only three times.

Memories of the silent dinner table abounded; of her father giving her irritated glances as she wept and looked down at her dinner plate.

He used to dissect his food, cutting the meat into very small pieces and putting them to one side. Then the vegetables, the potato. Clinical dismemberment of food. He would select this piece, then that; put them down again, prise them off the fork. The food would be stone cold by the time he finished it, and he would eat it morosely, making a small revolted face at its congealed state, chewing like a cow with cud. He drank tea while he was still eating: she heard it going around his mouth. Why don't you just pour your tea on your plate and mash it all up together, she wanted to say. Mash it up! Baby food. Easier!

'Have you something to say?' He would turn and look out of the window, in the direction of Hugh's farm.

Something about the dream now alters and shifts. The country around them has been telescoped down, the long, long tunnel of light beyond them. The treeless slopes of the farm dip into a deep V, and the house, their house, slips into the dip, the table slithering towards the window, the knife scraping on her father's plate, the chairs crashing over, slipping towards the dark well of the farm, where Hugh is standing . . .

'Eve!'

The windows bevel, shrink, and then shatter without a sound. The glass is sucked inwards, and she has time to think, *How beautiful it looks sweeping in like that, glass sucked into a tunnel with a thousand reflections of colour* . . .

Then the pieces come flying towards her.

No time to put her hands to her face to protect it from the glittering shards. The window is a glass bomb, a bouquet of glass fragments opening in blossom. She can't even close her eyes. All the thin nails of glass will go straight through her, straight through her eyes, straight through her neck, straight through her head.

Cover the precious artery pulsing in your neck. She can't. No time. No time to raise her hands either to her face or her throat. Father's face will appear on each thin piece of glass, cutting her.

'Eve!'

Buried under all this devastation in the dark.

The window is gone, and the long funnel of the land, and Hugh standing as she rolled towards him. The darkness rolled in and lifted her up.

I'm covered in all this broken stuff.
I'm dead, perhaps.

Momentary sensation of holding that shattering window as one holds the balloon of a brandy glass, or the round rubbery wall of a birthday balloon. Holding it close and praying it would not burst. My God, the terror. Everything bursting and exploding, and she had been holding it. Her responsibility. It had been her job to hold it all together, hold it safely, to keep it under control. If you are *very careful, very good, very quiet, very very good; if you can be a good girl, it will not break.* Be a good girl. Be quiet. Be still. Hold it tight, and it will not break.

I can't hold it any tighter.
I'm afraid.
I'm so tired and afraid.
I *can't*, I can't!
'Eve . . . Eve!'

She turns her head frantically from side to side as the explosion blooms to its fullest and most lethal glory, trying to locate the voice in the whirlwind.

Her father is calling her from a long way off. From the pit of a well, from blackness.

'Eve! Eve! Eve!'
No more!
No more, *Jesus Christ!*

Her own screaming woke her up. And then she heard the voice.
'Eve! Eve! Eve!'

Someone's hands were on her arms, and the unaccustomed feeling of those hands threw her bolt upright in the bed. Sheer terror. She was breathing as though she had run ten miles, and she was burning hot. For a second she began wildly brushing at herself, trying to dislodge both the hands and the million shards of glass that were all over her naked body. She dared not move too much for fear of shifting her legs, buttocks, back, hands into some new pool of shattered remains, a sea of splinters.

'Eve . . .'

But it was not her father any more. It was Jon.

'Oh, God . . .'
'What is it? You were shouting.'
'Glass, glass . . .'

'There's no glass.'

'Something: it exploded. Glass everywhere. All round here.' She was whimpering, brushing her fingers experimentally over the thrown-back sheets.

'All the glass . . .'

He wrapped his arms around her. Shaking, she allowed herself to be held, frightened still of moving an inch.

'Dad . . .'

'I'm sorry, but he's not here,' he said, kindly.

He, too, was warm, but smoothly, softly warm, like a rug laid before a fire. His skin was perfectly smooth, and to put her hands on it was like putting her hands on moving silk. It smelled nice. Comforting. She could feel the muscles in his back moving as he altered his position on the bed, drawing himself up to his knees. She dropped her hands and rested them on his shoulders.

'Better?' he asked.

'Dreams,' she said. 'Terrible dreams.'

Then she remembered the last few hours.

She put her face to his shoulder, so that he wouldn't see her expression.

She remembered washing in the bathroom, shamefacedly washing at the sink in a hurry, too embarrassed at herself to even look in the mirror. *He is only nineteen, you are a fool, what have you done?* While he was downstairs in the kitchen, she had gone down the stairs, tiptoeing, snatching up their discarded clothes like a thief, piling his at the corner of the landing, bundling her own in her arms, stuffing them in the washbasket. She had grabbed a robe from the door hook and tied it tightly around her, red in the face. She'd wished she had a door on the landing, with a lock, to lock him out. And as Jon had put his foot on the first stair, she'd prayed he would go; her stomach had promptly tied itself into a hundred knots.

He had come up, with a tray on which he had put two coffees, and a little glass filled with daisies. He must have gone out there in the nude, in the garden, and picked daisies! She started to laugh, forgetting her he's-nineteen-and-I'm-thirty-something-knocking-forty shame. His ridiculously broad grin – like a cartoon rabbit – set her off in a stream of giggles. He put the tray on the floor, took three steps, and threw her on the bed, kissing her on the face, the neck, pulling down the robe, laughing against her laughing, kissing her hands and fingers and wrists . . .

Hardly half a dozen words had passed between them all evening, all night. As she had turned over in bed with him at her side, she had seen the blue luminous dial of the clock. It was twenty to one. There was no moon that night, nothing to see, no shapes to make sense of. Only the figures. Zero-zero-four-zero. Blue light rigid in the black.

The stairs, the bed.

Somewhere since then, some explosion, some implosion, shattering inwards. Perhaps the explosion was them. God knows, there had been none in this room before. Ever. Perhaps the explosion was in her; her release.

She shivered. She looked at him now, and loosed his hands, and swung her legs over the side of the bed.

'Go back to sleep,' he said.

'I must get some air,' she replied.

He squatted on the bed behind her, his hands flat on the sheet. Like an athlete waiting in the starting blocks. She went to the window to open it and, as she did so, she looked out.

Hugh was standing on the track below.

'God . . .!'

She leapt backwards, hit her ankle on a chair, cursed again. 'Good God . . .'

'What is it?'

Jon was getting up.

'No – no! Get down!' This a hissed whisper. She waved at him with both hands.

'What's up?' She stopped dancing in agony, and tried to peer out of the window from where she stood. 'It's Hugh,' she said.

'Eh?'

'Hugh. Hugh Scott.'

'You're joking,' he said. 'What, out there? At this bloody hour?'

'Yes. I saw him. He's—'

Jon started to laugh.

'Will you shut up!' she said.

'It's the middle of the night!' he protested. 'What is he, mad?' He started walking across the room towards the window.

She grabbed him. 'Oh, please, he'll see you! Don't look out. Don't look out. He'll see you . . .'

'What if he does?' he said. 'What's it to him?'

It was as if he had thrown a bucket of hot water over her: she blushed from head to foot. For a reason she could not fathom, the thought of Hugh knowing that Jon had slept with her was terrible. More than embarrassing . . . 'Jon, please . . .'

He touched the side of her face. Ghostly hand swimming towards her in the gloom, taking, it seemed, twice as long as it should to connect with her face. His index finger tracing the side of her cheek to her chin, resting eventually on her lips. 'You're afraid of him,' he said.

'No . . .'

'Yes.' He cocked his head at the window, a surreal square floating freely in the room. 'What's he done?'

'Nothing. Well . . . He's just always coming here. He's very good with Dad, and I feel I can't say anything. Hard to explain . . .' Her voice came unnaturally loud. She straightened herself up, hopped on to one leg, rubbed at her ankle. 'It's the visits, all the time, that're getting to me. The way he looks at me . . .'

'At this time of the morning!'

'No, of course not.'

But Jon had already gone to the window, angry. He opened the lock, swung the glass open, and leaned out.

She looked at the long line of his back for perhaps thirty seconds, her heart in her mouth, fear prickling down her own naked spine like the tremble of shattered glass against her skin, as Jon turned his head this way and that in the darkness. Then he closed the window and walked back to her.

'There's nobody there.'

'What!'

'Nobody. Take a look.'

She edged toward the frame. Very, very faintly, she could make out the line of the track running between the field and the hill, suspended like a pale rope. The crop moved infinitesimally, picking up the faintest of currents over the long slope of the land. Over the last hill before the sea, a line of lilac was lying low in the sky.

'He *was* there,' she said quietly. 'I don't know why, but he was.'

Jon went and lay down. He stretched out with his hands behind his head, watching her.

'They say in the village he's a bit peculiar,' he said. 'The first time I saw him, he looked grey. It was daylight, the sun was out, and he was this . . . funny colour. I thought he was ill, but it's not that, is it? He *always* looks like that.'

Eve walked, slowly, to the edge of the bed. 'Someone else said that to me recently,' she told him. 'I don't notice it. Perhaps I've got used to it. The only thing I feel . . .' And she stared above Jon, stared at the wall without really seeing it.

'What?'

'I feel as if my skin . . . goes *cold* when he is near me . . .'
Jon held out his arms.
'Why don't you come back to bed,' he said softly.

Eleven

It was nine o'clock the next morning.

Hugh had two visitors.

They came almost together: a woman who was organising a summer fête at Hillshead Bryce House, two miles past the village, and who wanted to use the bottom wall on Hugh's field to put up a sign advertising the event; and a rep from a machinery company.

Hugh was standing in the entrance, gradually edging the woman back towards the road, agreeing to everything she asked, his hands in his pockets, a frown on his face. The woman was sidestepping, holding a sheaf of handbills, asking him not only to set up the sign, but also to come on the day.

'We need nice able-bodied gentlemen any time, especially setting up and taking down—'

'All right.'

'And the marquee. Last year you were—'

'Set up the marquee.'

'Would you?' She pumped his hand, after holding out her own, and he grudgingly pulled his hand out of his pocket. She felt like a wet fish. 'Would you really? That's so kind. We ordered the marquee last week, and do you know—'

He saw the rep's car coming.

Oh, bloody hell.

The red Sierra flashed its headlights at him.

'Do you know, they've gone up two hundred per cent in one year, do you think they could have made a mistake? You know Major Emmsberry, don't you? I phoned Major Emmsbury—'

The Sierra's engine flicked off. He saw the rep gathering his books off the passenger seat. He was from Yeovil – a widower who worked seven days a week, admitting frankly that he hated to go home. Once, Hugh had even given him Sunday lunch, and now the least the man expected was an hour's talk and a cup of tea. *Of all the people to come*, Hugh thought. Of all the *times* to come.

Hugh's eyes flicked desperately to the cottage.

'It can't be right, can it?' the woman chattered on. 'Only last June when they had the fair at Saftwell—'

In the sunlight, he saw the rep raise his hand behind the glass of the windscreen.

There was no noise from the cottage.

'And what about tomorrow?' asked the woman.

Hugh dragged his eyes back to her. 'Eh?'

'Is tomorrow all right? I can see you're busy. What about tomorrow afternoon? Or I could bring it up today. I have to come back this way to pick up Roger. What about this afternoon?'

'All right.'

'Oh, that's super.'

The rep was getting out.

Still no noise.

He looked at the man shoving the car door closed, the cottage with its roof with the U-shaped sag, the yellow sign on the door. Sometimes the rep sold him chemical. Once they had unlocked the cottages, searching for the supplier's label on a delivery. Green mould had traced the pattern of flock wallpaper along the deserted and lifeless hall, the cottage had felt crushed and small, the ceilings lower than modern height, the hall much narrower, the cellar so much, much deeper . . .

The yard was perfectly peaceful. You could hear the horses beyond the trees, the call of birds in the copse a quarter of a mile away. Sun drenching the ground, causing a deep shadow even now. Hugh stared at the rep.

'Today?'

He shot a glance at the woman.

'Yes,' he said, impatiently. 'Yes.'

He had no idea what he was agreeing to.

Because he had remembered something else about the rep with the Sierra.

The rep went to the other side of the car, whistling. He bent down and looked in the window. Grinning at Hugh over the roof of his car, and gesturing with his thumb to the back of the car, he unlocked the hatchback.

Despite himself, Hugh gazed at the cottage. He felt suddenly and violently sick.

They were going to hear Bill. They were going to find Bill.

Sun on the decaying thatch. Silence.

The rep's terrier dog bounded down out of the car and ran joyfully around the yard, tail wagging, his nose to the ground.

* * *

Bill was waiting.

He was waiting for something.

He knew exactly where he was, and he thought he knew how long he had been there. It was the second day. The days were light segments, the night a dark one. He held them loosely in his mind, three pieces of time, drawn in the way of junior geometry problems. He felt no panic or fear. It was merely a simple arithmetical problem. He could not remember finding his way in here, or falling. But the sensation of the two days and the one night were clear, and of mathematically drawn pieces of time, laid out in rows that shifted from time to time, like the pattern inside a slow kaleidoscope. Their shifting was not in the least worrying. Time had been doing that for a long while now. He was almost used to it. It was strange; it was sometimes lovely. He would wait for it to pass. As the sensation of being inside that kaleidoscope tube would surely pass.

He was waiting for Hugh to come back with the ladder.

Hugh had been there at first light, looking down into the cellar. Bill had been asleep, dozing lightly, slumped to one side in a sitting position on the floor. Hugh had pulled back the pieces of wood across the hole. He could not have been sleeping deeply, because the moment the wood scraped back, Bill felt immediately and totally awake, and pulled himself up. He went and stood under the hatchway and looked up.

'Hello, Hugh,' he said. 'I'm cold.'

Hugh's face was difficult to make out: behind the shape of his head, Bill could see lightened sky, the pale aura of day.

'Bill . . .'

'Got the ladder?'

'Yes, I—'

'Got the ladder, mate?'

Hugh, who was lying flat out on the damp ground, in the sea of dew-heavy weeds, his head and shoulders in the gap, stared down at him without moving.

'What time is it?' Bill asked.

'It's early.'

'Better get me out now, Hugh.'

Hugh said nothing. Then he shuffled backwards, crab-like. 'I will,' he told him. 'I'm going to. You wait.'

'OK,' Bill said.

Hugh put the wood back.

* * *

'William.'

She was looking over his shoulder at his fixing the tiles in the school foyer. It was a project he had set his class to do. She came in at the only time he had to himself, lunchtime. He did not look up at her, or touch her, even though she was his wife.

He stared at this picture that had flooded his mind, reliving it in every detail.

It was not his fault.

What she had done.

It was not his fault.

God damn you, don't *haunt* me.

'You get off and pick up that child,' he told her.

'I will. And it's not that child, it's Eve. I want to know—'

'Fuck it. Fuck it. See what you've made me do?'

'Refix it. It's still tacky. Don't get yourself in such a state.'

'Will you get out of here and see to that child?'

'I'm going. It's not *that child*. It's not any old child.'

'Why'd you leave her at the Bellamys' anyway? That Bellamy woman needs her head examining.'

'*You* need your head examining, darling.' She pressed her face to the side of his, laughing. She had always smelled of lemon – acidly sweet. 'She's only two. She won't come to any harm.'

'When she's fallen out of the Bellamys' window and stuck her face in an electric socket—'

'She won't. Julia Bellamy is perfectly capable. I have to do other things occasionally, you know. I'm not chained to the house, am I? Or am I? Perhaps that's what you'd like. Listen—'

'Go away.'

She got up off her knees, brushing down her skirt. 'You really are a perfect sod,' she said.

'I didn't ask you to come.'

'I just thought I'd look in and ask you.'

'I don't care what it is. Cook anything. It's all the same to me.'

Another tile fell away in his hands, and he caught it, looking at it in a fury of frustration.

'You really are, you really are,' she said, and the door closed behind her.

Hugh came back. The wood scrape, and the brighter light. 'Bill?'

He went to underneath the light.

'Hey, Bill. Catch.'

'What is it?'

'It's a cooler box I take with me in the tractor.'

'What's it for?'

'Can you catch?'

Bill held out his arms. The small Thermos box fell into his grasp. Green and white striped plastic.

'Open it up. I put a drink in it.'

He stared at the box.

'Why?'

'Why what? It's a drink.'

Bill looked up at the bright light with the human head. 'Why don't you get me out? Drink in your house is easier.' And he laughed.

Hugh shuffled back again, his head disappearing, the light blossoming. 'Back in a minute. You drink that. Back in a minute.' Hugh put the wood back. Splinters of light fell across the ceiling of the cellar.

Shaking his head, mystified, Bill opened the box.

When Eve woke up, there was no Jon.

She lay on her back and considered the silent room, the deeper silence of the house. No movement downstairs, no noise. Sunday morning.

She got up, and swung her legs off the side of the bed, into a patch of sunlight. She had not drawn the curtains all night. *Hugh in the darkness, and the crop moving, and the lilac strip of sky.*

Across from the bed was the wardrobe, satinwood, that had belonged to her mother. In the long mirror Eve saw herself reflected: thinnish pale body, blonde hair, small breasts. Her face was slightly flushed with sleep, her eyes large and dark. I look like a ghost, she thought.

She stood up and stared at herself, a small smile on her face. She was not bad, though, for nearly forty. There wasn't an ounce of fat on her. She was probably even bony. She could do with more weight... more of everything.

More of everything.

She looked down at her feet, smiling, thinking of him. Jon had left about an hour earlier, kissing her half awake, saying, 'I'm going home for a change of clothes, pick up some things. Will you be all right?'

She had struggled to wake, propped herself up on an elbow. 'How will you get there?'

He had stuck up a thumb cheerfully. 'With this.'

'Oh, Jon, wait. I'll get dressed.'

'No. You sleep. You need it. Rest. I'll be back this afternoon.'

She had slumped back, pressed back to the pillow by a quick, enthusiastic kiss; like being leapt on by a large puppy, all warmth and affection. He had gone down the stairs whistling; she heard him on the road, still whistling piercingly, and turned her face smiling into the sheet.

She looked again at the mirror. In this glass, she had seen this same body, touched by another body, the palest of shapes in the moonless night. He had touched her, in this room, in the rectangle of the mirror. She had woken up all the time, disturbed by his breathing, his hands on her. The closeness. Smooth milky satin. Soap on him, and some far drenched tint of smoke. A smell like sesame seed oil – ridiculous, not sesame seed oil – some other thing; something acid on him. In him. His mouth tasted sweet... odd. Apricots. Icing sugar. At some time in the night he had told her he was hungry – she told him about those icing-sugar rolls and coffee on the side of a lake – Interlaken, Thun, somewhere.

About midnight, he had made scrambled eggs and ham, coffee, raided a packet of jam biscuits, and she'd grinned at the three-year-old in him again. And afterwards he tasted of icing sugar and coffee and snow and in a whisper she'd told him about going to Europe, and French trains and Swiss trains, and the surface of that immense lake like white glass with the shoulders of green granite and houses balanced on the slopes hundreds of feet above, and then of nothing at all, only salt, only heat...

Nothing at all, and everything.

Everything.

She glanced at the clock. It was nearly nine. She stared blankly, thinking, *I ought to be looking for Dad*, and *I ought to ring Sarah, and the police.*

Her father was missing, perhaps dead. He had spent last night God knows where, certainly lost, probably cold, probably hungry. And what had she done? She had gone to bed with a boy half her age.

The woman in the mirror bit her lip, and two spots of high colour appeared in the centre of each cheek. Her eyes rounded at herself.

'I don't recognise you,' she said, to the ghost in the glass.

By eleven o'clock, she was at the school.

She had rung Matthew, explaining her father's disappearance. He had met her at the school gates half an hour later with the keys, waving aside her thanks. She began to explain that she would leave the money for using the photocopier on his desk for the morning, but he simply squeezed her arm.

'Leave the keys with Frank,' he said, nodding in the direction of the row of terraced houses where the caretaker lived.

'I'll see you in the morning,' she said.

He'd looked surprised. 'Are you sure?'

'I can't stay at home,' she said. 'It drives me mad to stay in the house. At least if I come into work, I'll be occupied. Hugh Scott is on the farm anyway.'

She went into the photocopying room, a cubicle off the cloakrooms. In her hand she carried a photo of her father taken about two years ago; she taped it to a white sheet of paper, and wrote 'MISSING' across the top. It gave her a peculiar sickening feeling: the one that had become almost second nature in the last two days. Underneath, she wrote his name, age, height. 'Last Seen Eleven p.m.'

She began to write her phone number, then, thinking better of it, she erased it and wrote, 'Please Ring Police with Any Information'. She held up the finished sheet and considered it, her father's lopsided grin, that of an ageing satyr, leering out at her. Pictures had never flattered him: they emphasised his heavy eyebrows, shading his eyes. He looked unsavoury rather than lost. In a moment of pity, she quickly added at the bottom, 'Mr Ridges Is Ill and May Be Confused. Please Help'.

She put the paper under the lid of the copier, and pressed '100', feeling guilty. She *would* put the money on Matthew's desk, no matter what he said. The light flashed rhythmically. She went out into the corridor, registering the unaccustomed silence of the place, smiling at the pairs of plimsolls knotted together and hanging from pegs, at the splodges of colour on the wall paintings, at the tiny-sized chairs, child-height handles and the floor cushions. She felt like an oversized interloper in a small world. She glanced across at the front door.

A face was pressed against the glass.

She nearly jumped out of her skin: her heart banged hard two or three times against her ribs, smacked out of beat by undiluted fear. For a second, she stared like one of the billy goats at the troll under the bridge, glaring through the gloom. Panic prickled in her mouth.

The troll knocked on the glass, and straightened up. She saw, laughing now in relief, that it was Sarah, standing on the windblown step in the shadow of the school porch.

Eve went at once and unlocked the door. Sarah came in, talking sixty to the dozen.

'What is it? You jumped like a bloody frog, you've gone absolutely white. Have you had anything to eat? Come across here – look, sit down in here . . .' Here, pushing Eve unceremoniously to a seat in the staff room, Sarah stood full-square across her as if daring her to stand up. 'I heard, darling, it's just *terrible* for you. What can I do?'

'Well, I just came in to do some copies – pictures of Dad. You could . . . I mean, if you had time . . . you could maybe put a few up around the villages? In the phoneboxes, at the garages . . .'

'Of course I've got time. I'll do it after lunch. Listen, where's the coffee? Where's Matthew's decent stuff? I know he keeps something better than that cat's pee.' And she began ferreting about in the cupboards, saying, 'Jesus, look at that cup,' and, 'How long has that bloody sugar been there?' Eve watched her affectionately, thinking, thank God for you. I can't sink while Sarah's standing on the side yelling instructions at me. And she imagined herself, drowning in this dreadful sea, or falling over the cliff of yesterday evening, and Sarah bawling from offstage, *Keep your head up, watch your bloody feet!*

As Sarah handed her a cup of Matthew's treasured and hidden coffee, a thought occurred to Eve.

'How did you know?' she asked. 'About Dad?'

'From the dead sheep.'

'From . . .?'

'Sheep, sheep. Baaaa. Hugh *Scott*.'

'Ah.'

Sarah took a long gulp of her drink. 'Yes, I couldn't get a reply from your phone – d'you know it's off the hook? I was actually ringing to invite you and Bill to lunch, and I had this strangest premonition, listening to that phone, that all was not well, so I drove over. And when I got to the house, there was Don Giovanni on your step. He said you promised to ring him.'

'Oh, God.' Eve put her hand guiltily to her head. 'I clean forgot. I took the phone off the hook last night.'

'Well, of course, he hardly puts two words together, as you know, but I gather all about Bill, and I tell him you're probably out looking, and he stares at me like a landed fish – he's so terribly smooth, isn't he, poor duck. Sweeps a girl right off her feet. He said not a hello, not a goodbye, stomped off along the track, and then lo and behold on the way back just now, if I don't see Matthew . . . Eh, voila! Here I am. Listen, you look tired, Eve. Really tired. Why didn't you ring me yesterday? Surely you've not been driving all over the countryside on your own?'

'Well, actually, no . . .'

Eve stretched her legs and looked at them rather shamefully. There was a weal of bright orange paint down one side of her skirt. Her feet were bare in sandals. She felt ragged and unwashed and gloriously pleased with herself. This last thought, in its callous selfishness, was terrible. She put her hand to her face.

Somewhere, in one of those sixties books that bitched on about men, she had read of a man who so loathed his wife that, when she had died and was lying in the mortuary, he had burst out laughing at the sight of her blissfully silent body. His son had taken him home, telling everyone that it was a breakdown, hysteria, grief. When the man was alone he made himself a meal, drank several brandies, and went happily off to sleep in his empty bed.

That man came back to Eve right now. She had a desperate longing to burst out laughing, and go on laughing until it was all out of her. She smoothed her face with her hand, biting on the inside of her cheek. She tried to stop herself without daring to look at Sarah. Get a grip, she thought. A grip! She turned and looked out of the window.

'Eve . . .?' Sarah had stood up as Eve stood, and now came alongside her, trying to peer into her face.

'You're right. I'm tired.'

Sarah's eyes narrowed. 'Who went with you yesterday?'

Eve looked down at the windowsill. She ran her finger along it. 'It was Jonathan Davies,' she said.

'Jon Davies!'

'Don't go making a big thing of it. I met him in the market yesterday, and he offered to help, and it seemed a good idea.'

'I wouldn't dream of making a big thing of it. Never crossed my mind.' She paused, smiling. 'Though it obviously crossed yours.'

Eve glanced up. Sarah saw the spark of something different in Eve's face at once.

'Well, well, well,' she murmured.

'You're completely wrong, Sarah.'

'Oh yes?'

'Yes.'

'Of course. Silly me.'

'He was just helping.'

'Yes, I can see that.'

Eve turned away. 'I must see to the copies. They'll be finished now.'

Sarah came after her and, at the door, laid her hand on Eve's arm. As Eve glanced back at her, she said, 'Be careful, won't you?'

'What do you mean?'

'Just . . . careful. Don't get drawn in, will you? It's a bad time – your father missing. You're vulnerable.'

Eve said nothing.

As they stepped into the corridor, the phone in the head's room began to ring.

At last, they had all gone.

The woman, the rep, the boy, and the sodding dog.

Sodding dog! He'd thought it was going to the cellar straight away. It had run round the yard madly, tail wagging, and made a beeline for the cottage. The woman had been walking back to her car. The rep had been saying something about traffic, the morning, God knows what else . . .

'Don't let him go over there,' Hugh had said. Panic seized him: he was going to be found out. He was going to let Eve down.

Something that felt like a seizure had gripped him: his vision had blurred for an instant; he'd felt himself go rigid. God *damn them, damn them!*

'Call that fuckin' dog back!' he'd cried.

The rep, mid-sentence, getting a cigarette packet out of his jacket pocket, had stopped. 'Eh?'

'What – what's-its-name. Dog . . .'

'Eh? You mean Pepper?'

Hugh had made a frantic swimming motion with one hand. 'Pepper!' he'd shouted. The dog was fast disappearing round the back of the cottage. Hugh had spun on his heel. 'Call him, damn it, call him!'

The rep had stared at him, an inane smile on his face. He'd put the cigarette, unlit, into his mouth, and searched for a match. 'OK . . .'

A light seemed to flash on in Hugh's mind. 'I put poison down,' he'd managed to say. 'Rats. For the rats.' A great red flush of colour had spread into his face. He could feel it. He'd strangled out a smile. 'It's rat poison. Your Pepper—'

The rep had run forward. 'Why didn't you say so?' he'd grunted out. 'Pep! Here, Pep!'

It seemed hours before they'd left him in peace. In reality, he supposed, it had been less than thirty minutes. The longest thirty minutes of his life. He felt as if he had aged five years. And, to cap it all, that bloody boy had appeared, that Jon somebody, Latham's sidekick. He had wandered into the yard as the rep was leaving, calm as you like, hands in pockets, out of bloody *thin air*. Hugh had gaped at him, and Jon Davies had said, 'I was around here, and I thought I'd drop by and ask about that job. You said I might be able to give you a hand.'

Hugh had stared, his mind now a buzzing, short-circuiting blur. 'Job?' he'd said.

Jon Davies had smiled, glancing about. He'd caught the rep's eye, nodded at him. The rep had called across, 'You picked a bad day, boy.'

Jon had looked back to Hugh. 'Yeah?' he said.

Yeah. Just like that. '*Yeah.*' Bastard. Bloody cocky young sod, swanning into the yard as if he owned it, grinning all over his face, looking about, interested, like he was laughing at him. Hugh had thought he was going to choke, to keel over there in the dust of the yard. Everything had rolled as if in a heat haze. His hands had felt bloated; the rim of the sweatshirt felt tight against his neck. Then, dredging up the memory from some distant recess in his head, he'd remembered that when Latham had been doing the last field trial, he had said something to Jon about giving him jobs to do, especially at harvest. The boy had been looking steadily at him with that smile on his face. And something else: a double-crease frown of interest, twin lines between his eyebrows.

Bloody young bastard. Yeah. That's how they taught them to speak at college these days. That's what an education did for you. What was he looking at, anyway? What was he looking like that at him for? *Young sod. Bloody cheek.* He'd tried desperately to clamp down his temper.

'Yes,' he'd managed to say, at last. 'Yes, all right. Well . . .' He had been seized with a sudden inspiration. 'I got to fix a board in the low field, fix it on a fence. This afternoon.'

'I can come back then. That fits in,' Jon had said.

Fits in with what? Hugh had wondered.

'Go down the low field – it's a mile. On the bend. I'll leave the board and the fixings where I want it up. Or – or, come back tomorrow.' His mind had started racing now, trying to deflect the lad from coming back anywhere near the yard and the cottages. 'Yes, in the morning. That's better.' Then he could check what Jon was doing. He himself had other plans for this afternoon. And, with this thought of Eve, Hugh's face had lightened and relaxed.

They had gone, all of them, eventually, and that was all that mattered. He'd got rid of them. Rid of them. Thank God.

The yard had reverted to its sleeping square of sun, the heat notched up a little. He went indoors, making sure no one was about as he stopped alongside the cottages and listened. He went indoors to the house, feeling sick and lifeless, holding the door-frame for support. He felt he had been twisted on a rack, twisted out of shape.

He stood in the kitchen, his hands flat on the work surface by the sink, and he stared at the cottages.

Just for a second, then, he thought he saw something move by the cottage back entrances fifty yards away. By the rubbish piles, the wire and the bales – he thought he saw something *crawling* there. He closed his eyes, breathed slowly, and reopened them. He thought that he had seen a human hand trembling and lurching along the ground like a white spider, feeling its way. A fluttering and clutching movement – but there was nothing there.

It was OK; it was OK. There was nothing there at all.

After a while, he felt able to pour himself a drink of water. He washed the glass, dried it, and put it away in one of the antiseptically neat rows in the cupboard. Then he turned his back on the window.

He didn't know how to do it right.

That was the trouble.

It wasn't that he wouldn't do it for *her*; it was that he didn't know *how*. Not how.

Bill was a big man. Hugh spent a moment calculating his own size and strength against Eve's father's, if it would come to that . . .

He had seen Bill in a rage so bad that the old man had kicked a hole in a wooden door. Last November. Hugh had not been there when it happened: he had arrived about half an hour afterwards, in time to see Eve, shaken and white, keeping her father at bay in his room. The old man had kicked a hole in the toilet door because he could not fathom the lock. Only an ordinary bolt in an ordinary sapele door; and yet he had managed to kick it through. He was talking, talking, talking . . . and searching all over his room for something – what, neither Eve nor Hugh could understand. They had watched him at the door as you watch animals in zoos tearing food to pieces.

He tried to calculate the odds of Bill getting himself free.

For a sane man, it would be difficult. For a young man, it would be difficult. There were no handholds, and nothing to make a ladder or a step from. The walls were slippery with grime and damp. It was dark in there: hard to see how to climb, where to climb, even if climbing were possible. The hatchway where the original wormy ladder had been was fifteen feet above Bill's head. No rope, no leverage. Too high to jump, even for a sane man. Even for a young man. And Bill was neither young nor sane.

No, it was not keeping him there that was the problem. It was keeping him quiet. Until it was finished.

Maybe he had put too much in the drink of coffee in the cooler bag. Aspirins were no good. He knew that aspirins wouldn't make a man go to sleep. It had been all he could find in the kitchen cupboard in that hour before dawn, in that panic.

Nevertheless, it must have made Bill groggy. Groggy, when he hadn't slept much the night before. Groggy enough to make him sit down and shut up.

Hugh pressed his hands to his eyes until he could stand the fluttering of geometric shapes – squares, light and dark – no longer. Why hadn't Bill called out? Had half a dozen aspirins made him go to sleep?

He mustn't give him any stuff like that again. After all, when he was found – when Hugh let him be found – they might do a post-mortem on him. They might open him up. They might find things that he had taken, been given – even aspirin. How would you explain away aspirin in a man who had eaten nothing for days? He mustn't give him nothing like that.

But to keep him *quiet*.

He could – what? What would keep him quiet?

He could climb down there when he was asleep, and tie his arms up, his mouth up. Then, afterwards, he could climb down again and untie him, so that when he was found he'd look like nothing had been done to him.

And Bill might wake up. He might wake up and catch hold of him and throw him against the wall – and maybe get Hugh's ladder and get up it. Then, before he could do anything, Bill would raise the ladder and he instead would be trapped down there; *he* would be the animal, and Bill would be hanging his head down through the gap and laughing at him.

No, no . . . can't get down in there. Won't get down in there. Going into a dungeon, into a place where you could be forgotten. For always and always.

Hugh put his hands up over his face. *I can't do it. I can't do any of it.*

I can't do it.

He went to the back door, pulled his greasy old Barbour jacket off its peg and went out. He kept his face resolutely away from the back of the cottages.

She stood at the far wall, leaning against it and watching him.

She was very clear in this dim light, and very white. She was smoking a cigarette and smiling at him, almost taunting him. She knew he despised women smoking. Hated it with a vengeance. 'But *you* do it,' she'd say. 'That's different,' he would tell her.

And there she was now, drawing on the cigarette, narrowing her eyes at him, taking it out of her mouth, letting the smoke wreath upwards, over her hair and face. For a moment, it looked as if she, too, were composed only of smoke.

His wife was a strong woman. Nevertheless, he could have put his hand – one hand – around her neck. Just one hand. He had done, once. She had only looked back at him with that extraordinary composure. Taunting him again. Do it. Go on, then. Do it. I won't make a sound . . .

She had on a V-necked sweater; very tight. White slacks, white sandals. In the pocket of the slacks, she had tucked a pair of white-rimmed sunglasses. Very Fifties. Thick white rims. Very black lenses.

'Hello, Bill,' she said.

Smoke, smoke.

'Hello, my darling husband.'

No . . .

'Hello, Bill. What's the matter?'

'Piss off.'

'Hello, Bill.'

He walked briskly to the back. When he turned, she was still there.

'Hello, Bill. What's the matter?'

He glared at her; furious, helpless.

'Oh Bill,' she said, smiling. 'What a mess you're in.'

He advanced on her, one hand outstretched. This time he would clutch that neck. He would squeeze that neck. He would, he would . . .

Within six feet of her, he stopped.

'Hello, Bill. What's the matter?'

'Stop it!' he cried. Fear had suddenly touched him. Very cold, to the bottom of his soul. 'You're not here,' he whispered. 'I know that. You're not really here.'

She pinched the tip of the cigarette, and let it fall to the ground. The few bright shreds of burning tobacco were dead before they hit the dirt. 'What are you going to do about me, I wonder?' she asked. 'What can you do?'

He saw that she was standing in the one small knifepoint of sunlight that could get through the hatchway high above.

'I'll kill you, that's what,' he said, tearful. He stared down at his feet. The toes of his shoes, all grey-green as if they had been in water and not cleaned. The toes of his shoes and the grimy grey socks and the hems of his trousers, brown and green, seemed suddenly pitiful to him. 'I'll kill you if you don't get out,' he said, raising his face. 'That's what!' he screamed. 'That's what!'

She put her hands behind her back. Not smiling. Not laughing. 'Oh, Bill,' she said. Quite calm.

Fists clenched, he began punching the sides of his legs. Thudding knuckles on the side seams of the filthy clothes, battering the thin old-man's thighs under the material. She wasn't to know. She wasn't to know that he wasn't as strong as when she last saw him. She wasn't to know that he'd grown thinner. Thinner under his clothes. His clenched fists had always stilled her before. Shut her up. The thudding of his fists on his rigid legs would still her now. He saw her look down at him, as if she had grown. She seemed to fill the cellar. No smile or any grimace of fear came to her face. It was cloudy, the smoke hanging in the air.

'Oh, Bill,' she said sweetly. And her voice had a hundred echoes. 'You know that you can't kill me.'

She leaned forward, until her face, larger than it should have been, her body, larger than it should have been, pressed at him in an undulating wave of smoke.

'Not again, anyway,' she said.

Twelve

Jon went through the Sunday morning streets, trying not to dance. The seaside town was barely awake, even at ten o'clock; sun slanted across the pavement in white stripes, between the Victorian terraces. He felt like the only man on earth, his steps echoing off the shopfronts. Every now and then, looking up a side street – five-storeyed narrow houses, split into holiday flats, shops below, attics above with the flat-topped dormer windows like hooded eyes in the roofs – there was a glimpse of sky and sea, a flash of a sign on the promenade. He turned the corner towards his flat, which was up an alley two streets back from the beach.

There was no one about, except for the old woman who walked her dogs on the sands; at the corner of the run-down terrace, he waved to her, and she nodded back in his direction. He wanted to run up to her and throw her bodily in the air, and start the manic dogs yapping; but he did not. Instead, he leaned by the front door for a second, shirt loose over his jeans, T-shirt scratchy at his neck, his thumbs looped in the belt of his jeans, and grinned at the world.

He went up the stairs two at a time, and let himself into the bedsit. Going over to the window, he pulled back the curtain and opened the window wide. Light poured into the room: in the distance, he could hear the church bells ringing.

It was still the same place, but it was not the same. Everything had changed since yesterday. He felt too big for the room; too big for the sofa bed and the tables and chairs, too big for the walls, the sill, the glass, the line of the street he could see below. From this window, the roof of the next house was only twenty feet away: he felt he could easily leap the gap and climb the oblique angle of the slate, and sit with the seagulls on the ridge tiles. The idea made him laugh for a second, and he passed his hands over his face, over his hair, as if trying to wake himself from sleep.

He looked down at his hands and arms, under the rolled-up cuffs of the shirt. Miraculous hands. He went to the sink and stared at himself in the mirror. Miraculous face. She saw something in that face, read something in it, and he tried to see what. Something of value, of worth;

something remarkable. The elements that made up *him* appealed to her – this configuration of lines and shapes that she had touched. It was nothing short of amazing.

He looked about himself: a room painted white over striped wallpaper, with the indentations of the stripes still showing through; a carpet of indeterminate colour; a sink, a cooker, a fridge, a wardrobe that rocked when he opened its door. And a sofa bed, red and black striped, with the material worn thin on the edges. Yesterday he had hardly noticed it. Now he saw every strand in the fabric, every fleck of paint. It seemed intricate and marvellous. The way white looked against red. The way light curved over objects. Marvellous . . . wonderful.

He tore off his shirt, T-shirt and trousers, and went down the corridor naked to the shared bathroom, trailing a towel after him, and whistling loudly all the way. Someone in the flat opposite muttered, perhaps cursed him, but he didn't care. He simply whistled louder.

The water of the shower was lukewarm, running to cold; the pipes in the wall clattered. It made no difference at all to him: it would have made no difference if the moon had fallen into the sea and the sun had frozen. All the paraphernalia of the world had dwindled to less than nothing; there was only one thing that mattered, and that was getting back to Eve. *She* mattered; every inclination of her voice, her head, every movement of her fingers, the expression in her eyes, was weighed down with extraordinary significance. The earth and everything in it had shrunk down to one face and one body and, by comparison, the petty affairs of life on earth were as fragile and transitory as dreams. *She* mattered. That only.

He scrubbed himself vigorously, shampooing his hair and, turning off the spluttering water, rubbing himself dry with the grunting carelessness of a dog shaking and rolling on grass. He had the absurd feeling that he could run up the bathroom wall, over the ceiling and down the other side. Nothing was impossible. He stopped towelling, and stared at his feet. *He was in love.* That's what songs were about. That's what they wrote poetry for. That's why there was music. *That's why people did those things.* It was all down to this – the feeling he had in his stomach, the pressure in his chest, the feeling that he had wings – like those of biblical angels – folded at his back, that would at any moment flex and carry him upwards. The whole ludicrous, stifling feeling of it. *He was in love.*

'Bloody hell,' he told his feet.

In his makeshift kitchen, he took out bread and butter and marmalade, and began eating them as if his life depended on it, stuffing great chunks into his mouth. He was starving.

As he ate, he planned. He would pack a bag. By three or four he'd get back to her. The fifteen miles between them were nothing: he would have walked them gladly. Thumbing hadn't failed him yet, though. He wanted to stay with her until her father was found. Finishing off the bread, he paused with a cup of black coffee – he'd forgotten milk – half-way to his mouth.

His arm froze unconsciously in that pose: Hugh Scott's face, blandly grey, with its intense grey eyes, asserted itself in Jon's small white room.

There was something incredibly *odd* about that man, Jon thought. It was not just rumours. Not just gossip. When people said that Hugh Scott was strange, they were not just being idly malicious. They felt real disquiet. Real distrust. There was something peculiar even in the way the man walked, hesitation plugging each step, the footfall very heavy. There was something peculiar in his hands, fleshy and large, that hung at his sides as if they did not belong to him, but were burdens that he dragged with him, like a bunch of keys hanging at his belt wherever he went. And, worse still – here Jon lowered the coffee cup, and his face lost the smudges of wry amusement it had worn while he considered Hugh – worse still were Eve's tense smiles at the mention of Hugh's name. And her dream last night, of Hugh standing on the track below her window and staring at the house.

It was that, more than anything, that had prompted Jon to go via Hugh Scott's farm on his way back this morning. Curiosity had itched at him, and turned his feet down the lurching gradient of green hill that was Hugh's. Coming into the farmyard, where Hugh had been centre stage, looking sick, as the rep's dog cantered about in the sun, Jon had had the impression that he had walked into some kind of crisis. He could actually *feel* the fear coming off Hugh as clearly as if he could see it: electricity arcing and pitching from the man. He noticed that Hugh's eyes were moving all over the place, almost rolling, like a man in the grip of a fit; two or three times, his eyes, and then his head, would turn towards the two derelict thatched cottages at the yard's edge. Hugh said that there was poison down; the rep retrieved the terrier, making a joke about the dog's love of ratting, but not of traps . . .

And still Hugh Scott stood in the yard, transfixed, his face flecked by colour around his mouth, around his neck.

Stepping into the sun of the yard was just like putting your feet and hands into a cold pool of water. Jon had even looked about himself, to try to see what the matter was; where the feeling of coldness, of *not-*

rightness came from. Everything looked normal, yet... Cold pool, wall of cold, cold smoke; that eerie, godforsaken coldness dominated Hugh Scott's yard even though it was drenched in early sun. The two did not go together: cold and light, like Hugh's blank drained colour. Cold and light.

Shaking his head, trying for a moment to free himself of the under-the-skin distaste of that image, Jon set about packing. He could hear people stirring on the street below: it was now mid-morning, and the families were beginning to make their daily invasion of the beach.

His heart raced as his hands folded the clothes into the bag. In a few hours, he would be in Eve's house again, in her arms, his arms around her, her skin against his. He had no idea how long it would last, or what would happen when her father came home, or what people would say when they found out. And he didn't give a toss. Not a toss. He was not going to leave her. Not going to leave her *not going to leave her* danced in his head: they would find some way. They would make some way. She was not someone he could lose.

'Eve,' he whispered.

And the sound of his own voice jolted him, and made him smile.

He wondered – his hand zipping the bag, his feet making for the door, his mind already on the road back to her house – he wondered, just for a second as he turned the key in the lock, how long he could possibly stay as happy as this.

Thirteen

Hugh came to the school at two o'clock.

When the phone rang at Eve's house just before lunch, it had been his voice on the other end of the line. Eve had answered, apologising for forgetting him, while Sarah made disgusted faces at her, miming the actions of hanging up, and turning away with a smile.

When Sarah went home, Eve walked round the village of Petherell, sleepy in its Sunday quiet, tacking posters of her father on to the hall noticeboard, in the telephone kiosk, in the bus shelter, and handing them out at the pub. She spent an hour in this pilgrimage, and then went back to the school.

Hugh had insisted on picking her up and taking her to Threlfall's farm. It adjoined Hugh's land, and covered the highest ground in the district, stretching for several miles along the hill-tops. Hugh seemed to think Bill might have gone as far from houses and roads as he could. She supposed, sitting waiting for him in the silence of the school corridor, that it was as good as any other theory.

At two exactly, she saw the Land Rover pull up. But, just as she was about to stand up, something about Hugh caught her eye. He was in the driver's seat, but the engine was turned off. Partly screened by the enormous buddleia bush by the gate, it might have been easy to miss what he was doing.

He was talking.

But not *just* talking.

Sometimes, when Eve told a story in class, she would glance up and see a child mimicking every word of the story; snarling as the story tiger snarled, waving as the story goblin waved. If it was a story that they knew, she would hear words whispered a fraction of a second before she actually read them out loud.

And Hugh was talking like that. It was like watching a tape being rewound again and again. A video tape of a conversation, but seeing only one of the people talking. Hugh was reacting, then adjusting that reaction. Playing the same imaginary scene again. His unseen partner was somewhere in the middle distance, beyond the windscreen of the car. As she gazed at him, fascinated, he leaned forward, one hand across the wheel, and smiled. Hugh playing at romantic hero. The smile had the roguishness of Rhett Butler. It looked so peculiar that Eve started to laugh. Oblivious to the fact that he was being watched, Hugh immediately slumped back, frowned, and then repeated the action, this time with a little more friendly concern on his face. It was the sort of smile you might give a mirror. *See how attractive I can be. See how sweet. Gonna knock you off your feet.*

The moment passed. Eve got up, gathering her bag and the remaining posters, hugging them under her arm. She saw Hugh register her movement; he jumped from the Land Rover and came walking across the playground, almost to attention, smiling. As she went out of the door towards him, she felt extraordinarily tired. All she really longed to do was to go home and sleep.

'Hello, Hugh,' she said tonelessly.

He took the things from her. 'Get in,' he said, looking delighted. 'Get in.'

It was mid-afternoon by the time they were over at the Fifty Acre of Threlfalls'. They stopped on the ridgeway and looked down into a landscape of wide rolling fields that fell away from the summit on either side, like waves parting before a ship. The top of the farm gave a good view of Chesil Bank, a white stone line holding back a flat blue sea.

Far down in the valley, all that moved was a tractor, looking like a toy stranded in a great ocean of grass.

'Lovely today,' said Eve.

Hugh went on ahead, a rucksack held awkwardly over one arm, head down, as if on a route march. Ahead was the copse of woodland. Eve struggled over the stile, realising as she did so that, for some time now, she had not been looking for any signs of her father. She had been doggedly tramping in Hugh's wake, letting the strong wind push at her as it came over the hill, a great warm hand nudging her forever sideways as she tried to walk.

'Hugh,' she called. 'Hugh.'

'Sit up ahead,' he called, pointing, but without looking back.

'Thanks a lot,' she muttered.

It was a remote spot, about a mile in any direction from the road or a house. Eve knew the place only vaguely. From school lessons, she knew that there was a stone circle here somewhere, and the Ordnance Survey showed small brown etched squares on the hill-top – a Neolithic hut enclosure, now hidden by the copse. Eve walked to the hedge, where Hugh was holding open a gate.

'Do you really think he might have come this far?' she asked as she drew closer.

Hugh shrugged, waving her through. She set her mouth stubbornly at his impatience. *I'm not one of your damned horses*, she thought. *Telling me what to do. Damned cheek.*

The stone circle was just the other side of the gate.

Its appearance was so sudden that, for a second, it took her breath away.

There was a raised mound close to the hedge. A kind of gatehouse to the circle. Except that it had two enormous stones set into the head, raised on their end like gravestones. Which is exactly what they were.

'The Ewe and Lambs,' she said.

The Neolithic grave was well nicknamed: it looked exactly like a grey animal guarding a lesser flock. Behind the upturned piece of granite, the smaller stones figured a rough circle. Some tipped over flat; others, too big to be tipped, looking as if they squatted on the ground. A green enamel sign claimed government ownership. The grass was clipped short by weather and sheep. It was a pale yellow ring. Eve walked to the middle.

In the centre it was curiously still, as if the slipped stones were able to keep out the wind. She sat down, and fought a diabolical urge to sleep.

As a child, first learning about the way the world turned like a ball in space, she had lain down in the garden on the lawn, clutching the ground to save herself from falling out into space. She had thought that she could feel, far down in the soil, the groaning of that ball, grinding on its axis, imagining it to be like a ball speared on a metal stick. And the world hauling itself around the stick, dragging every house, every tree, every living thing with it. The terrible burden of turning in the abyss, with all these humans hanging on its skin for dear life, gave her an attack of the wildest vertigo.

She had the urge now to lie down and listen to it again. Here, of all places, she would hear the world revolving and groaning, as if the centre of the circle were a window into the core.

'Up,' said Hugh.

She looked at him, as she lay propped up on one elbow on the turf. Then, dumbstruck by his rudeness, she realised that he was giving her an order.

'Up.'

'I beg your pardon?'

He caught hold of her elbow and, too surprised to protest, she allowed herself to be pulled to her feet.

He pointed towards the sea.

'See that green? That green bit?'

'Where?'

'That green, all over there. That field of linseed rape. That field of barley. That field of wheat. That one, and that one—'

'Yes, of course. I see them.'

'Mine, they are. Every one.'

She gave him a crooked, puzzled smile. 'Yes, Hugh. I know they're yours.'

He started to laugh. 'Gives you a funny feeling, eh?'

He dropped her arm, and waved both of his, the rucksack abandoned at his feet.

'Gives you a feeling,' he said. 'I did all that. I sometimes think, that's what *I* did. You see? All that land. Fantastic.'

She smiled. 'Yes, fantastic.'

Abruptly, he sat down on the nearest stone. 'That's the sort of deal you get. Can't grumble at that, can you? I should say not! Better eat this, then,' he said. 'Got a lot in here.'

She began to chew on the sandwich he gave her – a doorstep of bread and ham. She was dumbstruck, both disturbed and amused. Hugh was like a great boy, playing at being in charge. As she swallowed the food without really tasting it, she thought, *Deal? What deal? And what about Dad?* Hugh was staring at her happily, his mouth working over his food, not quite shut.

'All right, is it?'

'Yes thanks.'

'Have any breakfast?'

She had to think. She remembered Jon immediately, and looked down. 'Just coffee.'

He nodded. 'Thought so. Tuck in. I got to look after you.'

The wind swept and dived at them. Shadows of clouds scudded over the valley.

'Do you think he's been here?' she asked.

'Who?'

'Well Dad, of course. Bill.'

He snorted. 'No.'

She stared at him, at the derisory laugh. 'You don't?'

He finished his sandwich and rooted about in the bag for the next one. 'Bit of a long shot.'

She swallowed, staring at the top of his head, tousled grey hair that looked as if it had been cut with a pair of blunt scissors.

'I see,' she said coldly.

He glanced up. 'Never mind.'

She breathed down her annoyance. Deep breath now. So he had brought her here – insisted that they come here – as a wild-goose chase. Typical of him. Typical, obtuse, blinkered-faced Hugh. 'Well, maybe we ought to look now we're here. Look in the trees, under the hedges,' she said. 'He likes anything historical. You know, anything archaeological, like this. He might have come. There might be something.'

This time, Hugh didn't bother to answer. Just another snort. *Fat chance*, it said.

'Anyway,' he blurted out, after a second or two. 'I want to talk to you.'

He held out a slice of cake in the palm of his hand.

'No, thank you. What about?'

Shrugging, he took a bite of the cake, smiling at her. Never taking his eyes off her. He made her wait until his mouth was empty, until the cake was all gone.

'Bet you can't guess.'

'You're right. I can't.'

'Ha. But bet you *can't*. You should though, by now. Something extra special.'

'Oh?'

'Yes.' He brushed the crumbs off his lap, fastened the bag, put it down at his side, and sat facing her with his hands planted on his knees, grinning from ear to ear.

She was not to know about the pact, the pact he imagined they had made together to get rid of her father. He needed help with it, but dare not ask her, afraid that this would make him seem helpless and incompetent. The pact loomed horribly large in Hugh's mind. He kept seeing Bill, at the bottom of the fifteen-foot drop, staring up expectantly at him. He could get round it, he *would* get round it, somehow. If she could just help him with reassurance, with her hand in his, her smiles . . .

'Got a book out of the library,' he began.

This time, she laughed. 'A book. That's it?'

'Yes. A "How-to" book.'

'How to what?'

'Get married.'

'Get . . .'

He began to nod rapidly. 'Get married. Get married. All what you do. You know: customs, that sort of thing. Who does what. Who pays for what.' At this point, he stopped. 'Course, there'd be no question of that. I'd pay. No question. But flowers and cars and things. Banns, all that.'

She merely sat staring at him. Then, 'Who are you getting married to?' she asked.

She thought that he must have met someone recently – that some woman had come along at last and swept him off his feet, just as she had always imagined it would happen. That was the way it was with these men who had been alone for years. They fell like chopped trees, she thought. They crash into marriage. Maybe he had been trying to tell her before and she had not listened. A wave of relief, carrying a little picture in it of Hugh, standing on the path outside, in the darkness, washed over her.

He stood up. He spoke very slowly.

'We've known each other for a long time,' he said. 'And I reckon it's time now. Neither of us are getting any younger.'

She gazed up at him, a half-smile on her face, still not understanding.

'Eve, I want us to get married,' he said. 'Shall us get married? I wanted June. But it'll have to be September.'

Her mouth must have dropped open. She sat gaping at him like a landed fish. He took several steps towards her.

'It can't come as no surprise, Eve,' he said. 'You know it's been on my mind. For a long time. You know, don't you? I want to look after you, Eve. And it's much better together. I can't look after you while you're up in that house and I'm over the track. I can't even see your house unless I come up over the rise. I don't *want* to keep coming over there, Eve. I'm tired of it. I want you to be where I can see. Look after you properly, see? Properly.'

She leapt to her feet as he came at her, his arms outstretched. She stepped back; he lunged forward, trying to grab at her.

'Oh, Hugh.'

'What's the matter?'

'Oh, Hugh, please. Please don't.'

He was pawing at her arms, prising them from the straight-jacket grip at her side, trying to make her reach up and hold him, return his embrace. 'Here, Eve,' he said. Clasping like this, his breath swarming over her face, he whispered, 'I'm always looking after you, you know. Always thinking of you. You know what I do?'

She shook her head dumbly.

He gave a little laugh. 'I ring you up sometimes. Just dial your number. Then put it down. I don't – you know, I don't want to disturb you, Eve. I put it down before it clicks to ring. But when it's finished dialling, I know I've got through to your house. *Your* house. Gives me a nice feeling. I just lift the phone. It's a red phone . . .'

Eve swallowed. A disgusting taste had floated into her mouth: the acid taste of fear.

Hugh was looking over her in his arms, as if he had somehow got hold of this glorious prize and could not believe that he was actually in possession of it. He stared over her body and face and hair and shoulders with a lunatic smile.

'I don't half like looking at you,' he said. 'I come and look at your house even when you're not in it.'

Eve felt her bottom lip begin to tremble.

He began to nod, delighted.

It was enough.

She brought her right arm up, crooked at the elbow, warding him away, her fingers and palm turned outwards to push at his chest. Frankly, she didn't even like the thought of touching him even to get him off her.

Her fingers slithered on the waxed surface of his coat. The zip felt cold. He suddenly seized her, pinning one arm to her chest and the other at her side.

He pushed his face at her, trying to kiss her. She leaned backwards, tucking in her chin, terrified even now of offending him, this great square bulk of a man. He pursed his mouth like a child's imitation of a kiss, like someone who has only watched others kissing, and his face smothered her. She felt his lips blotting at her mouth, pushing, pushing.

He was incredibly hot, as if boiling inside his skin. Even his breath was hot. She wrenched her face to one side, starting to wriggle in his grasp to dislodge his arms.

'No, Hugh . . .'

His strength was frightening: she could not break the hold on her. She tried to walk backwards, and discovered his left leg locked behind hers. *Oh Christ*, she thought. And the stupidity of it all hit her. *We must look like a couple of all-in wrestlers*, she thought.

'Hugh, *please!*'

One moment they were staggering around, and the next they had fallen backwards. She didn't know if they had simply lost their balance, or if Hugh had meant to push her over, but the force of him landing on top of her thumped the breath from her body, and she flailed her arms, crucified, on the ground. A piece of stone under her felt as if it had cracked her spine.

He started pulling at her clothes.

Winded, she couldn't speak. She brought both hands up and began hitting him.

He fumbled under her top, clutched her breast. Then, with his other hand, he pushed up her skirt. He tried wrenching her briefs down, forced his hand between her thighs, and began groping her, trying to get his fingers to her as though he were delivering an animal through a difficult birth. She had a wild and disgusting vision of his hand inside her, twisting for leverage, pulling at her, dragging some bloody knot of flesh into the open air. And all the time he was hissing her name in her face, spitting on her skin. In the still grass circle older than time, the world at last groaned underneath her.

She screamed.

And it was as if he had been punched in the face. He rocked back on his heels and stared at her, gasping, his face bleakly shining.

She opened her mouth, and before any second scream came out, he scrabbled backwards, pulling down the fluttering material of her skirt, edging backwards on the grass until he was about ten feet away. And there, abruptly, he drew his knees up and clasped his ankles, as if to lock himself in place.

She lay on her back, trembling violently, her head twisted to one side. She could not move; she was shaking too much. But she lay with her eyes fixed on him, watching for *him* to move. After a few moments, she managed to get on to her side, then to her knees. She never took her gaze off him.

Watching, waiting, she edged back until she was propped against one of the gravestones at the rim of the circle.

It was a long time before he said anything.

Then, without raising his eyes to her, he said, 'We're going to get married, Eve.'

God help me, she thought. *God get me down off this place and get me home and help me, please . . .*

'Hugh.' Her voice wavered and fell. She cleared her throat. 'Hugh, listen. I can't get married to anyone. I don't want to get married at all.'

He shook his head. 'That's not true,' he said.

Not true! Jesus!

'Every woman wants to get married,' he said.

She thought of the unspoken, private ambition she had, one day when her father was no longer there, when she could read without interruption; paint, cook. Play the piano without knowing he was listening critically. Perhaps even go and live abroad. Stop racing against the clock. Feel the peace.

'You got to have children,' Hugh said.

'But, Hugh . . .' There was her voice climbing again. She checked herself. 'Hugh, I don't want any children. I never have.'

He looked over the hill, away from her. In profile, his face wore the expression of a sulky child. 'You would once you was married,' he said. He told her as if revealing some eternal truth, some elementary law of biology that she had not grasped. A fact of life.

She rubbed her hand across her face, feeling desperate. 'Hugh, you never told me any of this,' she said quietly. 'You never mentioned a word of this before.'

Please God get me down off here.

Get me down off this hill and I'll never ask for anything, anything, ever again.

Hugh's head wheeled back towards her. His face was flushed a purplish colour, a terribly unhealthy colour. 'You knew!' he said explosively. 'Don't say you never knew, because you did!'

Lord. Oh Lord.

'I – well, you've always been a good neighbour, Hugh, to me and Bill, and . . .'

He sprang to his feet, shouting. 'Don't say you never knew!' he yelled. 'You bloody knew. You bloody did!'

'Well, I—'

He was upon her in a flash. 'Don't you lie about it,' he shouted. 'I know and you know. Don't say that isn't right!'

She looked up at him, really afraid now. Really afraid of what he might do. Her whole body went cold.

And the pity and the irony and the idiocy of it was that this poor devil of a man was right. When she thought about it, he had done everything he could, in his fumbling way, to show her what he felt. He had been like a deaf mute, miming love, counting it over to her, trying to show her. All his sad little gifts that had been such irritations and embarrassments.

'Hugh, I'm sorry. I don't know what to say,' she murmured.

He dropped to his knees in the grass, and grabbed her by both arms. His face lit up.

'You don't have to say nothing. Nothing at all,' he said. He tripped over his own words, stammering. 'You – you – you got to take your time,' he said. 'I know that. That's a lady's privilege. Ladies got to keep a man waiting a bit. I know that. That's like a tradition. I don't want answers right here like this.'

And he smiled at her broadly. He leaned forward, kissing her cheek as she shrank from him. If there was an aghast look on her face, he did not notice it.

'But there isn't no use in waiting all our lives until we're old and grey, is there?' he told her, grinning. Almost laughing. 'No, you take all the time you want. Say, what if you tell me by – well, what do you want? Say a week . . .'

'Hugh.'

'Well, then. Two weeks. Or a month. It could be a month if you like.'

She looked in his face, flecked with that awful high colour. Grey eyes that looked as if they never slept. A great square scrubbed face with its reddish neck, and cropped greying hair.

All at once, she saw how he would look at fifty, sixty, seventy. He would never lose that stubborn, blank look. Saw him wrenching at a cable drive to a cutter, an engine; imagined herself standing at his door. Saw him doggedly bent over his books, figuring out meat auction prices and straw and feed; and her hand putting a cup of tea at his side.

Oh God, this was ridiculous . . .

Suddenly seeing a way out, she took his hand from her arm.

'Hugh.' Very softly and kindly, she spoke as to a child in class who could not understand. 'Hugh, dear, I can't possibly think of being married. You do see that, don't you? I can't think of being married while Dad is missing.' It was the only thing she could think of to say.

'While he's missing.'

He repeated it like a child, too.

'Yes. You do see that, surely? I can't think about marriage just now. And when Dad comes back, when we find him, I have to look after him. You know how he hates other people in his house. It would be misery. That's no way to start a married life.'

'What if you put him in a home?' he asked.

She looked at Hugh closely. The way he replied was almost eerie. She got the feeling that they were hardly speaking the same language. It was as if he had slipped into some parallel world, and was aping her from behind glass, mouthing words. There was something not right about him. Not right.

Even though she had often dreamed – fantasised, really – about putting her father into care, she saw plainly that now was not the time to say such a thing to Hugh.

'No, I wouldn't do that,' she said firmly. 'There's no question of that. I would never put him in any institution.'

They sat opposite each other, Eve still propped against the gravestone, Hugh squatting, rocking backwards and forwards on his heels.

'What if he's dead?' he asked.

He was just like a five-year-old, *just* like her five-year-olds. *Oh dear God. Let me out of this.*

'Hugh, I don't want you to say that.'

'Well, what if he's got killed?'

She got to her feet.

'I don't want to talk about it. Hugh, wherever Bill is, he's my father. My father.'

She took a pace sideways.

Hugh did nothing to stop her. He was still rocking, tilting gently back and forth.

'Hugh, I'm going to walk back down now,' she said. Her heart knocked in her throat. She tensed herself for Hugh to make some sudden movement. 'OK, Hugh? I'm walking back down now. I want to go home.'

She turned her back and started moving. Her legs felt wooden, rigid. Her feet slithered on the grass, as if she were walking on ice; the muscles in her thighs flickered and jumped. She prayed violently that she could get a head start. Prayed that Hugh would stay where he was, at least until she was in sight of the Threlfalls' house and farm. It wasn't too far. Not far. *Please, please, please,* she prayed. *Let me get away . . .*

All the time, all the way to the gate, all the way past the gate, even when Threlfalls' farm came into sight on the slope below, even when she walked down the fringe of their wheat field and she could hear sounds from their kitchen – the rattle of plates, the dog beginning to bark – all the way, she was terrified that Hugh would come running up behind her, taking her arm again, pulling her back. She imagined his arms sliding around her neck and dragging her off her feet.

Hugh watched her go with quiet satisfaction.

After a minute, he followed her, keeping her in sight. But he did not try to catch up with her. He was content to wait for his answer.

At the stile, he stood for a moment, gazing at the way he had come. He wouldn't forget that place.

That ring, like a magic ring.

Fairy circles. A lucky place for him.

'Marry me if it weren't for her father,' he said.

At the top of the slope before the farm, seeing his Land Rover parked in the lane, he quickened his pace. And by the time he caught up with Eve, he was running.

He did not see her flinch as he came thudding up behind her.

All the way, he had repeated it to himself. 'If it weren't for her father, if it weren't for her father, if it weren't for her father . . .'

It wasn't very often, lately, that those pieces of time came together and made any sense.

Segments of wandering time, some light, some dark. Very clear, each in their separate compartments. But not clinging together. No sequence. Time melted and flowed. Backwards, forwards, never stopping. Time melted and drained into the ground. Time stood up in walls. Only sometimes, sometimes, did they mesh together in order: day following night, date following date.

When they did come clear – like now – Bill found himself standing and simply staring at it: a wonderful sequence of days and weeks and months where all the events held together and made sense. At such times, he would feel as if he had been asleep and, waking, saw the lunacy of the dream. The kaleidoscope of shifting time in the dream.

And time – waking from the dream – was holding together now.

Bill stood under the hatchway of the cellar, looking up. The sun was at its height, or perhaps just past it. It looked and sounded like afternoon: a dry, warm, late spring day, of which all he could see was a shaft of light, inching its way across the ceiling and the floor. Bill put his hand to his throat, and winced. He had been shouting for the last two hours, on and off. Shouting at the top of his voice. Now his throat ached terribly. Felt as if he had swallowed razor blades. And his mouth was dry – drier than he had ever known it. A pain in his stomach that was now much stronger than plain hunger. A permanent pain, a contraction of the stomach, a cramp: sometimes dull, like toothache; sometimes worse, much worse. As if his stomach was pushed back against his spine.

He thought, from time to time, that he could smell food. Chocolate. Gravy. Eggs. Marmalade. All kinds of bloody strange food. Food he didn't even like, the memory of which brought a taste – not saliva – into his mouth. Like the aftertaste of an illness. Flu. A cold. Like antibiotics. That taste. There was nothing left in the small Thermos that he had found on the floor. He had a vague recollection of Hugh having given it to him, but when – exactly – he could not be sure. Perhaps this morning. Perhaps an hour ago. Perhaps yesterday . . .

For the hundredth time, he cursed the other man.

He was being left here: that much was obvious. Left to stew in his own juice. Bastard. Fucking, fucking, fucking bastard. He would smash that stupid face of his. He would smash his face. He visualised his fist connecting with Hugh's aimless, expressionless face. Cut him and hurt him, he would. When he got out.

He stared around himself in the cellar.

It was about twenty-five feet back, he reckoned. At the very back wall, there was no other hatch or vent or window, even though the cellar must run right under the whole house. And it was pitch black for at least ten of those twenty-five feet.

Half-way down the left-hand side – left-hand if he faced the hatch above him – were a set of wooden steps. Eighteen steps. He had counted. Ending in a locked door. He had spent the last half-hour at that door, trying to get it open. If it could ever be freed, it would open *into* the cottage. He had pushed, thrown his weight against it, tried to fiddle the lock, wept, beaten it, cursed, even prayed. On his knees, praying for it to open. Just a fraction. Just a tiny fraction. Just a splinter. Just weaken a bit at the hinges.

But it was solid oak, and must have been two or three inches thick. The lock was rusted and was a great Victorian contraption: solid, and welded shut by time. The hinges were of the same manufacture: enormous, scaled with rust. The door-frame was oak, too. Built to last, those cottages. Built like mausoleums.

Then a terrible thing had happened. Breathing on it, begging it to open, the wood beneath him had cracked. He had not seen, in the dark, the worm-eaten blocks of the stair steps, eaten through till they looked like balsa wood.

But now, as the top stair cracked, he knew straight away, lucidly, clearly, that they were rotten right through. He got up and stumbled back down, away from the noise of the crack. The stair trembled with his weight, and he felt a ripple pass through him. Afraid, and painfully aware of the drop below, he had almost fallen back down the treads. He leapt off the end, on to the dust-thick floor. The stairway sheered right across at the top, quite neatly. The rungs crumbled inwards, collapsing in one piece sideways and crashing to the floor, where they raised a knee-high wall of grey dust. Only the top tread stayed where it was, cemented to the bottom of the door.

He went over and looked at the fallen wedge of steps. The drop had cracked many of them; he could see, now, the pattern of decay in them.

Neat little burrowing creatures, woodworms. Neat little job they did.

Then, in a sudden fury, especially at his own objective thoughts, he kicked the triangular edifice. Splinters of wood flew off. The wood was damp and fragile.

Exhausted, frightened, Bill sat down on the floor. He must get out of this dark place and go home. He wanted just to go home now: he fixed *that* at the front of his brain. Go home. Going home. Get home.

Bloody fool. Bloody old fool! Stay in a cellar! Fall in a cellar in the first place – damned bloody old fool that he was.

Get home. Go home.

Got to get *home*.

He glanced up at the thin light coming through the hatchway.

It was about seven or eight feet above his extended fingertips. He had tried it. Even if he had jumped, there was no way he could reach the lip of the sill. He might have once – as a lad – been able to launch himself at that light and get some sort of purchase. But not now. He had attempted it about an hour ago. Got bruised to buggery for his trouble. Cut his hand. Scraped his arms and legs. Hurt both his knees. He had just fallen back into the pit.

The walls of the underground room were built of brick. Something porous and grainy with age. There was a lot of green mould and lichen, growing in round clumps in the cracks. A lot of spider webs, too. Thick grey with them. Must be a thousand spiders in this cellar. All sizes. Little spiders like a speck on a fingernail. Bigger ones with those bulbous sacs on their backs. Bigger ones still with great long legs, pale as pale, skittering across the long reaches of brick. House spiders, the kings. Fit into the palm of a hand. A thousand spiders . . . and him. He wondered if they ran across him when he was asleep. Ran into his clothes.

Or hair.

Or mouth.

He had been awfully frightened of spiders when he was a kid.

Wouldn't sleep in a room with a spider in it.

No, *sir*.

Got over it when he was thirteen or fourteen. Used to grab them to throw at girls. Didn't much like them, though.

He flicked his gaze around in the dark. Into the dark. Into the far utter black of the cellar, where nothing could be made out. No shape, no light.

A thousand spiders. No, sir. No, *sir!!*

He tried to smile. Been in hysterics if he were five. Hysterics . . .

The ones with round sacs on their backs. He had caught one in a curtain once above his bed. Crushed it – frantic – with thumb and forefinger. It had *popped*, squirted. That sac.

Oh God. He slapped his hands together. The noise smacked around the room like a gunshot. That's better.

Don't get funny now. Don't get funny. Get *out*.

Rubbing his forehead with one grimy finger, he tried hard to think. Tried to . . . now, *think!* You . . . you *think*, Chrissake. Think what they kept in here. When it was built. Coal, probably. Wood. Maybe an animal. He had heard of parts of houses being used for animals, way back. But then, not cellars. The gable ends of houses, above ground. Not cellars.

This was a storeplace of some kind. So huge. It must have been coal. It was certainly cold: no one could have lived here. The floor looked dusty and chalky, like earth, plain earth, dotted with lumps of stone. The natural bedrock of the country here; chalk. Coming up through the floor. Like a cave. A cold place . . .

Cold!

He jumped to his feet. Peering through the gloom, he searched what he could see of the ceiling. The ceiling was wood, wasn't it? He couldn't see. Couldn't *see*, oh God, must be wood. Wood floorboards above. Must be wood. Beams. Filthy black, but . . . They *hung* things, didn't they? Hams. Meat. Poachers' rabbits. Hung things.

Suddenly, he stopped. Opposite the stairs, about half way down the room, screwed into a thick beam that ran crosswise, he saw what he had been looking for.

Ten feet above his head. About six foot from the hatch. Four – no, *five* – iron hooks.

Thick felty grey with webs.

Hugh drove her home.

As they turned into the drive, they saw the police car standing there.

'Dad,' said Eve, under her breath. 'Oh, Dad . . .'

The young constable got out as she did. 'Afternoon,' he said. 'Nice day.'

'Yes,' she said. 'Have—'

'I'm sorry. There's no news.'

Then, over her shoulder, he saw Hugh.

'Mr Scott, isn't it?' he asked.

'Yes.'

'Ah, sir, I've just been down the farm to see you. Hope you don't mind; I had a look around.'

Hugh walked forward until they stood in a small ring together. 'I don't mind,' he said.

The constable smiled, his gaze flicking back and forth between them. 'Only they asked me to look over – wherever Mr Ridges might have gone. Outbuildings, and so on.' He turned to Eve. 'I had a look in your sheds again.'

Eve felt faint. The ground seemed to swim up to her, then recede. As if she were on a ship pitching at sea. 'We checked the sheds,' she replied.

'Of course. But the idea is, that he might wander, and come back to the places you've already searched. So it's best to go on looking, every day, places that—'

Eve forced a smile. 'I see. Of course.'

She glanced at Hugh.

He was staring at his feet. She noticed a vein throb at the side of his neck. His hands were clasped tightly in front of him.

'Would you like some tea?' she asked the constable.

'No, thank you . . . I must get along. Just called to see if you were all right.'

She did not ask Hugh.

The two men turned and went back to their cars. She watched them leave.

Only as she got inside, automatically locking the door and putting the key on the shelf, did she realise that Hugh had said nothing to her at all before he left. She stood in the darkness of the hall, thinking of him.

His face.

And hands.

She had to run to the toilet. She was violently sick.

Fourteen

Jon arrived at half-past four.

It was as if he had materialised out of nowhere. Eve stood looking at him on her doorstep – she had not heard a car, she had not heard a footstep – and was caught between shutting the door in his face and falling to the floor in gratitude. She felt as if she had been reduced to paper only held together with tape – and the tape was coming unglued.

I want to be left alone.

I don't want to be left alone.

But she neither closed the door or fell at his feet. She stood with her hand on the door's edge, obstructing him.

'Hello,' he said. He made a movement, as if to take her in his arms, and then, seeing her face, dropped his hands to his sides. At his feet, she saw a sports bag, obviously packed tight with his belongings. He stared at her, not understanding. 'Is it all right to come in?' he asked.

He was so young.

Lord . . . clueless. Young.

'Hugh Scott wants to marry me,' she said.

Jon began to laugh.

Switches engaged, turned, rattled, in her head. Switches connecting words. Not connecting words.

A phrase that a colleague used to use at school, way back, sprang into her mind. *You can't get there from here*, he used to say. *You can't get there from here.*

Then, abruptly, Jon was pushing his way in. She tried to stop him. 'Just go away, please . . .' His hand was on the latch. She tried unfastening it, helplessly smacking at it. His hands were nearly tanned. The memory of his silky skin, his tenderness and sweetness, reached up and assaulted her in return, and she suddenly wanted to be in his arms.

'Get there from here,' she whispered.

He had shouldered his way past, and was locking the door. They were enveloped in the artificial gloom of the corridor.

'... not standing on the step while you cry, for God's sake,' he was saying.

She hadn't realised that she was actually weeping. With both palms, she wiped her face. 'Don't look at me,' she said. 'It isn't anything. It's just the last three days. It's too much.'

'What did he say?'

'Who?'

'What d'you mean, who? That sod Hugh. Who else?'

She attempted a smile. 'Don't take any notice of him.'

Jon gripped her arms. 'I do take notice. Look at you . . . When was this? This afternoon?'

'He came up to the school. He had a picnic packed, as if it were some sort of jaunt. He wouldn't look for Dad, and we got all the way to the top of Threlfalls' . . .'

She wanted to get out of the dark, but Jon was standing across her. 'And what?'

'He just said. As if it were understood. He just announced that we were going to get married.' She looked into Jon's face at last. 'Crazy. Crazy.'

Jon turned away and went into the kitchen. She followed him. For a while he stood looking out at the fields.

'And?'

'And what?'

He turned round. 'What did you tell him?'

She started to laugh at the absurdity of it. 'What do you think? I'm not marrying him. I'm not marrying anyone.'

Jon's face was expressionless. She took a chair and sat down.

'He must have thought he had a chance,' Jon said. 'You must have talked about it before. A guy doesn't just assume . . . You might have told me. Last night . . .'

She swayed her hands about, madly trying to push his assumption away. 'You don't understand,' she said. 'He's never said a thing before. Never! I know it sounds unbelievable. It's just – all so . . .' She flung her hands down in exasperation. 'It's a nightmare.'

It seemed an age before Jon reached over and touched her on the arm. 'What's this?'

She looked where he was pointing. A long scratch marked her forearm. 'I don't know.'

'It wasn't there this morning. Hugh do this?'

'No, I don't think so . . .'

'You don't *think* so? You mean, you can't be sure?'

'Look, it doesn't matter—'

Jon thumped the table with his fist. It was the first time she had ever seen any kind of violence in him; anything other than his usual quiet sweetness of temper. He looked stifled, as if his rage was about to choke him. 'It *does* matter!' he shouted. 'He takes you up there and you come back with marks on you, talking about bloody marriage—'

'It isn't anything. It's nothing.'

'That *fucking* Scott!'

It was the first time she had heard him really swear. She hated the sound of it: from Bill, it was normal. But not Jon. It was as ugly in his mouth as the word was possible to be.

'You don't understand,' she said. 'Hugh isn't important. I've known him for years. He gets intense about stupid details: it'll pass, I'm sure it'll pass. Nothing's right at the moment, it's all messed up and strange. It isn't his fault . . .'

Jon's mouth worked soundlessly for a second. Then, slowly, he tapped the mark on her arm with his index finger. And, despite herself, she drew back.

With his right hand he held her face, gently, cupping the jawline. His eyes ranged over her: eyes, hair, mouth. Trying to see into her; working it out. When she looked away, the pressure from the hand increased until she looked back. She could have shrugged him off, pushed him away. But she did not.

'I can't stop thinking about you,' he said quietly. 'I don't want him near you.'

She opened her mouth to speak, to object that it was not that simple. He leaned down and kissed her.

She didn't want him to see inside her. She felt so fragile, so wiped out, so thin inside, so breakable. Her common sense told her that no one could give her peace but herself, and yet she clung on to him, this quiet stranger, who seemed so infinitely younger than her: that in itself was terrifying. He offered a refuge she felt she did not deserve and ought not to take. But it was so wonderful inside the sanctuary of him.

Don't look at me. There is no reflection.

Don't drink from me. Don't touch these locks. Don't touch, don't touch . . . Leave me alone.

For yourself, your own sake. Leave alone . . .

Both hands holding her face. He was whispering something. It didn't matter what. They were just words. His arms went around her, enclosing her, clutching her to him as if he were drowning and she were the rock. She was pulled to her feet. He kissed the side of her face, too

fast; eager and clumsy. He raised her hands, kissed her fingers.
Don't look at me.
You're too young to help. Too young to know.
He brushed back her hair, smiling, every movement one single, extended embrace; a single kiss. She relaxed into him, letting go. Tired. So tired. Too tired to hold back.

They got to the door somehow, and then no further. She undressed him where he stood, and he let her, his eyes level with hers. His skin today was slightly burned from the sun, on his shoulders and arms.

'I caught the sun, thumbing,' he said.

'You are two different colours . . .'

'I got hot. No one stopped. I sat on the verge at the by-pass roundabout . . .'

She stepped out of her own clothes, trembling slightly. Hugh's face kept leering at her, imposing itself on Jon.

'I don't like you to hitch lifts,' she said.

'I'm all right.'

'You never know.'

'I won't . . . I won't again . . .'

'Just for me . . .'

'You . . .'

She closed her eyes.

Take me away.

'Oh – God!' She spoke without thinking, a reaction to his hands.

'What's the matter?' he asked, drawing back. 'What did I do?'

'Nothing, nothing.'

'Don't put your hands up like that. Are you hurt? What did I do?'

'Nothing. Jon—'

He stared down at her. 'What the hell is that?'

'It's – just a bruise.'

'Just – Jesus Christ!' His eyes grew wide with surprise. '*He* did it. Christ! He did it!'

'It was an accident—'

'Accident!' His voice rose to a shout. 'Accident! You call that an accident! What the hell was he playing at?'

'He – just – got the wrong idea – before I could—'

Jon sprang back like a cat, his face red. He made a motion with his head, a hugely frustrated motion, both fists at his temples, as if wanting to tear his hair out. 'What the hell *is* it with that fucker! I'll kill him. I'm going down that fucking farm, I'll *kill* that bastard—'

'No, no . . . Jon—'

'He tries to *rape* you, and you defend the sod! You defend him! He hurts you, marks you, you *defend* him, I don't get it—'

He was almost incoherent with rage.

She stared back at him.

Stupid as it sounded, she had not put a name to it. Not called it rape. A mistake, yes. A farce, yes. An humiliation for both her and Hugh, the poor struggling bloody fool, the utter humiliating mess of it—'Oh, Jon, I don't know . . .'

He turned her head, so that she had to look down at herself. 'Well, I know!' he said, furious. 'I know what's it called.'

She drew her arm up across her face. Tears welled up that hardly belonged to her: they spilled out of her, without effort, without sensation. She tried covering them up, stopping them; they ran through her hands, too many to be coming from her, impossible to be so much – so much water. Pouring from a fractured well.

At once, he wrapped his arms around her, whispering, 'I'm sorry, I'm sorry . . .'

'I didn't know what to do,' she told him. 'It was – there's no sense in it . . .'

'You've got to stay away from him,' Jon told her. 'Will you try – try not to see him? Tell him anything, but don't see him. Don't go anywhere alone with him. Please, you've got to take care of yourself . . .'

She couldn't reply. Couldn't voice the words.

I can't. You take care of me. Take care of me, please.
You do that. Because I can't. Not right now.

It was evening.

He was so, so thirsty.

Thirsty. He would die without water. Had to have water. Live a long time without food, but you had to have water.

Bill thought of the adverts on television. He would have laid bets that he had never taken a blind bit of notice of them; yet here they came, taunting him.

Pictures of yellow-bright pints of lager in a cold, cold glass, and pints of bitter with an inch-deep foam head, and bottles of milk dancing down the street, and pictures of sea and rivers, and cans of lemonade, and glasses with four clinking ice cubes, and hands cupped around mugs of coffee, and teabags dipped into cups, and water pouring from spouts of kettles.

His mouth ached, trying to summon up enough spit to salivate.

Thirsty.
Thirsty thirsty thirsty . . .

Hugh could hardly wait to get home.

At first, speeding away along the track, his heart pounding, he had been in a terror that the police constable had heard something, seen something at the farm.

Then, breasting the rise, with the Land Rover leaping and jerking through the ruts, he realised, of course – coming out on to the top of the hill and the last light of day opening like a wide white flower in front of him, and the far rim of the sea – he realised that the constable had seen and heard nothing of Bill. Otherwise, he wouldn't have behaved as he did; he wouldn't have *been* where he was, said what he did. No, no. He was safe. There would have been not one, but a whole bloody posse of police asking questions.

The Land Rover slowed nearly to a crawl as he thought about it. Far down in the dip, he could see the roof of his house and the roofs of the outbuildings and cottages, crowded together like conspirators beneath the trees. Wait a minute, now. Wait a minute. Think.

He slammed his hands on the steering wheel.

God damnit, *whatever* happened now, he was safe. He was safe, safe, safe, safe. Eve was going to marry him. Eve didn't want her father. Eve wanted rid . . . Oh yes, rid to be married. Said as much. To him, to him!

The words careered around his head. Voices deafening him. To me, to me, to me. Getting married. *Here's to you, my fine young man, here's to you, my darlin'.*

'My darlin', my darlin', here's to you, my fine fine darlin' . . .'

He didn't know if it was a song or not. Not a real song. It didn't matter: it was now!

Down the slope he went, picking up speed. Dust rose behind the jeep, a cloud covering him, a sheet drawn over him. The Land Rover skewed into the yard, and he turned off the engine and listened, in delight, to the silence.

That's right, Bill old boy, that's right old boy, you keep stumm, just a bit longer, done all right till now; keep stumm just a bit longer old boy old boy old boy.

'My darling, my darling, here's to you my darling . . .'

He slammed the Land Rover door. Felt like doing a jig in the yard. *Do a jig in the yard – it's my yard!*

He clicked his heels in mid-air, laughed, and fell against the bonnet, laughing still. *Can't dance for toffee, can I? Have to learn to dance. Take* lessons. Take Evie over to Bourne Pavilion and Tivoli Park and wherever she wants to go, dancing, whatever she wants, dancing.

He looked at the cottage.

No sound.

His face stilled. He stopped dead, but the faint smile remained. Perfect, undiluted peace ruled the yard. The gods were running with him. Running with him to suffocate the old bastard down there in the dark. Nobody wanted him. Not even his daughter. He was just used up and useless, a weight, an encumbrance. They said that the children at his school were frightened of him; unpredictable, one day pleasant and the next day a bastard.

Nobody wanted him. His time was all gone.

A song drained out, a low whisper, from Hugh; drained out in a whisper and filtered across the yard.

'Evie is my darling, darling . . .'

And it was *then* that the idea came to him.

Dark was beginning to crowd the cellar.

Bill was standing with his back to the wall, the hatch above him.

He was trying to calculate how he could reach the meat hooks and, once he had his hands on one, if he could swing from it and manage to touch the hatchway.

It had been three-and-a-half hours since he had first noticed the hooks, but he now stood gazing at them, unaware of the passage of time. It was slipping about. Losing it. He tried hard to concentrate on the shape of the hook.

So very thirsty.

He was six foot two. Used to be three. He had shrunk. A small smile touched his face. Everything about him had shrunk. Brain especially. Six foot two . . . he looked from the hook to the upper patch of light. It was about – what? Eight feet or ten from the hook to the hatchway. Nearly two feet short. If he swung hard, and if the hook held, and if he could get to the damned hook in the first place, if if if . . . If he swung hard, he *might* catch the sill . . .

No. What would happen then? Just be suspended like a bloody fruit bat between the hook and the sill, nothing to grip. He was no fucking Olympic gymnast, for Chrissake.

What then. What?

So . . . Oh God, so thirsty. And the spiders.

Stop. Think, think.

He looked vaguely around him. Part of his concentration swooped away, urging him to lie down, to rest, to sleep and wake up in his bed, whispering, like an evil spirit; that if he released the dream, it would be just a dream, and he would wake up and it would be morning. *Let go and lie down and you'll wake up somewhere else . . .*

He took a deep breath, bit his lip. Couldn't be tempted. Had to think. Wasn't a dream. Was real.

Help me, help me!

The broken ladder from the hatch, snapped in two pieces. Each piece was only about three feet long, because it had only come halfway down the wall; which was why, in his surprise, he had pulled on it, finding no other rung, trying to get back out. It had snapped.

No piece long enough, even if he wedged it against the wall, no piece long enough to get him to the sill, even with hands extended.

It wouldn't hold him, anyway. Matchwood.

Matches and fire. Fire and heat. Heat and steam. Steam and water. Water . . .

He put both hands over his face. Despair, huge, blackened, deadly, engulfed him.

It was only just a little way to that light. Just a stupid, small way. Just ten feet away, up there and out, were the back yards of Hugh's farm, his house, the front yard, the stables. Just a few *yards* away. He could hear traffic, from time to time, as well: cars and lorries going along Hugh's back road. Just thirty or forty yards away was a house, a house with a kitchen as the first room you walked into, a kitchen with a tap in it, where water flooded at the turn of a handle. Water pipes must run just a few paces from where he was now: pipes full of water. Full of water. Oh Christ, just a few short yards away. It was so . . .

Few yards might just as well have been a few miles. Few *hundred* miles. Thousand miles.

God help him.

His eyes rested, without thinking, on the rotten wood stairs from the back of the cellar.

Broken stairs.

Time shifted in and away, a bevelled mirror. Hall of mirrors. End of the pier mirrors, each throwing a different reflection of himself.

All of a piece, except here where he had kicked—

A cry escaped him.

All of a piece.

All of a piece: stairs!!

It was a beautiful plan. Such a beautiful plan.

Lovely.

Hugh whistled as he walked to the stables. Lovely lovely lovely lovely lovely.

He opened the first door and looked in the tack room. Shadows rewarded him; and the neat, pricking smell of his own care. He polished all the tack regularly, as you ought. Everything done as you ought. The horses were rigorously cared for and groomed and kept clean, as you ought. He always did what he ought. Today was no exception.

He walked into the gloom, and looked around him. In the far corner cupboard, an immense oak corner case drilled into the wall, he kept every remedy ever prescribed for the horses. His father had done the same and, in this locked niche, were dozens of bottles, paper packets, droppers, some of them very old. He had never allowed the vet to see the cupboard, because he knew that he would say that the whole lot should be thrown away.

But you never knew when a thing might come in useful. He had poisons in here for rats, rabbits, mice, enormous great brown bottles of linctus; faded boxes of oils and vaseline and polish and all the combs and brushes and mending wire and thread and coarse cotton: a regular chemist's shop. Unlocking its door, he looked at the collection proudly.

You never knew when a thing would come in useful.

Like now.

His hand went immediately to what he wanted.

He brought down a cube-shaped wood box, about six inches square. Amazing that he had not remembered it before now. But then . . . He stopped, gazing into the half-light of the stalls. He had not known what Eve wanted, before.

Now that he knew, it was easy. Easy to remember.

Images of the cold room at the top of his house wreathed about him. Cold flesh, cold floor. The phone, the cards, the snatched mementoes of Eve's life. Little things he had picked up – stolen, then – from the house. She had never missed them. Soon, he would no longer need the room that had satisfied him for so long. Because he would have the real thing. For years, the room was all he ever thought he would have of her. As they both grew older, and Bill got worse, it had come to him that she needed him, and that her very dependence drew her close, so that it became possible, imaginable, that he could have the woman and not the cards and the boxes and the clothes: the *woman*. From that moment, he never laid his hand on another girl. They all seemed so pallid compared to the promise of Eve.

And she would love him so much when she knew how long, how faithfully, how patiently and quietly, he had waited for her.

For the time to come.

And the time was now.

His fingers smoothed the surface of the lid. Inside the box was a faded paper packet, folded. He broke its homemade seal, and took the bag out.

There was a sudden, odd odour, reminiscent of fruit – like melons. Written on the side of the packet was a label prescribed by the vet some time before. A spidery brownish script. His father used to give this stuff to the horses before they were castrated, to calm them. Hugh himself had used it on his own stock, and knew that it was effective. He remembered his job of mixing the same thing for his father. It used to turn yellow in clear water. They used to put it in a bucket and let the horses drink.

And they would drink, *especially if they were very thirsty.*

CHLORAL HYDRATE, it read.

Administer one half to two and one-quarter ounces in drinking water half-hour before handling.

The white crystalline mixture seemed to smile back at him. Hugh gave a deep and profoundly happy sigh. Shared secrets.

He pressed the box and the packet to his chest and crossed his arms over it, smiling hugely.

Shared secrets. So very good. And a sweet passage to oblivion.

Gasping with effort, and with the excitement of getting out, Bill hauled the stairs to the hatch.

They were heavy; very heavy.

Small pieces came away in his fingers, shards of worm-eaten wood. Parts of it were crumbling in his hands. He was reminded, heaving and panting as he pulled, of long-buried bodies that crumbled when exposed to light. The stair ladder was like that – stood there a century, slowly decomposing in the darkness. And the moment these things were touched, they fell to pieces.

'You don't have to hold out long,' he whispered, as he pulled backwards, his feet slithering in the grime. 'Just one minute. Just seconds. Just long enough to let me fuckin' well climb up you . . .'

Under the hatch, he looked at the top tread, which had come away from the wall. Rusted thick nails protruded from it, bent and cracked. The batten that the tread had been attached to was still beneath its step on the wall, the tread had sheared from the batten. It looked like dust. Sandy, reddish dust.

He ran his hands, squinting, over the ladder. Twelve steps. On one side, the underneath strut that supported the treads was cracked in two: it hung from the underside like a broken arm. No matter, no matter. There was one the other side. All he had to do was to put it to the wall.

He sat down for a second, trying to regain his breath. For Christ's sake, he was stupid. What was he? *Stupid.* He had sat there and looked at those stairs, lying cracked in the back half of the cellar, for what must be the best part of . . . what? Was it an afternoon? Or a day? It was so hard to tell. Sometimes the cellar looked like a room, sometimes a street. The hours lifted and danced. The minutes dragged like days. He held his hands in front of him, the fingers spread. Digits for counting. Since childhood; counters carried in fists. But even on his hands, he failed to count the hours. Here in this room, this pit, this street. Sometimes it turned into a room on a winter evening, where Eve's mother stretched on a chair and regarded him through opaque, clouded, wretched eyes. Sometimes the barred-light classroom at the dreg-end of the day, his counting fists pressed to his throat in the last suffocation of patience. Sometimes his own child's schoolroom where he figured times and weights and impossible arrangements of mathematical shapes.

He was back at the beginning, where, childlike, he figured time. He could feel the grain of the desk under his skin. The smell of ink. The smell of his own parents' rooms. Time catapulting backwards and taking him with it.

The cellar receded and shrank; the cellar bloomed out again, real and present.

He dropped his hands. Got to . . . get the ladder up. Up, up.
Where?
To the light. To the air. To the water. Water, air and light.

Shambling, confused, he got to his feet. Got to get the ladder up. Tensing himself, he gripped the side and pulled. It was so heavy, so heavy: it wavered. He grabbed. He leaned on it, and the tread on which he was leaning snapped. Snapped under the pressure of his shoulder. *Godamnit!* Yelping inner panic. Yelping squealing silent inner panic. Sweat sprang out, cold, from every pore on his body. Ice cold. He lunged for another hold. Wheeling the length of the stairs around towards the wall. They fell against the dark brick with a thick, clunking sound. The bottom rung jiggled along the ground; he tilted himself backwards, on his heels, to halt it. In the centre, the rungs were split. It made a broken, splayed 'V' against the wall.

He stepped back and looked at it. Broken in the middle. But it only had to hold for a few, a few precious seconds. Please, please God, *please God*, only a few small seconds.

He would have to scramble. Scramble up it like a sodding squirrel. In the gloom, in the shadow, Bill grinned a slack, unhappy smile. A rictus of a smile. A death's head.

Oh my Lord my God. Lend me a little lightness. Just for six seconds of my life. That's all I ask. Sweet, sweet, merciful God. Only six short seconds of lightness, speed and agility.

Before time collapses in on me like a house of cards.

Fifteen

'I don't know anything at all about you,' said Eve, across the bed.

Jon paused. He was sitting, eating an apple, propped up against the pillows.

'What's to know?'

She made a face. 'No, come on. Don't say that to me. You sound like some film—'

'What film?'

'You *know* what I mean. "What's to know."'

He finished the apple and dropped the core on a newspaper at the side of the bed.

'OK.'

She regarded him levelly.

'I don't know anything about you,' she repeated. Then she spread her hands, to include the room, the house. 'You know about me. But I don't know where you live or who your parents are or what you like to do . . .'

Jon started laughing. 'You want to meet my parents!'

She slapped him, softly. 'You know exactly what I mean.'

'You mean a girlfriend.'

She hadn't meant a girlfriend at all. She sat back on her heels.

'No girlfriend,' he said. 'Not recently. We split up.' He gave a great, drawn-out sigh and, by way of acknowledgement of her intense gaze, a smile. 'I come from a place called West Bickett,' he said. 'Kent. I went to University because . . . there wasn't anything else I wanted. I thought it would come to me—' his gaze fell on her, speculatively – 'what I wanted.'

'Brothers, sisters?'

'No.'

'Didn't you want to go home – when you had to leave college —'

A low laugh, far back in his throat. 'No. You haven't met my mother.'

'No.'

Mother. Eve fought down an impulse to ask how old Jon's mother was. Forty? Forty-five? Maybe younger. She could be thirty-five. She could be *younger* than she was!

Jon put his hands behind his head. His eyes fixed on some point beyond the window: the rolling dip of Hugh's field.

'Dad was in the Army,' he said. 'A sergeant. We moved around a lot. Hanover. Rheindahlen. Osnabrück. And Berlin. Ten months in Berlin. He was posted back to Aldershot when I was about nine or ten. Then they split up.'

'What does he do now?'

'Who, Dad?'

'Yes of course, Dad.'

'Got out of the Army and went to Tenerife. He works as an insurance salesman. The ex-pats out there. That's how he got into it.' Jon turned his gaze back to Eve. 'He's got a Spanish woman; she's OK. They get along – you know, they have fun and do things. I see him three or four times a year . . . you'll have to come with me next time.'

'And your mother?'

'Mother.' He seemed to savour this word with irony. 'Yes, well. It depends what month it is, what year it is. You never know with her.'

'Why?'

He shrugged. Ignored child. 'She likes enjoying herself. I don't think she ever wanted to get married – I kind of forced the issue. She doesn't stick at anything for long . . .'

Eve began to clear the mess from the meal they had shared. Shreds of bread, crumbs of cheese. One day she might get to cook a meal and eat it with Jon. Or even go out somewhere with him – what a luxury *that* would be. To go with him on a date, an evening out, to the cinema, on a walk, to the pub. He watched her.

'Your Mum sounds fun,' she said.

'Having a grown-up son doesn't do her any favours.'

'No. But—'

'But what?'

Devil's advocate spoke up for Jon. Eve considered as she tried, rather in vain, to tidy the bed.

Nineteen and running away from responsibility. Into debt at the first chance; fallen at the first hurdle. He would go home again soon, perhaps to show Mum what a naughty boy he could be. He would go back to University soon, too: it was the autumn term in less than four months. Back to the bars and the libraries. Student cards and pints of bitter; counting the pennies to be good this time. With all the quickfire optimism of immortality; those sidespent smiles towards middle age, and regularity, and hesitation.

She looked at him now, as he sat on her bed, gazing out of the window. She must seem old to him, surely? When *she* had been nineteen, she remembered classifying anyone over twenty-five as slow-moving dinosaurs with coagulating opinions. They were foreigners from another world, tied to houses and jobs and children and cars. She recalled clearly that teenage contempt for the sheer slowness of adults, their conservatism, their fear of the new. She used to look at older women in their stiff dresses and American tan tights, always carrying handbags, their hair lacquered, their faces grained into expressions of weariness. At nineteen, she had promised herself that she would never be like them. In some ways, she had kept that promise, helped by changing fashions: she never wore tights, never had her hair set. In other ways, she was sure she was unable to keep the promise. She was sure that fatigue, a kind of ironic acceptance of life, showed in her face, despite all she did to conceal it. She still felt free, free in thought, in opinion, free to think creatively, inside her skin. But the face . . . oh, Lord! The joke of time. Wearing a face – not lined, not old, but with the first sign of her father's obstinate square jowl, with the deep line beginning on each side of her mouth – a face that was a traitor, some other woman's face.

She saw that Jon was now looking at her. Inadvertently she straightened herself up and smiled self-consciously. *She* might feel the same on the inside. But on the outside . . .

'What are you thinking about?' he asked.

She laughed. 'I shouldn't tell you,' she said. 'But I'm thinking about age.'

She sat down, and glanced across at the mirror in the wardrobe, the same one she had watched herself in that morning. As she did so, Jon moved across the bed until he was sitting behind her, and his face appeared, resting his chin on her shoulder.

'You've got lovely skin,' he said.

'Have I?'

'Pale. Nice.'

'Jon . . .'

'There's only one thing wrong.'

'What is it?' she asked.

From behind, his hand circled her face, smoothing the line between brow and chin. She waited for some painfully honest comment on that other woman's face.

'You don't show anything.'

'What do you mean?'

'In your face. Your face is closed up. I can't tell what you're thinking.'

She turned to face him, and kissed him. 'Oh, Jon,' she said. He took her hands in his, turning them over to look first at the back, then the palms. 'Does it really matter?' she asked.

'Maybe not,' he said. 'Anyway, I feel like I've known you a long time.'

She had to spoil the moment: the words were out of her mouth before she could help it, and she hated herself as soon as she heard them. 'You don't know how old I am,' she said.

He let her hands rest, stroking her fingers. 'No,' he said. 'I suppose you're thirty-five or so? I don't know. I'm really not interested.'

He looked her straight in the eye. 'But I'm interested in why you look down, look away, when I'm close to you, and I'm interested in what makes you stay here in this house with that – with *Scott* about; and I care about what hurts you, and what you need, and I'm interested in what you think, and if you're happy.' His voice had dropped almost to a whisper. Raising her arm, he kissed the inside of her forearm, slowly and delicately, from wrist to elbow. Momentarily, she turned her head from him, as his mouth moved over her shoulder, her neck.

He slid from the bed and on to his knees and began again, at her feet, brushing the skin with his lips with no urgency at all, visiting each contour. She lay back, sighing, wishing the sensation could last, reaching down to draw his head towards her. He obeyed her, following her hands with silent understanding. After a minute or so, she raised her arms and crossed them over her face, shielding her eyes, smothering her own cries.

She did not see him pause, frowning. Or feel him falter as she hid herself from him.

Hugh walked to the back of the cottages, humming softly to himself.

He carried before him, held out in his hands like an offering, a glass jar. It had a screw lid, and contained a thick, yellowish liquid.

He got to the hatch and looked down at it.

There was a snuffling, shuffling, inhuman noise inside. Like an animal. Pushing aside the creepers of the blackberry bushes, he edged sideways to the cottage.

He got to his knees, placing the jar carefully on the ground next to him.

'Bill.'

It looked very dark in the cellar. A sense of its size, its looming darkness that stretched back so far, pushed up into the still air of the evening.

'Bill?'

Trying to accustom his eyes to the blackness, he hung in the narrow rectangle. There were pieces of wood on the floor: big pieces. Not just the hatch ladder. Other pieces, all broken up. The snuffling was louder now.

'Bill, you there?'

Of course he was there. Where else would he have gone?

Maybe he *had* gone. Got out.

The thought crushed him. *Got out.*

'Bill! Bill!'

Into the faint circle on the floor came a human hand.

Hugh was silenced, watching, thinking for a second how like his nightmare image outside that hand looked. The hand edged and stuttered, as if searching. It passed over the shards of wood, picking little bits up, trembling, letting them fall.

Bloody Nora, those are the steps off the other side, Hugh realised. *He's only pulled down the other steps and tried putting them up here, and they've broke . . . You poor old bastard, you.*

As if dragging the body after it, the hand brought Bill into the half-light.

He looked utterly defeated: a wreck of a man washed up on the cellar floor from some unimaginable storm. His face turned upwards; a face drowning at the bottom of a well. It had no real expression; it was merely a drawing – a not very able drawing – of a human being. The planes were flattened as if two-dimensional; the hair matted to a slick of dirty grey. Eyes that shone like blue marbles, like pockets of blue gum, bluish snail's-trail moisture; filmy, grey in the flesh.

'Hey now, Bill,' Hugh said. His voice seemed to boom. 'You thirsty?'

It sparked an immediate response. Voltage seemed to flicker – snap, jolt – through the body beneath.

'Thirsty, yes,' said Bill.

Hugh wriggled a little further in. 'What you been doing then?' he asked loudly. 'What's all this with the ladder?'

Bill gazed down around himself.

'You broke up those steps, Bill.'

'Ladder steps . . .' Bill said. He looked back up at Hugh.

And if ever Hugh's resolve wavered, it was then.

Bill's face creased like a child's. Tears welled in his eyes and spilled down his skin; tears that Hugh would never have guessed – never, never, in a thousand years – Bill possessed. Men like Bill never cried. They made others cry. Weep and thrash and cry, yes. Bill had made Eve cry a hundred times. He had seen it. Seen the small Eve knuckling her eyes on the doorstep of the house, running to the corner of the garden to throw herself into the sheltering shadow of the hedge. Seen her eyes fill with tears as Bill called her filthy names as the illness got worse. Seen Eve's face scored by a hurt that went deeper than mere expression, that drew the long lines down at the side of her mouth, that brought the hollow, set line of forbearance as she guided Bill's hand in an ordinary task. He'd seen Eve cry and Bill shout at her when she played the piano, or did any small thing wrong as a girl; seen him turn his back as she said she was sorry and tried to hold his hand for forgiveness.

He had been told that Bill made children in his class cry like that. Parents went to the school and complained.

And then there was Eve's mother . . .

Hugh's eyes narrowed. And yet here he was. That consummate heartless old bastard, crying. A perfect picture of misery.

Hovering in the air over him, Hugh was the divining angel. Bringing his reward for the tears.

'It broke,' Bill gasped out. 'I put it up there, and they . . . I tried to climb them, I thought they might hold, I wasn't quick enough. I tried. They broke, broke . . .'

Gasps, sobs. Pitiful.

Hugh reached behind him, and found the jar. *Got to finish this now. Get it done with.* He pulled the jar alongside him, and curled his fingers around it. The glass was cool to the touch. Rounded and cool. Clean and cool and clever.

'Bill. Here, Bill . . .'

The old man wiped his face with his dirty hands.

'See this, Bill?'

'I . . . I see it, yes.'

'Drink in it f'you.'

'What is it?'

Hugh laughed. 'Wouldn't have thought you could pick and choose, old man. Don't matter, do it? All I had in. A bit of lemonade. Thought you might like to drink it while I go get my ladder.'

Bill stared upwards. A paroxysm crossed that face. 'How bloody fucking long does it take to get a fucking ladder!' he yelled.

He came right to the wall, and stretched his hands upwards, clenching and unclenching, as if he would scale it if he could. 'I'll . . . tear you . . . tear you to pieces, you bastard!' he screamed. 'You – you come down here, bloody coward, come down here. You come down here, I'll tear off your fucking face!'

'No no no no.' Hugh made a soothing sound, the sound a mother might make to a child in a temper tantrum. Bill was *his* child now. His frantic little child, locked in the dark for his crimes.

'No no no no.' He held out the jar. 'I've only been gone a few minutes,' he said sweetly. 'Couldn't find the ladder – only the old one with the rusty extension. Knew that wasn't no good. I made you a drink in the meantime. Cos I took the new extension ladder over to the Top Barn to fix the roof last Tuesday. Got to get in the Rover to get it, see? So I brought you a drink. In the meantime.'

Bill's eyes were fixed on the jar. 'How long?' he whispered.

'Only be twenty minutes.'

'No! How long since you were here last?'

'Oooh . . .' Hugh made a great show of wriggling his arm through and, balancing, looking at his watch. 'There now . . . about half an hour.'

'Half an hour?' whispered Bill. 'Only half an hour . . .'

And he began, falteringly, to laugh. And cry.

'What's the matter?' asked Hugh.

Bill shook his head, back and forth, back and forth, a limp and ragged unjointed doll. 'I thought it was two days or something,' he said. 'I thought it was two days. I was sure . . . I thought there was a night, I was sure . . . Two . . . two . . .'

And he put his hands to his face and let the rage go, in a long and pitiful cry of relief. 'Oh, my God . . .'

At last, drawing his sleeve across his face, he looked up again at Hugh. 'I'm sorry about the steps, Hugh,' he said.

Hugh smiled. 'That's all right, mate. Don't you worry about them. I knew they was rotten.' And he grinned broadly. He held out the jar just a little further. 'Think you can catch it? Don't want it to smash on the ground.'

'No, no. I can catch.'

'Sure?'

Bill passed a dry tongue over even drier lips. 'Yes, Hugh. Thank you. You throw it. I'll catch it. Thanks, Hugh. I will.'

'Ready?'

The jar swung to and fro, a moon swilling in a parched sky.

'Yes. Throw it, Hugh.'

Hugh couldn't resist one last agony. He withdrew the jar; saw the panic cross Bill's face; saw the old man's hands flutter in desperation.

'I better not throw it,' Hugh said, grinning.

'No! It's all right. I'll catch it, I know I will. You throw it, please Hugh . . .'

Please. How many times had Bill said that word to him? Maybe only four or five times in his life. Hugh couldn't help the laugh that gurgled out of him: this was like teasing a dog, or pulling the wings off flies when he was a lad. Only better.

'I think I'd best lower it, so it don't break,' he told Bill. 'What d'you think? Don't want it broke an' all over the floor, do you?'

Bill's tongue ran over his lips. His voice was cracked. 'No, all right,' he whispered.

Still chuckling, Hugh reversed through the weeds. He lay on his side for a second, laughing to himself, a great surge of exultation passing through him. *I got you now, you old sod. I got you now.*

He took a piece of cord from his pocket, and knotted it in place around the lid. For a moment, he dangled the jar with its precious contents experimentally in his hand. Then, satisfied, he wriggled back into the gap. This time, as he gazed down, he found the smell from Bill doubly revolting. It smelled like the old man had wet himself. Or worse. *You filthy old bastard,* he thought.

'Here, Bill.'

A little squeak of appreciation came out of the old man; a sorry, helpless little sound, like an animal whimpering. Bill held up his hands.

'I'm going to lower it on this cord, Bill.'

'OK.'

'Ready?'

'Yes, yes.'

Hugh edged the jar down. It swung tantalisingly in mid-air, the colour of the liquid inside itself darkening as the jar descended into the cellar. Hugh watched, holding his breath. The moment that it was in Bill's hands, he let the cord go, and it fell, a white worm, at Bill's feet.

Might strangle himself with that, he thought. Then, *No he bloody won't. He's too thirsty to bother with it. And once he's drunk what's in that jar . . .*

Bill looked up at him.

'Thanks, Hugh,' he said. 'Thanks ever so much.'

And Bill began carefully, trembling, to unscrew the lid, and let out the sleep of the dead.

***

'What are you doing?' asked Jon.

Eve looked over her shoulder. She was in her father's room. 'Trying to find something,' she said.

Jon came in, rubbing a hand over his face. 'I fell asleep,' he said. 'What time is it?'

Eve had sat down on the floor next to her father's trunk: the one that he had always guarded so furiously against her. She knew that he kept his insurance policies and other papers in here, and had allowed him yet one more idiosyncrasy of keeping it secret from her. She glanced back at Jon.

'I don't know,' she said. 'Ten? Eleven? I haven't got my watch. Are you going?'

He looked offended. 'Do you want me to?'

'No. I thought you'd want to. That's all.'

He came and stood over her. 'There's nowhere else I want to go,' he said.

They looked at each other for a long moment.

'What're you looking for?'

She shrugged, turning back to the trunk. 'I don't know really. I feel like Sleeping Beauty putting her hand to the spindle.' She laughed. 'Forbidden fruit. He never lets me near this thing.'

She smiled wryly at herself. More than once, Bill had accused her of wanting to see him dead so that she would inherit his money. A five-thousand pound insurance policy on his life, with a dozen get-out clauses. And a house beginning to crumble for want of maintenance.

She opened the lid. It was not locked, and, at first, revealed nothing out of the ordinary. There were some blankets for the bed; half a dozen fifties records; some travel guides; old Minutes of the Archaeological Society. Under these, as Eve lifted them out, she found holiday clothes; shorts, swimming trunks, long unused. And two boxes.

The first was the one that he hated her to see: the strongbox containing the policies, the house deeds.

'What's in the other one?' Jon asked. He had come to look over her shoulder.

She took it out.

A cardboard shoebox. Fifties shoes, price nine shillings.

'I was looking for a book,' Eve said, thinking aloud. 'He's had this book, a red one. Like a desk diary . . .'

She took the elastic band from around the box, winding it around her wrist.

'Perhaps I shouldn't do this,' she murmured, hesitating.

'If it gave you a clue . . .'

She looked down at the shoebox. 'I suppose . . . He reads *my* letters, you know. If I leave them lying about the house. I have to hide them.'

'There you go, then.'

She grimaced. 'When I got up, I was thinking of the teachers Dad used to go to conferences with. He was in the Union, you know. I wondered if he had a list of their names in here. They were from all over the country. I wondered if he might have tried to get to one of them.'

'Worth a look.'

She opened the box, saying, 'I feel like a thief.'

Inside, there was a handful of letters.

Slowly, her heart curiously sinking, she opened the first.

It was a long envelope in an expensive linen-feel paper. The handwriting, to the school, was looping and black. A strong, determined hand.

Sandalfield

Bill,

    Sorry, Thursday's become impossible. Ring me between six and seven tomorrow – Monday,

Celt

Eve stared at it, puzzled. She turned the page over and stared at the blank side. Such a short message.

'Celt?' she said, wonderingly. She squinted at the signature. 'Am I right? Celt? Is that a name?'

Jon read over her shoulder. 'Celt,' he confirmed. 'Sounds like a nickname – or something shortened.'

Eve studied the envelope. It was postmarked London. 'It could be from someone he'd met – at a Union thing,' she mused. 'Where is Sandalfield?'

'Never heard of it.'

There was another the same, undated. She drew the stiff page out of the envelope.

Sandalfield

Bill,
Believe me when I say that you do! You do, whether you like it or not, whether I like it or not, whatever is before us, you do you do you do! This is like an accident that happens to people. One doesn't go looking

for it, nor expecting it. It simply occurs . . .

Mark was back yesterday and we were at Glyndebourne – not my choosing, so heaven help that frown – business, of course. Rather a nice evening, though. But not ours – not belonging to you and me.

There is talk of a holiday. It's always June. Must I make an excuse?

I can hear you laughing, you absolute devil. Satan in disguise and both of us utterly mad. Satan must help us. The Lord won't.

Don't ring. You know how Mark is. The arguments are tedious.

I will ring the school this week.

Celt

'It's a love letter,' said Jon.

'No, it can't be. What does it mean, "Do"? What does he do?'

'Love her.'

'No . . . no.'

'It is. Look: "not ours", "both of us". It's a love letter. Mark must be her husband. He sounds under her thumb, poor sod.'

Eve stared at the postmark: 9 July 1959.

'Two years before my mother died.'

It was impossible to read the placename, which had been smudged.

'I don't understand,' she said.

'She sounds well-off,' Jon remarked. 'Glyndebourne. I bet Sandalfield is the name of her house.' He came round to the side of Eve now, trying to catch her expression. 'You didn't know about her?' he asked.

Eve rested the letters in her lap. 'Maybe it's a friend,' she said. 'Mother could have known her.'

'Why would she make such a point of ringing him at the school if she were a friend of them both?' Jon was fingering the paper of the first letter. 'This woman had money,' he said. 'The paper. The handwriting. The *way* she writes. Are there any others?'

There were not. Fragments of a puzzle.

Eve reached down, pulling out the last folded sweater, a faded newspaper, folded to a page where there was a photo of a school play. One of Bill's old classes, probably. The bottom of the box was chipboard.

'Well, no book,' Eve said.

Jon got to his feet. He smoothed his hand over her hair. 'Do you want something to drink?' he asked. 'Anything I can bring you?'

She did not look at him. She was acutely aware of her being at his feet. 'Coffee? There's a bottle of brandy in the cupboard. There's some cold meat.'

'OK,' he said.

He touched her lightly on the shoulder as he left.

She turned back to the trunk, ready to put the things back. As she knelt there, she drummed her fingers absent-mindedly on the base. It didn't sound odd at all, but, as she turned slightly to get the first item, and leaned inadvertently on the chipboard, the corner slanted upwards. She looked down at it, and laughed outright.

'Good God,' she said to herself. 'Arise, Sir James Bond.'

She pulled the board back, intrigued. It revealed another six inches of trunk – this time, its real floor, pitted and marked with age.

And the red book.

She frowned, and touched it. It was a desk diary, the kind you might be given by a company rep at Christmas. It bore the figures, 1961.

'Hello,' she murmured. 'Hello . . .'

She lifted it out, and opened it.

As she turned the first page, she saw at once that this was a continuation of some other book, some other diary. Almost mid-sentence, the handwriting began at the top of the page, ignoring the appointments sections, the moon phases, the lighting and tide tables. It seemed, principally, to be notes for the garden – names of seeds and plants, and planting times, and shopping lists. Interspersed with the most mundane housekeeping details were little notes: notes that became larger, longer, and more expressive as the pages went on.

At the top of the third page, the text ran:

. . . sent back in for making a noise. Poor thing! She was heartbroken. It really is hopeless of that odd woman Matthews to allow half the class in and half out and expect to keep control of both. By the time we got home Eve was quite unconcerned, and telling me . . .

Eve!

. . . how to purl stitch. She's much more opinionated these last six months. One day, I'll get her a special book of her own to write these things in. Had to see Mr Jarvis about the meat bill. We waited ages for the bus and it broke down half-way here. Eve delighted. We could see Scott and son tramping the top field – two red squares, red necks, red ears. Bill late back again. Eve wants to make a shell collection—

'What is it?' asked Jon.

He was standing in the doorway, with a tray on which were two glasses of brandy and a coffee pot with two cups.

'It's my mother, my mother . . .' She put a cooling hand to her face. 'There was a false bottom to the trunk. It was hidden in it.'

He put the tray down. 'You're joking.'

'No—'

'What's the big secret? What was in it – coke or speed or something?' He was half laughing. 'The Crown Jewels?'

'I don't know why he should hide it,' she said, taking the brandy glass he offered. 'I didn't know she kept a diary. He never mentioned it.'

'What does it say?'

'Well, that's what so strange. Nothing revealing. Just little things about me at school. I'm—' She checked the last page she had read – 'I'm eight,' she said. 'That would make it 1961.' She raised her eyes to Jon's. 'Nineteen sixty-one was the year she died.'

He came and sat close to her, on the floor. 'What was she like?' he said. 'Can you remember?'

'No. No, that's the sad thing. Just snatches. Images. I wish he'd given me this. And there must be others, or were. It would have been nice to read them. It would have made her . . .'

'Closer.'

'Yes. Closer.' She fingered the book, touching her mother's lines, the faded blue ink, the curling loops of the letters.

'What did she die of?' Jon asked.

'A kind of pneumonia, I think.'

'Unusual.'

'Maybe not so much for the year.'

He looked down at the pages, and pointed to her own name. 'Odd to see yourself written about like that, too.'

'Yes.' Then, softly and affectionately to herself, she said, 'I remember those shells . . .' She flicked through the pages while Jon sat next to her, his coffee cup balanced on one leg. Her mother kept a rigorous record of the garden; it was obviously an occupation she loved. She was a list-keeper, too, and a village gossip, taking a fresh delight in absurd family arguments and misunderstandings. She kept a record of the storms, frosts, droughts; days of sand and grass and chalk; of soft clarity, of curtained fog. Eve felt a tremendous charge of affection, seeing the hill through her mother's eyes, in the moods which she herself was constantly drawn to, the shades of the crop, the enormous breadth of sky.

'I would have loved to have read this,' she murmured. 'Loved to have had something of hers. Why didn't he ever show it to me?'

Her voice trailed away.

The month the pages had come to was March.

The angular, jerky handwriting, full of dashes and exclamation marks, and scrawled occasionally at the side with reminders, suddenly became smaller and applied with more pressure.

Eve started her own strawberry patch. Very proud. Watered with a plastic seaside bucket. Got a letter from Inland Rev. Lambs and ewes brought into Scott's top pasture. Eve asking to go up – I shall have to brave the rednecks. Risk another slavering from Scott senior – he really is an old lecher, dreadful, those purple-red hands, the frayed cuffs sticking out under the jacket. Scott Junior at his back, watching. Like some godawful Chad peering over his wall. That boy has horrid eyes. What a bloody terrible pair! Today spent all day with Anne while Bill went with Chris to the Cheltenham conference. Back at six in the foulest mood. Did the ironing this evening and cut Eve's hair.

Rednecks! The Scotts. Rednecks, watching over the wall.

Writing on, her mother reached up to her from the page, alive and bright. The diary was full of Eve and much less so of her husband Bill. Her mother's obvious adoration of her child clasped Eve's face in the two loving hands of the open book, and kissed her through time, smiling. The sudden sensation was crushing, like a real touch. Eve held her breath, as if to seal and retain it. So fleeting, so strong and sweet.

Another page. Here was May. A Wednesday.

A change of ink, to black.

. . . sat and looked at this wretched wheat. If only Scott had not taken down the chestnut trees at the top of the road. They were at least a green line, breaking up the skyline. All the candles they had that looked so nice. They were – a hundred years old? More. Now he is burning them in his bloody Aga. Bit by little bit. He ploughed over the tumuli. May bad luck strike him. Beast beast. The son comes and looks over the fence at Eve, like a bloody toy soldier standing there. Hardly says a word. I'll tell him to push off next time. I want to leave this house. Go into town.

Eve raised her eyebrows at the change of tone, at the new disjointedness of the sentences.

He'll never do it. Doesn't want to. Won't do it for me . . .

Turning another sheet, the handwriting dwindled: it became very strained and small and composed. Almost a month had passed since the May entry.

It was June 1961.

She knew that her mother had died in the summer, and, with Jon's hand stroking her arm, Eve felt a sudden tightening in her throat, waiting to find the entry that marked the beginning of her mother's illness, waiting for the reference to feeling ill.

> *... daresay have overreacted, Bill says so, but then what does he know, never here, doesn't care ...*

'Hold on,' said Jon, as she tried to turn the page. 'Christ, you read fast.'

> *... found them at last, walking down the track, and this revolting boy holding her hand. Going to show her the animals, he said. Big square face and hair that sticks up, the sight of Eve's hand in his, why I can't say, just disgusted me. Marched them both down to Scotts' farm, boy Scott protesting all the way, done nothing, etc. Dreary dreadful place they live in, the mother like a mouse, never spoke, twitching every time Scott Senior yelled. Gave as good as I got. Won't have the boy taking Eve off like that. Animals! He should know! They live like animals down there, I doubt the boy has been in school more than half the term. Talk about bloody* Cold Comfort Farm *...*

'Hugh,' said Jon. 'That's Hugh.'

'Yes.'

'Taking you off. Well, he doesn't bloody change, does he?'

'I don't remember him doing that,' Eve said.

'Mental block.'

She smiled. 'No. Just one of those things you forget. Seven is a blur, isn't it? Seven or eight.'

They dipped their heads and read on.

> *... as if that wasn't enough, as I came out of the house – there's a smell in there, absolutely bloody indescribable – damn me if the father doesn't sidle up and try putting his arm round my waist, all in sight of the boy, all in sight of Eve. I slapped him. Still can't believe I did it. Slapped the old bastard there and then. The look on his face was worth it.*

Eve started to laugh, saying, 'Good for you,' and then stopped abruptly, seeing Jon's face. 'What is it?' she asked.

'Don't you see?' he said. 'Doesn't it make your flesh crawl?'
'What?'
'His father did the same to your mother. Touching her.'
She frowned.

Eve turned another sheet, drinking the last of the brandy. Almost a month had passed now since the last entry.

It was now July.

> ... she came last night, on her own. I waited at the gate and I knew the car. White. She was very – upright – sure of herself. Cool. I had put Eve to bed and she asked after her. How she bloody dared! Looked at the house – like an estate surveyor. 'Of course you know why I have come,' she said.

'Celt,' whispered Eve. 'It's Celt, isn't it? Come to this house.'

> ... Glasgow brogue – he says Edinburgh – she peeled off a pair of driving gloves. She had a silk taffeta frock, must have cost a packet, big roses on it. So this is her. In the flesh not so daunting. Oh, money. Money all over her. But not such a giant, not so frightening, face to face. It would be worse I suppose to be faced with some tarty coarse bitch from town. A young girl. At least Bill fucks a grown-up.

Eve caught her breath. The obscenity – so out of character from what had gone before – summed up the bitterness of the paragraph.

> I am to understand that Bill will not come home. Species of relief. But then perhaps with her he has no moods. Perhaps only with us, with me. Poor little Eve. I know he will want her to visit. She won't visit. I will die first. She will not go to them. To her. Over my dead body. Not Eve in her house, watching them. Not to be tolerated. I can't kill over Bill but I will kill over Eve. I don't want to hold, don't want to grasp. The touch of him would revolt me anyway – greasy and cold, like old food, old love got sticky, foul-smelling, old flowers rotted in a glass. Thank God he is not looking at me tonight. I can't bear his looks. Looks looks looks. All he has to do is leave me alone. That is all he has to do. Not come near Eve. That is all that remains for him to do.

> This sick interview in the garden. How dare he send his messenger for his things, how dare she come and do his work for him? I made her wait

and look at that empty field, like I do. Not over my doorstep. Let her wait. I gave her his two flight cases and the portfolio he's kept since college. I put Eve's photo in it. His Latin primers and survey maps and Roman Society books. God save me from the bloody aqueduct and the Neolithic causeway camps and the early Christian burials. At least I won't have to do that any more. I won't have to drive out with him to some spot and stand at the roadside looking at some hump in the ground and pretend I care about it. I shan't have to listen to his bloody lectures on them again – what he knows, what he knows, so clever. Let her listen. See how much she likes it. The bloody ice queen. I am sick to death, sick to death . . .

'My God,' said Eve. 'My God, my God.'

Her father had gone – actually left home over this woman. The woman in the garden. The woman in a roses dress, in gloves, in a white car. The woman from a house called Sandalfield. Eve had no doubt that this must be the one who signed herself 'Celt'. Why had her father not come with her to collect his belongings?

Cowardice on his part. Courage on hers. Courage, or that cold self-possessiveness her mother saw.

'You know why I have come.'

Supercilious bitch!

How her mother had not slapped her face, slammed the gate shut, locked the door on her!

I have to look at this empty field.

She had been closed away, imprisoned, by her husband. Shut out from his feelings and his life, made to feel unimportant. *Just like me*, Eve thought. The blood ran cold through her veins: for a second, she actually felt it, freezing, coursing into her heart, turning her arms cold. Her father had shut her mother away, turned her from him, betrayed her. Then, alone – the smug Scottish bitch must have gone back to her husband, or left, or – that didn't matter; what mattered was that *her father spent the next thirty years alone with his daughter*. Freezing her out, closing himself from her, cutting her with that look he had, cutting her with his indifference, with his voice, bullying and belittling her as he had done to her mother.

All over again. All over again.

Her mother's daughter. How she must have reminded him of her mother, the same looks, possibly the same kind of voice, the same build and expression.

I have to look at this empty field.

Her mother had been so lonely. Eve looked up, out at Hugh's land, the same land, sloping away, the track slicing through it.

That beast.

Those animals.

How her mother had hated the Scotts. That was another thing she had never realised, never been told, never understood. Her mistrust, her unease with Hugh was not hers alone. Her mother had felt it. It was not fantasy, as her father had so often hinted. Her mother had felt threatened too, and yet been left exposed to the Scotts all day. She had felt exactly the same gut-level instinctive aversion to both the man and the son.

Eve looked at Jon. His face wore a sad, almost apologetic expression.

'No wonder,' she said to him. 'No wonder he kept this from me. And lately, he's been looking for someone at night, saying it wasn't his fault, asking me to find her . . .'

'Do you think he meant your mother?'

She shook her head. 'I don't know. If Mum died of pneumonia, perhaps he came back to nurse her, or look after me, and then Celt left him. She doesn't sound very caring, does she? One whiff of discomfort, she was gone. Then Mum died.' *And he was left with me.*

Jon bit his lip. 'Maybe – at night, when he was looking – maybe he was looking for this other woman. Celt.'

But Eve hardly heard him. She was staring at the book, her last sentence churning over in her mind. *And he was left with me.*

'He must have hated me,' she whispered.

'No,' Jon whispered.

'Yes. Yes. He must have *hated* me.'

Jon stroked her arm. 'You can ask him about it when he comes back,' he said. 'He might remember. It might be good for you, good for him. He's been looking for it, maybe looking for an answer. You can talk about it.'

Eve fought down a taste of acid in her mouth. 'I don't want to talk to him about it,' she said. 'Even if I could get him to make sense for two minutes put together, even if he were normal, even if I had *ever* been able to talk to him about anything . . .' She stopped herself, her voice that had been threatening to break. She took a deep breath. 'He left my mother. He left her. How could he do that?'

I can hear you laughing, you Satan, you devil.

She laid her hand over the page, over her mother's agonised script. Had her mother seen it coming, that great black blanket of the future, where everything she was, and wanted for Eve, and needed, would be obliterated? Had she sensed it, creeping across the terrible empty wheat field, clutching for her daughter through the hedge with thick, squarish fingers; had she sensed it, in the cold white car and the overblown roses?

Over my dead body.

Eve turned, looked at Jon. A thought had occurred to her, so terrible, so inconceivable, that she couldn't put it into words. She leaned forward, burying her face in Jon's shoulder, saying nothing, her heart hammering sickly in her chest.

If her mother had died of pneumonia . . .

If.

Bill had a dream.

The kind of dream that comes only rarely – a gift from the angels. A dream of soothing, lulling motion: water, rippling and falling. The rising of waves.

At first it was all pure fantasy, and he stood back, impersonal, watching himself, perfectly aware that he would wake.

The sea in which he found himself was blue. But that hardly began to describe it. It was a clear, light, glowing colour, shifting with refracted light. It was the blue of a gemstone held up to the winter sun; ice, in geometric cubes and slices, and each face a whitening mirror. It was the blue of cornflowers, with a tissue of green dropped across it. Looking down, he saw his own body walking through the sea; walking through it, with no sand or rock or shelf beneath him. Walking through water, buoyant and clear-headed, with no sense of effort at all.

The sun was shining, the sun of the Mediterranean, high and gold and limitless. He saw the light brown skin of his own arms, a skin untouched by age, the skin he had had at twenty or sixteen or as a child. It struck him with joy that he was young. He flung himself into the water and, sinking under it, opened his eyes. All around him the ripples spread. He was the centre of the world, of the universe. He switched and flipped and turned like a seal. Easily, wildly, freely. Echoes rebounded from him: phosphorescence sparked from his fingers. He burst up through the surface of the sea and saw the drops, fan-like, arching above him.

Just at that moment, the current shifted. He found to his dismay that it was no longer easy. When he pushed, the water pushed back.

He began striking out as he had swum in life, grunting with the exertion of fending the water away. Waves began to roll, lifting him, dropping him. And then, just as he thought that he needed to find land, just as he felt the first tugging of fright in the incessant strength of the ocean, he suddenly sensed a pair of arms pass around him.

He could not see his rescuer: they were behind him. They passed their hands under his armpits and lifted him up, so that once more he could see the long, long line of the horizon. He let himself relax, and he floated and drifted once more, allowing himself to be taken where the arms wanted him to go.

An island appeared out of the sea.

It was as simple as that. One moment not there – one moment there. The shoreline was a soft white sand. There were no trees, and no people. No boats; no sign of life. Just an arc – a shape like a curved smile of sand – in the empty and vast sea. There was only a single building that almost occupied the whole sand-shelf, its white stone foundations almost touching the water, the sand fringing it neatly like a skirt. It was made of glass. Impossible to see inside. It merely reflected the burning sun.

His feet touched the sand: the arms around him vanished. As soon as he got his balance, he turned to thank the person who had brought him to land. But they were gone; and there was no ripple in the water, no footprints in the sand, to show where they had been.

There was a flight of white steps leading into the house. They curved slightly. Everything was curved. The arc of sand, the steps, the walls of the house. A silent shining white boomerang of glass in a silent sea.

Wonderingly, he put his foot on the first step. It was icy cold.

Sixteen

Bill's body was heavy. Too heavy.

Hugh lay beside the sleeping man in the darkness, groaning, gasping for breath.

He had hauled him up the metal extension ladder from the barn, which had been put in place with the greatest difficulty, pushing it through the hatch and trying to avoid Bill's prone body beneath. Then he'd climbed down into the cellar himself, heart in his mouth, throat dry, tying Bill's hands together, looping them over his neck. Now, ten minutes later, they lay side by side at the mouth of the hatch, in the weeds and brambles, stretched on the ground.

Bill was where he had wanted to be for so long. Up in the open air. Out of the nightmare.

Pity he would never know it.

Hugh considered, staring at the slack grey face next to his own. They were lying like a pair of lovers together on the gritty earth face to face. Hugh smiled.

Poor old sod, he thought.

It was not so much the weight that was the bother, but the extraordinary looseness of the body in its deeply sleeping state. Bill was like a sack of wet sand. A puppet made up of wet bags of sand, his fingers hanging loosely open. His head lolled. Spittle looped from the open mouth. The eyes, though closed, Hugh knew to be rolled back in the head. The breathing of the body was so slow that it was hardly perceptible.

He had given him a lot. He was not sure how many ounces. But a lot. Enough to roll a horse. Let alone a man.

Gaining more of his breath now, Hugh leant on one elbow and looked down at Bill, his expression filled with loathing.

Nothing but a useless bag of flesh and skin and bone. William Ridges had ceased to be human.

Bill climbed the steps slowly.

It seemed to take an awfully long time: the more effort he put into it – to wrest his feet from one step to another – the worse it was.

He tried to step aside, out of the dream, telling himself that this was the usual stuff of frustration and nightmare. The running on the spot, the tearing of the feet from mud into mud, the sliding backwards towards some unseen enemy that breathes on your back. But he could not.

He could no longer escape the dream.

There was no handrail; and so he laboured, the breath now scorching his chest. At first there were only ten or twelve steps; but then, as he looked up, it seemed that there were twenty. Or more. The muscles in his thighs screamed; his ankles and joints ached. And each touch of the steps was agony, because they were so terribly cold. And yet he could not – not even for his life – increase his speed.

By the time he got to the top, he was on his hands and knees. Now, his palms ached from the cold as well as his feet. He stood, shaking from the exertion, on the top of the flight, wringing blood back into his fingers.

He looked about him.

The terrace of the house was white. It described a shallow semi-circle. There was a set of French doors, closed. The pattern on the marble floor was vaguely swirling; faint shades of blue, like veins, in the pale.

He put a hand to the top of his head. It seemed to be on fire. It was actually hot to the touch.

I'm getting heatstroke, he thought. Can't feel my fingers, can't feel my feet. But I'm getting heatstroke. Have to get under cover. Get in the shade for a minute. Get inside.

He glanced backwards. Nothing to be seen anywhere but the flat blue sea, without a ripple.

'Painted ocean,' he murmured. And turned back to the glass.

As he watched, the doors opened. They were much larger than they had at first seemed. And they rolled, rather like a piece of soft material rolling in on itself. The room beyond was impossibly huge: a great low, light hall. It had a glass roof through which the sunlight fell in dappled underwater clouds, exactly as the sea outside had fallen away from him in muted ripples. There were dozens of tables, all set with floor-length white cloths and white and pale yellow flowers. Lilies in great waxy bouquets, with long stamens of gold, floating on water, with thick and lush green leaves supporting them. Silver shone in the light. Above, at the edge of the glass ceiling, swags of white damask lined with the same pale-gold silk were draped to the floor.

On every table there were settings of food. Not meals, for their displays were too opulent. They were like theatrical tableaux. Fruit of every description. Slices of every imaginable meat. Jugs of cream. Wine, row upon row. Fish, lobster, shellfish. Bread in a dozen shades, from the black of schwarzbrot to the dense white of English loaves. Food . . . Holy Christ, food and drink everywhere. It was a gourmet's paradise, a scene from a glutton's heaven. And everything so fresh, so appealing, so perfectly clean and new. The frosted droplets of condensation on the bottles. The skin of the peaches. Everything, everything . . .

His mouth watered. In fact, it watered so much, and he found himself so suddenly aware of his own extreme hunger and thirst, that he actually had to put his hand to his face to counteract the spit swilling in his mouth. And it was while he was doing so, and dipping his head a little from embarrassment, that *she* stepped forward.

She had not altered at all. Not at all. She was tall, almost as tall as him. Very erect and calm. That lovely reddish hair.

It was over thirty years since he had seen her, and yet she looked absolutely the same. Thirty years, he thought, watching the fluid and easy motion of her walk, since that last argument, the last fight on the doorstep of the house. It might have been yesterday. She wanted everything out of him. Not just leaving his wife and child and home; she wanted the last speck of himself, the last drop of blood and the last grain of his soul. She wanted every second, all to herself. At first it had been wonderful, the urgency in bed so marvellous, her greed for him intoxifying. Then, it had begun to suffocate him, and he felt that first misgiving that he had done something irrevocable. He had been torn, even before that terrible day at South Branks. And when that day had gone, and its aftermath, she had still had the temerity to come, waltzing down the path as she waltzed and danced now, her head held high, and that insistence on her face. But he had drawn the line; he wanted his life back, his power over himself that she sucked from him like a spider. He wanted to be in charge again, not drugged by her rapacious appetite, cheated by her demands, agonised by her impatience sarcasm. He had fought free of her.

Only to find her again here, at the end of the motionless sea, at the top of the ice-cold stair, in this impossible room.

She walked a little way, and then stopped, and crossed her arms, regarding him with that old, gluttonous smile. It was a very sardonic expression. He remembered it with painful clarity.

'Celt,' he whispered. 'Celt.'

'Hello, Satan,' she said.

'Celt! I . . .'

He stepped towards her, and then stopped and looked down. He was not dressed. Not in anything at all – he had not realised it. His flesh was smooth and hairless and roasted brownish pink, like a baby coming in from the sun after playing too long. His nails were long: he felt as if he were salt all over. Worst of all – the most horrible part, the nightmare of it – was that he was sexless. Completely sexless, without a mark. Below his waist he was smooth and featureless. His legs merely met his body in a waxy contour, as on a doll. No lines or birthmarks or patches.

I am not me, he thought.

I'm not . . . finished. Not right.

The discovery appalled him more than he would have thought possible. His whole identity vanished: without this body, the familiarity of his own skin, his own flesh, he was nothing. Nothing at all. Tears of shame and frustration welled, and ran down his face. Unchecked. Unwanted.

Celt was still looking at him. Her smile unchanged.

'What's happened?' he asked her.

She began to laugh. 'We are all the same,' she said.

And she peeled back the thing she had on – some diaphanous, floating thing, some dress. She peeled it back and let it fall. It had no fastening. It dropped as if it had a will of its own, and dissolved before his eyes.

Celt's own body had no breasts, no pubic bone, no marks of ribs, no hollow of shoulder-blades, no joint at the elbow or knee or ankle, no hairs, no marks, no blemishes, no tone at all. It was as if she had stepped from a warm bath and, with a body made of wax, the warmth of the water had melted her into this shape.

'My God,' he groaned. 'What's the matter with us?'

Celt sighed, and began to turn away. As she did so, she lifted a small green grape from a waterfall of a thousand other green grapes, all the same, a wall of fruit.

She did not look at him again, but let her remark drop; over her shoulder as she walked. 'You are dying, darling,' she said calmly. 'Dreaming and dying. That's all.'

It was three miles to the wood.

A track ran from the back of Hugh's farm, below the ridge of the hill, about half-way up. It skirted the lower slope, and then stopped abruptly after about a mile and a half. Here, a small stream – so small that it invariably dried in summer, and was now little more than a trickle – crossed the track. On the other side, there was no way forward for a vehicle. The track degenerated into a weaving, scrubby line, densely overgrown in places, between hawthorn trees stunted by the wind that swept up the hill.

Here, Hugh got out of the Land Rover and opened its back doors. Squinting for a moment in the darkness, he stared down at Bill's curled body. At last, with a grunt of effort, and grimacing against the touch of the slack flesh, he laced his arms under Bill's from behind, and pulled him forward. By hanging Bill head down over the tailgate, he got underneath him and hauled him on to his back, looping the tied arms over him. As he did so, he noticed that Bill's hands were icy cold. He checked the binding – a piece of soft cloth.

It'll leave a mark, he thought.

And there followed another farce – heaving Bill backwards, untying the binding, and then having to carry him by fireman's lift, Bill's head hung down his back, his hips over his shoulder. As he finished, he heard Bill give a faint gasp, like a child's cry. He stopped dead, and listened. Bill's breathing was faint, irregular, and very shallow. Ineffectual . . .

Crossing the stream, Hugh followed the path. It began to climb upwards slightly. After a while, it came out into a clearing. A low fence dissected the land, separating scrub from rough pasture. Here, in the topmost field, surrounded by low trees, Hugh occasionally brought calves or ewes or lambs. There was nothing in it tonight.

He climbed the stile. Bill's lifeless feet danced at Hugh's back. As Hugh climbed, so Bill climbed. As Hugh ran, so did Bill, his knees flexing, his hands loosely circling.

After the narrow field, another stile. This time, the wood was thicker. Hugh's breathing came loud and rasping. This was a patch of conifer plantation. It was only very small, a dark green patch on the hillside, hardly visible from the lower road, slipped into a fold of the hillside.

Hugh went only two or three hundred yards in. And finally, on the carpet of dry pine needles, in the silence of the trees, he dropped Bill's body.

Bill turned from the room. His head was heavy, full of blood.

I'm dreaming. It's not real. It's only a dream.

He had dreamt like this before, usually after drinking, and he had discovered a knack of waking himself up. Now, standing at the french doors, the dreadful room at his back, looking out over the sea, he commanded himself to wake.

Usually, he could sense his dream self and his sleeping self coming together like two unfocused images. As the images merged, he would open his eyes. Sometimes, only for a second, some picture from the dream would superimpose itself on the real picture of his room.

I'm going to wake up. Any moment. Any moment now.

As he watched the sea, it changed. The blinding light faded, and the surface of the water went black. He thanked whatever powers there were that he was to be released; he would soon be conscious again. The sky became concave, pressing down on the waves. White tops began to show, but there was no storm. Only a grey suffocation as fog rolled towards him.

Fog on a summer afternoon.

With a snap like a shutter closing on a camera, the scene changed.

Bill sprang forward with a choked cry, running to the edge of the parapet. It was not going to stop, the dream. It was going on, relentlessly on. He clutched the cold stone of the ledge. Trying to shout, his voice froze in his throat.

Fog on a summer afternoon.

The curtain of mist closed down on where he stood; the sea, silent, came up to his feet. Some of the sand remained, but only some. And it was a sand – not white, like before – but horribly familiar, oh God, *horribly* familiar. A strip of dark gold-grey sand at the foot of a shelf of pebbles.

He knew the fishermen were somewhere behind him, but he could not see them. They stood on this bank and fished for mackerel that came in enormous shoals right up to the beach, casting long lines into the churning water. The land shelved away sharply here – only ten yards out, you could not feel the bottom. Red flags on the coast path warned against swimming.

He knew this place.

He knew this place, God help him.

'Please, he whispered. 'Oh please, not this.'

The fishing boat, which had been on its way east to west along the coast until it saw the thing floating in the water, was now anchored a hundred yards out. He could see it, a black line with a square cabin, outlined in the mist.

'This fog comes down like nobody's business, don't it?' said a voice behind him. 'You'd never credit it, would you? Two miles in, it's sunny. Dead funny, isn't it? I never saw nothing like it.'

The woman from Birmingham. The woman on holiday from Birmingham.

God shut her up. *Please God, dear God, shut her up.*

He fixed his eyes on the boat.

Another was coming in, a little motor boat. The police launch.

'What are they doing?' asked the woman at his shoulder.

'Pulling somethin' in,' replied her husband.

'What – fish?'

'Nah, don't talk daft. Not fish. That's the police, that is.'

'Is it?' A pause. 'What're they pullin' in, then?'

Bill turned sick with panic and fear, and scrambled up the beach of the dream, his eyes closed. Stones slithered and spun under his feet.

Don't show me that again, God!

'Oh please, don't show me, don't show me,' he whimpered. Don't . . .

Fog on a summer afternoon.

. . . show me that!

Hugh put the sticks together.

Taking the match from its box, he lit the small fire, crouching over it until a thread of smoke began to rise.

Then he sat back and watched it, scuffing earth up around the edges so that it could not spread. From the pockets of his jacket he took a handful of things and put them beside Bill's body. A plastic bag that had a few slices of bread still inside; a pack of cigarettes; a half bottle of Gordon's – very old, all he had left in his living-room cupboard – and Bill's watch.

Bill was lying flat on his back, his mouth open. He was snoring slightly.

Small communion in the night. The fire cracked; he added pine cones, needles, anything that would burn. There were plenty of fallen sticks. The dense green odour of the wood clouded around them like fog.

He knew there were deer in this wood. Quite a few deer. There were foxes, of course. And rats. He sensed their silent audience. The deer would not disturb Bill for a few days. Foxes were different; more curious. More courageous. As for the rats . . .

Bloody things, rats. He despised them. He had always been fastidious about keeping them off the farm. But they ran riot in a place like this. Or would do, when they scented Bill.

Hugh put his head on one side, and regarded the old man. Can't hurt anyone now, can you? he thought. Can't smash doors. Can't run away and lead her a wild-goose chase and come home as if nothing had happened. Played that card once too often, didn't you, you old bastard? Keeping me at arm's length from her. You and your foul mouth. You and your superior smirk. I'm good enough to do jobs for you, but you'd stop me soon enough if I made a move for her. You and your fists. Used them on her and would have used them on me, given half a chance. Keeping me away. You – and that wife of yours, even. All that time ago.

Pity about her.

They said you did her in. Common knowledge, it was. Wonder if you ever told Eve what they said about you?

Things had changed now though, by God!

Without even bothering to hunch down close to the body, Hugh screwed open the cap of the gin bottle, and, from about five feet up, poured its contents at Bill's face. After about three or four seconds, the old man began to choke: Hugh grabbed his collar and hauled him up, and jammed the neck of the bottle in Bill's mouth. Alcohol spattered the grey skin; it shone in the fire's reflection like oil. Bill sputtered and caught his breath. Even the gagging now was slow and laboured, a grudging reflex reaction. Eventually, Bill was allowed to fall backwards, with a thump. He landed on one shoulder, the arm crooked under him. He looked like what he was: an old drunk left to rot.

Hugh threw the bottle into the fire.

They brought the body into the hut. It had been in the water for two days.

'Currents,' said the police. 'Lucky she came into shore, really.'

Lucky. Holy Jesus, *lucky!*

He sat in one corner. She was wrapped in an oilskin: shapeless. Nothing showed.

They had rung him at home. Not the police. The local paper. Body found offshore at South Branks. Any comment? A woman. Any comment?

He did not remember driving here; hardly remembered leaving eight-year-old Eve at a friend's, barely registered the taut expression on that woman's face and the way she protectively pulled Eve into her side, putting her arm around her. *Anyone would think he was some kind of monster.* They blamed him for leaving Eve and her mother, and for all the fuss since. For her disappearance. And now they would blame him for this. How was he to know? She had always been a strong person. How was he to know what she would do? No one could have guessed she would do this. He couldn't believe it himself. He stared at the oilskin, feeling sick. *It had to be an accident.* No matter what anyone said, he couldn't accept that she would drown herself. She was a strong swimmer. She must have got caught by a tide; and that thought helped him a little, lifted the black burden of guilt for an instant.

She'd been upset lately, it was true, and that thought hid a greater guilt, worst of all, the guilt of lying about her distress. She had not been upset, not *upset*, he knew. Look in my heart and tell me the right word, the correct word for her tears. Find the photograph of her face tucked in your disgrace like a memo in a family album – find the *right* word. My mistress and I deranged her. Inflicted a wound that tore a hole in her strength and good humour and spirit.

Last week, for instance. The people at Eve's school had rung to tell him that she sat in the school corridor all morning until the school secretary took her home. They said she was dazed, as if sleepwalking, and talking about Celt.

Upset.
Liar.
Murdered.

And now, she had gone. No matter how much he looked again, he would never find her. He would never be able to tell her how much he regretted what he had done, how miserable he was with Celt, how terrible his life had been since leaving. The sight of her, lately, shouting in the street and after them, coming to the house and banging on the door, had wrenched him in two. He had taken the coward's way out each time, turned away to shut out the noise; while Celt ranted and raved at him to do something about his wife. But he could do nothing; nothing except hide in the house, drowning the noise in drink, wishing it were over. And he wrote her letters. Cold, dry letters asking her not to come to the house any more, *because it annoyed Celt . . .*

It was not his fault.

He could say that to himself, a private litany. He could keep that thought in his head for years to come, protecting himself.

Protecting himself against the truth.

But he would never again be able to look in the eyes of his child. Because *she looked just like her mother.*

'Can I see her?' he asked, from the corner of the shed.

They all stared at him. It speaks. 'Do you want to make an identification?'

'I want to see her.'

They ushered the others out.

Poor little place to put her: on a bench in a hut. It was used as an information hut, for the birds, for the beach, for Chesil Bank. Posters of shells and seagulls and seagrass. Neolithic man casting a fishing line. Glass case with flint arrowheads. The swannery. The Fleet. The sweep of the chalk hills to the sea. He gazed at the posters as they pulled back the cover from her body. Began to read, helplessly.

Since time immemorial, man . . .

Her eyes were open. Dull glass balls. Witch balls, the kind they used to hang in the windows of Victorian houses to ward off evil spirits: swirls of glass. Eyes in the light.

She was naked and grey. Blue, even. Bloodless fingernails and lips. He touched her hand. It was ice. She looked very thin and slight, all the wiriness in her arms, the tension in the set of her head, the line of the mouth, gone. She looked almost like a child.

He looked away, back to the far wall.

Since time immemorial, man has fished from the beach ahead of you . . .

'Is this your wife?'

He groped behind himself, to find the chair.

'Yes,' he whispered. The oilcloth closed over her. 'This is my wife.'

Hugh looked back through the shadows.

Bill was nothing more than a crumpled line on the ground. The fire was almost out, burned down. It was nearly half-past three, and in another two hours – probably less – it would be light.

'Good riddance,' Hugh said. He fastened his coat, shrugging his shoulders up and down to get his circulation going again. Then he squatted down and felt the ground. Dry as a bone. No footprints. No marks.

Turning away, he began to walk back to the Land Rover.

There was nothing now. Nothing. He was suspended in the air. Greyness, that might have been cloud, that might have been sea, supported his floating body. He could not turn, not even his head. He was paralysed.

When the arms came, he was glad to feel them again: human skin touching his, wrapping themselves to him, guiding him gently. Then, very slowly, they began to pull him down.

The grey folded over his face: he held his breath. No air came, no sound, no warmth, no cold. No sensation of drowning. Only the folding and folding of the grey. He felt himself dropping with increasing speed. The arms tugged and pulled.

He looked down and saw with dread that they were *her* arms: the drowned arms, the arms with white fingernails, with blue-grey flesh.

A sudden terror swept through him, in case he should inadvertently turn and see that face, that frozen face pressed to his, her dead lips at his mouth, those awful marble-glass eyes staring into his. He tried to struggle, resist the pull. Tried to wriggle out of the grasp.

But it was no good. He had no strength at all, and no substance. No power at all. It was over.

Vice-like, the dead hands dragged him into oblivion.

Seventeen

It was Monday, and Jon arrived at Hugh's at eight o'clock.

He had walked from Eve's house, over the track, through the fields on each side. The morning had at first been dull, with grey clouds scudding fast; just as he breasted the rise and looked down through the sparse woodland to Hugh's farm, however, the day changed. The wind eased, and the sun filtered through.

Now, in the yard, he looked about himself.

It was unusual that Hugh was not about. That day when he and Latham had come down to the house, Hugh had said how he liked to be up and working by six. Jon stood and listened intently. No sound from the house itself, and the windows were all closed. The Land Rover was parked by the back-door step. For a second, Jon ran his eyes over the vehicle, trying to place what was unusual in the way it was parked; but he could not. Instead, thinking that, if the Land Rover were there, then surely Hugh would soon turn up too, Jon wandered across to the stream bridge and sat down on its coping wall, swinging his legs over the water.

The stream ran brown over sand and flint. Not deep enough for larger fish, it was nevertheless fringed with the first growth of watercress. For some time Jon sat, watching the stones in the shallows, the light on the water, thinking of Eve.

She had woken very early that morning. The sound of the shower had roused him and he had rolled on to his side, trying to see the clock. Five-forty; grey morning light through the room. He waited, half asleep, until the water stopped. She came into the bedroom, towelling her hair, and walked to the window.

'Couldn't sleep?' he asked.

She jumped, turning round. 'Did I wake you?'

'It doesn't matter.'

She turned back to the window, laying the towel on the chair, looking out at the fields.

'I can't stop thinking about Dad,' she said.

He got out of bed. 'The book?'

'The book.'

He wondered what comfort he ought to offer; if any comfort were possible. Perhaps it was not surprising that she was already awake; perhaps, instead, it was surprising that she had slept at all. Father missing. Mother reaching out from the past. He considered her profile. 'What will you do today?'

'Mmmm?' She looked back at him. 'Oh – go to school, I think. I can't leave them in the lurch.'

'I'm sure they'd understand.'

'I know they would. But it's not just them. It's me. I can't bear to stay here alone.' She paused a second, biting her lip, then turned and smiled. 'Are you going to see Hugh?'

'Yes.'

'Don't . . . say anything, will you?'

'If you don't want me to.'

'Don't get into an argument.'

'About what?'

'Yesterday.'

He reached to touch her hair, still wet and clinging to her throat. 'If you say so.'

She had smiled, holding his fingers.

He did not say so. If *he* had *his* way, he would like to beat the living daylights out of Hugh Scott. The man was a bloody coward. Mental. Making her afraid – *and marking her.*

Fury swirled for a second in his head: he imagined beating an apology out of Scott, seeing that bland grey face colour and crease. Making him promise never to touch Eve again.

Don't . . . say anything, will you?

His hands clenched on the stone of the bridge. Taking a deep breath, he looked up from the water.

He had never known a woman like Eve. She gave so much, with such frenzy, with such urgency, as if snatching at life as it flew past her; and yet, she gave nothing at all. Even close to her, even in the very depth of loving her, she would reach the moment and abruptly close her eyes, turn her head, shutting herself from him. She spoke his name only rarely, and she would draw her arms across herself. At first he thought it was as if she wanted to hold the sensation into her; then, especially last night, he thought it was to build a barrier between them. One little stone in a wall, two little stones in a wall. Soon she might be able to build the wall higher, shutting him completely from her. Perhaps in a month or two she would shut her arms over her *before* he touched her.

He frowned, rubbing his hand across his face.

It was not that she did not want him. Not that she did not like him, need him. He knew that; he *felt* that, in her hands, in her lips, in her head buried in the curve of his shoulder. It was that . . . she would not *give*. Give herself. In the very act of giving her body, she took away what was more herself than any other part, the thing that some called the heart, and others the soul, the thing that was really her.

It was too early, probably. Too soon. He couldn't expect a woman to launch herself, body and soul and heart, like that, even if he would give himself to her, body, soul and heart: he didn't expect that price, or exact that price. She need not pay him anything at all, if she chose. She need not lie against him, touch him, reach for him in her sleep. And yet she did. She travelled this far with him, and then, at the gate, turned away, refusing to step forward with him, meet his look, go with him.

She'd told him last night about her father.

After the book, as they'd sat for a while downstairs, she'd told him about Bill's illness and what he had been like before. She'd told him a little about playing the piano. She'd told him how Bill was: loud and overbearing and immoveable and funny. Caustic. Wicked, selfish, dry. Dry and cold. As she had spoken about his coldness, her hand in his had shrunk a fraction.

She had told him that, ever since the illness, when her father became particularly confused, he was capable both of venom and tears. How, in tears, he would try to hold her hand and stroke it.

She had looked down at their clasped hands and told him that she could never bear this final too-late intimacy of Bill's. She could bear, had got used to, the insults and the wanderings and the furies that blew out like storms. But she could not get used to her father trying to hold her hand and stroke it, all the while his mouth trembling, trying to fabricate an affection that she had wanted so often as a child, and had long accepted would never come.

I can't bear him touching me like that, as if he wants me to love him, as if he wants to be the baby and I am to be Mum, and I am supposed to cuddle him and make him better . . . and her smile had been bleak and tired.

'I wish I knew where he was,' she said.

It had hung between them for a long time, until they had gone to bed.

Thinking of this, Jon found that his eyes had fastened on the Land Rover at Hugh's back door. And suddenly, with a flash of inspiration, it occurred to him what the matter was.

It was parked around the wrong way.

It was facing the yard, not the house. Hugh usually parked it facing the other way. He had seen him do it: seen him drive in and park, without bothering to reverse. Jon stared at it, mildly puzzled. It looked as if Hugh had driven in from the opposite direction – from the woodland, not the road. From the hillside, not the track. From a dead end . . .

Shaking his head, still wondering about it, Jon got down from the bridge, brushed down his jeans, and walked away, towards the stables.

The horses were nowhere to be seen. They must have been taken to pasture early, or had been left out all night. Maybe Hugh had taken the horses to pasture beyond the copse, up the hillside. Where the conifers were, that way, and that was why the Land Rover was parked back to front.

A door to one of the outhouses stood open. He glanced around himself: at the closed house, the derelict cottages, the empty yard. The open door led to the stables, through a tack room. Almost aimlessly, he wandered into it.

It took a moment for his eyes to become accustomed to the darkness of the room. It was obvious that it had been recently tidied and swept: cobbles showed through, copper-faced in the early light. Jon looked around himself, feeling a thread of something unusual, or out of place. Feeling some activity, recent, out of sync.

He saw the key in the door of the wall cupboard.

That was peculiar; it was not like Hugh, so pedantic and careful and prissy in his ways, to leave a key hanging in a door.

Jon stepped forward, peering at the cupboard. That key ought to be put away. Some instinct made him open the door and look inside.

Eve phoned in sick.

But she had only been half expected anyway; the head was already taking the class.

'Come when you're ready,' was the message.

'I might be in this afternoon.'

She stood at the bottom of the stairs, her hand resting on the phone back in its receiver on the wall. From the recess on the landing, her mother stared out from the photograph.

Eve turned on her heel.

Something had been picking at the corner of her mind from early this morning, something that had woken her at first light. It was not going to let her be until she faced it. There was only one other place in the house where something secret, something private, might be stored. She went out to the shed and brought the stepladder. She hauled it up the stairs only with the greatest difficulty, cursing as it bumped the paintwork and scraped the walls. It was a heavy, outdated, wooden stack. Right at the head of the stairs, she opened the steps, and pulled them under the hatchway to the loft. There was no loft ladder: this was the only way up.

Pushing aside the hatch, and swaying slightly on the steps beneath her, she pulled herself up into the darkness of the roof-well. She knew there was a light somewhere to the left, and she fumbled along until her hand came in contact with an old-fashioned switch, grainy and sticky with dirt.

Only the palest pool of light came on; she looked around her.

The loft stretched the entire length of the house. Here and there, boards had been laid down over the beams. Eve got herself through the gap and shuffled warily along, looking to the left and right. Old clothes, broken frames, two stacks of books, a useless television aerial lying on its side, the water tanks with a shedding cover of fibreglass. Then, close to the far end, she saw three tea chests, standing side by side.

The boards gave out: the chests were balanced on the joists themselves. Crouching, she got over to them, carefully placing her feet astride each beam. The first seemed to be full of curtains: she vaguely recalled her father stowing them here when they had bought new, maybe ten years ago, for the living room. The outdated damask, dark red, smelled appallingly musty. She leaned to look in the second.

Envelopes stuffed with paper stared back at her.

Leaning her elbows in the soft, dusty, yielding pile of the curtains, she reached for the first few. Her hand snagged on the metal rim of the chest.

'Damnit,' she said, and sucked the scratch. Tucking the first two or three large brown envelopes under one arm, she worked her way backwards, to where the floorboards would at least let her sit down.

And here she squatted, under the bare electric light. She heard birds skitter along the ridge tiles of the roof, just an arm's length over her head.

Solicitors' letters, after the separation.

There were about a dozen of these: from both sets of lawyers. Her father's and mother's. Talk about the house, insurances, her own custody and care. In the fourth letter, his visits to Eve were fixed at two a month. There was some complaint about the disconnection of the gas supply mixed in, prosaically, in the same letter.

Then, in the same envelope, a tied bundle.

Blue envelopes, blue writing paper.
The first page was missing: her father's hand.

Money is not the issue. Time is the issue. I cannot keep coming to the house. If you have a problem with the Scotts, or whatever problem you have, you must talk to Evans. That is what you have engaged him for. That is his purpose. And to ring Adriane and complain in that most offensive way, and to insult her, is not at all productive. It will not do you any good. If I say a thing, I mean it. Please have Eve ready at ten o'clock on Saturday morning.

This is the receipt for the gas burner. When the men come, tell them it is still under guarantee, and you will find the guarantee in the box in the drawer next to the boiler. Pass the bill through Evans.

I can't help what the school wants. If you remember, I am employed as a teacher and, whatever my domestic circumstances, I remain employed as a teacher. Do not ring me at the school unless there is a genuine emergency with Eve.

Excerpts from another life.
 The blue envelopes lay at Eve's side as she read each letter, putting it face down in a pile. Her mother had kept everything he sent her. She took them out, glancing briefly at each one. Stray paragraphs reflected back at her. Letter after letter.

Don't come again. What's the bloody point? What is the point? You only embarrass yourself and cause all sorts of distress all round. The thing is over. I will not see Eve want for anything: on that you have my assurance. If you need something for Eve, you have only to ask. The telephone will be kept on. I know you need the telephone for practical purposes. But I don't have the money for any car, and where you have got this notion for a bloody vehicle – of all things! – I simply cannot imagine. If I had the money, you would have the car. But I do not have a penny.

I am sorry about Eve's flu. When she is better she can go to Poole theatre if she likes the play so much.

Please do not come to the house. What is the reason for standing in the street? Why don't you answer the phone to me? Please don't stand in the street. You are making Adriane a nervous wreck, and moreover she is angry. If that is your intention, then you have achieved it. For God's sake have some pride and don't stand in the street.

'Oh God,' whispered Eve. 'Oh God.'

That there had been some sort of breakdown, some sort of conflict, was obvious. The blue letters stopped; in the remaining half-dozen were merely references to payments of maintenance, extremely formal. Little more than business receipts.

As she tried to loop the elastic band around the letters, the rubber – already perished – snapped. Each envelope bore a mark where it had been held together. He had probably thrown them in here without even reading them again, knowing his own handwriting.

Eve looked about herself with a dead feeling.

What a pompous, sickening sod he was to her, she thought. The way he wrote to his own wife. Eve could exactly imagine the way he talked, as if still lecturing a class. She could visualise the freckled fists, the large fists, closed at his sides. As they were when he spoke to *her*. 'Whatever the domestic circumstances I am still employed as a teacher . . .' 'On that you have my assurance.'

What a cold bloody way to carry on. The letters must have enraged her mother, made her despair. She had obviously followed them about, went to where they were living. Tormented and haunted them. 'Adriane a nervous wreck . . . moreover she is angry.' Good! Let the bitch be angry! Yes, that must have given Eve's mother some fleeting, thin satisfaction. The precious bloody Celt angry. Arguments between him and his mistress.

'She may go to Poole Theatre if she likes the play so much . . .'

She could not remember any play, any theatre. Funny. Perhaps her mother did not take her, after all.

Eve considered, her eyes fixed on a cobweb hanging over her.

I wouldn't go either, if some pompous husband deigned to give permission, she thought. Actually given permission to go! To spend money, she supposed. How she would hate having to ask. 'If you need anything you have only to ask.' Making petitions for clothes, for food, for outings, for any kind of small luxury. Dependent. How thoroughly demoralised she must have felt. Small, wretched, begging like that.

Poor mother. Standing in the street.

In the half-darkness, Eve edged back to the tea-chests. She put the envelopes back where she had found them. She made her way back to the hatchway, where she sat for a second, looking down into the drop of the stairs, her feet hanging over the edge.

Her mother never got a chance.

She had died that same year, 1961.

She'd died after he had left her, after she kept Eve jealously to her, resenting him, hating him, haunting him.

Eve closed her eyes, trying to get her thoughts in some kind of order.

She'd died that same year. But of what?

It was only as Eve was putting the step ladder away that she thought of a death certificate. Standing in the darkness of the hall, she considered, hands on hips, looking at the floor. There had been no certificate in the box of house deeds and insurances. She had her own birth certificate ever since applying for a passport years back. Her father's was in the box she had found yesterday. But her mother's birth certificate – come to that, their marriage certificate – had never been seen. And she knew of nowhere else to look.

She went into the kitchen and, absently, filled and switched on the kettle, staring out at Hugh's immense rolling field and the road.

Pneumonia, bronchitis. From a healthy woman to that. And in the summer. To die of that in the summer.

He had once said that, in years past, there had been no medicine like modern antibiotics to treat such illnesses. She had always accepted the explanation. Until now.

Doubts, like the slithering encircling of a snake, closed hard around her, jumping from an infinitesimal seed to a living, breathing, growing vine, clouding out the light. She opened her eyes on to the silent kitchen. Her own hands – alive, alive – pressing on the workboards beneath her fingers. She was alive and real, in the real world, in the possible world. Jon's mouth kissing this hand and this finger: *that* was real. Life life. Life now and breathing in the present, the new world. Her father, old and demoralised and selfish and stupid and so painfully, disgustingly small.

Turning on her heel, she went to pick up the phone. 'Directory Enquiries.'

'Hello. I want the number in London of the place where they record deaths. It isn't Somerset House any more, is it?'

'St Catherine's House? Births, marriages and deaths?'

'That'll be it.'

She wrote the number on the memo pad alongside the phone, bit her lip, looking at it. Then she dialled.

The switchboard, and then a disembodied voice, Asian or Indian.

'Can you tell me . . .?' It sounds so stupid. 'The cause of death, on a death certificate. It's recorded on the certificate?'

'Always.'

'What if someone weren't sure? If the doctor weren't sure of the cause . . .?'

'The cause of death would go on after the coroner's verdict.'

'Oh. Right. A coroner. And would that be straight away?'

'It would depend on the case. A suspicious death, maybe – if the death were last year, say, and the coroner didn't give a verdict till this year . . .'

'I see. But don't you have to have a certificate before a body could be buried?'

'Then the body would be kept in storage until the coroner's verdict.'

In storage. A suspicious death. Faint bells, the tolling of bells, in the back of her mind.

Death knells.

She shut her hand to the side of her head, as if to crush out interrupting voices.

'And . . .'

The conversation ran haphazardly ahead, and she followed it, not knowing exactly where it was taking her. Now she was actually through, she felt loath to break the link. She could hear voices in the background, a rattling of files or metal cases. Distant traffic.

'So, if I had a copy of a death certificate, it would say what caused the death . . .'

'Always. In one way or another.'

'Even, eventually, a suspicious one.'

'Suspicious. Suicide. Murder. Whatever. In one way or another. Some say it in a kinder form of words. They wouldn't say, "He threw himself under a bus", you understand? But in one form of words or another.'

'But it wouldn't say something like pneumonia if it was a murder or a suicide or whatever?'

'The cause of death would be recorded.'

A murder or a suicide – or whatever.

'Thank you.' Slowly, she replaced the phone.

She arrived at Hugh's house a quarter of an hour later.

She came by car, into the empty yard. Sun split it straight across: the cottages were in a deep shadow, the barn in a blinding slice of light.

'Hugh,' she called as she slammed the driver's door shut.

It had been as she was drinking the first scalding sip of coffee that she realised that Hugh would know.

Hugh had been about ten or so when her mother died. He had never said a thing about it, never commented, never reminisced. She had never heard him say, 'I remember when your mother was alive,' or anything like it. But then, Hugh always said very little. He talked, often, in a kind of shorthand, and you read between the lines, if you could be bothered. Hugh's closed face often made you want to close up too; to hide from him as he hid himself.

But that didn't matter this morning.

All that mattered was the sudden, absurdly simple answer, like a flash of recognition – 'how could I have been so stupid not to think of it before!' – that Hugh would know.

'Hugh!'

There was no reply. The windows of the house were closed; so was the big back door.

Irritated, she turned to the barns and stables.

'Eve?'

Jon came out from the nearest door. His face darkened as he confirmed that it was her. She walked towards him.

'I know what I said,' she began. 'But I have to ask him something. I won't stay long.'

'I thought you were going to the school.'

'So did I. I will, in a while. I decided to look in the loft. Dad's papers.'

'Find anything?'

She looked at the ground, sighing. 'Yes.'

'Bad?'

'Yes.'

'Oh.'

She shrugged slightly. 'Bad like a bad dream.' She cocked her head towards the house. 'Is Hugh here?'

'No. I've knocked at the house.'

'The Land Rover's there.'

'I know. But the horses aren't. Perhaps he went for a ride.'

'Not with all of them. He'll have them in pasture.'

Jon made a face. 'I don't really care where he is. I don't want to work for him; I think I'll tell him that, when he appears.'

She reached for his hand. 'Don't lose your job because of me,' she said.

He smiled. There was a silence. Eve looked about her. 'It's almost eerie,' she murmured. 'Hugh's *always* about. If you can't see him, you can hear him.'

'Like the Evil Eye. Like Big Brother. Hugh around every corner.'

She laughed. 'Paranoid.'

He slipped his arm around her waist. 'Living next to him would make anyone paranoid. How have you stood it for years? He's got my flesh crawling after a week.'

She leaned back, against his grasp, smiling at him. He locked his hands behind her back, braced his legs. She made a mock-movement of falling, loose, like a doll, her back arched, her arms hanging by her sides.

He kissed her back-arched throat. She slipped half beneath him, laughing, pretending to be a dead weight. 'Hold me up!'

He passed his locked hands upwards, catching her under the arms. For a second, he bent over her, his face within a couple of inches of hers. Still smiling, she searched that face: its smooth contours as soft as a child's. Eyes fringed with the strange light lashes; brown pupils, like soft tar, Latin-looking, doe-like. Eyes searching her own.

'I love you,' he said.

'No, Jon. That's not love.'

He pulled her upwards, so that she was standing straight. One arm went around her, pulling her towards him; the other cupped the back of her neck, the thumb gently stroking the line of her throat and jaw.

'Why don't you believe me?'

'Well, next year . . .'

'Not *next* year. *This* year. Now. Why don't you believe me?'

She tried placating him with a gentle finger on his mouth. 'Next year, it'll be someone else; I know that. There's no need to make promises to me. I know how it is – how it is for *anyone* when they're nineteen. Next year . . .'

'You've got a crystal ball? You see into the bloody future, is that it?'

She stopped, surprised, at his suddenly offended tone. 'Look, Jon – it's not you. It's just life. I don't say you don't mean it. But—'

'I'll show you how I mean it,' he retorted.

'No!'

He had not exactly lifted her off her feet – they scraped the ground. She lost her balance. 'Jon, don't be silly . . .'

He kicked open the door behind him, the door to the tack room. The door to the feed and the once-locked cupboard. He hauled her over the threshold, his arm under hers, the kicked door shut behind them. The scent of leather and oil washed over her: pungent, almost acidic.

'Hugh might come back,' she said.

He released her, stepping back, touching her at arm's length. His hand traced the length of her own arm, and dropped from it, trailing her fingers.

'I am so sick of hearing that man's name,' he said. 'I'm sick of hearing it from your mouth.'

She looked at him, sorry.

She couldn't say the word 'sorry'. It was too small. Hugh seemed nothing – a breath, a shadow, a silhouette – at this moment.

'Can't you think of anyone else?'

That was more like it. More of what she expected. A small boy, petulant, hunched against rejection.

She gave him a sad smile. 'I don't know what to think,' she said, quietly. She leaned on the wall, weariness washing through her. Today had all the reality of a dream – today, yesterday, the day before. A world knocked out of course. She tried to find words for this boy in front of her who felt so much. The strength of his emotions were obvious, from his eyes down to his feet set wide apart on the stone floor. She loved him, in that moment, as one loves a child who fiercely protests that boys can fly and that angels exist and that straw can be turned to gold. She wanted to believe him, and mourned her lost ability to, mourned her cynicism in the face of his conviction. Wanted and needed to trust as he trusted, to take the offered hand, to accept what he said. She tried to find words.

'Nothing makes sense,' she began. 'I lost my father and the idea I had of my father and I lost my mother and what he told me about her. And I—' She stared, bleakly, at a point above Jon's head, not wanting to look into his face. Beams notched into one another in the lintel above the door at his back. 'I feel as if I stepped into a maze. You know, like the one at Hampton Court. There was one in a place with a fairground once. Somerset, somewhere. It was winter and you could see through to the outside. It was only a beech hedge. You could see the outside, but you couldn't get out . . .' She dropped her eyes to his, embarrassed by her own confession. 'It's like that. I can't get out . . .'

He had not moved an atom. He might have been stone.

Then, slowly, he drew his sweatshirt over his head. He unbuckled the belt of his jeans, unzipped them, and stepped out of them. His skin was dark in the shadow of the room. He passed his hands lightly over himself: down the length of his body, across his hips, resting them finally on his thighs.

'There's no maze,' he whispered. 'There's a way out of everything. There's no maze . . .'

Tears sprang to her eyes.

He walked to her, put her hands on him, caressing her hand, caressing himself over her hand. She was standing against the wall. His naked feet slipped, braced for purchase, on the stone cobbles of the floor. She was wearing a short skirt that morning, and he reached gently under it and took off her briefs. She stepped from them as if hypnotised. Then he dropped to his knees, ran his hands up her thighs, and put his mouth to her, forcing her legs apart with the pressure of both thumbs on each thigh.

'Jon . . .'

It was too much: too searching, too deep. Almost too much to offer. It was not as it had been with Hugh: she did not resist him; she wanted to find the place he tried to show her, the place where children never grew old and wheat metamorphosed into light, spinning through her fingers to make magic. She *wanted* to let go, and feel this love bearing her up in its arms. She felt forward, into the dark of themselves, reaching for some understanding, some light and faith, past the caresses of his mouth and hands. For half a minute she struggled with him, gently pulling at his hair, at his shoulders, to get him to release her. Then came the waves: pitching, rolling. Swarming in from the dark corners of the room, lifting her from her feet, carrying her away. His hands, moving up, searched for her. Waves of deep blue, waves of light. Smothering sweet waves. He touched her breasts: she tried to bend over him. Whatever he needed. Whatever he wanted. Suddenly, he stood up, fastening his mouth on her breast like a child searching for its life. Her knees buckled: she had been on the very point of orgasm.

'Oh, Jon,' she urged him. 'Don't leave me.'

He plunged into her. She cried out, and then her mouth shut, afraid of making any noise. She closed her eyes. Jon's hand shot from her breasts to her face. He pressed his fingers to her temples. 'Don't close your eyes,' he ordered her. 'Look at me.'

She obeyed him. 'Oh my God, my God . . .'

He did not stop. Did not alter. He bent his head and looked at themselves, coupled against the wall; he bent her own head between his hands to look, too. Her back thumped helplessly against the rough plaster.

The waves snatched her up and flung her forward, anchorless, powerless, into the storm.

'Look at me, look at me, please look at me,' he whispered, desperate.

She looked: saw the impossible in his gaze, felt the power pass between them. He arched his back and drove into her deeper than ever. She cried out, lost, drowned. Her hands dug into the flesh of his shoulders.

Only a minute more, and it was over.

He kissed her with a passion, kissed her face, kissed her neck, shoulders, lips, eyes. He wrapped his arms tightly, protectively, around her. Their breaths ran raggedly together.

'No maze,' he whispered, finally. 'No maze . . .'

The walkers had been out since breakfast.

Setting off from Abbas Tithe, they had walked the long hill southwards, the river in the valley beneath them. And, although it was a beautiful morning, they were not happy. Not happy at all.

It was a group of four lads. There had been six of them until Buckland Frewton the night before, when there had been a row about two girls and getting to the coast by some better form of transport – namely, the bus. It had almost come to blows. After all, walking for a week and then having a week at the sea had only seemed like a good idea when they'd talked about it in the pub. Tramping for eight hours a day had turned out to be a different matter. Now, the four that remained were only held together by the dogged insistence of the ringleader: a spotty youth called Andy Prentiss. A Queen's Scout and in line for a Duke of Edinburgh award, he already considered himself an authority on the rigours of outdoor life. The others, trailing in his wake, considered him merely a pain in the neck.

Nevertheless, Andy had managed to retain a vague semblance of leadership, and had sense enough to have promised them a pub in Petherell village for lunch. As Petherell drew nearer, along with its alluring pints, he decided to leave the footpath shown on the Ordnance Survey and strike out slightly west, so that they would come to the road. 'Cut a couple of miles off,' he told the rest of them.

'Bloody marvellous,' was the only reply.

Down off the scrubby hill-top, they came to a wire fence. Beyond it lay a small conifer plantation. The four of them stopped and looked up and down it.

'No stile,' said Matthew Wright.

'We'll get over,' Andy said.

'Get ripped to buggery.'

'No you bloody won't. It isn't high. Only five foot. Get up on each other's backs.'

The laconic one of the four gave a snort of derision. 'What about the last one? Pole vaulter or what, then?'

'We ain't meant to get through, that's what,' said the fourth. 'Private.'

Andy drew himself up to his full five foot seven. 'We won't do any damage,' he told them. 'Get your fucking selves over.'

The others smirked at each other behind his back. Andy Prentiss said the F word. Andy Prentiss. Andy Virgin Prentiss said the F word. Things were looking up. Maybe by Bourne he'd loosen up enough to find his way to a shithouse without a compass.

They obeyed.

Not without falling down, cracking up on the other side at the sight of Matthew hanging from Andy's shoulders like a chimp. They sat in the needle and fern floor on the other side of the fence, sniggering. They ate the last of the cheese and crisps they had bought at the shop. And then, still shoving each other and laughing, they got up to go on.

It was only after about four or five minutes that Matt spotted something ahead of them, to one side of the wavering, obscure path.

It looked like a bundle. A bag of something. Big bag, like a bag of rubbish thrown away.

They stopped.

'What's that?'

Something moved near it, scuttling away through the bracken, the stringy pale growth of dandelion.

'That was a rat. See that? A fuckin' rat!'

They all looked at Andy. He squared his shoulders. 'Course it was a rat,' he told them. 'If some idiot puts a bag of rubbish out in the middle of the country, rats will get at it. Stands to reason.'

They peered for another second.

'What kind of rubbish's in that, d'you reckon?' asked Matthew.

Coming closer, they saw the small ashy mound of the fire.

'Someone's been camping out,' said Andy. 'They maybe . . .' A couple more footsteps. Then his voice died away.

Bill Ridges lay on his side, facing them. A big man, his arms crossed in his crotch, his knees drawn up tightly to his chest, foetal position, his head turned slightly upwards, at an awkward, cranked angle to the neck. The mouth was open as if gasping for breath. A thick line of vomit ran from the mouth, over the neck of the clothes, the left shoulder, and on to the ground. Chalky coloured and solid. Even as they watched, the flies settled on it again. The face was grey, puckered. The eyes open. The hair matted, bunched up on either side of the head like a thin clown's wig. One shoe lay apart from the body, as if kicked off by accident. It balanced on its side in the edge of the fire, in the whitish fringe of ash. There was a green glint of glass from a bottle in the burned down sticks and embers.

'Fucking hell,' said Matthew. He was the first to speak. The others stood clutching their stomachs, willing themselves not to be the first to be sick. The tall one at last lost the battle and, holding on to a tree, turning away from the rest, he said goodbye to his breakfast, the cheese, and the half bag of salt and vinegar crisps.

'Is he dead?'

Andy shot the culprit a withering look. 'Course he's bloody dead.'

'What's he doing here?'

They stared again.

'Looks like a tramp.'

'Old boy, ain't he?'

'Got to be a tramp.'

'Alky. Meths. That's what they do. Cider . . .'

'Got no shoe on, there look. No shoe.'

They edged a little nearer.

Close to, they could suddenly see what the rat had been doing. Feasting on the stream of vomit, he had started on the mouth and cheeks of the face, and the right eye.

'Oh, bloody hell!'

'Jesus.' Another turned away, holding his hand to his mouth.

'Look at his eye . . .'

'Shut up.' This from Andy.

'But look at his fuckin'—'

'Shut the hell *up*.'

The remainder of Bill's face looked up at them, pleading in death. He bore an expression of bewilderment and fear, a cloudy approximation of terror.

They said nothing at all for a long time.

And then, as if one body, they edged around him, skirting him by eight or ten feet.

Looking back, as if half expecting the sorry corpse to spring to its feet and start after them, they began to run down the path towards the farm.

'Hugh?'

Eve stood at the back door of the house, after knocking softly on the frame.

Inside, in the kitchen, she could hear Hugh moving about. She did not like to go in, or look in the windows. There was no radio on, no sound other than that of running water. She could hear the sound of a brush, a scourer, in the metal sink.

'Hugh? It's Eve.'

The scrubbing sound stopped.

'Hello, Hugh? It's Eve. Can I come in?'

A silence. Then, 'Door's open.'

She came up the step, opened the inner door, and saw him. He was right by the door, at the washing-up drainer, a Brillo pad in one hand. He looked somewhere near her – over her – and then, swiftly, away. The scourer resumed its steady, circular course.

Sun lit his hair and showed its thinness. She could see the pinkish scalp, the slight thread of vein pulsing.

'Good morning.'

He did not reply.

'Did you get up late? Jon's been looking for you.'

Hugh shot her a glance, directly.

'Sleep in?' she asked.

'Maybe.'

Scrape, scrape. Metal against metal. Nails on a blackboard. Knife across a plate. Eve's skin goosefleshed for a second. 'Oh, how can you stand that?'

He stopped. 'Stand what?'

She nodded at the drainer. 'That awful noise.'

He put down the pad. Without bothering to wash the soap away, he moved from the sink. For a second he stood at the table, soap dripping from one hand, the other placed flat on the wood of the tabletop.

She picked up a teatowel, and handed it to him. He began to dry his hands.

'Hugh, are you OK?'

'Yes.'

'Are you sure?'

'Yes.'

'Only –' she came around the side of the table – 'only you don't *seem* all right.'

He finished wiping his hands, folded the cloth into a small, precise square.

Embarrassed, confused, she looked around the room. 'Shall I make you a drink?' she asked.

He was staring at her, like a child who is both afraid and disappointed. The bottom lip of his mouth clamped over the top. She was terrified that he was about to actually weep.

'Look. You – you sit down here, and I'll make us a drink,' she offered, smiling.

He held the back of the chair, but didn't move.

She turned to the still soap-wreathed sink, taking up the pot, turning on the tap. Outside, a field down from them, a car passed along the road under the archway of chestnut trees. Their white banks of candles dying, they were in deep, full leaf, and breathtakingly lovely.

'I came down to ask you something,' she said, her back to him. 'I came to ask . . .'

But, for the moment, she did not get the chance to ask him anything.

Hugh moved at her back, towards her. One hand hung loose. The other, clenched in a fist, knotted at his chest. The upper fist, as she let the water run fast from the cold tap, came fractionally upwards, over the shoulder, inch by inch, in a soft, smooth, flowing motion . . .

'Good God,' Eve said, leaning forward.

There was a boy running down the tack, from the hill. 'Who's that?'

After the first, who was running with a rucksack bouncing ludicrously on his back, side to side, side to side, came three others. They ran raggedly, desperately, as if their lives depended on it, as if they were being chased by the devil himself. Their shadows split the ground in their wake, black dashes on the green.

A voice came drifting with them.

'Hey,' the first boy was shouting. 'Help up here! Help up here. Hey!'

Eighteen

The police arrived quickly: within an hour, a stream of vehicles had passed up the track. Eve stood outside the house, watching, with Hugh at her side.

'I'm walking up there,' she said at last.

'No. Better not.'

'I've got to sometime.'

'They'll come and ask. Leave them to do their business.' Hugh's eyes were fixed on the top of the track, where it disappeared into the shoulder of the hill.

The boys were up there somewhere, closer to her father than she was. Strangers, everywhere. Strangers finding him when all their looking had failed.

Jon was up there, too. In Hugh's place.

'I looked up there two days ago, at night,' Hugh had said. He said it two or three times, holding Eve's arm, as if to convince her. 'I walked all along that hill.'

There was nothing to summon up, it seemed. No distress, no grief. She could only think of her father wilfully sitting down to a fire and a drink, while she watched for him from his own bedroom windows, only a mile or so across country.

'He maybe didn't know where he was. He might have walked round in circles and lost his bearings,' Jon had said. They had stood, the three of them, by the door of the house, waiting, discussing him. Not a single expression of dismay between them. They might have been talking about a family pet found at the side of a road; less than a pet, in fact. Some stupid animal that had wandered into the traffic.

'Miss Ridges ought to stay back. I'll stay with her,' Hugh had said.

Jon was taken up there.

Jon. Who knew him least.

Bloody vigil at the side of the track, Hugh's hand cupping her arm. He never released his hold.

It might have been his own father, the way he looked. Ashen, drained. Eve realised, faintly shocked, that she pitied Hugh at this moment more than she did the dead man lying on the hill.

'You found *your* father up there,' she said. 'Wasn't it there? Up by the lambing field?'

Hugh did not take his eyes from the hill. 'No. He was down at the Blackcross field. Down by Witchams'.'

Hugh's father had died of a massive stroke, about ten years ago. Hugh had once told her that he'd found him propped up at a gate, sitting with his breakfast in a box on his lap, his eyes open and glazing. It had been winter and he had died early in the morning. There was frost on his clothes.

Hugh had clutched her more tightly. 'You all right?'

'I feel sick,' she admitted.

She sat down on the ground.

Beside her feet, crawling towards the brown leather sandals, a ladybird staggered across the dust and trodden strands of grass. She watched it spread its wings, beat them – black unfurled from a red umbrella – and take off into the air, a weighed-down helicopter, black body, red gloss wings. It fell back on to her feet and began labouring across her skin. She forced herself to look up at Hugh, who had edged so close that his boots were now touching her shoes. She drew up her legs immediately, with a little pinched grimace he did not see.

'Hugh, I came to ask you something this morning,' she said.

He looked down.

The ladybird lumbered on, fighting down a forest of hair.

'What did my mother die of?'

He seemed genuinely shocked. Even amazed.

'Why?'

'I was looking through Dad's things. I found letters. What did she die of?'

'Why now? It's a long while past. Gone.'

'Hugh . . .'

'I don't know. He must've told you.'

'Hugh . . .!'

'What'd he tell you?'

'He told me a lie. He told me pneumonia. I know it can't have been pneumonia. I know he was seeing some other woman – went to live with her.'

'I don't remember.'

She squinted up at him, against the sun, shading her eyes. 'You don't remember the woman, or you don't remember my mother dying?'

'I was at school. My father told me. I don't know, not really.'

She stood up.

'You shouldn't be thinking about that now,' Hugh said. 'Try not to think of anything like that just now.'

She shoved his hand away. 'Don't patronise me,' she snapped. 'I've a right to know. He – ' and she nodded, cruelly, abruptly, up the path – 'he never told me. He always lied to me. My mother went, and he lied to me, and now he's gone and the lie's still there and I want – ' she made a brushing, seething, wriggling motion of her shoulders, as if the memory had settled on her and was picking its way over her, like the red-and-black Toyland beetle creeping across her flesh – 'I can't stand any deceit. I need to know, before they come down. Before something else comes between it, before I have to see anything else . . . I've got to know.'

Hugh did not look as if he had understood this speech. His mouth worked slightly, as if repeating it to himself.

She took one of his hands. 'Please . . . please.'

The touch straightened him. Electric shock. Freezing water. She couldn't even begin to read the expression in his eyes.

'She drowned,' he said. 'In the sea.'

'The sea . . .'

Salt water and her mother's face next to hers.

'They had an inquest. The police came to get a statement off Dad. I remember them in the house. About her . . . state of mind, like. State of mind.'

'Was it an accident?'

'No.'

'Suicide?'

'There was an inquest. In town. I know Dad went. Your father went. Dad said a woman went. It was after a few months, I know. There weren't no burial for a long time.'

No burial.

'But she's in St Augustine's. In the graveyard.'

'It was only after months. I know it was a long time . . .'

'Where did they find her?'

'They said she'd gone in at the cove – Boss Cove. On our land.'

'Suicide.'

She sat down again – the wall held her up. She rested her head on it, the sun beating on her face. The ground tilted for a while – ship rocking at sea; waves pulling gravity – dear sweet God, my poor mother . . .

'She used to go and stand at their house, you know,' Hugh said.

203

'They had a house at Blandford somewhere. She used to leave you with Sharon Watts's mother in Petherell, and go and stand outside their house all day.'

Eve opened her eyes.

The world still rolled, a camera shifted to a wrong angle, the frame skewed, the roofs slanted precariously on the cottages. In the field over the road, the turning tractor described two-thirds of a trapezium in the wheat. She remembered vaguely. A stay at Sharon Watts's house, the old dog they had, the swing in the garden, and the noisiness of their meal times; staying there maybe a week or more . . . was that when it happened, when her mother . . .?

Suicide.

Bastard.

I don't care if it is you lying in the open up there alone and dying and sick and lost, I don't care.

I hope you *suffered.*

A WPC came out of the house. 'All right?'

'She's sick,' said Hugh.

'The doctor is coming down,' said the girl.

Eve pressed her face into her hands.

Hugh saw Jon come down the track first. He was walking, though a white Land Rover followed, bouncing through the ruts. He was taking deep draughts of air, his hands shoved into his pockets. When he saw Hugh ahead of him, he slowed, his eyes narrowing. The older man stopped and waited, acutely aware of the faces of the police in the car slowly drawing alongside.

'Is it him?'

'Yes.'

'What . . . what's he like?'

'Dead. What d'you think?' Jon made a move to go past.

Hugh looked from the car to Jon. He restrained himself from grabbing the boy's arm, thinking that he would willingly murder *him*, willingly put his hands around that neck. Jon's eyes flickered over him as though in distaste. He saw something in that casual, dismissive look. Sensed something, other than the animal sense of the younger and taller boy to the older, thicker, broader man. Thin black dog next to the tired father. He saw it in that look. The dancing disgust of the young for the weathered, the exhausted, the worn.

I'd snap your fucking neck for nothing.

For nothing. Like – *that!*

Never mind what you've done . . . you . . . you . . .

Biting the inside of his cheek, swallowing down the recall – flesh in shadow and Eve's keening, rising voice . . .

'What did he look like? What was it?'

Jon stopped, glancing back at him. The Land Rover rolled by: they stepped aside.

'Well? Did he break his neck or get an attack or what?' What they say?'

Jon eventually looked down at his feet. Eve was coming up the track, walking quickly, almost running.

'He choked on his own sick,' Jon said. 'He'd been drinking. There was a bottle up there.'

And he turned to walk away.

Now that the police had gone past, Hugh risked it. Grabbed Jon by the arm. Warm, smooth arm.

. . . snap the fucking neck like *that!*

'You keep away from Eve,' he said. 'She wants peace and quiet. Don't go disturbing her.'

Jon stared at him. Level. Slight smile.

Like that!

'I won't upset her,' he said. 'I'll ask her.'

Hugh's grip tightened.

Don't care what she did with you. It was a mistake. You forced it. I know you forced it. She don't know what she needs. I know. I know her from a long way back. Before you were born, even. It'd take a minute, maybe less. Just like a big cat. I wrung a few cats' necks in my time . . .

'I'm taking her back on up the house,' Hugh heard his own voice say. Too loud. 'She asked me to take her back up the house and run her out to the hospital, up the police, all what needs doing. You got no car – you can't help her. You'd best come back tomorrow.'

The boy stared him down. He was obviously thinking – but what, was impossible to say. He looked as if he were calculating something: some mental mathematics. Some problem of weights, physics, balances.

Then he turned quickly on his heel.

Eve was almost upon them. Hugh stood in the drive and watched him meet her. Jon stopped by her a second, said a few words. Eve's face whitened, and Hugh saw Jon momentarily hold her hand. Then another whispered word. Eve looked at Hugh. And Jon passed her, releasing her hand almost longingly. Hugh's eyes settled on their fingers as Jon stepped to one side of her. As he turned his back to leave, Eve stared ahead, along the path.

Caught between the two of us.
A fly between two webs.
Not for much longer, Hugh thought.
Not much longer.

Nineteen

That night, on the way back from the hospital, Hugh asked her to stay with him.

Eve looked across the twilight of the car, as the road began to dissect his land, and the neat hedgerows sped past.

'What?'

'They'll be up at your house.'

'Who will?'

'Paper people.'

Paper people. She had a fleeting image of cardboard figures crowding the garden, the doors.

'Newspapers.'

She smiled, and looked out, away. 'No they won't.'

'I bet you anything.'

'No . . .'

'It was on "Look South" tonight. TV news.'

She turned again. 'Was it?'

Hugh nodded, changing gear as they came to a junction. 'I saw it on the TV in the waiting room. At the hospital.'

Paper people.

'Well, they have to go home some time. I'll be all right.'

Hugh's hands flexed on the wheel. 'You want to come down to my place?'

'No, Hugh.' After yesterday, after his hands on her, the stone circle. Eve's gorge rose. *No.* After tonight, she never wanted to be with Hugh again. She'd only accepted his lift because she'd felt too wrung out, too trembly, to drive. She'd wanted Jon . . . but Jon couldn't drive. And Hugh was so bloody determined . . . she clenched her hands on her lap. She wanted to be alone. Just alone. 'I want to go home.'

'Or a hotel . . .'

Irritated, she rested her arm on the window, her chin in the palm of her hand.

Hugh's foot had eased from the accelerator; the Land Rover began to slow. He was thinking, his eyes fixed on the road. Disconnection.

She closed her eyes, shutting him out, shutting out the images from the hospital mortuary that rolled in after the imprint of Hugh. She tried to think of a world untouched by any of this.

Sarah's voice had been unnaturally subdued on the phone; she had never heard her speak so softly.

'Eve, the radio news, at lunch. It's not . . .?'

'Yes,' she said. 'It was Dad.'

'Oh, Eve. I'm so awfully sorry.'

Eve had let the receiver rest on her shoulder. She was only in the house for a moment, collecting her bag before Hugh took her to the hospital. Picking up the ringing phone had been an automatic, reflex reaction.

'Eve, shall I come out to you?'

Eve explained what was happening.

'Let *me* take you. Not Hugh.'

'He's already outside, waiting. It'll be OK. I came in for my bag. I just want to get it all over with quickly, Sarah.'

'Shall I come and make a meal? It would be ready when you got back.'

'No, Sarah. Honestly. I just—'

'I know. I know. You can do without people twittering about. I know. Look, promise me. Promise me absolutely that you will ring the *moment* you need anything. Don't ask Hugh. The last thing you want is that vulture hanging about. Will you ring me? Please.'

'Yes.' Eve managed a smile. 'Oh – maybe you could ring Matthew and tell him, I don't know when I'll next be in? I'll try, but—'

'Will do. I'll speak to him right away. Don't worry.'

'Thanks, Sarah.'

'Take care of yourself. I'll check later. See you soon.'

Eve replaced the phone. Hugh had come and knocked on the half-open door. 'I'm coming,' she had responded, dully.

That had been four hours ago. Now it was well into the evening. The road dipped, and they saw her house in the silent lee of the hill. Sure enough, in the rapidly fading light, they could still make out the roofs of three or four cars parked along the track. Hugh was still driving slowly, evidently digesting her refusal still.

'Can't you see how it would look?' she asked irritatedly. 'Me staying with you, or you with me?'

Hugh's petulant, closed expression was worse in profile. He pouted, like a baby. 'Won't be letting them know anything that isn't right,' he said.

'Oh, for Christ's sake!' she snapped. The man was the limit.

Through the window, the house was drawing nearer. A police car was among the others. Several were lumped up on the verge, wheel ruts through the grass.

Hugh plunged the Land Rover down through the gears. A bird, flying suddenly across the car, weaved and dipped. The people – the paper people – came forward, almost apathetically, white faces in the dusk.

'Hugh, you've got to leave me alone about that,' she whispered. 'I don't want . . .'

He turned in at the gate; put the car fumblingly, by accident, into reverse. It stalled. The policeman was waving them through. Eve put her hand across her face. Someone knocked on her window.

She had been about to say, *to marry you. I don't want to marry you.* But the burden of explaining, of pointing out what was impossible, intolerable . . .

They got to the door, somehow. It seemed Hugh expected to be allowed in: there was a brief, fumbling pantomime on the step as she put the key in the lock, and Hugh stepped forward with her; in the sight of the people behind, she deliberately stepped across him to bar his way. He stared down at her, too close. Too close and breathing on her.

'I'll be all right. Thank you for driving me there.'

He seemed to accept the rebuff, following her eyes as she glanced towards the crowd behind them.

'Oh – OK,' he said, nodding. 'Right. I'll go home and –' he lowered his voice, as if telling her a secret – 'I'll ring you up, in a minute. Make sure.'

She said nothing.

She got inside and slammed the door.

The phone did ring.

It was an hour later. She had gone around the house, closing all the curtains, locking all the windows. In the kitchen she made herself the world's worst sandwich: dry brown bread spread with yoghurt. It was all there was in the fridge. She ate it mechanically, hardly noticing how terrible it was.

Without putting on any light, she walked through the rooms on the ground floor, a glass in her hand. Pausing at the cupboard in the living room, she poured a huge Scotch into the glass and drank it back in one go, like medicine. A book lay half open on the floor; a book, a pair of shoes, a carrier bag stuffed with cue cards from school. She walked upstairs, blank. At the door of the bathroom she peeled off her clothes, letting them drop, kicking them to one side. She poured cold water into the sink and stuffed her hands into it. Then she put her face under the water. Its outrageous cold made her stand up, and the drops ran down her. She felt that she was melting. Inhuman. Stranded, bleached out, a negative on a piece of celluloid, all wrong shadows, curling in heat, cracking in cold. The bathroom was green: a green blind, green vinyl wallpaper, a green sink and bath, a straw-matting floor. She was dead in a green sea.

My father is dead.
My father.
I saw him tonight, in an underground room.
The phone began to ring along the corridor, in her bedroom.
'Hello.'
'It's Jon.'
Jon. Jon.
'Are you OK?'
'No.'
'What are you doing?'
'Drowning.'
'What?'
'No, forget it. Drinking.'
She could hear him smile. 'Anybody there?'
'The world. Come and see the peepshow. Grieving daughter. Respected member of the local teaching community found on hillside.'
'You watched the news.'
'Just.'
'What happens now?'
'Oh Christ. An inquest. The police. Another inquest.'
'Another?'
She looked at the carpet, her mother's death and inquest now intruding. The carpet was flock pink. She would change it. She would change everything. She would go. She would never look at the field again, or watch for cars, or water the chalk garden. Leaving. Drowning. Drinking.
'Can't you come out here?' she asked Jon. 'I want to tell you something. About Dad.'
'What?'
'Something Hugh told me.'
There was fractional silence. When Jon spoke again, his voice had gone up a notch: subdued excitement, perhaps. Heightened feeling. 'I've got something to tell you, too. About your friend there. Hugh.'

'Hugh? Look, better not over the phone.'

'It's getting to you. Getting persecuted. They won't tap your phone, you know.'

'No . . . I know. Don't laugh at me.'

'I'm not.'

'I can hear you smiling.'

'I'll come out now if you want me.'

She rubbed her hand over her face. *If you want me.* 'No, look. Better not. It's too late. It's complicated. It's all a mess. Come out tomorrow. Not to the house. There are people here.'

'Why don't you come to me?'

'To . . .'

'This flat. Come to the flat.'

She wrote down the address, which she ought to have known. She scribbled on the only thing near her, which was the back of a tape cassette.

'Eve?'

'Yes. I'm still here.'

'I thought you'd vanished. I meant what I said today. I love you.'

She smiled at the phone, unable to reply, but choked with a feeling of sweetness: pity and gratitude and affection. He waited a while and then spoke again.

'Go to bed now.'

'I will.'

'You sound like a bloody "Thunderbirds" puppet.' He laughed, very softly. 'Go to bed. Sleep.'

'I will.'

Putting down the phone, she was struck by a thought.

She went into her father's room, and looked down at the box where he had kept her mother's last diary and the few letters from his mistress.

The box, lumpish, stared back.

Stepping towards it, it felt as if this was where all the cold was coming from. She stretched out her hand, and the box seethed back, a wave of such intense pressure and cold, it was like walking into a wall. Her father seemed to spring up from it, full and alive and in voice. That yelling, cursing voice. Black voice from the piano scales, the music sheets, the white keys; water dripping from the keyboard and the flat of his palm swinging towards her, followed by his other hand, balled to a fist. He had knocked the air out of her that day that she poured water into the piano, while the languid paintings of her mother looked on, helpless. He had chased her round the room like a demon.

Laughing at me, you devil.

That's what the woman had called him. *The devil.*

She got to the box, and flung back the lid. 'Oh, you miserable, miserable, man,' she whispered.

The upper sheets in the box leered back at her: alive, writhing, letters scattered across the pages. All his meetings. All his passions. All his crude little megalomaniac, I-know-better-than-you bloody faces, that welling voice, those hands. Closing on hers, arched in a span across the music. Moulding her small hands in his. The slack hand in hers, stroking hers, in an old age haunted by his disease and unease and fear. Shrinking from the hand in hers.

She tore the papers out of the box. His letters, Celt's letters.

They were easily destroyed, the secrets. She wrenched and tore at them until they were little more than grains of paper, small grains of lust.

She turned her attention to the cupboards, the wardrobe. Here hung his public self: the blazer and the jacket he wore to the Archaeological Society, and at school. Leather-patched elbows. The must-musk smell of his body ranged in silent rows. Checked shirts. Collar frayed on a pink striped background. Black polo-neck sweater. Flannels. A yellow waistcoat. Lord of the sodding manor, stretched in a row on wire.

She pulled them all out, every single thing, and heaped them on the floor. The hangers rattled behind.

The hatred and the cold possessed her. There was not enough of it. There would never be enough to repay him: never enough cold, never enough misery to repay the loss. Of him, of her mother, of time. Of all the things that should have been in the place of their frozen lives. No way back, no way to a little human warmth and pleasure and understanding. Most of all, no allowance for weakness. No way past the pompous black mausoleum of himself. The grave of her mother.

She stood in the street and shouted for him.

She stood in the street and *begged* for him.

But he was shut away. In his private prison, the secure, cool darkness of self. Afterwards, in old age, a second defence came and secured the barred castle gate: a defence of illness, sealing him away for ever. He paced around inside, a convict pacing a single exercise year in the cold. Deaf, dumb, blind to everything but himself and the irrational demands of that inner demon. Illness shut tight the castle gate, for all time. Behind it, he begged, like his wife had begged, for a little love; but no one heard him. People had forgotten he even lived inside there, inside an oubliette of his own making.

I want to talk to you . . . I want a little love, a little love . . . Her father's voice might have been her own. Or her mother's. Cries for attention.

Eve pulled the clothes out on to the landing and threw them down the stairs. Some of the shirts caught around the last steps, the banister.

After them, she threw the photograph. He kept a photograph of himself – not her, not her mother – on his own bedside table. At the stone floor below, the picture bounced on its engraved silver rim. Then the glass splintered.

As she turned around – almost dark now – she caught sight of her mother, smiling from the ledge.

Mother pushing her hair back from her face, isolated in time.

Grasping the wood support of the balustrade, Eve sank to her knees. Naked, alone, she gazed at her mother until the image danced and shrank and flickered. Sobs were dredged up from the horror inside her: they overcame her, animals in the darkness snatching at her flesh, pulling her downwards. Her whole body began to shake. She was alone, a child in the world, both mother and father vanishing into darkness. The face of her mother, the salt smell in her arms, the smell of lemon, the dandelions in her arms, the heat in the garden, lost. Her father, lost, drowned by his sickness, drowned by his greed, and nothing left at all for their daughter, stranded on the shoreline while they both drifted from sight. Nothing remaining of them. Nothing to frame and hold. Nothing to cherish.

She collapsed inwards, rolling herself tight against the floor, the wall, grief claiming her at last.

'Daddy,' she whispered. 'Tell me things. Oh please tell me things. Talk to me, Daddy. Please come back and talk to me, Daddy.'

Hugh had locked all the windows too.

Tonight his routine was doubly important.

Very important not to miss a lock, a key. For the tenth time he went back and looked at the kitchen, making sure – for the tenth time – that the plugs were out, the switches off, touching the black rings of the hob with his fingertips. Just to make sure.

In the hallway, he touched the smoke alarm. Just to make sure the batteries hadn't run down. Its deafening response didn't bring a flicker to his face, other than a slight nod of satisfaction. Just making sure.

He closed all the doors behind him.

Upstairs, folding his clothes into the laundry basket, he took a shower as quickly as he could.

He didn't want to think until he was ready; and to be ready, everything must be done. Clean, in order. He towelled himself meticulously, not looking in the mirror. He put on pyjamas and a dressing gown, tying the belt slowly. Carefully.

On the landing, he turned away from the door of the room, *the* room, as if he couldn't bear to see it. Even acknowledge it was there. It did not belong to today. Tonight.

Not tonight, when there was so much to think about.

He went and sat in the chair in his bedroom. Oak, with a hard back and seat, and two carved armrests, it gave him a quiet pleasure. This was the right place. No one coming. No one here. He understood what Eve had meant by wanting to be alone, at home. Perhaps she, too, was sitting quietly.

Like two statues observing one another across a room. A room made a little bigger by their separate lives; a room a mile wide. But still, sitting looking at each other. A chair facing a window or a wall.

He had told the police that Bill's body had not been there when he'd last checked the hill, which had been a day and a half before. He said he had seen no sign of any human disturbance. No fires or tracks. No litter. He had heard no sounds. There had been nothing unusual.

In a sudden inspiration, he had told the officer that he had spent the last couple of days laying rat traps in the cottage cellars, and in clearing out the tack rooms and the stables. But the police had not seemed interested at all, really. They said there would probably be a post-mortem, although that was not certain, as the man was certainly ill and deranged, and had shown all the classic signs of severe and advancing senility. He could quote their words. GP to be consulted, of course.

Of course, he had agreed.

He had to describe the last night, when they had been playing cards. He had made a great thing of saying how angry – violent, even – Bill had seemed. Irritated at Eve's going out. 'He got angry very quickly,' he had said, watching them write it down. 'He was always wandering off, like to spite her, so she'd have to go looking. Then he'd forget – once out, like – he'd forget what he'd done. Could change his mood. Be very polite. If she found him, he'd come home with her, without knowing, properly, who she was. Just to be polite, like.' Hugh had sighed – almost a bit too casually. He had corrected himself and leaned over the table in the police station. 'I reckon he might of done that, you know,' he said.

'Done what?'

'Gone with somebody he met. Some tramp, maybe. Just gone with them, walked off. He would, you know, if he was in a good mood. Just ramble off. Strike up conversations with people right on the street. Walk alongside them. They would be a stranger, right on the street . . .'

They got bored with him.

Clever that. To make them bored with him. Cut the interview short. Spoke a long time to Eve. Sent them home.

Nobody had been about, not up in the yard of the farm. The only thing that had been wrong with the house was that, in his anxiety to get Eve in the car, and with all those people milling about, he had forgotten to lock his own door. He had another key, of course. When he got back to the farmhouse about nine o'clock that evening, he had been unlocking the kitchen door when it suddenly struck him that he had not gone through the act of *locking* it before he left. It was the confusion, the shock of them finding Bill so soon. He had hesitated on the doorstep in the twilight, looking about himself. Then he'd noticed a piece of white paper tucked behind the metal box he put there for the milkman. Drawing it out, he'd seen that it had been written and signed by a WPC Martin. *Mr Davies locked the house and gave us the door key. We have it at the station if you would like to collect it,* it read.

For a second, Hugh's head had swum. Anger at their bloody cheek had overwhelmed him. Touching his door, maybe even looking in his kitchen. Bloody intruders. He'd scanned the note carefully. The time had been printed at the bottom beneath the signature. Two-thirty p.m. They had locked the house in the afternoon. Jon and the police had been there until then. Heat had washed over him, with a sudden panic. He had left his house, the farm, *the cottages*, here on their own. For anyone to see. To look in, to inspect. He'd tried, wildly for a second, to think what they might find. If he had left anything. That morning, before it was really light, he had cleared the cottage. Cleared the old cellar ladder. Even if they had looked in the cellar of this house, they would only have found evidence that he had recently been cutting up wood for kindling. Wood that was now bagged in polythene sacks. Nothing else. Nothing to show that Bill had been anywhere near the house, let alone in the cottage cellar.

As a precaution, he'd rushed to his own house cellar, gone down the steps and turned on the electric light. Nothing. The bags of kindling – the cut-up pieces of Bill's worm-eaten steps and ladder – were lying untouched where he had left them, the loops of the top of the bag still neatly tied. No one had been here. No one had looked.

He had gone back up to his kitchen, breathing more easily. There was nothing to get excited about. Nothing to worry about. All that had happened was that the policewoman had been given the house key by Jon Davies, and she had taken it to the station for safe keeping. If they had found anything, or were suspicious of him, they'd have been here waiting for him when he got back. Asking him questions. But no, there was just the routine little note. Key at the station. Locking and safeguarding his property.

Nothing to worry about.

As a last precaution, however, he had gone over, in the dark, to the cottage. Looked at it a long time, his heart thumping dully in his chest. The ladder was there, that was all. The metal extension ladder from the barn, up which he had hauled Bill's heavy body on his back. But that in itself was nothing. Plenty of houses and farms had ladders lying about. Even if they asked, he might say he'd been checking the cottage roof, or something. The fact that he'd left the ladder there was not important. Then, edging out backwards, he'd scuffed the weeds from side to side, so they were not flattened so much. He'd taken the ladder to the barns and locked it away.

And so it was finished.

Complete.

Nobody cared, not even Eve.

Her face had been rigid, closed, all day. No tears. Nothing. All along he had been right about that. In a day or two, when her tiredness had gone, she would look around herself and see. Nothing stood between them now, not when she came to her right mind. Her usual mind. Not when she weighed it all up. The boy was . . . the boy was . . .

Hugh fought to find a word, a place for what Jon was.

He was a . . . shadow. A kind of mistake. He was nothing. Not a man, not an owner of anything, not with a place – a house, any possessions – he was a kind of . . .

. . . smoke.

A fire lit on a summer night, making the colours of a garden grey. A fire lit on a summer night.

Hugh looked down at his knees.

Eve didn't want a boy like that – with nothing, that had nothing, that was only a shadow – coming into what was theirs.

This was his land, his house. And Eve – this too was his, marked out for him for so long that it was unthinkable that some stranger, little more than a cloud casting its momentary rushing shadow on the field beneath it, should have any power to come between. Not into the picture. The drawing he had made of the future. No other figure materialising in the picture of Eve and himself and their family, here in this place. It was all his. He had done what Eve asked.

And now nothing would alter the future.

He got up and went to the bed, pulling back the covers.

In this bed, Eve would lie. He visualised her length, her colour, her naked body, lying on the stretched sheet. No dirty fumbling in a shed. No *mistakes*.

He had come down that morning at five. An hour's sleep, if you could call it sleep. An hour's restless dreaming. The first thing he had done was to go to the cottage, to get the cooler box, the glass jar, and to see to the smashed pieces of stairway and remains of the cellar hatch ladder. He'd carried the box and the jar in one hand, dragged the pieces of the ladder in the other. Half-way along, he'd dropped the ladder, put the box and the jar down, and picked up the wood again. The cooler box was now in his kitchen, and the jar – he hadn't noticed the jar. It would be inside the box, probably. He'd check that soon. Then, from six till eight that morning, he had axed the pieces to firewood in his own house cellar and bagged them up: they were now stacked in the house, under the stairs, waiting for the Aga to burn them, piece by piece.

It was as he came up from his cellar into his kitchen that he'd seen, through the window, the door of the tack room open. It must have been some time after eight. Hesitating, thinking that he had done it himself, he'd thought he heard a sound.

A panic had coursed through him, a gut reaction. Thinking the sound was Bill, in the cellar, calling him.

He had walked across the yard in a kind of dream, a sleepwalker. Subdued voices had come from the stable block. He had looked through the trees to the bottom road and seen Eve's car slewed up on the verge. She had parked low down in the yard, almost on the road. She had walked up, and gone into the stable.

He had still been trying to think why when he'd heard *his* voice. The lad, Jon Davies.

He had forgotten he was coming down today. He had had lads like this before, hanging about the place. Especially with harvest coming up. Looking for odd jobs. But, with the thought of Bill lying a mile or two at his back, he wanted no one about the farm for a week or so. If no one found Bill by then, he would 'find' him himself: he had already worked that particular scenario out. Even more of a hero to Eve if he found her father, and made a thing out of his being dead. Sorry, like. A big thing that he had found him but couldn't do anything for the old man. He had written the scene already in his head, casting himself at the centre.

Jon was to be deterred.

There had been a silence: he'd increased his pace, his soft shoes making no noise on the gravel. Just as he'd come level with the window, he'd heard Eve cry out: two voices, then, in a kind of urgent harmony. Two voices.

He'd looked in through the grimy window, its pockets of thick bubble glass in a cast-iron frame.

The exact picture of them would not erase itself from his mind. The exact placing of her arms around his neck. Their lowered heads. The opened braced legs of the boy. The colour of him. Two white ghosts on a dark wall.

Eve had thrown back her head, and Hugh had leapt back from the window.

Afraid to be seen.

It was on *his* land, in *his* building, and he was afraid to be seen.

Blood had thundered in his head. The world had raced, yellow on green, brown on yellow, white on green, white on black, as he'd run across the yard. The door was a great block of red paint, the brass door latch, the brass letterbox, reduced to gleaming bands in the gore. He'd shoved the door open, slammed it shut. He'd leaned against it as if a whole legion of devils were hammering on the other side.

He had never been so angry, never so angry before.

He had gone to the hall and unlocked the gun shelf – dropped the keys, lost them on the dim floor, scrabbled for them, swearing – and taken down the shotgun and had fumbled and sworn again over loading it, and shoved the breech home and gone out through the kitchen to the step.

And looked over at the yard and the tack room door.

He had savoured what he would do. Three seconds of perfect revenge. He would repay them for using him. He saw the bullet go through the smooth back, and into Eve. It would tear a hole in that back and cut him in half. Her too. Not finish them off at all. Leave them to lie there. 'He was raping her and I tried to stop him . . .' He could say that. They would believe him. If they did not, he would be taken away. Eve, too. The boy had ceased to exist, even in the three-second picture.

One oiled barrel in his hand could destroy her, and himself. Take away the present and the future. The children. Long after Eve and the boy were dead, he too would die. But alone.

The barrel of the gun had dropped. It had swung in his hands, swerving over his own feet, knocking against the stone. He'd rested it, wiping his eyes. Hard to think. Hard to think.

The next thing was, this idea he had always had, since he was fifteen or sixteen, maybe before, this idea of the way it would be with Eve. It was no fiction. It was real. The thing was, the thing was – the barrel nicked the scraper at the doorside – Eve. There *was* no future for him, no idea of life at all, without Eve. He'd turned his back on the yard. Disappointment, thick as nausea, had swept over him.

The gun had gone back to the shelf, the keys turned the lock.

He'd gone back, grudgingly, and looked at the tack room. They would come out, sooner or later.

He would wait.

She wouldn't have come looking for the boy, would she?

There was at least an even chance she had come looking for him. Sooner or later, they would come out – there had been no rape in that attitude, that bowing of heads, those leaping, soft voices; that was what destroyed him – sooner or later, they would come out, together, and she would come up to the house, even together; and he had to get past this moment, this destruction, and find a way past. A clean path. Clean path. He had pushed down his disgust.

Still, when she did come – not together; she left him behind – he had been washing at the sink, cleaning, and she'd come to the door . . .

Holy Christ, at the sight of her so close, when she'd turned to fill the kettle and looked out of the window, he had come so very close to taking her out of this world.

Even then, he might have killed her and killed himself. The loaded shotgun for himself. His own fist for her.

Then he had thought of the boy. Or, rather, the ghost of the boy – smoke, shadow – had come into the room, and he'd thought, Not us. Not *us!* But *him.*

Almost immediately, Hugh had found an excuse for her.

The trouble was, there was always a man who wouldn't respect weakness in a woman. There was always a man who would come into that place and try to take it from her, try to work on it. No patience. No willingness. No time. He would always come, the outsider, the thief, and take what was not his. The weakest had no defences against thieves. Eve had no defences.

There was always some animal – and he had seen plenty: the fox circling the heifer as she delivers the feeble calf – ready to take the defenceless. And that was where you laid a trap.

He had laid a thousand quick traps. You took the rabbit from the net and bent the neck under your thumb. Two hands, opposite screw.

The dull sick snap ended that verminous error. Throw the body to one side. Start on the next. Life throws up vermin and thieves . . .

He lay down on the bed and pressed his face into the sheet, inhaling its clean scent. It would be different for her when she came here.

He only had to make the path clear. Like the laying of hedges, the trimming back of verges, the straightening of tracks. The clean broad sweep of the turning lines, the stripes in the fields. Made clear and perfect. Mathematically perfect. Every yard accounted for. Every last seed and grain forecasted, counted, weighed. Every head on the straining green crop. Charted against a timetable. Cleanliness and accounting. Everything stripped and clean. Down to the last blade of grass, the last brick, the last tile, the last drop.

There were poisons to kill what you did not want. Or machines to dig them out. Or tools to scythe them down.

And a hand, his hand, waiting on the wire for the boy Jon.

It was after eleven when Eve saw the headlights of the car turn off the road and into the drive. She was still sitting on the stairs, wrapped now in her dressing gown and nursing a drink on her knees. She had started sometime after ten, to try to fold her father's clothes, to make the house tidy; but she had not got far. She had been sitting on the same stair now for over an hour, the arched window on the landing throwing its faint light over her.

For a moment she thought of Hugh. *He's come back.* Immediately she knew she would not open the door to him: she would ignore his knocks. Then she realised that Hugh would come along the track and, anyway, the low sound of the engine below was not the Land Rover's. She wondered if it could be Jon, having a lift from someone. In the next second, however, she heard Sarah swear under her breath as she stumbled on the gravel path that dipped to the back door.

Eve licked her finger and wiped under her eyes: even in her drink-slow state she realised she must look a mess. She retied the sash on her wrap slowly, balancing the glass on a tread of the stairs.

Sarah's knock was brisk and businesslike. As Eve got to the hall, she heard her friend's voice. 'Eve? It's me.'

She opened the door.

Some comment died on Sarah's face. Her eyes ranged over Eve, taking in the glass and the traces of mascara and the pile of clothes and belongings at Eve's back. Sarah stepped over the threshold, gently guiding Eve with a palm in the middle of her back bringing Eve through from the door to the kitchen.

'I don't suppose you've eaten.'
'There isn't anything.'
Sarah opened a couple of cupboards. 'Tomato soup,' she announced.
'No.'
'I agree it doesn't enhance Bell's, darling. But beggars can't be choosers.' And she opened the tin and spilled the contents into a saucepan, eyeing Eve all the while. Eve sat on a chair, her arms propped on the table in an attitude of terminal weariness.
'See you've been having a clear out.'
Eve didn't reply.
Sarah tried a different tack. 'I was at the Ladies' Circle and that damned Florence Beecham gave this lecture about seedheads. I thought we'd never finish, and on the way back, I thought I'd just come past, and when I saw the light—'
'About *what?*'
'Sorry?'
'A talk about what?'
'Seedheads. Thistle things.'
'What for?'
'Well, quite.' Sarah stirred the soup. 'Apparently one sprays them with gold paint at Christmas and then one's guests arrive and foam at the mouth over them and declare how wonderfully artistic you are.'
'Good God.'
'I know. But I keep telling myself, we raised over two hundred thousand for St Matilda's Hospice, we can't be all bad. If one or two of us are going ga-ga, one can't be blamed . . .'
She put down the spoon on the side of the hob and stared at Eve, who was sitting in the same chair, unmoving, while tears ran silently down her face. She left the soup and came striding across, saying, 'Oh Christ. What is it? Is it the clothes? Shall I clear them away?'
'No, no.'
She sat down next to Eve and placed Eve's hand between her own. 'Tell me.'
'Sarah, you wouldn't believe me.' Eve wiped her face with her sleeve, looked in the pocket of the wrap for a tissue, and failed. Sarah promptly got up and tore off a sheet of kitchen towel, gave it to her, and sat back down.
'Try me. If I can suspend reality for Florence I can do it for you.'
Eve's smile was ghostly.
'Is it the police?'
'No. They've been very kind.'

'Was it . . . identifying, you know—'

'No.' Eve looked up, past Sarah, past the kitchen, into some indefinably cloudy past, trying to find what it was, out of the last two or three days, that cut her most. 'Sarah,' she said. 'Did you know that Dad had an affair, in the year my mother died?'

'Did he? How d'you know?'

'I found some letters. I asked Hugh.'

'Oh, and I suppose Mr Scott was terribly thoughtful and gave it to you with both barrels.'

'I bullied him into telling me. These letters—'

'When was this?'

'The letters were last night. Hugh told me the rest today. This morning. While we were waiting . . .'

'Oh, Christ.'

'Yes. But that's not the worst. My mother committed suicide over it. She drowned herself. *And Dad never said a word about it.* All these years, he's let me think she died of pneumonia. Pneumonia! And there must be other people in the village who knew, and never mentioned it . . .'

'Well, perhaps they thought it was best left unsaid. Nobody wants to hurt a little girl. And things were different then. Things were hushed up. Adults *didn't* talk to children. And then time passes, and there are other scandals.' Sarah sighed. 'People do keep skeletons in their closet, you know. I mean, Duncan's grandmother never spoke to her sister, and nobody knows why to this bloody day.'

'But *Dad*. He lied to me. He pretended it was just some kind of illness, when he knew that all the time it was *him*. What he had done. *That's* what took Mum away from me. And all these years . . .' She blew her nose on the kitchen paper, wiped her face. 'All this time, I used to ask him about Mum, *and all the time* . . .' She stopped speaking, unable to trust herself any further. She heard the child weeping in the sound of her own voice.

Sarah sat without saying a word for a full minute, her face full of pity. 'I'm so sorry, Eve,' she said finally.

Eve looked at her, took a drink, and finished it.

'Want some more?'

'No, that's my third. Or fourth.'

'Soup, then.'

'If you say so.'

'I do.'

Sarah got up and dished from saucepan to dish expertly, putting it down in front of Eve, and actually putting a soup spoon into Eve's hand. 'Eat.'

'You haven't heard it all yet.'

'Eat first.'

'Hugh Scott proposed to me. He wants to marry me.'

Sarah's face went completely blank for a moment; then, like a switch being thrown, she burst out laughing. The roar of laughter knocked Eve sideways: she had forgotten it could be funny. All she connected with Hugh's offer of marriage was the stone ring, the feel of his hands on her thighs, the bile that rose in her throat. It didn't seem possible to her that this could ever be even faintly amusing.

'Oh but – but really, he *couldn't* be serious. Not really.' Another peal of laughter. 'Oh, but how *dreadful!*'

'It was. It *was* dreadful.'

'But he can't think in a million *years*—'

'He does. He does. He's got it all worked out.'

'*No!*'

'I went up to Threlfalls' with him to look for Dad . . .' Her voice faded again, and she stopped, swallowed, before carrying on. 'He talked as if it were understood between us.'

'Well, I hope you put him straight.'

In the background, in the living room, the phone gave a short, faint ring; a single cut-off note. Sarah turned her head, listening, waiting to see if it would ring fully. It did not. Eve appeared not to have noticed. 'I tried,' she was saying.

'Tried? What do you mean?'

'He didn't seem to take it in. He tried to kiss me, and—'

'Oh, Lord.'

'That's not all. He seemed to think – I mean . . .'

Sarah, realisation dawning, gripped her wrist. 'Eve—'

'It's all right. Or rather, it's *not* all right, but I'm not hurt. I just screamed, and he dropped me and seemed . . . really dazed . . .'

Sarah still had tight hold of her, but her mouth had dropped slightly open with shock. 'I knew there was something wrong with him,' she said at last.

Eve gazed down at the rapidly congealing, untouched bowl in front of her. 'He's like a child,' she said, faintly. 'A great, lonely child.'

Sarah shook her head. 'Well, I must say, you're rather generous about it. I hope you've told him to bugger off.'

'I'm sure he's not actually dangerous, it's just he's – stupid, helpless . . .'

223

'Sorry. You'll have to run that by me again. This is the man who's attacked you. You feel *sorry* for him?'

Eve smiled, resting her head on one propped hand. 'That's what Jon said. He thinks I ought to report him.'

Sarah sat back. 'Jon.'

'Mmmm.'

'Jon's been here.'

'He was here, last night, after I got back. He . . .' Eve looked up, suddenly realising that Sarah knew very little of what had passed between her and Jon.

Sarah was nodding, slowly, trying to absorb the look on Eve's face. Finally, she said, 'Well, congratulations. Is that in order? Is that what one should say?'

'Don't be angry, Sarah.'

'I'm not angry.' She grabbed the now-cold dish, stared at it in disgust, and took it to the sink. 'I'm not angry,' she repeated, over her shoulder. 'Good heavens, it's nothing to do with me. You have had a busy old time, haven't you? Jolly good luck, I should say.'

'Please . . . don't, Sarah.'

'No, I mean, gosh, there's absolutely *no* harm in it, is there? A young boy like that is *just* the kind of stalwart you need at a time like this. Reliability itself. Not a hope of him running off and leaving you. Didn't I warn you, yesterday? A lot of good *that* did. Marvellous.'

'Sarah, please. Stop it. He's very gentle, he's very kind . . .'

'Oh, I'm sure. Where is he, then, this paragon of virtue, this knight in shining armour? Down the pub?'

Eve stared at her hands on the table. 'He couldn't help today. I had to – identify Dad.'

Sarah was merely nodding.

Eve pressed her face into her hands. 'Sarah, don't judge me,' she whispered.

There was a long silence, punctuated only by the sound of Sarah washing and drying the dish and glass. The house seemed to press in on the scene in the kitchen, blackness blinding the windows, the fridge and freezer in the hall humming like a sleepy animal lying against the door. All Eve could think of, behind her laced fingers, was Jon; of him drawing the sheet over her and smoothing her shoulder. She longed for him, for the drug-like tranquillity of his touch.

Finally, with a great sigh, Sarah turned from the sink. She folded the teacloth into an efficient square and laid it on top of the boiler.

'I'm just going to collect up that stuff on the stairs,' she said. 'Shall

I bag it? I'll bag it. Then I'll run you a bath.'

Eve did not reply.

Yet as Sarah passed, she relented, laying a hand on Eve's shoulder: Sarah's ultimate sympathetic gesture. It lingered there longer than usual.

'What on earth am I meant to do with you?' she murmured. 'You absolute poor utter *bloody* fool.'

The next day was hot, unseasonably so.

Eve got up at seven; drank a cup of tea for breakfast, and was out, driving to Jon's, by eight.

She walked through the streets, checking the piece of paper with his address. The flat when she found it was no surprise: she knew he had little money. She went up the narrow stairs and knocked on his door.

He was awake and dressed.

'I can't stay long,' she said.

'Why?'

'School – Dad. Things.'

As she passed him, he said, 'How was it?'

She sighed. 'Terrible. Newspaper people were there when I got home. Somebody was arriving in a car when I left today. The phone rang eleven times before eight o'clock,' she murmured. 'You have no idea.'

As he closed the door, he tugged her back towards him and kissed her. She drooped, still, in his arms, unresponsive. He let her go.

His window gave a view of a narrow back street, with the esplanade and the sea at the end, a small peephole between the houses. As she glanced out, two girls passed beneath on their way to work. They were carrying the local paper and both reading the front page. Eve knew that she and her father were on that page. There was a faded and out-of-focus picture of Bill, dressed in a suit and tie, standing by his school gates. It was almost twenty years out of date. She rated halfway down the third paragraph. A smaller picture showed the copse where Bill had been found, and the four boys standing by the stile, trying hard not to grin.

Jon was bringing her a cup of coffee.

'Sometimes . . .' she said.

'What?'

She brushed his cheek, smiling. 'Nothing. Just sometimes.'

'Wait till I show you what I found,' he said. He held his own mug in two hands, shifting from one foot to another, as if about to break into a dance. His face was lit up. 'Bet you can't guess.'

She had been through some conversation like this recently: 'Bet you, bet you.' It struck a dull, unpleasant chord. 'Jon, for God's sake don't play games.'

He sat down abruptly. 'What do you know about Hugh?'

'Why?'

'Come on. What?'

'Most things, I suppose. Why?'

He grinned. 'This is the guy who wants to marry you. Come on, you must know quite a lot. Ever been in his house? You must have.'

'Only downstairs. Look—'

'Think you know him well?'

'What's all this about?'

He leapt up again, put his cup on a table. 'Wait here.'

He went out of the room. She heard him rummaging about in the small kitchen, bringing something out of a cupboard.

She looked about the room. She had been imagining some kind of student bed-sit: posters, stacked magazines, dirty floor, unmade bed, dusty windows. Instead this single room was something of a revelation. It was almost bare, with a terrible red Wilton carpet that was threaded in parts. But the walls were painted white, recently. He had one armchair, sagging, and upholstered after a fashion with an Indian rug slung across it. A red and black striped sofa bed, a wardrobe. One table – black – spread with maps. One table lamp, brass, with no shade. There was a Bakelite radio and a green Bakelite clock, collectors' pieces. She leaned forward and looked at the maps, and the books beside them.

The Causeway Camps of Neolithic Britain. Ritual Landscape. The Bronze Age Burial.

She smiled. One of the maps, an Ordnance Survey, was spread open, half hanging off the table, at the Dorset coastline, the scoop of the Fleet at Abbotsbury showing uppermost.

'I didn't know you were a walker,' she said as he came back.

'Not walking. Landscape.'

'Ah . . .'

'It's too good to miss round here. That's why I came down in the first place. Best place in the country for burials – Bronze Age. Do you know there's tumuli marked on Hugh's land?'

'Yes, I knew that. He and his father ploughed them over.'

'He's got no feeling for the dead, has he?'

'Sorry?'

'No respect for the dead – or the living. All he thinks of is himself.' He handed her a paper bag. 'Have a look inside.'

She brought out three or four items: a pair of tights, still in the cellophane wrapper. A postcard. A pack of small tissues, the kind you could buy at station bookstalls or newsagents'. A library card.

'This is my card,' she said.

It was an old cardboard one: the library had gone over to computers about a year ago. She recognised the stamp. 'It must be three or four years old. Where did you get it?' She smiled up at him, bemused.

'Look at the others.'

'Well? Did you buy them?'

'No.'

She turned the bag over, looking for a mark, a clue. 'I give up. You got them from my room. I don't understand . . .'

'Not *your* room. Another room.'

She shrugged her shoulders. 'I've lost you.'

'Hugh's.'

She frowned at him. 'Hugh?'

He was biting his lip, biting back a smile of triumph.

He kneeled forward, picking up the tissues. 'I went inside his house yesterday. I went upstairs. He's got a room, a locked room, up there. You . . .' He closed his eyes for a second, as if to conjure it up. 'You wouldn't believe it.'

She stared at him.

'It's a shrine,' he said. He threw down the tissues and picked up the postcard. Venice. 'Look.'

'It's mine.'

'Yes, yes. Look. It's dated 1981. You went to Venice in 1981? Look, your writing. *We went to the Gallery* . . .'

She took it from him, read it, replaced it in the pile in her lap.

Jon, on his knees, grasped her hands. 'He's got a whole load of stuff up there. No bloody carpet, no furniture, no curtains. Just an empty room. There's a couple of boxes filled with all stuff like this. Postcards from you, going back years and years. Some clothes. Have you noticed any clothes going missing? There's a pair of old shoes up there, Eve. Shoes! All laid out, neatly, in these boxes: *your* things. I bet you things you missed and then forgot. He's taken things from you and *kept* them.'

She looked down again at the pile.

'He's got a phone in there. A red phone. It's connected up. Who does he ring when he goes in there?'

Eve shook her head.

'Does your phone ring at night? Does it ring and then stop?'
'Sometimes. But that happens to everyone.'
'How often?'
'How often what?'
'Oh, Eve, for Christ's sake, come *on*. How often does your phone ring and then stop? Or you pick it up and there's no one speaking?'
'He told me – I think he told me . . . he dials our number . . .' She rubbed her forehead, confused.

Jon gripped her arm, to stop her. He stared up at her face and knew that she was only dimly grasping the significance of what he was trying to say. She looked a little punch-drunk, a little hungover, certainly very tired. He tried to rein in his feelings, to be aware that he had to lead her gently towards what he already knew.

Hugh had taken Eve away very quickly yesterday: Eve, shocked and silent, had merely followed him listlessly.

The sight of her getting into Hugh's car had incensed Jon. He'd still ached from her, had wanted simply to carry on holding her, protecting her. It had been terrible to let her go, more terrible to see Hugh pause before he got into the driver's seat and look back over the roof of the car, to give Jon a smug, small grin that said, *I've got her.*

The police had been concerned with the boys, with the GP. No one had stopped him when he went into the house.

For something to do, to make it appear that he was used to the place, he had filled the kettle from the tap and plugged it in, watching all the time out of the windows. No one had challenged him. No one had even looked into the kitchen.

He had been struck by its cleanliness: the order of the cups on the dresser, the neatness of the way they were arranged. There was none of the dross of a busy household, or the occupational grime of a working farm. Not even letters flung on the worktop, or magazines or newspapers, or bills, or washing or books. It might have been swept clean, like a showhouse. There was no dust on the sills, no coffee rings on the table. The taps gleamed as if new.

Bemused, and intrigued, he'd stepped into the hall. The same smell of cleaning had assaulted him. Disinfectant. Polish.

There were several rooms on the ground floor: living room, study, a shower room, a dining room. The dining room was almost painfully new: a reproduction Regency table and six Regency chairs, their pink and cream striped seats still wrapped in polythene. A mahogany unit with nothing in it but a silver plate trophy, engraved 'Young Farmers Darts 1971'. Jon had smiled thinly as he'd put it down. They'd said at the pub, when he had been playing that night, that Hugh Scott used to play; he had even been captain of the team one year. The trophy stood alone on its shining shelf, a memorial to a time when Hugh Scott had some kind of a social life. Jon turned and walked from the room, feeling its nakedness and loneliness.

In the hall, he'd paused and looked up the stairs.

No one would know.

Hugh Scott would never know.

He'd wondered for maybe a minute about the ethics of creeping round Scott's house in this way. He felt like a thief or, worse still, some voyeur gloating over an empty life. Then the marks on Eve's arm and thigh came vividly back to him. He had put his foot on the step determinedly, and gone up.

He had half expected to find a darker side upstairs: some clue to Hugh's self that was not revealed in the more public places below, some sign of cruelty. But the upper rooms were almost feminine: two, one of which was Hugh's, were fully furnished, the other two only carpeted. Jon had stood at the door of Hugh's and looked at the bedspread and the frieze around the walls, and the dressing table. It was as if he were expecting a woman: of the two wardrobes, only one held clothes. Of the two chests of drawers, only one was full. The other merely had lined paper down, and a little bag of lavender in each drawer. *He's waiting for a wife*, Jon had thought immediately. And he'd known with a sensation like a blow to the solar plexus, that the woman for whom these drawers and this wardrobe and this mirror were waiting was Eve.

He'd had to hold himself very straight for a second; he'd had a sudden urge to tear the place to pieces, tear the paper from the cupboards, smash the wood doors to splinters, erase any promise of Eve that the room implied. But he let the feeling pass, reminding himself that Eve thought Hugh was to be pitied more than anything.

And he could see that the room *was* pitiful. Sad and pitiful and a sign of weakness and blindness; the dumb blinkered blindness of a horse put between the shafts of a cart, and pulling it without question.

He'd left it, his mouth dried and feeling slightly tacky and sweet, as if he'd drunk medicine, heavily saccharined to make it palatable. The soles of his shoes had seemed to cling to the carpet, as though Hugh's devotion clung to him, tangibly, like glue. The feeling was gruesomely unpleasant: he'd felt he would need to wash.

He'd wanted to get out of there as soon as possible.

He'd stopped at Hugh's door, to get his bearings. And seen the far door and, by some miracle, the glint of something metal on the picture rail alongside it.

He had almost not gone to see what it was. It had been that close. Almost turned away to go down the stairs. That close to not finding the room with the red phone . . .

He had found that the glint of metal was a key. He had unlocked the door next to it. Hard to recall, now, exactly what he had felt as he had looked in that room. Hard to conjure up. It was not amazement – not exactly. Far back in his mind he had imagined something like this – been waiting for it as he climbed the stairs. It had not been surprise, not even anger; hardly even horror. He'd felt a kind of sickness, a kind of grief. Eve's past stapled and pasted and collected in these boxes, on this bare floor. Eve's thoughts marshalled into line and pored over. It was as if Eve herself had been kept in here, a prisoner, chained to Hugh's need. As if, for years, she had been put in a small wooden prison and never been allowed to develop or grow. The breath had seemed to go out of him: it had felt hard to breathe at all. Trying to get air where there was no air. A dead room, with a red phone on the floor. A red phone like a pool of blood, with its red cord curling back to the junction box like an umbilical.

He'd picked up the first three or four things he found, wincing in disgust at the very touch of the hoard.

He had gone out, locked the door behind him, put the key back exactly where he had found it, and gone downstairs, all the time feeling that thready sickness of suffocation. Through the hall. Through the kitchen. Out into the air, where people still walked up and down. He had seen that the police had roughly cordoned off the farmyard: there had been a few cars turning up already. Neighbours, maybe. Press, certainly.

'Has he left his house unlocked?' the WPC had asked.

'Yes,' he'd said.

'Are you staying about till he comes back?'

'No . . .'

At that moment, he'd have given anything not to have to go in the house again. Not to have to stay even at the door. He had stepped down and begun to walk vaguely away, pressing the key into the policewoman's hand. 'You'd better have it,' he'd said.

He had gone to sit on the wall of the yard, in the shadows of the cottages. It had been a long time before he had been able to look about him.

Now, here in his own flat, he tried to think how to describe that feeling to Eve. She sat back with a mild, rather disjointed look on her face.

He spoke slowly, deliberately. He wanted her to see – to *feel* – Hugh going into that room.

'He goes in there,' he began, softly. 'He rings you up. He rings you up from the room where all your things are. I've heard that phone go in your house. I've heard it click several times, even in the short time I've been there. He gets *near* to you that way. He comes and looks at you. Don't you see? Don't you see?'

Eve shook her head slowly.

She knew she ought to be disturbed. But the only emotion that came was a terrible compassion for Hugh Scott. All those *years*. She laid the postcard of Venice across her knees and considered the picture. She remembered actually writing this very card on a bright, cold, breezy morning, sitting on a bench by the Santa Maria dei Miracoli. A little girl had been chasing a cat towards the theatre behind; in the street a shop selling bronzes and jewellery.

It was all faded now.

'Dear Hugh,' she had written. 'You should see the colours here. Terracotta and green, faded red. This is a picture of the Tiepolo Papadopoli Palace . . .'

There had been a time when she had talked to him about colours. He'd had a book about painting from the library, she remembered. She had said, when she came back, how much he would like Venice if he was interested in painting. The brightness of the blue. They had fenced round the subject rather embarrassedly whenever they met, he telling her, very formally, about art exhibitions at the Arts Centre. He had asked her to go once, and she had refused. There had been something on at school; it had been a relief. She had laughed with her father about it. The relief of not going with Hugh. Then, even more awkwardly, she had arranged to go with a couple of the teachers, and it had slipped out in talking to Hugh that she had seen the thing after all: she could still see the surprise, like a blow, on his face, when he understood that she had gone after all, but not with him.

And now, looking back at that time, it dawned on her with utter poignancy that Hugh had only got the book from the library because he sensed *her* interest in art. He must have sat at home, dutifully learning the names of painters, reading the names of paintings and galleries so that he could pretend an enthusiasm he did not feel. All to surprise her. All to catch her attention.

She wondered where the books on paintings had gone. Taken back to the library. Forgotten in a drawer. One more ploy that had not worked.

She looked up at Jon.

He was so young and sure of himself.

She put the things back in the bag, folded the top over, and gave it back to him. 'You shouldn't have gone in there. A locked room. It was private,' she said.

He frowned at her, tilting his head to one side. 'You knew all about it,' he said.

'No, I didn't. But now I know, it doesn't . . . well, it doesn't shock me.'

Jon got to his feet, looking dumbfounded, rebuffed. 'You bloody amaze me,' he told her. 'You really do.' He lifted up the bag, and shook it. 'This is weird, do you know that? It's criminal. He's stolen things. He ought to be reported to someone.'

'He's not dangerous. Just sad.'

'Sad . . . Oh, right. Just a sad man. I get it.'

He wheeled around and snatched up, from the mantelpiece, a glass jar and a small paper box.

'I'm a criminal, then,' he said. 'Because I did more than that. Know where I got these?' He didn't wait for a reply. 'I got this –' he held up the paper carton – 'from Hugh Scott's tack room. It was out of place on a row, on a shelf.'

He stood with his back to the window, grasping the bottle and box in front of him. 'When you get a crossword clue, and the word's on the tip of your tongue. You know? Didn't fit. Didn't know why. Just didn't fit in with him, his tidy places. Left in an unlocked cupboard.' He shook his head, almost laughing now. 'And I didn't even know why I took it! I just took it. Had a feeling. When he went off with you yesterday – did he tell you, he ordered me, really gave me an order, not to talk to you? – I thought, right. Right, I'll have a look round. While he's not breathing down my neck. Did you see his face when that boy came down the path? Did you notice it? Did you see him go white? He went bloody white, Eve. White! And I thought, hello. What's *he* worried about? Not you. Not me. He's *afraid*. He rocked back on his heels, you know. I came from the stables – what? Thirty seconds after that boy first started shouting. You were next to the house. And Hugh *rocked* back on his heels when the lad said about an old man up there; he *rocked*. I thought he was going to faint.'

Jon exhaled, caught a breath. He held up the cardboard box, and read from it, slowly.

'Administer half to two and one quarter ounces in drinking water.'
He looked up at her. 'Know what this is?'
'No, I...'
'Chloral hydrate. It's a sedative. Prescribed – here – for horses. It's got a –' here, he brought the box close to his face – 'funny smell. Like melons.'
'And you found it... in the stables?'
'Yes.'
'I'm sorry, I don't see what that means. I don't see the connection.'
'You will.' Jon lifted the glass jar. He looked at the specks of liquid inside then, gently, he held it out to her. 'Open the lid and smell that,' he told her.
She did as he said.
There was a stale, but recognisable, smell of melons.
'Where did you get this?' she asked.
He came and sat down, facing her. He put the box on the coffee table.
'From the path between the cottages and Hugh's house,' he said.
There was a knock at the door.
Jon got up to answer, looking back at her. Eve sat with her glance flickering between the jar and the box, trying to make sense of it.
He opened the door to a girl of his own age.
'Hi. Want anything?'
'No... no.' He stood in front of the door.
She tried to look past. 'Got visitors?'
'Yes.'
She began to smile. 'Who is it, your Mum?'
'No.'
'I won't show you up. Promise.'
'Look, it's not my mother. It's just somebody I know.'
She leaned against the door-frame, smiling. 'Aren't you going to let me in?'
He shook his head. 'Kindly piss off, Fran,' he said. 'I don't want a thing from the shops. I told you.'
'I'm not going to the shops. I'm going to Mike's. Did you want his tapes, or what? And don't tell me to piss off. It isn't polite.' She placed a forefinger on his chest, and drew a line, downwards.
He stepped back to close the door.
She was too quick for him, put her foot in the crack, and shoved him to one side, edging her body past him.
'Hi.'

Eve looked up.

'Hi. I'm Fran.'

'Hello.'

'I'm downstairs. In the shop.'

The girl was tall, rangy, and blonde. Her hair was a tangled, sharply cut bob. She wore white leggings, a white T-shirt, a day-glo pink band twisted around her waist.

'Well . . .' She turned and winked at Jon. 'Must be going. Nice to see you. Both.' As she slid past Jon, she smothered a laugh and whispered, 'Pervert.'

Eve said nothing. Slowly, she put the glass and the box back on to the table.

As Jon closed the door, he said, 'Where are you going?'

'I've got to go. I couldn't be long.' She looked down at the table again. 'What are you going to do about these?'

He came alongside her. 'Listen, don't get upset about Fran. She's nothing. Don't look like that. One of my mates knows her, honest to God. Don't take any notice.'

Eve smiled.

He put his arm around her shoulders.

'Look, I *must* go.'

'Not like this.'

'No, I must. Let me go, Jon.'

'I can see you're pissed off with me. What've I done? Is it Fran? Don't take any notice of Fran. Is it the sedative? Look . . .' He picked up the glass. 'I'm trying to find out for you. For your sake. It wasn't very clever going into the house. But he left it open. The key to the room was just hanging next to it. It wasn't like breaking in. You can see that, can't you? This Scott, he's not—'

She unpicked his fingers from her arm.

'Eve . . .'

'I just need to think.'

'What's there to think about? Come with me to the police.'

'The police!'

'Just tell them about this. The jar. The box.'

'They'd laugh you out of the place. Come *on*.'

Jon began to lose his temper. 'What's so stupid about it? What's so funny? Why did Hugh put a sedative into a jar? He hasn't done anything with the horses. They weren't sedated, were they? Why did he want it? He mixed up a solution of it, and *now there's only a few grains left.*' In frustration, he grabbed her arm tight. 'Where did the rest go?

Did he spill it? Did he give it to someone?'

Eve made a tossing motion of her head that infuriated him further.

'Eve, you—'

She stepped away. 'I've got to go.'

'I don't want you to.' He passed his arm round her waist, and held her face, and tried to kiss her, pressing his body to hers. For a second, she responded, despite herself. There was such oblivion in him: blindness to the rest of the world. She took strength from him. He was never tired. It was never over. It just grew and doubled and bloomed, a mad vine suffocating all else in its path.

At last, she pulled back from him.

'He's not . . . safe,' Jon said. She saw, with a sinking sensation in the pit of her stomach, that he was completely serious.

'Oh Christ!'

Jon's face reddened. 'Of course he isn't! What about him and you the other day? Don't tell me you've forgotten it. Don't tell me you'll *ever* forget it. If that isn't dangerous, what is?'

She bit her lip. Then, in a low voice, she said, 'He won't do anything again. I know it.'

She looked at him levelly. She wondered if she would ever be able to communicate with him what changes she had gone through in the last week; felt a fleeting, fragile link to Hugh, who had known her for so many years and never, in all that time, changed at all. 'You're jealous,' she murmured. 'That's all it boils down to.'

'Jealous!'

'Jealous of this lonely, stupid man. He's no threat to you. Leave him alone.'

Jon had flushed a deep and angry red. 'I've a good reason to be jealous,' he cried. 'Hugh this. Hugh that. Protecting him, excusing him things. He comes in between us, and I don't want anyone between us, not when . . .'

His hand had worked, lingeringly, then more forcefully, between her legs. She closed her thighs, he prised them open, his fingers searching, finding . .

'Let me,' he whispered.

'For God's sake. For *God's* sake—'

'Let me. Let me—'

'Jesus!'

She backed off from him, breathing hard, pulling her clothes down. 'Will you let me alone!'

'But I—'

She slammed her hand to her forehead, turned it to a fist. 'What *you* want, what *you* want,' she said, trembling. 'You and *him*. You and them all. It's all what *you* want – nothing to do with me.' She turned away and stood facing the window. She was actually shaking.

'I only want to help you.'

It forced a laugh. 'Help me! Oh Christ, yes. Help me. You all want to help me, don't you? You and Hugh both. I wish you would just leave me alone.'

'You don't mean that.'

She swung round to him. 'Yes I do. I want to be just ... *left* ... *alone*.' She spread her hands, helpless. 'My father died yesterday. Can't you just understand that? Can't you appreciate what that means? *My – father – is – dead*. I find out he's a liar and a ... a ... almost a bloody *murderer*, for God's sake.' She almost bent over double, as if this memory of the letters would never leave her, and had the power to crucify her, agonise her.

Jon was standing perfectly still. In the silence, he gazed at her with a mixed expression. Grief and anger. Offended.

She hoisted her bag across her shoulder, shaking her head.

'He's something to do with it,' Jon murmured, stubbornly. 'I know it. I can see it in him. What about the way he looked when the boy came down—'

'No! It's a fantasy.'

'It's no bloody wilder than that room.'

'That room.' She gave a great sigh. 'When you're forty and had your griefs, maybe you'll look at Hugh Scott differently.'

'I'll never look at him differently.'

'All right. If you say so.' She started for the door.

'I won't.'

'All right.'

'He did something with your father. To get him out of the way, to have *you*.'

'Jon, that's rubbish. Utter rubbish.'

'No. I'll prove it.'

'You can't prove it because it didn't happen.'

At the last chance, he stood between her and the door, where her hand rested on the lock. She gazed at him sadly.

'I'll prove it.'

She opened the door.

On the way down the stairs, she heard the door open again. She thought he was going to repeat that phrase – waited for it as she stepped down, almost at the street.

Or, perhaps, call her back. She might even have gone.

Just before she stepped into the street, she thought, *I wonder if he's right*. Absurd, because he could not be right. You read about such things, but they happened to other people; to people who, when the thing was investigated, probably had a long history of mental illness, or were well known for making threats. She and Hugh Scott were not like that. Even this issue of the marriage was nothing more than a passing phase: something that Hugh had become focused on, something he clung to. It was like the painters, the books. His interest would wane and alter. As for the room in his house . . .

She suddenly saw herself, reflected in a shop window opposite, caught in a framework of small, rectangular panes. Her face had a deeply preoccupied expression, twin frown lines deep between her eyes.

You look so tired, she told herself.

And that was all it was. Stress, exhaustion, worry. Seeing things that were not there. Worrying needlessly.

She fought down a need to run back up the stairs, throw herself into Jon's arms and go to bed with him – a panacea against all ills, a shield against the future, a curtain drawn between themselves and the outside world. She realised that she had been hiding behind Jon perhaps ever since her father had disappeared; and knew that she could not climb the steps either to use him like that again, or to renew the argument about Hugh.

She sighed, the force of it shaking her body.

And, feeling ill, feeling old, she walked out into the sunlight.

Twenty

Jon sat on the harbour wall, watching a boat bring in a catch of crab.

It was eight o'clock at night. The pubs were beginning to fill, and couples and families passed along behind him, remarking on the boats, on the water. He sat with his legs swinging, his hands drooping between his knees, thinking of Eve.

When he thought of them at all – Eve, Hugh, himself – he thought of stepping into a dark room, where at any moment he could fall. It was like that now. Half in and half out of darkness, feeling the way; certain that, at any time, his foot would step into air and he would topple over, losing his balance.

'Take 'em up,' called the man in the boat beneath him.

The bucket of crab came swinging through air, and landed six feet away from him.

On the top of the bucket, the catch danced clumsily across each other, searching for a way out. Their pincers waved as they knocked blindly against their neighbours like drunks at a ball. Some got to the side and wobbled on the plastic rim, feeling for purchase. Looking down at them, Jon wondered what the ones on the bottom of the bucket felt like. Poor devils... they were probably already dead. Were there any on the bottom, crawling, as this one nearest him was, upwards, past the dead bodies of others, to get out?

Poor blind devils.

He had seen a pit like that once, at a manor house in Kent. You went along a long underground tunnel to a kind of dungeon, about twenty feet square, cut into chalk. The inner room of the pit was dark grey; there were no windows, and the world had receded down the tunnel into a tiny loop of green. Turning into the heart of this prison, there was a niche in the solid rock. The lady of the family, five hundred years before, had been taken to this room and walled alive into the niche. For adultery.

He had been about fourteen when he'd seen it. He had thought it was very funny. He and a friend had got thrown out for making choking noises while the guide was trying to speak.

It didn't seem so funny now.

Now he felt *he* was being pulled into some dark cell, some drunken, formless dance. *He* would be endlessly circling between Eve and Hugh, fumbling to find a solution, a better way before they became sealed in the dark together.

He had to free her of Hugh.

'Can y'shift?' asked a voice.

It was the fishermen: they were standing, breathing heavily, hands on hips, waiting to get past him. Twelve buckets of crab writhed around them.

'Sorry,' he said. He got up, shoved his hands in his pockets and started to walk.

The trouble was, he did not know her well enough. Eve must think that was important; she thought that the years she had known Hugh counted for more. More than their last days. Because it was only days that they had been together, it counted less than Hugh Scott. Hugh was to be trusted, or at least given the benefit of the doubt, because of time. Just the passage of time. Perhaps she was afraid of being caught – being walled in – too.

It wasn't fair. Unconsciously, as he walked, he pulled a face of the utmost frustration. He couldn't give her years. He couldn't give her time: he had none. No currency to barter with. In the scales dominated by days and months and years, Hugh weighed heavy; Jon weighed nothing at all. She had to trust him some other way.

And he only knew one . . .

Yesterday, they had come close – when she looked in his face – to the heart, the centre. He wanted to find the centre and catch her there. Yet he touched her, and she slipped through: always this draining and slipping away. It was a shield; *that* much he understood. A shield not of instinct, but of habit. And he wanted to tear down the shield, to wake her, like the prince in the story, with his kisses; wake her to dances, wake her to run. Wake her to him, him, him. She had been shut away so long, she dared not look past the bars.

His love seemed very small at that moment. Powerless, and futile. It was just a fiction, after all, the prince with a kiss; his kisses had failed to wake Eve, failed to lift her and help her. She was turning, slowly, back to the house, back to Hugh, slipping back under the invisible bounds of his influence.

He did not know what to do. She was vanishing, and he didn't know how to go forward, what else to give her, what else to say to her, how to deflect her. He wanted to *free* her: that was the one large, coherent, definite thought in his head. He couldn't bear to stand by and watch Eve deciding that she wanted to stay, living life as she always had, dependent on Hugh, living in the same house, folding in on herself, reducing her world by choice and not because of her father. It made him feel claustrophobic, breathless. He couldn't be a spectator while Eve took the line of least resistance for the rest of her life, when he knew that what she wanted was so much more.

She wanted to travel; she wanted to go back and see Italy, and France. She had even told him, during one of their long dark-hours conversations, that she would like to live abroad for a while. When she talked of leaving here, or of painting, or of music, he saw a transformation come over her face: her eyes lit up, her face became animated, he could see the person that he thought of as the real Eve leaping out of the expression, out of the sentences. As she spoke, he was already ahead of her, paving the way, running with her into the future, leaving the empty fields and Hugh's bleak track far behind.

But if she would not even believe what he said about Hugh; if she wouldn't even listen, or admit the smallest grain of doubt about him...

He looked back at the buckets on the quay being loaded into a lorry. Light flashed on the evening water: the tide was ebbing unseen under the bridge, under the passing feet, pulling backwards into the sea.

He frowned and turned away.

He turned into the busy back streets, and headed for the first pub he saw.

He wanted a drink. He wanted *several* drinks.

At the Steamship, he met a girl. She was on holiday. She came from Wales.

He bought her a drink, and she bought him one. There was a band playing recycled classics from the sixties. The girl was very small, very round-faced. She wore black and shouted at him over the music. She had one earring: a savage-looking spike of copper which glittered and rolled in her dark hair as she talked. In the silences, she asked him about football and he asked her name. It was Melanie.

'You can call me Melly. Or Mel,' she said.

They went on to another pub.

When they came out, it was nearly twelve, and she wanted to look at the sea. Going along the narrow street, he was conscious that they were weaving, falling off the kerb. They began to laugh, clutching each other for support. Above them, in the cloudless sky, a full moon hung directly ahead. They staggered drunkenly through the slices of shadows, through a calm night as warm as the tropics, following the scent of salt.

On the promenade, they stopped at the unicorn. It was a Victorian statue, depicting the town coat of arms. A unicorn holding up a shield, with a gold wreath around its neck. He sat her down on the step, under the unicorn hooves – outlined in silver in the moonlight – and kissed her. She kissed him back enthusiastically, dragging him down next to her.

'Oh!' called someone, over the road. 'Give the poor cow some air!'

She laughed. 'You aren't half nice,' she said.

They went down on to the beach.

The tide was in: the broad, white sweep of the beach rolled away as far as he could see. The waves made a faint sound somewhere below them; an exhausted, half-hearted stroke at the shore.

They sat down, in dry and silky sand, behind a burger cabin. It was white, with huge signs painted on it. A menu ran down the wall, roof to sand. 'Sausage and Chips, Sausage and Onions, Sausage and Egg, Egg and Chips, Egg and Beans, Beans and Chips . . .' Plates of steaming food were painted on the hoarding behind his shoulders.

She unbuckled his belt, dextrous. Quick.

'Aren't you nice,' she said. 'Warm.'

He gazed at her dark face. Moonlight.

'I've got an uncle somewhere in Wales,' he said, slurring the 'S'. 'He's my Dad's brother. He lives somewhere off that road. The Heads of the Valley.' And he copied the way she spoke, with her musical lilt. He started to laugh and she shushed him.

'Someone'll hear.'

She was lifting up her skirt.

'Merthyr Tydfil,' he said. 'Aberdare. Mountain Ash. Abercynon, Pontypridd . . . ouch!'

'Sssssh, ssssh.'

He leaned his head against the lurid plates.

'Beddau, Llantrisant, Radyr . . .'

'Barry.'

'No, Jon.'

She began to laugh, between gasps. 'No, you doombrain! That's – oh – that's where I live.'

'Cardiff girl.'

'I got to stop. My legs hurt.'

'Lie down.'

'You are nice . . . you are . . . nice . . .'

242

It was all over in a rush. She gave a little drone of disappointment, and he obliged with his hand. He was told he was nice, several times over. And over. His arm ached.

Afterwards, she got up, stumbled, stepped out of her knickers and went behind the hoarding.

'I gotta wee,' she whispered.

He got up and walked away, down towards the sea.

Drowning and dying, drowning and dying.

The waves slopped around him, whispering slavishly, like voices in sleep, the murmured remains of conversations, the ashes and dregs of dreams. Out on the horizon, a boat with a small blue light was tacking east.

He heard her, behind him, calling.

The water came in over his shoes, and soaked him. He made no effort to get out of the way. He simply watched his shoes fill with water.

He would go away tomorrow. He would go home.

Eve was already turning away, blocking him out; he was not fool enough to wait until she ignored him completely. Maybe – and here his heart sank like a stone – maybe she would even marry Hugh. After all, the man pestered her enough. He did a lot for her; made himself indispensable. And he had a lot of money, and had known her a long time. All those things counted, it seemed. Time and money, those precious commodities. Maybe that was why Eve turned from him even in his arms, closing her eyes. Maybe it was because he was not the right person. He was not Hugh . . .

He stood looking down at his shoes, feeling so miserable that he was sick, the world rolling and tilting. It didn't matter. *It didn't.* He would get himself a girl like Mel. An uncomplicated, ordinary girl, who didn't obsess him, live in his heart, dominate his every waking moment. He'd go away, go home.

He looked at the flat-calm sea, and felt he was in a world of complete emptiness. A pitching, echoing world that only belonged to the dead.

And, for the first time since childhood, he began to cry.

Twenty-one

Three days later, the phone rang in Eve's house. She looked at it dully, waited, and then went to pick it up.

'Eve? It's Sarah.'

'Hello.'

'You sound rough.'

'Thanks.'

'Want me to come over?'

Eve sighed. She was sitting upstairs in her bedroom, still not dressed although it was nearly midday. The cars outside had gone, passed on to someone else's desperation.

'Eve?'

'You can if you like.'

'Has Matthew been?'

'Yes. He brought me some flowers, from the school. I told him, maybe next week . . .'

'They don't expect you, I know they don't.'

'The children will miss me.'

At the other end of the line, Sarah frowned. There was nothing left in Eve's voice.

'Of course, if you're not alone . . .'

She heard Eve laugh. Low-pitched. 'I'm alone.'

'I thought . . . Jon . . .'

'Jon's left.'

'Left? Left where?'

'Left *here*. Gone home. Kent.'

Sarah snapped to attention, kicking away the cat that was trying to wind around her legs. She stopped mid-way through lighting a cigarette. 'How long for?'

There was a long pause. 'I don't know.'

'Well, what did he say?'

'Nothing. I rang last night. His landlady said he'd gone to Kent. Left a note; it didn't say anything about coming back.'

'Oh, Christ.'

Another silence. In her room, Eve lay back, her arm thrown across her face. 'Listen,' she said. 'There's no need to pretend sympathy. I know what you thought. You said he'd do this.'

'Well it isn't as if I *wanted* to be right, darling. Still, just leaving. At a time like this!'

'I suppose it was my fault. I told him he was wrong about something. I suppose we argued.'

'What about?'

'Hugh.'

'Ah.'

'Not . . . not quite like that. It's too complicated.'

'Did you tell him about last Sunday?'

'Yes.'

'What did he want you to do?'

'Tell the police.'

'And you won't.'

'It's just not that simple.'

'Eve . . .' A pause, considering. 'Maybe he couldn't handle that. He *is* only very young and inexperienced, darling. He might take that as some kind of personal insult, that you wouldn't report Hugh.'

'I know, I know. But it isn't even that,' Eve said wearily. 'Jon's got this bee in his bonnet. It sounds ridiculous, but . . . Jon thinks Hugh had something to do with Dad's death.'

Another, fractional, pause. When Sarah replied, her voice was low-pitched, intrigued. '*Does* he, now? Interesting . . .'

Eve stared at the phone, then replaced it to her ear. 'You mean you think there's something in it?'

'Eve, Hugh Scott is certifiably peculiar. You've lived too long in that man's shadow to see it, petal. I mean, it's possible. What's the old saying? "When you have eliminated the impossible, whatever remains, however improbable, must be the truth"? Who said that, anyway? Was it Sherlock Holmes, or John Major?' And Sarah laughed rather forcedly. She got no response from Eve.

'Look, Eve . . . I'm going to jump in the car. Let's go out to lunch. I'll treat you to Marcello's in Blandwith. You can have the duck. It's fabulous. We can go shopping in Temple's Arcade and buy something outrageous and useless and expensive.'

'I don't know . . .'

'Well, I *do*. You can thank Duncan's credit card for its generosity later. Get moving.'

Eve's voice was weak, her laugh throaty. 'OK.'

'We can eat a box of chocs on the way. And I'll bring some Kleenex. Better safe than sorry. Bastard men. Don't you know his home address in Kent?'

'No. It's not such a big deal, Sarah. It's just . . .' Eve looked around herself. Tears filled her eyes, choked her. She had to swallow them down, squeeze them away. 'Oh, Sarah . . . It's so quiet in here without Dad.'

Sarah heard the tears. '*Two* boxes of chocs, *four* Kleenex. Hold on, I'm getting in the car.'

She didn't even wait for Eve's subdued reply. She put down the phone and, as the cat came back for more, she hissed at it, stubbing out her cigarette savagely on a Chinese plate at the same time.

'You bloody men!' she said. 'It's all take, take, take.'

It was only when – as an inspired afterthought – she took the three-quarter full bottle of Bell's from the cabinet, she heard Eve's small whisper again. She leaned her forehead on the window frame, sighing.

'Shit,' she said. 'It never rains. Shit.'

Twenty-two

It was the beginning of July.

A week had passed since Bill Ridges had been found in the woods above Hugh Scott's house. The post-mortem had been done; now they waited for the results.

In the farm and the house on the rolling down above the sea, nothing had been heard of Jon for eight days.

The weather was fine and warm, and they were due to bring the harvest in on the winter barley. It was Tuesday, and Eve was getting ready for her second day back at the school. As she stood at the window, a cup of coffee in one hand and a piece of toast in the other, she saw a van draw up at the gate. A man got out, holding a piece of paper in his hand, looking at the house nameplate on the roadside. She went out to him.

'Can I help?'

'Is it Miss Ridges?'

'Yes, that's right.'

'This Upper Towe House?'

'Yes . . . are you from Shaftesbury's?'

He opened the tailgate of the van. 'Yup. Where's best?'

She considered. 'Oh, out near the road? Just there? It'll get lost in the hedgerow if it's nearer the house.'

'Right you are.'

He set to work; she went inside. She gathered up her books, bag, and hat. She had taken to sitting outside, near the children, at lunchtime, in the shade of the Victorian elm – a last survivor – that was at the edge of the playing field. These last few days she had felt like an invalid recovering from some long, debilitating illness, a kind of fever. Now, moving about the kitchen, she sang softly to herself. In the hall, as she passed through the semi-darkness and opened the back door, she passed an enormous pile of bagged clothes, books, pictures, even little pieces of furniture her father had chosen and loved. A discarded life. Nothing in the debris moved her, touched her, not even his gloves, worn at the palms. Not even his records or his music. She had turned her face from him. She exterminated even his ghost. As far as she was concerned, she had lived all her remembered life with a lie.

When she came back out and got in the car, she reversed past the man from Shaftesbury's. He waved as she drew out into the road.

She switched on the radio, tuned to the early morning news. Life teemed out of the black plastic panel: wars in the Far East, riots in South America, hardships and injustice at home. She listened with only half an ear, drifting.

In the driving mirror, as she went along, she could see the red and blue flag of the 'For Sale' sign for almost a mile, until she dropped down the hill towards the village.

As she came in through the door of the school, the first children were already there. In the corridor, a small boy stood, knuckling his eyes. Others stood back at the door of the cloakrooms, waiting to see what would happen.

'Adam, what's the matter?' She put her bags in the staff room and came back out.

'Daniel Sherriff's got me rugby ball.'

'Oh dear.' She took his hand, looked down. 'What's this?'

'I fell down.'

His palms were badly scraped. Eve waved the silent spectators away; they ran out into the playground, squealing at each other. Adam stood, his head hanging, glaring at his feet, his face flushed. She took him to the sink in the Boys' toilets, where, after some coaxing, he washed his hands and soaped them.

'We'll go and find your ball,' she told him.

He looked up at her, drying his fingers on the towel. He was a diligent, careful child; his painting and writing lately had become almost excruciatingly precise, a fact which had not escaped Eve.

'He said my Dad wasn't in Australia.'

'Who did?'

'Daniel.'

'Oh. Did he?'

'Yes. He said my Dad . . .' He stopped.

She looked down at him, feeling sorry. Adam's father had left him, his mother and a younger brother six months before. His mother had told Adam, rather stupidly, that Daddy had gone to the other side of the world, whereas the whole village knew – excepting Adam – that Dad had only moved ten miles away with a girl half his age. Evidently Daniel Sherriff had chosen this morning to share this information with Adam.

She took him out into the corridor, and wondered for a moment what she should do with him. Today was a busy day; she had five sets of parents coming in for reports. The head himself had offered to do this work for her, but she had spent the last weekend gladly preoccupied, for most of her waking hours, with preparation. It had provided a much-needed and welcome anaesthetic; working at her desk from nine till nine left very little time – in theory – for thinking about Jon or Bill. She had told Hugh that she would be working on the end of term reports, and must not be disturbed.

Of course, that didn't stop him from ringing every day to see how she was. She kept the conversations as short as possible, resisting an impulse to wipe the phone receiver after she had spoken to him. For a reason which was hard to understand, his attack, which had seemed vaguely excusable at the time, now haunted her. The spectre of his face, his hands, her isolation on the top of the hill, loomed in her dreams. The thought occurred to her, over and over, *what if . . . what if?* What if she had not screamed? What if he had taken no notice of that scream? What if he had succeeded? And worse still, what if the violence had been worse?

She woke from such dreams and daydreams with a cold prickling of doubt. Perhaps Sarah and Jon were right. Perhaps her opinion of Hugh was wrong. Perhaps, perhaps . . . But she would shy away from the ultimate conclusion. Hugh might be unpleasant; even disturbed. But Hugh could *not* have murdered her father. She said it to herself, as she performed some ordinary, household task, as if the repetition would make her convinced of it. *Hugh was not capable of murdering her father.* She tried to rule him out of her mind: told herself that the only way to get through this was not to think about him at all.

And she had succeeded, until last night.

Last night, when Hugh had come to visit her.

Her stream of thought was interrupted by the pressure of Adam's still-clammy hand in hers. He stared up at her, confidently expecting her to come up with some magic formula to explain the world: the theft of his possessions, the theft of his father. She wanted to kneel down next to him and tell him she had no answers, no magic at all. She wanted to say, *Adults are fools, Adam. We are full of bloody secrets . . .*

Instead, however, she gave him a smile, and drew him closer by passing her hand across his shoulders. He allowed himself to be pressed, momentarily, against her.

'Listen,' she said. 'I've got some biscuits in my bag. Do you like those cherry and sultana ones?'

'Yes,' he said.
'What if we go in the staff room and have one before the bell goes?'
His face lit up.
'Right,' she said. 'Come on.'

If Bill's death was a form of release for his daughter, it was not quite the same for the police.

The case was passed to police headquarters, which were situated in the large seaside town about thirty miles away. There it lingered on a desk: not forgotten, not even closed. But hovering somewhere between the two, waiting to drop, come the post-mortem report, into an archive. The statement of Hugh Scott lay silently alongside Eve's and Jonathan Davies'; alongside the GP's letter, the coroner's office report, a fretwork of mere hieroglyphics on a page. Bill's body lay in cold storage, his face slackened and assuming the smiling rictus of death. The bones showed clearly in the face, as if the skin had been stretched over a sculpted approximation of life. Behind the eyelids, the eyes shrank. It was a bundle of matter, waiting – like his clothes, his books, his accumulated mementoes, his passions and resentments and curiosities – to be burned or buried.

No one had cared much for him in life, and no one cared much for him in death, it seemed.

The statements did not add a great deal to the facts of his death. Both Hugh Scott and Eve Ridges explained about his age, his illness, his disappearance. They detailed the searches for him. Eve's explanation talked of his wandering and aggression, his pitiable inability to recall routine things: how to wash, how to wear clothes. Not knowing the month, or the purpose of mundane household objects, like taps, or the sequence of growth in the garden and the fields around them, so that every day presented a baffling picture, totally divorced from the last day, of a landscape with no recognisable features. A desert into which he had, inexplicably, been plunged. Her identification of her father, the file noted, had been particularly cool, without scenes or tears.

Scott's statement went into enormous detail about his searches. He had a name for every field and dip of land: names that showed on no maps. His pride in his land – his small kingdom – breathed out of the recorded lines. Capricorn, Welt, Upper Groves, Witchams', Helpmeet, Flash. He explained that he and Eve Ridges were engaged to be married. There was no such comment on Eve's report. Hugh said, recounting the last night, that the old man liked to play cards, beating his opponent by fair means or foul. He recalled the cheating, the obscenities.

And the helpless body in the underground mortuary offered nothing: neither refusal nor defence. The fingers of one hand were retracted into a grasping gesture. Then they eased and extended. Alone in the dark.

It was only Jon's statement that held any interest at all.

He looked, and sounded . . . if not guilty . . . Just *something*.

The detective in charge of the case had spoken to the local sergeant and constable, those who knew the players in this drama. Of the three, it was the boy who was the outsider. The boy who . . .

Back home, the constable – on his night off – was thinking the same thing. A father of a young child, whose task it was to look after while his wife worked evenings in the supermarket, he sat this night, the bottle of milk jammed into the formless mouth of his son, staring down at the baby without even seeing it. Small fingers closed on his own, and an unconscious smile came to his face.

He was thinking, abstractedly, of love. Needing love like this. And that was when it came to him – the expression on the faces of the men on that lonely stretch of land.

As Bill Ridges' body had been brought down the track, both Hugh Scott and Jonathan Davies turned to look at the woman . . .

To look at Eve, who saw neither of them, only the jolting motion of the box in the back of the undertaker's car.

And both of their faces, looking at the woman, wore the same unmistakable expression.

When Jon got back to his flat, it was nearly dark.

He threw his bag into the room, and stood at the doorway, his head resting on his arm in an attitude of weariness. The room bloomed back at him: empty space. Blue evening light.

He had come down on the coach from Kent that day, making a journey he had sworn never to repeat. Never to see the flat again – or the farm. Or Eve. Or . . . *him*.

When obscuring the dilemma with women and drink had not worked a week ago, he had taken the London bus, to see his mother. As it had turned out, however, she had not been at home. Some other end of the country, their neighbour had said, handing over the door key they had been given. Scotland, they had added, making it a question. With the man she'd met two months ago.

The man was as much a mystery to Jon as any other aspect of his mother's life, and, frankly, he did not care who he was. In fact it had been almost blissful, walking into the house and throwing open the doors to the bare patch of garden. The covert silence of the house was good. The mismatched chairs and the formica table in the kitchen, and her collection of porcelain cats, all dusty.

Theirs was a thirties semi in a row of thirties semis, in a street of a hundred other houses just the same. The street stopped at a junction where a dual carriageway to London roared through. Today the sun beat on the back garden, and the traffic was only a distant rolling whisper. Jon had dragged a chair to the grass and sat in the sun, listening to the other sounds: children screaming down the street, a radio, the noise of a drill in someone's back shed.

He'd slept that night under a sheet culled from a creased pile in the cupboard. Wakeful and empty, the memory of Eve's hand had touched him. Desire had unexpectedly shot through him. His body felt rapidly on fire, and he had clamped his hand to his forehead, telling himself to shut her out ...

In desperation, he had transferred the sleepless night-time attention to the other ghost haunting the lonely bedroom. He thought of Hugh, and the paper carton and glass jar he still had in the bag downstairs. Jigsaw-puzzle pieces that did not match. Over and over again in his mind he had put them beside each other. Hugh's expression as the boy came sprinting towards him; the jar; the smell of sweet fruit ...

On his second day home, he'd rung college and left a message for his personal tutor.

Then, in the lending library in the High Street, on an impulse, he had gone into the reference section and looked up Chloral hydrate in a dictionary. In the deserted room, he had read:

Chloral, Chem. A thin colourless oily liquid with a pungent odour, obtained by the action of chlorine upon alcohol. Chloral hydrate ($CCl_3CH(OH)_2$) a white crystalline substance resulting from the combination of water and chloral, and much used as an hypnotic and anaesthetic ...

Imagine drinking something like that. He supposed you drank it rather than injected it. An oily liquid with a pungent odour.

Revolting, revolting. Perhaps if you put it in a drink of something else, he considered. Orange juice? Coffee ...

Push push push. No fitting into place. Jigsaw pieces.

Out in the street, he had walked without really seeing. The empty packet in an unlocked cabinet, a cabinet always kept locked, out of place from the neat rows, as though hurriedly – even excitedly – replaced. No, no. What would he use it for? Was it to do with Bill? It *must* be to do with Bill. Think of his face when that lad came down. It *must* be Bill. Had he seen Bill up there, maybe nearly dead, maybe sick, maybe drunk, maybe reeling, throwing up, and just turned and left him there and told no one? Perhaps Hugh had realised that Bill had taken the drug, and then gone looking, knowing he must be close. But why would Bill want it? From what Eve had said, Bill was angry, Bill was aggressive and violent, but he was not suicidal. Murderous, maybe . . .

Jon had cast his mind back to the morning Bill had been found. Hugh had had to ask if the old man was dead, so he did not know for sure. But he knew *something*. Bill had been drinking. A gin bottle in the ashes of the fire, the clothes stinking of drink. The green-bile acid sick on the neck, the face, the pine-strewn soil. A green-bile sick with flecks of yellow-white. Yellow-white patches. Hugh's face, turning white.

He'd stopped, pressing his fingers to his temple in the classic pose of the defeated, the puzzled.

And the jar on the path, between the house and the cottages. The morning that the rep had come with the dog, Hugh had looked much the same, as the dog ran round the cottages with that mad bouncing terrier skip, nose to ground. Round the cottages with nose to the ground, following a thousand scents. Round where the jar was on the path. To the back of the cottages.

He had bumped into a woman coming out of a shop, apologised, nearly walked into a litter bin, and had stopped, staring at the ground.

Laying poison for rats. That's what he had said. But there had been no traps. No carcasses cleared away. Hugh usually made a great thing of exactly where poison was laid, drilling it in that you had to be careful, lest the animals, like the horses . . . But there hadn't been any traps.

Only the flattened grass and weeds round the back of the cottages where someone must have walked. Where Hugh had walked. But why? Jon knew, as the police did not, that the grass there – even if they'd *looked* at the grass, which they wouldn't, why should they? – Jon knew that the grass and weeds there grew high, only a little pencil-thin path through them to each shed. On one of the days that he had been there with Latham Hugh had complained that the weeds grew like triffids, those science-fiction plants, the nearest he came to a joke. And yet last week at the first cottage they had been flat, walked over, not through. The only reason he would go up the back of the cottages was . . . to get wire from the sheds, to lay traps, to . . . what else? What else possibly . . . ?

They hadn't used any wire.

They hadn't done any jobs in that whole week. Hugh was too busy chasing Eve, ringing Eve, going for her to the school. Probably sitting in that fucking room... Christ, how could she take it so bloody calmly? That fucking horrible *shrine* up there, that church with her things in it. And the red phone.

She took it so calmly. Resigned, hypnotised.

Suddenly shaken, he had looked up from the pavement. Hypnotised. Chloral hydrate. He wouldn't – he wouldn't give the stuff some way to Eve? He hadn't been using it on Eve?

The tutor had rung him back that night. They'd fixed a date for the next morning. The last of Jon's debts had been cleared only the month before. Term began in October. They had spoken of the college, and Jon had conjured up its red brick walls and the lecture rooms and the refectories, and tried to place himself in them. It seemed dreamlike, impossible. Whenever he thought of his hand turning the page of a book, he thought of Eve's fingers over his fingers, the small, long-fingered hand with its deeply etched lines.

Jon had gone to bed alone, hungry because he had forgotten, after a sandwich in a pub, to buy anything to eat that night, and he thought of Eve, only Eve.

'Eve,' said Hugh. 'Scott.'

The man in the travel agency wrote it painstakingly down.

'My wife,' said Hugh.

He looked around at the posters, a blissful expression on his face, registering the date, 6 July, on the company sign on the back wall.

'Right,' said the assistant. 'Let me just read that back to you.'

Hugh caught the eye of a girl at a neighbouring desk. Wearing the company regulation suit, she was tapping furiously into a computer. She gave him the company regulation smile in response to his stare.

We'll be going in that computer, Hugh thought. He and Eve. We'll be booked in that computer.

He looked back to his own desk, where the man was politely waiting. 'Sorry.'

'That's OK. Let me read this back to you.'

Hugh settled back in his seat.

'Balcony, view, shower, WC, bath, full board, two persons, departing Gatwick, 5 September, returning Gatwick, 19 September.'

Hugh leaned forward, grinning. 'Wish I could stay longer.'

'Yes, indeed. It's a lovely place. Stunning.'

Hugh's voice dropped to a confiding whisper. 'My wife. A surprise.'

'Really? How nice. Lucky lady.'

Hugh's face lit up.

'Now, if you'll sign here, and here . . .'

The girl at the next desk, her computer input finished, was looking across at Hugh, her chin cupped in her hand. Hugh blushed. 'It's special,' he repeated. 'Special surprise.'

When Hugh finished writing, the girl said with a sigh, 'I wish someone would give *me* a surprise like that.'

It had been in the dead of night four days later that the answer had come to Jon. They say that if you stand too close to something, you never see it. Don't see the screaming obvious.

His eyes had snapped open. He had not really been asleep. For nights he had lain awake, staring at shadows, sleeping only fitfully in the early hours of the morning. And the answer had come to him at such a time. Two o'clock, and just drifting into the borders of a dream. He had lain rigid in the bed: the utter simplicity, the obviousness of the solution had taken his breath away.

How could he have been so stupid?

The cottages that Hugh didn't want the dog to run through. No traps, no rats. The flattened weeds. The glass jar on the path. And Hugh had had the *ladder* from the barn, he knew. Never given that a second thought. Let it drift by. Stupid.

Bill did not need a ladder. Bill did not take the drug from the cabinet. Only Hugh held the keys to the cabinet in the tack room. The ladder, the cottage, the jar, the weeds, the packet, the *white flecks* in Bill's drenched, dreadful pool of sick. A lot of *white* and oily whitish green.

White crystalline powder.

Jon had sat up on the single bed and stared, fists clenched, at the blank wall ahead of him. It was so clear. So clear. The ladder that lay in the middle of the flattened weeds at the back of the cottages.

Not Eve, but Bill.

Hugh had given the chloral hydrate to Bill.

Bill Ridges, in the *cellar* of one of the cottages.

Twenty-three

There were three men, besides Hugh, at the farm that afternoon. It was 7 July, the day after Hugh had booked his honeymoon.

Hugh was at the open end of the barn: stone pillars, with mushroom stones at their base to deter mice, supported a corrugated iron roof. The track ran up directly behind, and the team bringing the combine out from under its winter cover were having trouble negotiating the incline. They wedged the machine back; the driver, high up in the cab, watching with his hand on the gears. As it came out into the sun, it looked like some monster – some red beast – coming out of hibernation. It nicked the fence as they turned it. Smoke billowed across the track.

In the next shed, Hugh was supervising the towing of the header. The reel, lifted up as it was pulled forward, revealed the rows of tines: a medieval rack of spikes. Behind the spikes, the fingers splayed out as one long vicious hand, armed with the flat blades.

'Down right,' shouted Hugh.

The driver of the trailer leaned out of the window. 'Make up yer mind, then!'

'Down right. Bloody blind or what!'

The driver's head disappeared. He could be heard fluently running through his catalogue of the female body as the gears crunched. Hugh's idea of a serviceable trailer was a 1935 truck his father had bought from a debtor. The seats were cracked and the cracks stitched with cable twine. The driver's door bore a florid insignia of some long-dead feed supplies' firm.

The machinery was faultlessly clean: scrupulously oiled and wiped. Every inch. Every blade, every door, every switch, every inch of the table, the auger. Even the floor of the cab. The windscreen of the combine, the lights, the windscreen wipers. Hugh had had a radio and a CB installed. Sitting in the cab of the combine he became a king, the roaring red monster slaving at his back. The last of the harvest had been brought in at night last year: a humid night heavy with the threat of rain. Tractors toiling through the field, pierced by columns of lights from the combine, towards the drier.

King in a dark world.

'How'm I now?'

Hugh waved his arms. 'You got six feet. More.'

The ancient truck grated and shuddered; the trailer with its barbaric reel of blades heaved over into the hedge. Dandelion seeds spumed into the air, dust and torn leaves followed. Hugh turned away in disgust.

Coming at a brisk pace up the path was Jonathan Davies. The older man stared at the younger, sickness and fury rising in his throat. The lad stared back.

'Morning, Hugh.'

'Where've you sprung from, then? Thought we'd seen last of you.'

Jon smiled, looking about. 'Getting it going?'

'Winter barley. Should have got to it fore now. Still, better late than never.'

Jon went on smiling, hands on hips. He was wearing a pair of patched jeans, a shirt, a pair of wellingtons. Hugh's curiosity got the better of him.

'Where you been hiding?'

'I haven't. I just went home for a bit.'

'You never told us.'

'I had to sort out the autumn . . . college. Had to see about registering. If it was all right.'

Hugh's face literally brightened, like cloud passing off the face of the sun. 'You going back to college?'

'I always was.'

'Sorted?'

'October.'

The older man stepped down the path. He raised his arm, beckoning the truck driver forward.

'When are you starting?' Jon asked.

Hugh grinned. 'Think this is a game?' he asked. 'All this mucking about? Now, boy. Right now.'

Jon followed in his wake. 'Need any help?'

Hugh turned and looked at him. 'I give your job to another lad. You can't go disappearing before harvest. I got to know I got a team.'

They stood watching each other for another moment. 'I thought it was understood,' Jon replied, softly. 'You said you wanted me for harvest. You said end July . . .'

'Weather doesn't wait for a date.'

'No, but you knew I was coming. I came back so as not to let you down.'

Hugh's expression did not alter one iota. 'You already did. Left no word. Can't be doing with that.'

'I didn't know.'

Jon could not say what he actually wanted to say: that he had come back for Eve. And to look in the cellars. And to . . . He glanced away from Hugh, so that the intention might not show in his face, his eyes. To nail the bastard's head to the block. The bastard who kept a cell of her shoes, her cards. Who rang her in the middle of the night. Walked to the house in the middle of the night.

He stopped himself from reaching out and screwing his finger hard into the other man's chest, and saying, *I know you. I know what you do.*

Instead, he looked resolutely at his feet.

'I'll go ask at Abbots', then. Got to have a bit of cash, you see. Rent.'

Hugh gave a little tight smile of triumph. 'You can try 'em.'

'They're starting this week?'

'Your guess is as good as mine.'

Jon shoved his hands in his pockets. 'How's Eve?' he asked.

'Moving.'

'Sorry?'

'House up for sale. Moving house.'

'Where to?'

The truck pulled level: Hugh opened the side door and got up into the cab. The driver, leaning across him, gave a salute sign to Jon. For a second, Hugh looked down at Jon, smiling broadly.

'She's back at work,' he said. He slammed the door in the lad's face, and then leaned out. 'Tell you what,' he said. 'I'll give you a ring if I want casual.' The truck pulled away.

Jon stood in the track and watched it, a curtain of dust rising up, almost obscuring him from view. Head down, he walked ahead of the lumbering combine into the yard.

Revulsion swarmed over him for the smug, weather-tanned face in the cab. Yet, as he got to the yard, he saw that the truck had stopped again, and Hugh was leaning out again, looking back.

'Get up on the header,' Hugh shouted. 'Give you a day's work for a start.'

Jon did not question the change of mind. He jumped up on the rack tow and steadied himself on the back of the truck, then leap-frogged into the trailer itself.

Inside the truck's cab, the driver squinted at Hugh. 'Taking him on?'

Hugh grinned. 'He'll do,' he said. He nodded at the wheel, to show they should go.

And, as they dipped towards the road, every spring in the stitched seats straining, every square inch of metal rattling, Hugh leaned back and gazed at the way ahead with perfect satisfaction.

No better way to show him, he thought.

No better way to show him. Rub his dirty little face in it. *That'll teach him.*

The truck got to the corner, and Hugh had to put his hand to his face so that the driver would not see that he was almost laughing.

'Where's she going?'

It was a good joke. Bloody good joke.

If the mucky little sod wanted to see Eve, he could see her. Why not? Last request, like. The last request of the condemned man. They did that with prisoners before they shot them, didn't they? Gave them a last request. All right, so this could be Jon Davies' last wish.

The perfect solution had come to Hugh in that thirty seconds between refusing him a job and offering him one. It was not enough that Jon said he was going back in October; he might change his mind about that. No, it was better to make quite *sure* that he could never bother either of them ever again.

And it was such a perfect death, too. Out in the open, and all above board, and no mess – not like Bill. Not a fiasco like that. A good clean death. Far more than the little bastard deserved for touching his Evie. He would be finished with; a loose end neatly tied. Scrubbed out, cleansed out of their lives. And the best thing of all was that he could say it was all an accident. He could wait until the perfect moment. Wait until the lad was least expecting it; let him work a day or so, feel safe. Then . . .

As for Eve . . . well, if they should meet, she could even tell him herself where she was moving to.

For it was almost arranged. Almost done. She was moving into the farm.

As Mrs Scott.

That morning, in the local police station, the constable stopped his sergeant in the corridor.

'You know that death. The old boy.'

'Ridges?'

'That's him. Did the post-mortem come through?'

'Doubt it. It's up at Poole.'

'Can we see it?'

'What for?'

The constable let a secretary go by; they watched her pass through the swing doors.

'I had a thought. Just a thought.'

The sergeant laughed. 'You want to watch yourself, lad. Do yourself an injury.'

'No, sarge. It's about the lad.'

The other man sighed. He put his hand on the constable's shoulder. 'You can ring them. Make their day, that would. Pestered by some young sprog out of the sticks. Make their day.'

He walked off, still laughing. Then, at the door, he shrugged and waved his hand. 'Go on, why don't you? I'd be interested in it myself . . . better than the crossword.' He began to open the door. 'Then you can tell me your thoughts, Simpson. Your innermost secret thoughts.'

At the school, Eve sat in the sustained bedlam of thirty-one six-year-olds changing for Music and Movement, and thought of Hugh.

He had come up last night, as she had been sitting in the garden reading. He had walked all the way from the farm, and for a moment in the twilight, she had not been able to place the regular sound of his footsteps coming along the stone track. She had lifted her head and listened, her heart beginning to beat slightly faster, the beginning of a tightening in her throat. Soon, his head had appeared above the hedge. He had obviously been thinking, looking at his feet, for he had not looked up, and had made merely for the driveway.

'Hello, Hugh.'

He'd given a small jump of surprise. 'Oh, you're there.'

'Yes. Just reading.'

'I was coming to see you.'

She had brought out another chair, unable to bear him standing, as usual, to attention. Last night, the evening had been fantastically beautiful, with a heat haze lying in the contours of the hills, a deep grey margin of sky, and a pink and soaring vault of space above it. The land, with its full green weight of wheat, had looked like a carpet stretching for miles. In the garden, birds had fought in the branches of the apple tree, and flown, bickering, across the grass. Hugh had sat hunched on the edge of his chair.

'Did you go into town?' she'd asked.

'Yes. I went to them all. But only Wemsley's was any good.'

They had been talking about the undertaker: Hugh had offered to make the first enquiries. It had been useless trying to tell him that she would do the thing herself, and he had said – which finally, grudgingly, convinced her – that people might recognise her from the paper, and she would have to go through it all again at any place she visited.

He had told her the prices and sizes and finishes of coffin; the cost of hiring the cars; the flowers; all the astronomical burden of disposing of flesh. He'd looked at her almost embarrassedly, chin tucked in. 'I hope you won't mind,' he'd said. 'I booked it all up. And paid for it.'

It had really taken her breath away. She had sat staring at him, her mouth open. Then she had started to laugh. 'You're not serious?'

'I hope you don't mind. I thought about it a lot. I picked the best one . . .'

'Hugh – you must be joking! The price of these things . . . I mean—'

'That's all right.'

'It's not all right! I can pay for it. It's my father. I *must* pay for it.'

He'd looked away, as if she had accepted him graciously. As if satisfied. 'I'll pay for it,' he had told her, with an air of complete finality. 'Don't say no more about it. Forget it now.'

Sitting here now, in the midst of discarded small clothes – socks, T-shirts, skirts, and sixty-two battered and thrown shoes – Eve shook her head. Even now she was bemused, trying to work out how she could tell him that she could not accept. It was as if he simply went deaf when she objected. She would have to go into town and see the undertaker herself.

A small hand tugged her arm. 'Miss Ridges . . .'

'Hello, Cheryl.'

'I cut my knee.'

'Where?'

'Here – look. Yesterday. I got a scab.'

'Oh, I see. That's not too bad. It'll get better.'

The small blonde-framed face stared up into hers. Perfect angelic ice-blue eyes.

'Miss Ridges, is it your Dad who's dead?'

'Yes. He is.'

'I saw his picture on "Five to Six".'

'Did you?'

'And your picture.'

'Yes, well . . .'

The little hand gripped hers with concern. 'Why do they put them in boxes?' the little girl asked. 'Why don't they just put them straight in the ground?'

Eve got up, clasped the inquisitive hand in her own and walked to the door. As they reached the hall, she stroked Cheryl's hair. 'I don't know why they do that,' she said, finally. And she ushered the girl into the waiting crowd.

It was a quarter-past four when Eve got home. Coming along the road, she had been shocked – why, she wasn't really sure, as she knew it would be happening – to see the centre field, the one before the wheat, being shorn by the combine. A tractor and trailer shadowed its lumbering progress; a second trailer was waiting at the road gate, shuddering, with its cone of grain.

As she passed, she thought for a second it was coming out and, swerving slightly and touching the horn, she only had time to glance into the cab.

She thought she saw Jon.

Her car flashed past them in an instant; she looked in the mirror. It wasn't possible even to see the faces behind the dusty glass.

As she came to her own gate, her heart was thudding against her chest and throat: a choking hammer.

He wouldn't come back . . . would he?

She had had a feeling, from that first day of absence, that he wouldn't come back, and the feeling had not been painful at all, only a low-grade hollowness into which this unexpected peace had come. Despite all her efforts otherwise, she woke thinking of him, and went to bed thinking of him, and his face often asserted itself over the sea of children's faces, over drawings in blood-red ink or paintings of stickmen holding the hands of stick-women . . . She knew she missed him. But it was all silence. Grieving, if this was grieving. Silence, for the first time in years. The void of rooms. Jon joined her father, a figure behind glass. Perhaps the pain would come later. She stood and considered him, a two-dimensional outline.

She drifted, and it was wonderful. Not even to try. Just the days dropping into each other.

Going in through the back door, she picked up a pile of morning post: an electricity bill, a couple of free offers, a confirming letter from the estate agent, and a letter in a handwritten envelope. She opened it. There was one sheet of white paper.

Eve,
Sorry but I had to get away to think. I saw about college, but I can't go to college or stay at home without seeing you. Will you ring me at the flat? It's important.

Jon

It was dated the day before, and postmarked from town. She folded the letter and put it in the pocket of her skirt.

Perhaps when it was over. The inquest. The funeral. The house... But a boy of nineteen would not wait that long. It was now, now, now. 'It's important.' To him...

The selfishness of men. Lovers and husbands. Hands over hands, marking their boundaries, asserting their wants.

Hugh and Jon, Hugh and Jon.

They wanted her to stand on the sideline, while they argued over what was theirs.

Suddenly, the pile of clothes in the hallway caught her eye. It had been there for more than two weeks and it seemed to grow on its own: every day bigger, every day more of a shadow. She set her face; she put down her bags and the post on the floor.

From the outside shed she took a can of white spirit. She had no idea if it lit fires. It was all she had, and worth a try. If it was dangerous, she did not care.

Hauling the clothes and books and everything else that belonged to Bill from the dark mound in the hall took ten minutes. Sometimes she found herself running with her arms loaded down. The pile in the garden grew, at the far end by the gate that led to the track. Under it she stuffed newspaper and kindling. Out of breath, she scattered the spirit on, and threw a torch of twisted paper on to the pile. There was a momentary silence, and a sighing *whump* as the spirit ignited; then, all at once, the rest caught. In seconds smoke was pouring straight up in the windless evening. It was dark and smelled vile. The stench of the past, she thought, in a kind of satisfaction.

Burn the lot, fathers and lovers.

Soon, the fire had fully caught: it became all flame, and made a rushing noise. Bill's wood ottoman – the first thing she had laboured out with – cracked like a gun going off. She could see its red outline in the rest of the blaze.

She sat down and watched.

Twenty-four

The next day, at the local police station, the sergeant and constable regarded each other across a cup of seriously dreadful canteen coffee.

'And what else?'

The constable shrugged. 'He said they were making further investigations.'

'And these were . . .'

'Peaks. Peaks in the blood samples.'

'What did they want us to do?'

'He said he'd ring back inside an hour.'

The sergeant sighed and looked out of the window. 'Could be anything,' he murmured, thinking aloud. 'Could be the alcohol. Could be a disease. Could be anything.'

He looked back, drained the cup, and stood up. 'What about if I went out to see the lad?'

'What for?'

'I dunno . . . There's something. The lad and Scott. There's something.'

The sergeant smiled grimly. 'You want to stop watching Inspector Morse, you do,' he observed. But, despite his jokes, he took the younger man perfectly seriously; he had already begun to wonder if this case had more to it than met the eye. For instance, he had already made up his mind to make another visit to Hugh Scott, having had a visit from a Mrs Marsham that morning. This breathtakingly overbearing woman had informed him that Scott was not engaged to Eve Ridges at all – in fact, he had been making a nuisance of himself. She had suggested that the fact Bill Ridges had been found on Hugh Scott's land was 'thought-provoking'; that was the way she had put it. When pressed further, she'd admitted she had not a shred of evidence, but added, as if as an afterthought, that they might speak again to Jon Davies, who had gone back to Kent. 'I believe he too has an opinion on the matter,' she had said.

Thinking of that brief interview now, the sergeant could not resist a grim smile. These villages, he thought. Nobody could ever say his job was all cows and cars; you scratched the surface, you found a sore. Little private intrigues, little private wars. It was like last year, when two brothers barricaded their mother out of her house down Tyning Cross. All hell to pay, there was. Mother's boyfriend setting fire to the son's pigeons, and mother herself breaking a leg climbing up on the roof of the extension. You didn't need no TV; you had enough entertainment outside your back door.

He'd make a point of going up Scott's farm, and Eve Ridges'. Worth a visit. Worth a bit of a wander.

If not today, tomorrow.

He made a sweeping gesture with his hands, as if shepherding out a reluctant animal. 'Get back to missing handbags,' he told the constable. 'And do as you're told. Wait.'

When Eve got back from school, the phone was ringing. 'Hello?'

'It's Jon.'

'Oh. Hello . . .'

Silence filled the line. She could not think of a single thing to say. In the garden, the last of the fire was still smouldering, even twenty-four hours later, a thread of smoke against the green.

'How are you?' he asked.

'I'm . . . all right. I'm all right. Hugh said you're working with the harvest.'

'I am. I'm down in town with one of the drivers. They needed a spare part.'

She said nothing.

'Eve. I've been back two days. I wanted to . . .' His voice trailed off.

She clenched the receiver, looking down at her feet. She wondered where he had been for the last ten days, and who with, but felt she could not ask. She wanted to know if he had touched anyone else. Just if he had touched someone else. That was all. Just . . . The girl in white, anyone else . . .

'Did you get my letter?'

'Yes. I'm sorry. All the arrangements for the funeral, and this waiting for him to be released . . .'

She didn't say 'the body', as the police had said to her.

'Can I come and see you?'

'No, I don't think so.'

'Just a minute. Please. I came back to sort it out. I can't just leave it. I can't just leave *you*. I won't even come in the door.'

'No, I—'

'It won't hurt just to talk to me. You might just talk to me.'

'It's not that.'

A pause. She heard someone's car horn blowing in the background, filtering down the line. Voices.

'Is it over?'

'What?'

He raised his voice. 'Is it over? Is it finished?'

She said nothing. She pressed the mouthpiece to her own mouth, as if she had the power to touch him through the mechanism. Dear God, dear god, dear god; if only he knew.

'Can I come and see you tonight?'

There might never be another Jon. She was almost forty. Never another Jon.

'No . . . No.'

'In the morning. I must. I'll come in the morning.'

'Jon—'

'The money's running out. In the morning.'

There was a click, and the line burred. She put the phone down.

There was no point in seeing him. She would tell him to go. Perhaps not even go to the door to him. There was no point in opening what was already closed – and for what? So that he could leave again in October? Hugh had already told her he had secured a place for the autumn term. Open the door and let him in again, make a deeper cut in the first. For what, really? For what?

She leaned on the windowsill and gazed at the smoke. All her father's loves had gone; him too. It meant less than nothing. All the players were dead. She, too, could let go of her own need . . . like that. Like smoke. She could let it drift away, and then, she too would be able to vanish. Cut the rope. Disconnect. She would see her father buried, she would see the house sold. She would finish the summer term at school. And then, cut the rope. If she stayed any longer in this house, she would suffocate. She might as well lock every door and wall herself up in it. It would be the same. Walled up for ever in this bloody monument. She would go to Italy. She would go to France. She would be a tutor, a guide, a courier, anything. Live a little of the life she had forfeited. Anything, anything.

Jon.

By Christmas, he would forget her. And she would forget him. By Christmas, in Italy. By Christmas in Germany, wherever.

And she turned quickly away from the window, and switched on the oven, and opened the door of the freezer. Avoiding seeing herself, lying to herself, in the mirror.

It was eight o'clock when Hugh came to the door.

She was shocked to see him: she knew, in this weather, he should still be down at the harvest. Normally, he would work until dark, and beyond. And yet here he was, washed, dressed, and looking uncomfortable in a suit.

She smiled hesitantly at him. 'Hugh. Are you going out?'

'Just to here.'

'What, dressed up, for me?'

He actually blushed.

After school that day, she had been to the undertaker's, paid by her own cheque and, in return, received a cheque refund for Hugh's money. The manager had been totally baffled, but she felt that money from the firm – and not her – was the only refund that Hugh would ever possibly accept. Still wondering how to break this to him, she let him over the doorstep reluctantly. He walked straight to the living room, where he stood in the centre of the worn carpet.

'Well . . . Will you sit down?'

'All right.'

'A . . . drink? Tea?'

'No thanks.'

'Mind if I have one?'

'No . . . No, no. Go ahead.'

She went to the cabinet and poured herself a sherry, looking over her shoulder. 'Sorry about the mess,' she said. 'I was planning lessons . . .'

'Oh, yes?'

She sat down opposite him. 'I thought you'd be in the field still.'

'I left them to it.'

She frowned as she sipped her drink. *Leaving them to it* was not Hugh at all. Not at all. He looked as if he were ill, the colour gone from his face completely. As she drank, his tongue passed over his lips once or twice, like a reptile tongue flickering backwards and forwards. She looked away, at the pattern of the carpet, at the green beyond the window, at the vase of yellow roses, picked from the garden only this morning, and yet falling into disintegration, petals hanging over the glass.

'Had anyone to the house?'

'No one yet. They say it's a good family home, though. Not too far to town.'

He looked up at the ceiling, as if he could see through to the rooms above, considering. 'So it is. But not as good as mine.' And he smiled, as if sharing a secret.

'Yours? I suppose not.'

She finished her drink, and laid it on the table. 'Listen, Hugh. I've something to tell you . . .'

Suddenly, still grinning from ear to ear, he began to fumble in his pocket. He brought out a packet and laid it in the palm of his hand.

'For you.'

'What?'

'Open it.'

'I don't think—'

'Open it.'

She did as she was told, shrinking a little at that not-to-be-crossed tone, and annoyed that he had not listened to what she was saying.

It was a padded red ring box, velvet. Inside lay a solitaire diamond on a gold band.

He shifted forward on his seat. 'It's a good one. It's a twenty-four carat band and it's a nearly flawless stone. Flawless, mind. Diamond.'

'Yes, I see.'

'A good stone. Suit you.'

'Me?'

'Put it on, then.'

She looked up at him, her face stricken. He leapt from his seat, pulled the box out of her hands, the ring from the box, and gripped her left hand. He seemed to count the fingers, hesitating. Then he started to press the ring down over the third finger.

She leapt back. The chair lunged back with her, tipping. The carpet wrinkled under it. 'Hugh! Don't do that. Hugh, please.'

She wriggled her hand away, and he sat there, squatting on the floor, that leering grin on his face, the ring hovering.

Somehow she got out of the chair and squeezed past him. 'For God's sake, get up,' she said.

'Why? Here—'

'Get *up!*'

He shambled upwards, trying to hold her hands. She fought him off, as though trying to extricate herself from glue.

'Will you *please*—'

'But it's your ring. Here—'

'I don't *want* your ring! Please, look—'

'But—'

She got a chair between herself and the man who, it seemed, was moving irresistibly forward all the time. Some great grey bear invading the living room, his hands still holding out the ring, lost in his fist.

'Oh, for God's sake.' She closed her eyes, praying. 'Please try to understand, Hugh. I don't want to get married. Not to you or to anyone.'

'Eh? But you said—'

'Nothing! I said nothing!'

'You promised.'

'What!'

'Up on the stone circle. You *promised*! You said when your father wasn't around any more.'

'I said no such thing!'

'You did!'

She stared at him, aghast. *When your father wasn't around any more.* He was holding the ring between thumb and forefinger now.

'Oh my God,' she whispered, turning away. She rested her hands on the top of the piano, feeling its satin smoothness, its solidity.

'You – you're selling the house, aren't you?' Hugh asked. 'What're you selling the house for, then? Go on, then – tell me that! What're you selling the house for, if not to come and live with me?'

'Live with you?'

'Course!'

Eve blinked. Surely she wasn't hearing this. 'Hugh – I'm not selling the house to come and live with you. I'm selling the house because I'm leaving.'

He shook his head.

'Leaving. *Lea-ving*,' she repeated.

The shaking of the head continued. 'You can't leave,' he said. 'I booked it all up. It's all arranged.'

'What is?'

He looked up, forced a smile. It was so pathetic, it crushed her, suffocated her. 'I booked the fourth of September,' he said softly. 'And the Three Firs for the reception. I booked a nice four-course sit-down meal, Eve. I booked us up a honeymoon. You'll never guess . . .'

'Oh, Hugh,' she whispered.

His voice became urgent. The last grasp at her. The trump card. He stepped forward, hopeful. Desperate, 'Guess where I booked,' he repeated. 'Venice, Eve. I booked our honeymoon in Venice.'

'Oh, Hugh. Hugh . . .'

'It's a nice hotel. A real nice one. It's a four-star. It's got all en-suite. It's not rubbish. You like Venice, don't you? See, I never miss nothing. Nothing that you tell me. I remember it.' He touched the side of his face, at the temple. 'Remember it. What you like.' His eyes were fixed on her, never blinking. 'I even picked out a dress,' he said.

'Dress?'

'You like silk, don't you? I know that. See? I listen. It's in town. Silk. It comes down off the shoulders.' He mimed the cut of her wedding gown. 'Lovely, it is. You'll be lovely in it. I thought, when your picture was in the paper, they'd all say, that's that expensive shop in town, that dress. And it has a sash . . .'

She put her head in her hands. 'Oh no,' she whispered. 'No. Please stop. Please stop. No. No, no . . . Please . . .'

His expression was one of total and complete bafflement: then, like a switch being thrown, it turned dark. 'It's him – it's that bloody lad,' he said softly, in a strangled tone. 'It's him.'

'Who?'

'Jon Davies.'

'Why Jon?' A flush began to spread up her throat. Betrayal, betrayal.

'What's he got?' he asked in a throaty whisper. 'He's only a boy. He's going to college. You'll never see hide nor hair of him.'

'It's not Jon.'

'I seen you with him.'

'When?'

But he could not say it. He looked down at the ring. 'Talking to him.'

Relief flooded through her. She hung her weight on the edge of the piano, taking a deep breath.

'It's . . . not you. Not Jon. It's me. Just me. I don't want to get married. I don't want to have babies. I don't want to live here any more. It's been like a prison to me, Hugh. Can't you see that? All these years. Stuck here with Dad. A prison! I feel I'll go mad if I don't get out. Leave the house. Leave it behind. Just go. As far away as I can get.'

His face was working; silent, in an expression of terrible distress.

'Where?'

'I don't know yet. Abroad.'

'A – abroad?'

She straightened herself up, watching him. Between them stood the chair, the side of the piano, four feet of carpet. He stood in the gloom, the ring still partly outstretched in his hand.

'I never promised, Hugh,' she said. 'I never promised. You frightened me the other afternoon, so . . . If I made you think . . . Well, I'm sorry, that's all. You can't know how sorry I am. I never thought, never dreamed you meant it all like this. I really am sorry. So sorry.'

Very slowly, he put the ring back in the box, put the box back in the paper bag.

'Abroad,' he said, as if to himself. Then he carefully folded a margin of paper over the top, and creased it flat with his thumbnail.

He walked to the door.

She followed him, right to the back door, through the hall. He opened it himself, pausing at the back step to look out over the fields.

Somewhere in the great sweep of the wheat field, a lark was floating, dropping its liquid song. Nothing else broke the silence.

She came up behind him, embarrassed, trying to think of something else to say, glad that he had taken it so well, so calmly. She picked a piece of washing – a towel – from the floor next to the drier, and was folding it absently when she caught sight of his profile as he looked past the house.

He was crying.

There was no shaking of the body, or alteration in his face. No movement at all, other than the tears streaming down. They were as full as a child's, not the wrung-out retreat of an adult. He picked up his hand listlessly and wiped them from the side of his mouth, his jawline.

'Hugh. Oh, Hugh . . .'

He stepped sideways, avoiding her hand on his arm.

'Hugh, don't. Please don't.'

He folded the top of the paper bag again, so it had become a tightly wrapped square. Then he stuffed it quickly into his pocket.

'It's not that I don't think a lot of you,' she offered.

Once said, she heard the cruelty in it.

He heard it too. He winced as if she had struck him.

He walked away; she came down from the step. At the gate he got into his car, slowly. He sat for what seemed like a thousand years at the steering wheel, his hands gripping it. Then he turned on the ignition. She saw him wipe his eyes before he put the car into gear.

'Oh, God,' she whispered.

He drove away, along the track, at speed.

She watched him until he disappeared over the brow of the hill.

Twenty-five

Sarah sat across from her husband in the cave-like gloom of their living room.

Her expression was hardly one of loving devotion. Duncan was picking his teeth with a matchstick while reading *Management Today*.

'Duncan,' she said. '*Duncan*.'

'Mmmm?'

'Will you listen to me? You're not listening.'

He put the magazine down. 'What?'

She folded her arms. 'Why is it that you never listen to a damned thing I say? Why is that?'

'I *do* listen.'

'I could understand it if I nagged you. I could understand it if I rambled on endlessly about Safeway's or the price of wool. But I don't. Let's face it, we speak about six words to each other per week. And you can't even be bothered to listen to my six bloody words!'

Duncan smiled. 'You just used up a year's supply.'

She gave a sardonic smile. 'Very funny. Did you hear what I said?'

'Eve.'

'Did you hear what I *said* about Eve?'

'No.'

'Jesus Christ. I *said*, Eve told me that Jon told her that Hugh Scott did away with her father.'

'Eh? Jon who?'

'Jon Davies. He reckons Hugh Scott wants to get Eve so badly, he murdered Bill. Drugged him or something.'

Duncan began to laugh. 'Hugh Scott? Ridiculous.'

Sarah said nothing. She turned her attention from Duncan and looked steadily at the picture of the horse above the fireplace. 'I hate that sodding horse. I'm going to sell it,' she said.

Her husband sat forward. 'Not the Scott man who can't say boo to a goose? Wealthy git, looks like a tramp? And you can't sell it. Sell the cat. Sell the children. Not the horse. You mean the Scott man who came to the school barbecue with his bales of hay for the skittles and refused me when I offered to buy him a drink?'

'That's him. Farmer. Wealthy. Git. Well done.'

'Wants Eve?'

'Oh yes . . . He's been rattling on about marriage, if you like. Presumptuous little turd; it makes my blood boil. Eve's so calm about it, it beggars belief. If only you'd pay some attention I wouldn't have to go *over* and *over* this, would I? It'll never come to anything, of course. Not if Eve's in her right mind.'

'Naturally. Nice woman, Eve. And who's this Jon person?'

Sarah smiled broadly. 'If I told you that, dearest, you might revise the definition of a nice woman. Let's just say he has Eve's wishes uppermost in his mind. Or did.'

She considered adding that she had become so intrigued about what Jon had told Eve, and so angry about Hugh's haunting of her friend, that she had voiced her concern to the police. Duncan would certainly *not* approve of that, either. He would say something like, *Don't get involved with these people.*

Duncan himself, meanwhile, wondered about the faceless Jon Davies, decided he did not wish to get embroiled in this nest of vipers, and picked up the magazine.

'So you think it's all fantasy?' Sarah asked.

Duncan reached for the matchstick and inspected it thoroughly. 'Raving, darling,' he said. 'Raving. These people. Don't get involved.'

Sarah made no reply. Sighing, she went back to studying the painted horse with a look of unmitigated loathing.

Twenty-six

They had forecast thunder for the night, so Hugh brought the horses in.
    At the last box, as he closed the door, the mare turned round and thrust her head over the divide: he lifted his hand and let her nuzzle his palm, the soft lips straying over him. He could see this mare as human: a thickly built girl with dark hair and dark eyes. He had called her Gypsy for just that reason. That, and the dancing in the fields that she did, all alone. A featherweight mare with featherweight feet. He stroked her nose, and she fixed him with that intelligent look, her head averted, ears pricked forward. Above them, the clouds clattered, freight trains moving over tracks. It was raining hard twenty miles north.
    He went into the house and sat down wearily at the table.
    His father had said he would never marry. He had said it when he was only a boy, but he had never believed it.
    Not until now. Not until tonight.
    He had always imagined his own children, lots of them, running through that yard to the river meadow; and a big, willing girl in his bed. In his teens, the fantasy girl took the face of Eve Ridges, for no apparent reason. Before he had imagined a broad-faced girl, thick-handed, thick-hipped. Then had come Eve. She was always so thin, and vulnerable. In the summer, he could see the bones of her neck and shoulders at the neck of her dresses. She went on to St Kitt's, a girls' school fifteen miles away, because they specialised in music. He would see her on the bus, even taller, ever more wiry and white.
    Go and talk to her in her father's garden; she would smile behind her hand.
    Then, one night when he was twenty and she was starting the grammar school, he had passed the house and he had heard her playing. The windows of the living room had been open. It had been a night like this.
    Through the curtains, looped over the sill and caught on the brick and the ice-white clematis, he'd seen her back, hunched over the keys. The narrow little spine, the white neck, the long braid of light hair, tied

with a creased ribbon. Every detail, every detail. It had burned into him, unexpectedly. The little girl bent over the dominoes of sound, bringing that stream of notes out of the wood. It had been a Chopin Nocturne, he had found out afterwards.

Nothing had ever moved him so much in his life. Of course, he had heard her play before, but never anything like this. To be on his way back from a trip to town, where he had stood on the street corner for over an hour talking all kinds of rubbish with a crowd of lads, and then to get down from the bus, and hear, coming through the field, this lovely and terrible song . . . It had been like some sort of shock: a physical shock, a shock to the system. She had stumbled over some of the notes, paused, and repeated them . . .

The crassness and stupidity of the town had vanished, the voices of others. Here from the window came a life in flood, full of a sweetness without words. Nothing had ever touched him as she touched him that evening, her small body commanding this magic out of the house, running into him. It was a kind of sorcery. A pale little witch, her back to him, teasing him towards her as a fisherman plays on a line, tugging the catch through a current of opposing water. All the small jealousies and the ugliness of life had fallen from him.

He had stood by the garden, transported. And then her father had come into the room.

He had heard only his voice at first. 'What the hell was that?'

Her answer, fogged, unclear.

'You *don't* . . . look . . .'

There had been a repeat of the last refrain. Then Eve.

'No. *Listen*, listen. The man's talking to you. He sweated blood putting this on paper for you. Listen to him.'

The same refrain; the same repetition of the notes.

After a while, her father had gone out again. There had been a long, long silence. A muffled crashed chord, as if her fingers had squeezed despair out of the piano.

Then she'd begun again.

She was only young. Very young.

Why couldn't he tell her? The man who called himself a father. Why couldn't he tell her, *just once*, once, how clever she was, how sweet, how clever and pretty, to do such things, to play so well, just . . . *once*. No. It was beyond him. It would have choked him to spit it out. Why could he not tell her how proud he was; how clever she was, how sweet, his only child . . .

Unseen, even then, he had wanted to storm into the house and grab that terrible man by his throat and pin his head back against the wall. His fingers had itched to do it. It wasn't so much what he said, as the way he said it, with such a slow-burning irritation and loathing in his voice. He couldn't imagine how one human being could labour under such loathing and survive, let alone bring this sound out of her hands.

Strange. That night had been the turning point. He sat now, looking at his red hands and white knuckles, thinking of that night, and of how his whole life had altered after it.

He had begun to see, as he had never seen before, as if he had been blind all his life, that the world was a place of absolute beauty and stillness and perfection. It was a work of art, even in the fields and the colour of the fields and the light – especially in the fields. Subtle changes in the face of a green crop could suddenly make him stop, and watch the air moulding and altering it. He felt like God, putting his hand to the water and the earth.

It did not matter that she did not know what she had done. She had given it to him, the utter and wordless beauty of the world, the feeling that could not be summed up when he spoke – God knows, not him, not with his stupidity – but the feeling that poured from music and all the music that poured from under hands. She had given it to him, this unspeakable gift, like a key that opens a lock. The key does not feel, nor understand, the freedom that it gives . . . He blessed her, quietly, daily, for lifting him out of the ordinary and making him see. She had made him the private owner of the complete and fantastic world.

She had woken him. She had made him see.

Paintings and colour. He could not tell her. He would try to tell her, and he went to some exhibitions, and he tried to take her, so that he would find a way of telling her . . . but it failed. Everything failed. She did not see him as one person sees another. He was just Scott's son. He was just Hugh.

When she was eighteen, she had played in a Music Festival in Poole. He'd told her he was coming to see her, and she smiled – Jesus, that very polite smile she had – but of course in the concert she had never looked up. He couldn't have expected her to be looking for him. He'd accepted that she had to concentrate. But afterwards, though, she had never asked him what he thought. It was as if she had forgotten he had been there. Forgotten he was coming.

And she had gone away to college soon afterwards.

His father had laughed and said, 'A girl like the Ridges girl doesn't marry a farmer. She goes arty-crafty and sets up a pottery, or teaches in a college, or gets a job in a museum, and she'll soon be too stuck-up to give you a thought . . . If she gives you a thought now, *which I doubt*.' Hugh could still hear the sarcasm in his father's voice, and the drawn-out stress on those last three words. Which – I – doubt. He thought it was a great joke.

He had begun to hate his father for the way he talked about Eve. After all, what did *he* have, or do, to be so proud about? He had started to watch his parents as they went about their daily lives. His mother – small, thin, quiet – had long ago been overshadowed, cowed, by his father's careless bullying. She went about the house, relentlessly cooking, cleaning, washing, trying to keep a house clean that was too old, too badly maintained, to be clean. When his father was out, she often sat down and devoured those paperback romances, a bemused expression on her face, as though the book were describing something fascinating but entirely foreign. When she became ill at the end of her life, all she wanted to do was lie on the sofa and read those books.

Left alone with his father after her death, Hugh had realised that, although he *looked* like his Dad, he was, in character, more like his mother. He'd thought about it with a growing resentment. When Eve looked at him, she saw his father; the square, set body and face; she saw his father's colouring and she saw him doing his father's work, and she probably thought he was exactly, in his heart, as his father had been. But he was *not*: that was the *injustice* of it. Alone, working all day, isolated in the fields, he built a fantasy life that was all romance. He bent his back under the yoke like his mother had done, while he lived a different life deep in his heart. He fixed a tape deck on the old tractor, and would play classical music tapes, or talking books, while he worked. He bought Jane Austen, and Dickens. He tried not to be bored by the books; he tried to see their worth. When he went in the shop to buy the tapes on a Friday, he turned his face deliberately from comedy shows and pop music and anything lighthearted. It was like doing a penance. He wanted to improve himself, to be better, *for Eve*.

More and more as the years went on – and he was with his father for eight, between his parents' deaths – more and more, he couldn't stand the way his father spoke; he couldn't stand to watch him eat, or look at him at night, mouth hanging open while he dozed in front of the TV. He couldn't bear his father's dirty clothes strewn in the house, his filthy shoes and boots. He couldn't stand the stubble on his face, the reek of tobacco; or the cloudy, leaking stuff at the corners of his eyes that left crusted snails' trails on each side of his nose. The old man revolted him more and more.

That was when he had begun his collection; started it in a box under his bed. Started it with a postcard, and some flowers from her garden. Going to that box, handling her things, cleansed him of his father. It was a small pool of purity and calm. He felt clean and better and stronger just because of his box of things. And for a long, long time, it was all he needed or expected. Just to have her things, because he believed that he would never have *her*.

And his father had never liked Eve, or Eve's mother. He even said that her mother's drowning was a blessing. Like putting a sick animal out of its misery. He had never had time for Eve's mother, because she so patently shrank from them both. Hugh did not blame her. The sensation of his father's dirty arm around her, his breath on her face, would have appalled any self-respecting woman.

His father didn't mind the other girls, though. He liked Hugh bringing home the other girls. Thinking of him, Hugh knew the old man was a lecher. The girls knew it when he talked to them: they would eye Hugh warily as his father touched their knees, legs, arms. Sometimes he would even corner them in the darkness of the hall as they left; press himself up to them. His father liked girls out of the frozen little villages with their village-hall dances. Lumpish girls with bright faces and no conversation in them and no idea about anything . . .

No one ever talked to Hugh about cities or languages or history or music. Not like Eve could do. And yet they said he was too dull to stay on at school, and his father said it was a waste of time.

Eve had come home from college once with a lad. Her father had hated the intruder on sight; Hugh hated him too. They had gone out for a year or so; in the summer, Eve had gone to Europe with him. But by the Christmas of the same year, the boy had gone. Eve never brought him home again, and never mentioned him. The hurt in Hugh had healed a little. And when she had come home for good, and taken the job in the primary school, he had been so glad he had not lost her, he'd wanted to rush out and take her up in his arms and thank her. He was so glad. He had never told his father: he tried to be just the same whenever Eve talked to him. It did not do to let girls know you were too keen. So every other lad told him.

But just to know – to *know*, she was home, in the house. That was when he had started standing at the hill of the track, the mid-way point between their houses, and thinking of her . . . in there, in there. He would imagine what she was doing and what she was wearing. And sometimes she would play.

Even then, it had been like a pact between them. The music,

sweeping out of the house towards him.

And he'd begun really to believe, really believe, that there was not so much separating them. Just a little convention. And a few trivial years. Even if she had been to college, and he was a farmer, what did that matter? He was no fool. Farming was a bloody good livelihood. He was not a fool. Far from it.

And he had a good memory, too.

Good memory for a lot of things that Eve liked. The names of buildings in Venice, and the names of Blake and Goya and Manet, and the Chopin Étude in E major, with its frightening, haunting, plaintive poignancy and its fist of chords, taking your breath away just as your attention faded; and the Nocturne in E-flat major, her very favourite, that plagued him and possessed him and preyed on him, a little posy of harmony and fragrance that smelled rank and bitter as you pressed your face to the scent . . . Oh God, oh God, oh God, if she never had love, just a little pity, a little pity for him . . .

He laid his head on the table and wept. He had cried in front of her and never meant it, and now the tears took him over. He had waited so long, and done so much. He had murdered her father, as good as murdered her father, to get her release from pain, and he would have done anything . . .

The ring had cost almost four thousand pounds. And it sat in his pocket as worthless as sand.

He reached into his coat, took the carefully folded packet out, and stood up. For a moment, he looked about himself, as if he couldn't think what on earth to do with it. Then, in a flash, it came to him. He rushed to the Aga and opened the door, and pushed the packet inside, and stirred the ashes up to a glow with the iron poker. Grabbing wood from the pile, he shoved it in on top of the packet, and the paper caught light.

He slammed the door shut.

God *damn* her, God damn her . . .

God *damn her, damn her, damn her* . . .

He went out of the kitchen and rushed upstairs, taking them two at a time. He pulled the key from the nail and wrenched open the door to the back room. Out of breath, standing on the threshold, he did not notice that the things were not quite as he had left them. Any other night, the disturbance – slight as it was – would have leapt up and screamed at him.

But not tonight.

It didn't matter anyway. It wouldn't have mattered if the whole lot had been strewn around the room like confetti. It wouldn't matter at all soon.

He picked up the first box and up-ended it, scattering its contents on the floor. Cards and little boxes and underwear and stamps and dead flowers. He stared at the shrivelled head of a rose, and kicked it out of his way, furious at its weakness. Every fucking thing was weak in here. Every *fucking* thing.

Taking up the postcards, he tried to rip them in one go; but they were too small and the plastic was too stiff on them. He began tearing them one by one, sobbing in his throat. The pictures of Italy and Spain: shred them. Cut them, kill them. All the wasted time. Little sounds came out of him: whimpering sounds, a dog cornered. He swallowed them down, angry at himself. Red filled his eyes, drowning him. He picked up the red phone and yanked it from the socket, and threw it at the wall. It fell in two pieces – receiver and box – and he ran over to it, maddened, and tore at it, pulling the cord from the handset, the wire from the receiver, and, when it would still not shatter, he heaved it at the wall. Flakes of pink plaster sheared off at him. He did not care, it didn't matter. No one would live in this room, anyway. No one would sleep here. No one would love him in here, skin to skin at night, skin to skin in the winter afternoons he had painted in his head.

All that *waste*.

Time would never come again. It would run, empty and fruitless, into old age. *His* old age. Empty, empty, while boys like Davies had the women he wanted, and brought sounds from them he would never hear.

He would never hear Eve's voice in this room.

A shout came from him. It didn't have a form. It wasn't a word.

Raging, blind, he went to the second tea-chest that had held her things, and he lifted it up, and he threw it with all his strength, out through the closed window. The glass exploded, littering the room with shards and fragments, and he heard the chest impact on the concrete outside.

Not enough. Not enough.

Back down the stairs, slithering and slipping on them. He went to the gun cabinet and opened it, no fumbling this time, clean as you like, cold as you like. See me? Ever see me? Look Eve, look Eve, see me? Cold as you like. Nothing left to worry over.

There would be nothing left.

Out of the back door, leaving it swinging, he passed over the yard. It was dark now, and the air was almost unbearably heavy with the coming storm. It pressed like a suffocating bag over his mouth.

When he opened the first door, the old grey gelding that was standing in the corner flicked its ears, but did not move very much.

He went up to its head and shot it at point-blank range. The gelding tottered and rolled back like a drunk, its legs and flanks twitching. He fired again, and the bullet ripped a hole in the head. Blood poured out on to the straw.

In the next box was a hunter he kept for himself. At eighteen hands, it towered over him, its head veering about, terrified at the sound of the shots and the horse thrashing beyond the wall. He had bought this one a year ago; it had been expensive. Its breeding showed in its shining flank and well-formed nervous head. It was a stunning, precious animal. Only six months ago, the Hunt had offered to buy it from him.

He had to reload, and the thoroughbred kept trembling and rearing, trying to get out. In fury, with the gun cocked – he could have killed himself, never mind the horse – he launched himself forward and punched the great black animal between the eyes. Something in his own hand fractured; the horse, stunned, swung its head. He raised the shotgun and pulled the trigger. The recoil sent him off balance this time, and he was spattered from head to foot.

The little mare was screaming in the last box.

They say horses do not scream, but they do. They have voices like humans, in the last terror of living. Horses screamed in war, injured by fire or shells. The unearthly screaming, reduced, just like man, to the last indignity.

Gypsy was the hardest of all.

In the end, he went back to the house and got the handgun. Where she was lying wounded on the floor, her legs aimlessly kicking, he put her out of her misery with a single bullet to the brain.

He left the gun and the shotgun on the floor of the stable.

He went back to the house and took off his clothes, and smeared as they were with shit and blood, he put them, too, in the burning stove.

He showered the smell of the horses off himself. Then he dressed again, very calmly, very slowly, and went to sit by his window.

Hugh wanted to sleep, eventually.

When it was nearly four o'clock and almost light, he wanted to sleep. But he could not manage it.

Every time he put his head down, he thought of the glass blowing inwards, and the things he had kept for her for so long falling outwards, and the dull smack of them landing on the stone outside. He purposely did not think of the horses or the way they screamed. He thought of the smack of the box on the concrete, and the way the cards and the picture books and her clothes lay scattered in a fan shape under the window, gathering damp, gathering dew, and the way they would dry and curl in the daylight. And eventually they would blow to one side, or be eaten and carried away, or be grown over, and they would disappear. Maybe not for years. But they would disappear, in time.

He wished he could have slept that night.

At four, he got up and went downstairs and made himself a drink. It tasted peculiar, sour. He thought maybe it was his mouth that was sour. He had tasted something funny all night. Horribly bitter and dry and sour, as if he had been sick and not washed out his mouth.

Going out into the yard, he felt the air still and heavy. The storm had not come – it had passed east of him and left this humidity in its wake. The ground was parched, dusty. He glanced at the stables for a moment, thinking that he could still smell the horses' fear.

He got the petrol from the barn and took it into the house. Anyone watching him would have thought he was tending to some minor problem indoors – carrying out some routine job. As he walked, he swung the can casually against his leg.

He started at the top of the house, in the room he had kept for her. He went along the landing and into the other four bedrooms – his children's bedrooms – and out on to the top of the stairs, and down every step, into the hall. In the hall, he cursed the empty can, and went to get another. The second was not quite full, so he was more careful, sprinkling it over the inflammable things – the couch and chairs, the carpet.

By the time he got to the kitchen, that can too was finished. He let it drop, and walked out.

As he drove up the track, he thought he would stop – just for a moment – before he got to Eve's. He wanted to think, and gather his strength. After all, he would need his strength. He would need a steady hand.

He pulled over, and watched the distant house through the windscreen, emerging through the mist.

As time passed the sun rose, and the fog drained off, running like water past him into the valleys, where it drained away.

He sat for a long time watching the beautiful red disc swimming up through the haze.

When it was finished, later on that morning, he would go back and set a match to the house. He would sit in the top room. That would be appropriate.

He rested his head on his hands on the steering wheel, and sleep – sweet, blessed sleep – at last swept over him.

It was half-past seven, and Eve had just showered, when she heard the ring at the door.

'Oh, bloody hell,' she muttered, trying to peer out from the crack of the bathroom window. 'If that's you, Hugh, I'm out.'

As she got to the top of the stairs, it rang again.

She really did not want to see Hugh; and yet there would be no one else calling at this time of day. As she went down the steps, she tried to rehearse what she would say to him this time. Even if she tried to be kind, it would stick in her throat. Worse still, kindness would destroy him; and it was such a condescension to be kind. Rubbing her hair with a towel, she wondered if she ought simply to be cruel. Kind to be cruel. Very cold and off-hand with him. Perhaps she should just plainly tell him that she did not want to see him on her property again. Perhaps then he would understand, for once and for all.

It was a man at the door. She could see his shadow.

'Sod this,' she whispered to herself, turning the keys in the deadlock.

The shadow moved close to the door.

'Who is it?'

They did not reply.

'Who is it?'

The face came up to the frosted window.

Sighing, she opened the door.

'Where is he?' asked the driver.

There were four of them standing in Hugh's yard, waiting. For the last two days, he had been here to meet them at seven-thirty. Even – yesterday – given them a breakfast. The older two among them leaned against the fence, unworried. Hugh Scott was a moody character. All smiles one day and all murder the next. That's what he was – murder. Bloody murder.

The young driver looked in the kitchen window. 'He's spilled something,' he said.

'Eh?'

'He's spilled petrol or something in there,' repeated the man, turning back, cocking his thumb towards the house. 'Stinks, it does.'

The older ones shrugged, one of them pinching out the last inch of his cigarette, stuffing the tab behind his ear. The red ash spiralled to the ground.

'Quiet, today...'

They all listened.

There was not even the sound of the horses.

Had they thought of it then – had it been anywhere but Hugh Scott's – they might have gone to the stables to see. The big dark horse always made a racket, after all, whenever he was in the box and someone was in the yard. He had a whinny that could wake the dead. He would poke his head from the box, and push back his ears, and call at them in his aristocratic fashion, as if commanding them to come and let him out. Little mare used always to be looking out, too. Or at the meadow gate. She liked sugar, or an end of carrot, if you had one. Greedy, she was. If they had thought of it. It was funny, that hunter not making a noise...

But they did not think of it.

This was Hugh Scott's place. And you never knew with him. And he would tell you it was none of your bloody business, what's more.

The oldest hand on the team eased himself away from the fence. 'He'll be up at th'field, I bet,' he said wearily. 'He'll be foaming at th'bloody mouth.'

'He never said to go to the field. Who'd get the tractor up there?'

The older man raised his finger. 'I can tell you what he's done for nothing,' he said. 'He's taken them up there every man-jack of them hisself and he's waiting at the bloody field top, waiting f'us to get there, and he'll bawl you out for a lazy sod and what else, *that's* what he's done.' And, sighing, he made his way back to his beaten-up Escort. 'Get in,' he called to the rest. 'Else yer bollocks 'ull be in a bucket.' And he started to laugh, the laugh seamed in with a hacking cough.

'Something funny, if you ask me,' complained the driver as he got in the back seat with his mate. 'Off his rocker, if that's what he's done.'

The older man shoved the car into first, and it rumbled out of the yard.

The dust fanned up behind them, a thin curtain between them and the house, the stables, the cottages.

'Tell us something new,' he muttered.

Eve's mouth fell open in surprise as she opened the door.

'What are you doing here?' she asked.

'I told you I was coming.'

'At this hour!'

'I'm meant to be at work. I couldn't go the whole day, and once you're with Hugh . . .'

Jon let the sentence fall. He was staring at Eve, half smiling. She felt a sudden and shocking lurch of desire for him. It came from nowhere, out of nothing. It was like being drenched in cold water, or hot. It was almost nothing to do with them – as people, as these two figures standing at a door. It was separate and apart, alive on its own. Springing out of her, like some sort of parasite that had been living unseen, unfelt, inside her. And to think that, in the last few days, she had almost convinced herself that the feeling had burned out.

She turned away, fighting it down. God, please do not let me make a fool of myself. Please do not let him see. Give me this one thing, God. Please do not let me make a fool of myself.

She put the towel down on the fridge top behind her, and pulled strands of hair across her forehead and ears. 'I'm not even made up, or anything,' she said.

He did not reply.

She heard herself talking. Say anything. *Anything*. 'I'm still angry at you,' she said. 'You should have said you were going, at least.'

'Why?'

'Don't you know?'

'What was the point? You didn't believe me, you said I didn't understand, you didn't want me . . .'

'So you just vanish. You just piss off. Very sensible.'

'I thought so. At the time.'

She looked at her feet. 'It doesn't matter,' she said. 'I don't mean to give you the third degree. You should go where you want to go. Why not?'

He looked taken aback, even wounded. 'If you don't know the answer to that . . .' He touched her arm, very lightly, with just the tips of his fingers.

'Oh, Jon.' She leaned on the door-frame, pressing one hand flat to her face. Then she looked up at him, shaking her head. 'I don't know what to think of you. Really, I don't.'

'Don't think.'

'Oh, spare me, please. Go away and find a girl and just let me alone . . .' And she made a move to close the door.

He turned partly away, and picked up a plastic bag that he had put by the side of the door. He held it out to her.

'What's this?'

'It's the box, and the jar. From Hugh's.'

'The – Oh, for God's sake! I don't want them.'

'I don't care if you want them or not. You're going to have them.'

'Oh, really?'

'Just take them.'

She folded her arms, smiling grimly.

He gave a great sigh and put the bag down at her feet. Two cars passed on the main road, racing each other down the long decline of the hill.

'In winter, they don't take that turn,' Eve observed drily. 'Hugh fished two of them out of that field when there was ice.'

Jon appeared not to have heard. He was staring at her, his face set.

'I know you don't want to hear a word against him,' he said, quietly. 'I know you think Hugh is innocent. Everything I said. The box, the jar, the path to the cottage . . .' He took a deep breath, as if preparing himself. 'I think Hugh kept your father in a cellar in the cottages,' he told her in a low, steady voice. She made a face, a mock-horror face of embarrassment on his behalf. He ignored it.

'I think he gave him the chloral hydrate,' he continued. 'And he took him out and he put him in that conifer plantation, and left him there. I reckon he knew your father would die, more than likely. He counted on it. That's why he rocked back like he did when the boys came down that morning. It was what he'd been waiting for. Only it came sooner than he'd hoped. Sooner or later, your father would die out on that hillside, and he meant to see to it that he would get more of the stuff in that packet if it looked like he'd wander . . .'

Eve made a waving motion with her hand. 'Oh, that is really enough.'

Gently, Jon pressed his index finger to her mouth. 'I know you don't believe it,' he said. 'Maybe you'll never believe it. Maybe what you really want is to marry Hugh Scott. I don't know. I don't know, Eve. What you want. Who you want. I don't think you know yourself . . .'

He turned and looked at the field, gathering himself. Controlling himself as best he could. 'I want you to keep them,' he said. 'He was your father. This is your business. Until a month ago, it was nothing to do with me. You say you've known Hugh a lot longer than me, and I don't know – perhaps you're right. Perhaps there's something in him I don't see. Perhaps. So . . .'

He took a step towards her. 'So you decide. *You* decide. Here's the jar and the packet and all I told you, and if you can't see Hugh taking your father out of that cellar, if it couldn't happen, *never* happen, then all right.'

She was still shaking her head, frowning.

'You've got to believe,' he told her. 'Not me. You. *You've* got to believe. Otherwise it's no use. Can you see that? Can you understand? It's you.'

She stared down at the bag, feeling him close to her. Not looking up into his face.

'I don't care what they say,' he whispered. 'Hugh, the village, anyone I know, I don't care. In the end, I don't even care what Hugh did or didn't do. I don't care what happens or what they say, outside us. I only care what you want. What *you think*. I only care if you want to be with me.'

She met his gaze.

'Just that one thing,' he said, and he reached out and ran his finger slowly down her face. 'Just you,' he said. 'Just you. Nothing else. Nobody else. Just you.'

She held out her hands in a gesture of the limit of patience, holding him away from her.

'It will all be different,' she said. 'You're going back to Kent in a few weeks, and—'

'No,' he said. He took her hands, and forced them around his waist, drawing her up to him. His face was within an inch of her own, his eyes fixed on her. 'I don't want to stand outside, looking in at you. I don't want to have you from a distance. Or *think* I have you. Don't make the mistake of thinking I'm another bloody Hugh,' he said. 'I'm not him. I'm nothing like him. I'm never going to stand outside willing you to come out to me. You're going to be *with* me, and I'm going to be with *you*. I don't care where it is, if you move away from here, I don't care if it's Siberia or Tibet or fucking China, I don't care . . . And I don't care if you think – I don't know – I'm not old enough at twenty, I don't care, it doesn't have a time limit on it—'

He gripped her so hard, his fingers dug into her flesh. 'Is there a time, like an age, a birthday, when you say, *all right*, so I'm thirty, so I'm thirty-five, so I'm forty – so *now* I know, *now* I'm ready, *now* I can fall in love with someone and it'll be all right because I passed some signpost with a date on it? You've seen that signpost? You've seen something I haven't?'

He paused. She stared at him.

'No, you haven't,' he continued. 'You're just as scared as I am. Twenty years didn't make any difference. Not a bit of bloody difference! You're just as afraid it'll go wrong, and not just with me, with anyone. And no matter how many years tick off that clock, put on that signpost, you won't get any better at seeing who it is coming for you, and if they're going to be good for you, love you, care for you. *Nobody* knows that. *Nobody* . . .'

He swallowed, catching his breath. His voice dropped until it was barely audible.

'I'm twenty this year, but I'm not any age in my head. Neither are you. The only thing that matters is if you want me, if you can throw a dice for a second. If you can take that chance. Just a second. Throw a dice. You throw it, I throw it. I don't know if it comes up right. Maybe nothing comes up. Maybe everything. I want to be with you . . .'

Feeling her struggle, he held her harder. '*With* you. Not just now. Not just until October. Not till winter. Always, *always*, always . . .'

And he kissed her, urgently, but without force. She could feel him trembling. She put her hands to his face, and lifted him away from her, and looked hard at him.

'I love you,' he said. 'And you love me. I'll say it even if you won't. I know.' And he drilled a finger to his own chest. 'I – *me*. I know. I don't care what you say, or anybody else. I love you. That's the end of it.'

She began to smile; then, slowly, shook her head.

'Why can't you believe in us?' he asked.

'You know nothing about me,' she said. 'Have you looked behind me?' And she made a soft, helpless gesture into the darkness of the house. 'I don't look behind,' she told him. 'I daren't look behind. Like the children at school, in my class. They cross their fingers and pretend they didn't see the mask or the monster or the dreams. They feel it, they sense it, and we tell them it doesn't exist. Yet . . .' She frowned and bit her lip. 'And yet, they *are* there. All kinds of things. My parents. The past. I hear the beasts in the shadows. I can feel them breathing on my neck. You know, like the bears beneath the cracks in the pavement; the devil behind the door. And I can hear them, stalking me.' She put her head to one side, her breath coming in small, uneven phrases. 'I don't want that for you,' she added, finally.

He wrapped his arms around her, holding her tightly. 'I'll watch out for myself,' he said. And he kissed her.

'But I don't want that for you,' she repeated, tears filling her voice.

He ran his hands over her hair, over her face, lifting her head until she looked again at him.

'You,' he said. 'Bears, shadows . . . I don't care. I want you. All of you. You.'

She locked her hands behind his neck.

Love me a life, any life, better than this. Take me out of this life and into another, any life, your life . . .

'I'm going away,' she said. 'I mean, right away. Out of the country. Perhaps for a long time.'

'I know,' he said.

Softly, lingeringly, she returned his kiss.

'Let me come with you,' he said.

And they stood on the step, in the early light, their arms around each other.

'Where is he?' asked the driver.

They had come to the field top, shearing off from the track and down the rough edge. Here, in the slight depression of the land, was a shelter almost large enough to be a barn; under its roof the combine and the trailer and the two tractors were lined in a single, silent, military row. Nothing moved on the field, nor in the land beyond.

They got out and stared around them.

'Has he bloody vanished or what?' said the driver's mate.

The two eldest looked at each other. 'Better get started,' they said.

And it was only as they walked the last few yards to the barn that the driver saw the flash of a reflection on the track above them.

A moment later, they heard the engine of the Land Rover spark into life. It revved unmercifully. They heard the gears selected with a sickening crunch. Then they glimpsed the thin metallic line of its roof lurch forward on to the track on the other side of the hill. As they listened, it accelerated away.

They looked at each other.

'Was that him?'

'Must have been.'

'What's he playing at?'

The old man shrugged.

They listened to the Land Rover, racing down the track towards Eve Ridges' house.

Eve followed him to the gate.

'I'll be back as soon as I can,' Jon told her. 'I'll tell Hugh I'll finish tomorrow.'

'No, don't do that. Don't let him down.'

Jon smiled. He touched her face, raised her hand, and kissed it.

'Here he is,' she said.

Hugh's Land Rover came bumping down the track, too fast. They watched it until it turned the curve below the house, and slewed to a stop.

'I bet he's looking for me,' Jon said.

Hugh got out and came up the path. Eve thought he looked tired, greyer than usual. His hands were dug into his pockets, and his feet seemed to drag. And yet, despite his haggard appearance, he was – amazingly – smiling broadly.

'Hello, Jon.'

'Hugh. I was just coming down.'

'That's all right. No rush.'

He beamed at Eve. ''Nother nice day. Dry one.'

She smiled at him wonderingly, seeing the baffling difference in him to last night. 'Yes . . .'

'Going into school today?'

'Yes, I ought to get on.' She looked from one to the other of them, hesitating. Jon lifted the faintest eyebrow; she smothered a smile.

'I'll walk on down then,' Jon said.

Hugh fished in his jacket pocket.

'Here – take the Land Rover.'

'What?'

'Take the Land Rover. I'll walk back.'

'But I've only had a couple of lessons.'

'That's OK. Just go steady. Try it. I've got to go up and check the drier. You go on down. They're just starting.'

Bemused, Jon looked from the keys to Hugh's face. 'OK. OK, right. Thanks, Hugh.'

Hugh waved the thanks away, still grinning.

Jon stayed another moment: Hugh before him, Eve behind the gate. She looked at her feet, slightly shaking her head. Jon's expression of amazement was a picture. He started to back away.

'Well, right then, Hugh. Thanks . . .'

They watched him go. As he opened the door, he waved at Eve. Both she and Hugh waved back. Jon got into the vehicle, started it, and turned, very carefully. Then, at twenty miles an hour, he drove down the track the way Hugh had come. Finally, the Land Rover disappeared over the rise.

'Nice lad,' said Hugh.

Eve stared at him, wondering if he could possibly be joking. But it seemed he was not.

'Mind if I come in for a minute?'

'Well, I must get to school.'

'Yes, I know. Only a second. Not to bother you. Just a quick word.'

His smile – a smile she had seen so little lately – was disarming. He had all the open sweetness of a little boy in his face. It was almost as if her own pleasure, and that of Jon's, had flooded the garden, the gate, and even the man who came to the gate. Even Hugh. Touched him – like magic – and changed him. He did not even look as tired any more: a kind of brightness, a nervous friction, lit him from the inside. Her own joy was infectious. Dreamlike, she opened the gate, forgetting everything she had been thinking only half an hour ago. Forgetting even the night before, when this man's tears had so shocked her. As she walked up the path with him behind her, she remarked easily on the roses, and even pointed one out to him – a lovely lilac tea rose, in full flower. He reached down and stroked its petals, and she smiled.

They walked casually on.

In just thirty short seconds, she had opened the gate, led him to the house, opened the door – and let him in.

Twenty-seven

He came into the house behind her.

She walked straight through to the kitchen and went to the toaster, saying over her shoulder, 'I haven't had any breakfast. Do you want anything?'

He came in and stood by the door.

In one hand he was holding the back door keys; in the other, she noticed, a set of overalls – the kind he wore when he was harvesting. They were pressed very neatly, and folded. He laid them, slowly, down on the seat of a kitchen chair. But he did not put down the keys.

Her gaze flicked down to them.

'That's all right, Hugh,' she said. 'Just leave them in the door. I'm going out in a few minutes and . . .'

Her voice trailed away. He put the keys into his pocket.

'When did he get here?' he asked.

'Who?'

Hugh's face darkened. His voice brooked no hesitation. He took a step forward. 'He's been here all night,' he said.

She shook her head vaguely, still not understanding what was going on. 'You mean Jon?' she asked. She gave a little embarrassed laugh. 'No . . .'

She stared from Hugh's face to his hands. Next to her, the toaster cranked up with a dull 'thunk'; the smell of warm bread drifted into the room.

'I saw you,' Hugh said.

Eve shifted to one side, edging the table between herself and Hugh. Her mind raced haphazardly between Hugh and Jon, between the still garden and Hugh's hand on the petals of the rose, and the kitchen and Hugh's hands secreting the keys in his pocket. Trying to add up the equation, to let it make sense. But it did not.

His face was placid, expressionless, his voice very calm.

Behind her was the door to the living room: she fought down some primitive instinct to run through the door and slam it in his face.

'I saw you,' he repeated.

'I don't . . .'

'*Both* of you.'

'You . . . saw us?'

'I *saw* you!' And he slammed his hand flat on the table, his fingers spread. A plate spun a little, and rattled. Eve herself jumped like a cat, her feet lifting from the floor as if she had received a charge of electricity. As if the floor had suddenly become hot.

Hugh leaned on his hands, thrusting his face, now slightly blotched with colour – dark rose spots on his neck, paler rose spots on his forehead, as if the petals that he had been cradling had touched and stained him – towards her, his thick neck stuck rigidly between round shoulders.

'I saw you in my stables. In the tack room,' he said.

Understanding hit her like a blow.

He began to straighten, to move around the table. 'You played me along. I thought it was a mistake. I thought – I can let her make a mistake. One mistake. I can let that go, even though it killed me, it killed me, you understand? You know what it was like to look at you? I kept thinking of you, I kept seeing you, and I kept thinking, a mistake, God knows, I made mistakes, I can let her make one mistake when we're so close, and it'll never happen again, because she wouldn't *let* it happen again . . . I thought he . . . *got* to you, some way – but . . .' He frowned, and a look of utmost grief, of utmost betrayal, took over. 'But . . . you – you bloody bitch, he didn't take what wasn't already on offer, did he?' The voice had been calm until that very last word. Then, it ripped away from the man, ending in a kind of smothered, high-pitched cry.

Eve reached out, behind her, for the living room door.

Hugh had come around the table, and was coming at her, steadily and slowly, his eyes fixed on her face. 'You led me along, didn't you?' he said. 'Promising me God knows what. And all the time you was with *him*.'

'No. It wasn't like that. Hugh, listen . . .'

'I've listened enough!' he cried. And he pressed his hands to his ears, as if trying to force out some distant memory, some sweet chord that possessed him and drove him. A terrible bright red flooded his face.

'I could have forgiven you him,' he said. 'I thought we was together. I done what you wanted. I thought we was together . . .'

'Done what?'

Eve's hand fumbled behind her back for the handle to the door.

'Your Dad. What you wanted. Made sure he didn't come back. What you wanted . . .'

Eve's mouth dropped open.

'You . . .'

'Kept him in that cellar. I give him that stuff. I took him up the hill—'

'Oh my God,' she whispered.

He didn't seem to have heard her. He carried on, cutting through her words. 'I made sure for you,' he said. 'Just like you wanted. You never wanted him back. I took him away for you. I give you what you wanted. And all for us. You promised me . . .'

She found the handle; she pressed it down and turned around, and launched herself through the door in one movement, throwing herself towards the other door to the outside, the one that she always kept locked. She tore open the screen door and fell into the porch, reaching up for the key beside the window, tearing it down, forcing it to the lock, whispering, 'Jesus, please Jesus, Jesus . . .'

He came blundering through the room behind her. Something crashed as he pushed it out of his way. Flowers, water, she thought, pushing the key home, bruising the palm of her hand, the flowers and water and the glass vase. Roses and water—

'Help me, God,' she prayed.

His hands grabbed her shoulders, pinching the flesh hard through her clothes. She sagged at the knees, but still turned the key. The lock clicked, but, before she could depress the handle, he hauled her backwards, through the porch and into the living room, her legs and feet flailing against the door-frame and the floor. She tried to wriggle, squirming, out of his grasp, and only succeeded in coming face to face with him, half crouching, his face lowered to hers. She tore at his hands, first the right, then the left. It made not the slightest difference.

'Let go!' she screamed. 'Let me go!'

He did. With one hand.

He brought up his fist and smashed it into the side of her head, and the world receded for Eve; telescoping in on itself in a shower of dark flecks, the room became a round small hole. She fell to one side, and faintly felt a chair strike her under the arm, in her ribs. She slipped to the floor.

As she lay under him, Hugh looked back to the shattered vase. He took three steps across the room, swilled the last of the water and the blooms from the broken neck, and turned again towards her.

With the room shifting back, shifting forwards, Eve saw – as if from some enormous distance – Hugh coming at her with the glass, its cut surface refracting light. For a moment she had the insane illusion that he was carrying something burning and bright, a handful of fire or sparks: then the reality hit her.

She scrambled backwards on her heels, tottering and falling up against the first tread of the stairs. Panic-stricken, she started up: swaying and stumbling, she got half-way before he brought the glass down, hard, on the highest part of her that he could reach over her kicking legs; it landed in the centre of her back like a dead weight, a stone, and took her breath away. She gagged. It felt as if someone had hit her straight over the heart, making it stop dead. Breath leaked from her: she dug her fingernails into the thin carpet for purchase.

This set of stairs, the flight that had originally been the only flight up before the house was renovated in the forties, was painfully narrow. Two people could not cross on it – it was not like the big flight behind the kitchen. The walls closed in as she fought her way upwards; she balanced against them. At her back, Hugh was sobbing low down in his throat. He sounded like an immense dog panting after a long run.

She kicked back. She must have caught him, because she heard a small surprised noise. The labouring breathing stopped a second: she plunged forward, reaching the top. Never in all her life had she been so glad to see the stretch of open space. She clambered into it and looked behind.

Hugh was half-way up the flight, holding his throat with both hands. He was retching and spluttering. Just as she turned, he looked up, and an expression of the purest hatred, the blindest rage, filled his eyes. He let go of his throat and, still gasping, ran up the treads, his arms outstretched, as if ready to tear the skin from her, wrench her to pieces.

'No, Hugh, please . . .'

The begging went unheard.

She was ahead of him, but not for long. He floored her with a punch to the centre of her back, hitting the same spot so hard that she fell in an instant. He fell to the floor, knelt over her, and seized her hair, wrenching her head around so that her face was pressed in profile to the ground. For a second he paused, as if, having got her here, he did not know what to do with her. Then he lifted her head by the hair and crashed it into the floor. She whimpered.

He scrambled to his feet and pulled her, still by the hair, into the nearest room.

It was her father's: the gap where the box had been, and his nightside table, grinned emptily at her, as though taunting her. There was no more breath for words. The drab browns and greens of the room whirled past her, the squares of light from the windows. She felt herself heaped, like a sack of wet sand, on to the bed. Her legs dragged after her uselessly. Try as she might, she could not send a command to them to move. They were nothing more than lifeless pieces of flesh.

He turned her over on to her back. He brought his face close to hers.

Flecks of spittle were around his mouth. The broken veins on his face, so faint usually, showed up as a crazed network of livid lines. His lips looked grey, nearly black. Looking into the pale grey discs of his eyes, so flat, so lifeless, she could not believe that this was really Hugh. Even now, even now as he wrenched her backwards towards the pillows, the roots of her hair screaming and pulling out of her scalp, she could not believe . . . Hugh, Hugh . . .

'Please don't,' she said. 'Please, please . . .'

'Shut *up!*'

He straddled her, nearly choking the last of the life out of her. A dead carcase flung on top of her.

'You – don't – say – nothing. You say a fucking, a fucking word, I swear – you said enough, I'm sick of hearing, hearing you.'

She clamped her mouth shut, swallowing the shriek of pain. He had brought his fist into her stomach.

He did not intend to rape her. He did not want to have her at all. In that dark moment, all that Hugh wanted to do was beat the life from her. He did not want to soil himself with her. She had been standing on the doorstep – the bloody *doorstep* – with Jon, holding him in her arms, and he knew the boy had come after he had left last night, and spent the night with her, and fucked her here in this house, and she had laughed at him with his pathetic engagement ring and his best suit and his longing for her . . . Perhaps they had both laughed. Perhaps it had been a great joke, while he slaughtered his stock and swilled petrol over his own house, and thrown his life out of the glass of the window, and let it fall to earth.

They must have thought they were so fucking funny, his tears. They must have sat up through the dark hours, talking of how stupid he was . . .

With both hands he pummelled his fury into her. She writhed under him, her hands helplessly flapping at his fists. As he brought his rage smashing into her face, blood speckled him. She felt like a pulp wax face, a pulp wax body under him; squirming backwards, he smashed his fists into her stomach, her legs. But even that was not enough. Not nearly enough. His own hands were not enough. And they hurt him so much. He desperately looked around him for something to hit her with. Anything squat, square, bladed or heavy. A book. A lamp. Anything.

But Eve had stripped the room. There was only the bed and the empty wardrobe. Cursing, he stumbled away from the bed and down the long landing.

The bathroom.

Blades, bottles, razor, flex . . .

They turned to look as Jon came into the field.

He walked down to the tractor and trailer at the side of the combine. The driver in the cab, seeing him, let the engine die, pulled back the window, and leaned out.

'You're late starting,' Jon said.

'It's him,' said the driver. 'We've been waiting down at the house. He never showed up. Where's he bloody to now, then? You come in that Land Rover by yourself?'

Jon looked from one to the other. 'He's up at Eve Ridges',' he said.

There was a general groan. 'What's he say?'

Jon shrugged. 'Nothing much. He wanted a word with her. I thought he'd been out here. I thought he'd be angry at me not being down here – I thought that's why he drove down to Upper Towe.'

'He's never been down here himself.'

'Where's he been, then?'

The driver cocked his thumb. 'Parked up on the track.'

'Parked?' Jon laughed in disbelief. 'Why?'

The driver shrugged. 'Now, you tell me that, boy, and you win the sixty-four-thousand dollars. You tell me that.' He waved his hand dismissively. 'Probably looking at his field all night. I known him stay up all night at harvest before. Like a kid, he is. Too excited to go to bed, I reckon. Last year, *that* was. He's a bloody crank, that's what,' he added. 'Get on the trailer, now. Time enough's wasted as it is.'

Jon opened his mouth to object.

For a moment he thought of Hugh, standing next to Eve at the house.

He considered if he should go back; wondered what, if anything had passed between Hugh and Eve in the last few days. Nothing important – she would have said. There could have been no mention, any more, of marriage. She would have told him, wouldn't she?

The combine cranked into life, drowning out even his thought. The tractor driver was miming at him to get out of the way. Hugh seemed in a good mood today; his attitude towards them both had been friendly. His face, smiling and benign, flashed before him.

It would be all right.

He would go back as soon as he could – as soon as there was a break, as soon as they took the first load of grain in the trailer up to the drier. He would run back up the track and make sure she had got off to school all right.

Then he smiled to himself. She would laugh, probably, at the way he worried.

He ran to the cab of the trailer, and got in.

Twenty-eight

The sun was well up, and very warm, by the time Hugh came back to the field.

It was nearly ten o'clock, and they saw him walking slowly along the track, and coming in through the gate. Jon thought he looked like a bear; a toy worn by years of merciless childish hands. He looked tired; very tired. He was now wearing the overalls that he usually donned when out in the fields. His feet were dragging.

'The wanderer returns,' said the man alongside him, disgustedly.

The combine had almost finished the field, and was nearly back to the ridge of the hill. The first tractor was at the drier, along with its team. The second – Jon and one of the older men – had an almost full load, but they had stopped for the last minute while the combine driver complained of a problem with the header.

As Hugh came forward, he stopped and climbed up the side of the combine, on the narrow black steps and grid platform. The driver opened the door and spoke to him; the machine stuttered gradually to a stop.

Both Hugh and the driver got down.

'What's up?' said the older man alongside Jon. They, too, had got out of their cab and stood in the shorn field, sweating in the mid-morning heat. Clouds of dust from the grain and chaff hung around them.

The combine driver walked further away; they followed, sitting down at last in the shade of the hedge – a low hawthorn barely four feet high.

'Flints in the header,' said the combine driver. 'Get 'em out in a minute.'

He took out a packet of cigarettes; so did the older man. Hugh and Jon looked at each other for a moment, looked away, and then settled alongside each other in the shadow, their feet in the shallow ditch.

'You been busy?' asked the driver, nodding at Hugh.

'Some.'

'We came down to the house.'

'I was out early.'

The older man, behind Hugh's back, made a face, grinning, that said, 'I told you so.' Then, he screwed his index finger in at his temple, making the sign that the man was crazy. Jon glanced at Hugh. He was staring straight ahead.

As Jon watched, he noticed that Hugh's hands were making a washing motion: slowly lacing over each other, as you would if you soaped your hands before rinsing them. After a while, evidently aware that he was being observed, he stopped, and looked at Jon.

'Gone off to school,' he said.

'Pardon?'

'Gone off to school. Miss Ridges. Gone to the school.'

'Oh, right . . .'

Hugh nodded. 'Busy,' he said.

Jon pinched back a smile and stared at his feet. You poor old sod, he thought. She's right. You are just a poor sad bloody sod.

Hugh sat hunched over, his elbows on his knees, glaring at the ground in front of him.

'Well, that's it,' said the combine driver. 'See to that stoppage now.' And he rose to his feet.

Hugh suddenly looked across at him. Then he got up too. 'I'll see to it,' he said.

'Nearly done. 'Nother hundred yard.'

'I'll do it. You get off with Jim. Tell th'other lot to wait up at the drier. We'll come down when it's finished.'

The driver frowned. 'What for?'

'What d'you mean, "what for"? No problem. Get off down the drier and I'll see you in half an hour.'

'But—'

The driver looked from Jon to Hugh, from the combine to Hugh. Eventually, evidently deciding it was not worth the argument, he shrugged, pulled the older man by the arm, and went off to the tractor. Once out of direct earshot, Jon could hear them break into mumbled complaint.

Hugh turned to Jon with a broad and friendly smile. 'Give us a hand, then,' he said.

Matthew Streatham replaced the phone with a frown. 'No reply,' he said.

The Year Two teacher hovered in the doorway. 'And she never left a message?' she asked. 'Did you check the answerphone? Perhaps she had to go to Poole or something. Something about her father . . .'

Matthew gave her a withering look. 'I checked the answerphone twenty minutes ago,' he said.

He pressed a finger to his mouth and looked out of the window. 'It's not like her,' he murmured. 'Even two weeks ago, she always rang. Even when things were at their worst.'

He watched as a lanky girl from the nine-year-old class ran out into the playground, and enthusiastically began ringing the bell.

The school secretary poked her head round the door. 'Mr Fellows is waiting,' she said.

Matthew sighed. 'I'll try again at break,' he said. 'They'll have to double up at science today, that's all.' And, once out of the door, he was swallowed up in a stream of small bodies, hurtling in the direction of the classrooms.

The issue of Eve Ridges' absence vanished in the noise.

They stood in front of the combine, trying to see the obstruction.

The machine towered high above them; an immense red nightmare of blades, reels, spikes, with the bulk rising beyond that, and the cab on the front, looking directly over the header. On either side, it stretched out beyond them for another ten feet. Heat swarmed off the auger and the reel: it was higher than them, the reel a long barrel, like the barrel of a gun. Behind the reel, they could see the sections: the complicated arrangement of cutting blades, squat and blunt-looking now that the combine had stopped; lethal once it began work.

There was a stink of diesel and grease; under their feet, the field stank too, but with a rankness and sweetness mixed. It was like standing in a sauna doused with grass and paraffin: Jon found it difficult to breathe.

'There 'tis,' said Hugh.

He pointed past the reel, with its murderous spikes, to the cutting blades. Several flints were stuck there: a penalty of farming this chalk downland.

'Have to get them out,' Hugh said. 'Or they make the belt slip. Worse still, they get in the main machine. Bugger it up good and proper.'

Jon nodded. 'I'll get them,' he offered.

Hugh turned to him with a grin. 'Good lad,' he said, and patted his shoulder. 'Good lad.'

He began to move round the side of the combine, towards the steps.

'How do we go about it?' Jon asked.

Hugh started to climb up to the cab. 'I'll lift the reel,' he shouted down. 'You get under when I give you the sign. They'll worm out with a bit of fiddling, then we put the reel back down. Two-minute job.'

He paused on the platform and gazed down at the boy.

Jon looked very dark against the grain and the straw and stubble. He wore a black T-shirt and faded blue jeans; his black hair shone nearly blue in the strong light. He looked back at Hugh, hands on hips, with an interested, unperturbed expression.

The devil looks like that, thought Hugh. Not in a red cloak with horns on his head, breathing fire. The devil looks like a dark angel standing in the light. He looks young.

He opened the door, got into the seat, and started the motor.

The combine shook; the exhaust fumes trailed towards Jon, the wind blowing them forwards.

Hugh hung out of the cab window. 'I'll raise it up,' he yelled. 'Watch now. When I give you the thumbs-up, you go in. Keep looking at me. Make sure it's safe. Don't touch the blades till the thumbs-up.'

Jon nodded.

The reel lifted. Jon watched it rise over his head, the tines shining in the sun. Dozens of angled spikes, whose job it was to rake through the cut crop like a steel comb, forcing it backwards towards the blades, splayed out against the sky. They rumbled and trembled: the scent of the crop doubled and rolled over him.

As they came to a stop, the sections were clearly revealed.

Hugh leaned forward in the cab.

'All right?' Jon called.

Hugh's hand came up: thumb uppermost.

Jon ducked under the reel; in two steps he was at the blades. He reached his hand, carefully, to the first stone. It was a small sand-and-black flint caught near the centre. He wiggled it with his index finger, and it fell almost immediately. He caught it mid-air, grinned and showed it to Hugh, miming that it had been a good catch.

Then he edged to the left, glancing above him at the reel over his head.

He stretched out his hand for the second stone.

The police arrived at Eve's house at ten past ten.

As they got out of the car, they saw that the front door was open, and swinging back against the wall of the house. Its brass knocker clanged regularly against the brick.

The sergeant and the constable exchanged a glance. Inside, in the living room, they could hear the phone ringing.

'Anyone home?' called the sergeant, standing on the step.

As if in reply, the phone stopped.

They looked in the door.

A flower vase lay at the foot of the stairs, broken at the neck. In the opposite corner, the flowers were strewn across the hearth. A chair was flung to one side.

They took one cautious step in, looking carefully about them.

'Hello?' called the constable.

The sergeant nodded in the direction of the kitchen. 'You check that way,' he said.

The constable had only got as far as the hallway, when he called back, 'Blood in the kitchen, in the sink. Pile of clothes. On the tops . . .'

'Miss Ridges!' shouted the sergeant.

The constable reappeared at the living-room doorway. 'She's not down here,' he said.

They went up the stairs together. At the landing, they looked back down the stairwell, noting a long dark scratch in the wallpaper at the mid-way mark. On the landing itself was a trail that turned out to be water, running along the carpet leading from the bathroom to the bedroom on the right-hand side.

The silence in the house was profound.

They looked in the door of the first bedroom.

Eve Ridges lay on her father's stripped bed, on a blue-and-white ticking mattress stained deeply with blood.

She lay spreadeagled. She might have been asleep, in deep relaxation, if it were not for her head tilted backwards at an awkward angle. Water splashes were all over the bed, spreading the bloodstains from dark brownish-red to a delicate pink. At the side of the bed was a bowl and a flannel, the bowl half-full of water.

Someone had tried to wash the blood from her face.

That she had taken a terrible beating was immediately obvious. Her eyes were sunk in a puffed ball of flesh. Livid scratches and weals and cuts were all over the forehead, cheeks and neck. One particularly savage cut ran from the side of her mouth to her ear, a razor cut as though deliberately to disfigure. Her upturned hands on the bed showed how much she had fought off, or tried to fight off, her attacker. The palms were already bruised and swollen, the nails torn.

The sergeant looked at his feet, drawing a long breath.

Only ten days ago, the father. And now the daughter.

He pressed the switch on his two-way radio. 'Let's get an ambulance to this,' he muttered. As he finished his message, the constable caught his arm, pointing to the window.

'Look on that second field,' he said. They could see the red hulk of the combine clearly against the horizon of the hill. 'Isn't that Scott?' he asked.

He knew she was dead.

At first, for a minute or two, he had thought he heard a breath taken; a noise low down in her throat.

Hugh had dropped the razor, staring at his own hand as if it belonged to a stranger, the small defenceless choking sound from Eve touching him where all her screams had not. He had stared at her, at the stream of blood seeping from the cut. It wasn't too deep: he had thought he had cut her harder than that. If she had lived, it would have healed, perhaps even disappeared, in time.

But there was no more time.

Not for her, or him.

Or Jonathan Davies.

He had gone to the bathroom, washed the razor, replaced it on the shelf, and gone downstairs. At the kitchen sink, he'd filled the washing-up bowl with cold water and trudged doggedly upstairs. As he'd gone along the corridor some of the water had spilled, but he hadn't stopped to mop it up. He'd knelt down at the side of the bed and begun washing her face.

There was no more sound from her.

In the end, he'd sat back on his heels and gazed from her to the bed. Useless to clear it up. Useless to clean her. It was such a mess; so much blood. Her mouth was crusted with it; her hair too. He had brought her hand down from where it was crooked over her forehead, and laid it at her side. He'd tried to make her comfortable.

He'd gone downstairs, washed his own hands, neck and face, and stripped off his clothes. He'd put on the clean overalls. Then, feeling nothing more than a coolness – not numbness, for he felt the stairs under his feet, felt his hand on the handle of the door, felt the air on his face outside – but a coolness, a frigidity inside, like a draught from the Arctic touching him, he had walked down the track, leaving her behind for the last time.

Perhaps a thousand times – perhaps more – he had come along here, and walked home by himself. Count up the times from childhood to here: too many. She alone, he alone. It did not make sense. They could have had everything, if it were not for her father. If it were not for the boy.

The boy.

When he had reached the field gate and looked down at the crew by the combine, with Jon among them, he had felt nothing more than an infinitely weary sadness at the job he still had to do.

He was not afraid, or unwilling. It was simply the resigned hesitation of a man who has to put down an animal that cannot recover. Or a father who is forced to reprimand his child.

If only the boy had never come.

If only the clock could have been turned back beyond the first day, when he'd seen Jon and Latham on the trials field.

But it was useless to think that way. What was done, was done. There was no turning back. No shirking of the responsibility. Jon had come. The whole sordid play had run its course. And now he must finish it.

Sighing, he had gone down to the men.

Some jobs were unavoidable.

'All right?' called Jon.

He held up a second flint, then stowed it in his pocket.

Hugh, his hands resting on the wheel and the gearstick of the cab, motioned further to the left. Jon saw the stone, only a small one, stuck near the very edge of the sections.

He leaned down to it and tried to prise it loose with his fingernail, but it was stuck hard. He thought for a moment, and then got the second stone from his pocket and chipped at the small one gently. It rattled obligingly in the blades.

Above him, in the cab, Hugh leaned forward, saw the dark head bent at its work, felt the cold invade him. Felt the moment come, icy. His hand tightened on the switch, his heart slowed as if it were about to stop. The world stopped, too, hovering above his hand, waiting.

He pressed his fingers down on the switch.

There was a lurch as the mechanism responded.

The reel came down quickly, the tines glittering. As Jon flicked the stone into the palm of his hand, he only had time to wonder, in the briefest of flashes, what the noise above him was. He glanced up, and saw the row of spikes falling on him.

'Christ!' he shouted.

Hugh crouched forward in the cab.

The reel swung home with a tremendous thump: the combine shuddered.

He heard the boy scream, a scream like an animal caught in a trap. It was, too, he thought: a rabbit snared in a trap. As quickly as he could, he came backwards down the steps, and ran to the front of the machine.

Jon was alive, his mouth open, gasping, the whites of his eyes showing as the irises rolled back in his head, his hands clutching the spike that had entered through his chest, just above the ribs, in the soft and vulnerable depression of his throat. Another tine pierced his left shoulder; another his right arm above the elbow. The second row of tines had caught him just below the waist. Their pencil-thin savagery was deceiving. The boy squirmed, a fly in a web, an insect on a pin.

The agony would not last long.

Hugh turned away, oblivious to the high-pitched screaming of the boy. He began to walk.

He'd left the combine engine running, but it didn't matter.

Nothing mattered any more. Not now. He only felt very tired.

He reached the Land Rover, glad that these last tasks were done. He knew that he could go home now. Opening the driver's door, he wiped his face. If it was tears or sweat, he could not tell.

And did not care. He would be home soon.

And then, at last – at long last – it would all be over.

Twenty-nine

It was the second week of July: Monday.

The hospital ward was immersed in its usual ten o'clock tension. The consultant – late, and more irritable than he had been for weeks – strode out of the last side ward and into the sister's office.

In his wake, the two nurses raised eyebrows at each other.

'God Almighty,' said the first.

'No – but he thinks he is,' replied the second with a smile. 'He doesn't like patients telling him when they can go home.'

In that last curtained alcove, the female patient in question was sitting on the side of the bed. Having just argued for her discharge, she was trying, with infinite care, to put on her shoes. Trying not to bend too far.

The pain on the side of her head was still bad: they said it might go on for some time. As she lowered herself to ease on the sandal, a band, like metal, tightened around her scalp.

Eve raised her hand to the raised scar on the side of her face. 'God,' she whispered.

It was just over a week since Hugh had attacked her. A week of lying on this bed, being pestered first by the police and then by the press. During the last few days, she had been told that a second post-mortem had been carried out by the Home Office pathologist on the body of Bill Ridges, and it gave credence to Jon's story. The glass jar and the chloral-hydrate packet had been stored away as evidence. As had the photographs and samples taken from her house, and from the stables on Hugh's farm.

Sarah had given a detailed statement to the police. It recounted all that Eve had told her, and gave – with a few colourful asides – an excellent character for Jon.

Eve gazed out of the window.

So many lives, touching and crossing one another like an invisible network of paths. And sometimes you had no idea – no real, no true idea – of how you had touched another person. How you had altered them.

Until it was too late.

Wearily, she lifted the small overnight case.

'Will you be all right?' the sister asked her as she got out into the corridor. 'Have you got someone coming to collect you?'

'Yes,' Eve said. 'My friend Sarah Marsham. In a little while.'

They smiled at her as they said goodbye. Sympathy and intrigue crossed their faces. She did not blame them. They read the papers and listened to the news like everyone else.

She got in the lift and pressed the button for the sixth floor. A little boy, holding his mother's hand, looked at her bruised face with frank interest, his tongue hanging on his lower lip. He was obviously mightily impressed. He tugged on his mother's arm, and she frowned at him, turning his face to the poster on the lift wall to distract him.

The doors opened, and Eve got out. The directional sign opposite read: Six. Laboratory, Intensive Care, Chapel . . .

It was a quiet floor, especially in the east corridor where she turned right. As she walked, her body ached; the corridor seemed immensely long. She stood for a second at the door of the chapel, looking at the little altar with its seemingly makeshift potted plants and altar rail and its four rows of hard-backed chairs. She had spent a long time in here one day, coming in just as a thanksgiving service was ending for the birth of the new babies. The mothers, slopping past her in dressing-gowns and slippers, had shied away as if she were infectious. The highly communicable diseases of envy, desire, dread. And guilt.

In the window beyond was not the comforting green of a park or trees, but the more prosaic cranes of a building site across town. Real life. Real life.

Eve sighed, smiled a little, and went out.

The nurse at the desk of Intensive Care recognised her at once: Eve had insisted on being brought here as soon as she knew.

She went to Jon's bed.

He had been put in a side-ward off the ITU – a half-way house between the true emergencies and an ordinary ward. He did not look like a human being: not the human being she knew. He looked like a specimen for some medical experiment, an extension of the machines around him. On his cheek, the place where the ventilator mouthpiece had been taped showed a slight red weal. His eyes were closed.

The tines of the combine had missed Jon's heart, but collapsed his lung, and pierced the artery in his right arm. The one at the throat had damaged his windpipe; when the ambulance got to him – which was mercifully quickly – they said that the air had been whining in and out of him, making a sound like someone dragging breath through a broken straw. Thank God Jon had had the sense not to struggle, not to tear at the tines. Thank God he had kept conscious and upright, and not slumped . . .

Eve closed her eyes. All the time, she tried not to think of what Hugh had done. And *all* the time, she went back to it, playing the moment of the reel falling over and over in her head, as clearly as if she had been there herself.

The sister here said that Jon's survival was a miracle – only two years ago, they had had a case like this, an accident. And the man had died before surgery. The police knew all about it; thought that could be where Hugh had got the idea. Eve looked hard at the sleeping face; the dark hair. She reached out to touch it, as one would touch a talisman for good luck.

The hospital did not know – or would not say – if surgery could help Jon much more. There was nerve damage near the spine, the spleen. A major laceration of the intestine. A tendon neatly severed in the thigh. The list went on . . . on and on. They could only offer the opinion, whenever she asked, that Jon had come this far and the odds were on his side. He was a young man, and fit.

She couldn't help thinking that, if the police had not found them when they had . . .

Eve shut her eyes, trying to take away the image of Hugh standing over Jon, pressing the switch to release the reel. And the equally terrible image of Hugh, alone in his house, throwing a lighted match on to the floor. It had taken the fire service four hours to bring the fire under control. When they did, very little was left. They had identified Hugh only from his dental records.

Poor Hugh.

Even now, beside Jon – poor Hugh. They had told her that it was not her fault, but she felt that it was. Everything, her fault. They said that the feeling would go away in time. That it would heal.

A soft hand touched Eve's shoulder. 'Would you like some tea?'

'Oh yes . . . thank you. Has he been sleeping long?'

'Not long. It's the medication. You ought to go home and rest, you know. Come back later.'

'I will.'

'We're moving him on to the ward tomorrow.'

'Oh? That's good, isn't it?'

The nurse smiled. 'Very.'

They both gazed at the injured body before them.

Eve raised her hand to her own face, where the line of the raised scar ran from her mouth to her hairline. Her fingers explored it habitually. She dropped her hand, suddenly self-conscious. It was a habit she would have to break.

'I'll get the tea,' said the nurse.

Eve lifted Jon's hand to her lips. A flicker passed over his face. She longed to take him in her arms. She longed more than anything to tell him that he had been right – my God, so right – and that she had been wrong.

And she would.

Carefully, she laced his fingers with her own; fixed tight, like one hand rather than two.